DAUGHTER OF THE BEAST

DAUGHTER OF THE BEAST

E C GREAVES

First published by DieselPunk Creative 2022
Copyright © E.C. Greaves 2022

This novel is entirely a work of fiction. The names, characters and incidents portrayed in it are the work of the author's imagination. Any resemblance to actual persons, living or dead, events or localities is entirely coincidental.

A catalogue record for this book is available from the National Library of New Zealand.

Hardcover ISBN: 978-0-473-61487-4
Softcover ISBN: 978-0-473-61485-0
Kindle E-Book ISBN: 978-0-473-61489-8
Other Epub ISBN: 978-0-473-61488-1
First edition

For Charlotte.

Life is but footfalls in a forest.
Running toward something, or from something. It matters not.
Some charge brazenly through, some weave around,
but all must navigate the bracken of the forest floor.
To meander, or to stay in place, is to await the lurkers in the darkness—
those beasts that prey upon the slow and the lame.
For as long as you keep on moving, life is but footfalls in a forest.

- Old Gnome Proverb

TABLE OF CONTENTS

THE FOURTH STITCH - GROWTH

THE FIFTH STITCH - DISCOVERY

THE SIXTH STITCH - DESTRUCTION

BACK OF THE BOOK STUFF

THE FIRST STITCH

CAPTURE

DAUGHTER OF THE BEAST

i.

It would be the fifth time I'd killed this so-called 'knight', yet the fool just kept coming back for more.

A crackling cascade of sparks erupted into the sulphur air as I parried his blow with the flat of my axe, then twisted to lash out.

But he deflected my attack easily. Perhaps I had underestimated him this time; perhaps he'd actually been... *practicing*.

Controlled quick thrusts. A feint and then a backhand. His footwork, too, was impressive. But it was all too rehearsed, and he wasn't duelling some instructor's pet in the academy now. This was a fight to the death—back and forth atop the two halves of a giant rock that jutted like a broken and blackened tooth from the swirling, hungry magma below.

His order would not reach the Ebony Ziggurat, they would not find my master, and they would not stop the ritual of rebirth. Oh no. I wouldn't let them.

Every muscle and sinew in my body alight with fury, I roared and leapt forward, across the gap. He stepped back just in time to avoid my wild overhead swing, his feet skidding in the ashen dust, and sending pebbles of scoria and obsidian clattering into the fiery depths below. He was off-balance, but he wasn't defeated. Yet.

I pressed the advantage and swung my axe at chest height. But to my surprise he again managed to deflect the attack, and counter with his own: three lunges in rapid succession.

The first I twisted to avoid; the second scraped across my weapon, sparking once more as it went; and the final thrust caught me square in the stomach.

Ting!

It glanced harmlessly off my armour.

"What? That's dumb! You aren't wearing armour!"

"Am too."

"No Zynnie! You're a savage minion of the Necromancer. You're a monster, not a noble knight of the Faer-Reach. And besides, they don't even make armour for girls!"

"Perhaps the Necromancer got a suit custom made. Maybe he was sick of resurrecting his minions." I shrugged. "Then again, it's *you* who keeps dying. Who keeps resurrecting you, anyway?"

"See, this is why I hate playing with you. You just make stuff up and break the rules! You don't take *anything* seriously!"

Lleyden threw his stick into the brook, and sat down on the mossy rock in a huff. I sighed, cast my weapon away too, then sat on the other half of the great split rock, across from him. I dipped a toe in the water that gurgled happily between the halves. He frowned at me, then balled himself up like a hedgehog—only twice as prickly.

"What?" I asked him. But I knew exactly what he was going to say. And sure enough, he said it: "I'll just fight myself then, Zynnie."

"Oh come on Lley. Don't sulk. You know you love playing with me! You're the one who begs me to come," I reminded him, and threw a little balled up chunk of lichen at my friend.

"Well who else am I going to play with? Radu? Yaro?" he huffed. "Radu is only six summers old, and Yaro's mama won't ever let him come into the woods anymore... Thanks to you."

"Oh yeah, that's right."

It was ever since I dared him to stick his hand in that beehive.

I sniggered. It *was* pretty funny.

Lleyden smiled too even though he tried his best to hide it from me. He couldn't help it, I knew. He must've been remembering the look on Yaromir's fat face.

"You complain about Yaromir and Radu, but imagine how I feel. At least you have other boys to do stuff with—I'm the only girl our age," I said. "What if I invited you to make flower crowns and stare into the pond? Make up stories to explain the new patterns Mamochka sewed on my dress? Would you want to do that?"

He threw a balled bit of moss back at me. It bounced off my forehead.

"No, Zynnie. And I don't even know why you do stuff like that either. Those flowers are just flowers, your mother's stitching is just meaningless patterns—it's all dumb girl stuff, totally make-believe. And besides, Zynnie, you don't even look like a girl anyway. Makes it even weirder that you like any of it!"

"Well if that's the case, then I ought to stop worrying about all of that betrothal stuff Mamochka talks about with your mother too." I shrugged, and Lleyden nodded.

"You ought to," he agreed, then reached across the split in the rock to help himself to our lunch. "I don't want to marry you, or anybody else. I can't imagine anything worse than having to put up with your mother as well as you!"

I laughed at that. Her nagging was *far* worse than he knew.

"Zyntael! Your dress is ruined—and it took a summer to embroider! Zyntael Fairwinter! What have you got tangled in your hair? Oh what have you been doing with that boy again?" was what she would probably say when I returned today.

And what was it Mama had asked me last time—when we made potions of her herbs? Something really weird.

"Why do we do it, Zyntael? Why must mothers suffer children so?" and "What is it for, child? What does it mean?"

I had no idea what she was on about, but at least she didn't punish me for ruining her garden. I hoped tonight would be like that time, and not the usual nagging, extra chores, and no supper before bed.

Though perhaps two springtime adventures going unpunished in a row *might* be pushing my luck a bit—after all, I'd lost my sandals today.

"Reckon Mamochka will be cross again?" I asked Lleyden, between mouthfuls of foraged berries, and the cheese I'd borrowed from the pantry.

He squinted at the boughs above us as though the swaying leaves or the perfumed air of the glade held the answer.

"Well, my mama told me that yours is always annoyed at you because you slack off." Lleyden squinted at me. "Did you help with chores before you came here this morning?"

I watched a bee dance from flower to flower, busy with its never ending work amongst the spring blooms. I wished to never be like that poor, stupid insect. What a horrible life.

"No, I just left," I admitted.

"Then yeah, your mama will probably be cross again today." Lleyden shrugged. "You're such a lout."

I supposed he was right. But village life was so dull, and work only made it more so. Besides, it wasn't as though my parents really needed any help with chores anyway. They really only made me clean stuff, or tend to Zachya as punishment. For the most part, they seemed to forget that I existed unless I'd misbehaved.

3

"Mamochka has Magda to help her, and look after the baby anyway. That's her whole job," I told Lleyden. "You've only got to work because your parents are too poor to have servants!"

"Slaves, you mean."

"Whatever. Maybe if you become a wealthy knight you could buy some help. Or capture some in battle," I said.

"My great-great-great-*maybe*-great-grandfather was a wealthy knight, and he didn't have slaves or servants," Lleyden began. "When he slew the magnificent emerald dragon of these woods—"

"And got that scar on his face that was passed from son to son— yeah, I know. I've heard the story of your birthmark five dozen times now. Blah blah blah—didn't once keep slaves, despite all the money he got paid to kill the dragon or whatever."

I finished Lleyden's tale for him, then stared at him expectantly, goading him. "But then why are your parents just bakers, Lley? Shouldn't *you* be rich too?"

Lleyden knew I knew the answer.

"Oh *that's* right! Your father's uncle drank it all away, leaving your family with nothing as proof that it ever happened. Well, nothing but your dumb Magickal birthmark, that is. How very convenient. And honestly, Lley, that really is the best part of the tale!"

Lleyden kicked me. Hard.

"You know Zyntael, sometimes I wonder if your mama doesn't love you because you're horrible, or if you're horrible because she doesn't love you!" the boy hissed, then scurried away before I could hit him with something.

It was quite a hurtful thing to say—far worse than Lleyden usually managed. And only then, that was because it was probably true. But as hurtful as it was, I wasn't going to show it. I wasn't a baby; I was almost eleven summers old. And besides, even if she didn't love me, Mamochka said crying only made one uglier. And I really couldn't afford to risk it.

I so wished there were other girls my age in the village. There used to be, but Olyena died of fever two summers ago, and another family moved away when I was just a babe, taking their daughter with them.

I didn't know that girl's name, but my mother talked about the family a few times. She spoke of them fondly to other people, but she loathed them in private—because they were wealthy too, knowing Mamochka. Still, I sometimes wondered what that girl would be like. Probably boring.

No matter, I was stuck with Lleyden, as he was with me. Apparently for life, given our inevitable, impending betrothal.

With a heavy sigh, I forced myself to accept that fact, and then joined him in his current activity. But my mood was soon forgotten (along with the reason for it) whilst we chased woodland creatures, clambered over gnarled roots, wrestled in underbrush that hummed with insects, threw stones at birds, and foraged wild earthy mushrooms together until the sun began to burn orange in the undergrowth. It was then that we smelled the smoke.

Infused with the sweet and soothing springtime breeze, and carried from the direction of the village, it evoked excited thoughts of a bonfire and feast.

"Is it Solunstet already?" Lleyden asked.

"Solun-what?"

"The big spring festival. The one with all the singing. You know, when they burn that straw doll on the pole." Lleyden looked at me like I should've known all the names for all the stupid festivals. But I only ever cared about the feasts that accompanied them.

"Oh forget it," he said. "Let's go find out!"

He retrieved his favourite stick from where he'd tossed it into the brook, then hurried off down the path. I snatched up the remains of our food, and followed. Feast or no, I wouldn't want to waste good mushrooms.

I ate them, and Lleyden beat up bushes, as we followed the meandering trail through the woods. The closer we got to home, the stronger the smell of the festive bonfire became.

It was a little odd that there was no music, even if I hoped they'd skipped all that nonsense, and it wasn't until we'd almost reached the forest's edge—birds silent in the trees surrounding us, and the sun almost set—when I finally heard people shouting and crying out.

Not cries of jubilation and glee, however, but of terror and panic.

"Someone's lost control of a fire!" I told Lleyden, then started jogging, to sooner see the spectacle. "I bet it's your stupid oven again!"

And it was. Lleyden's father's bakery was ablaze. But that wasn't the only building that was wreathed in fire. Half the village was.

"Mama! Papa!" Lleyden cried out, and overtook me as I faltered. He attempted to run towards the inferno, but I caught his arm and dragged him backward into the bracken along the mouth of the trail.

I hadn't seen them at first, but now I did.

They strode amidst the chaos, armed with cruel blades and vicious spears; cackling and howling beast-things, like nothing I'd seen before.

They were moving from house to burning house—rounding people up. Searching for something.

Someone made a break for the forest trail, over the small wooden bridge and almost directly towards us. There was a hiss then a thud. He let out a grunt, stumbled, and slid face-down to a halt on the pebble-strewn path before us. And there he lay—with a black javelin lodged between his shoulder blades and jutting into the burning air.

Lleyden squealed in panic, and I clasped my hand over his mouth, urging him to remain silent and restraining him as he struggled to run. His blue eyes were wide and full of tears, which reflected the horror before us before spilling over my knuckles.

I took the stick from his hand and assured him that I would defend him. But we were as good as dead.

The largest monster bounded forward to retrieve its spear from our neighbour as the poor man stirred, and tried to crawl away from it all—towards us. And in the light of the burning buildings, I could see that it was Kyrill—the nice young man who helped Lleyden's father bake bread.

"Run!" he implored us, as the creature wrenched its weapon free. But I couldn't.

Despite being hunched over and crouching on dog-like legs, the monster was taller than any man I had seen. Scuffed and rusted plates of black iron, crudely stitched to quilted crimson cloth, covered its dark mottled fur. Its corded neck ended in a bestial, wolfish face—with wild white eyes, and large rounded ears. Black lips were parted in a wide and frenzied grin that slathered and frothed with terrifying glee. I couldn't have conjured a more frightening monstrosity in *any* of the stories I told to scare Lleyden.

But there it stood; a nightmare made real, and wreathed in an aura of violence and death.

I crouched in the undergrowth, staring at the thing, completely paralyzed by fear and awe as it reached over its shoulder and unhooked a massive cleaver from a strap upon its back.

The weapon was twice the size of me; a blackened and stained slab of iron—with one edge ground roughly into a wicked blade that ran up its monstrous length, and then angled up to a pointed hook.

The creature hefted the cleaver over its head with one massive arm and let out a cackling howl. Then it swung the blade down and ended its victim's struggle in an instant.

It lifted the body to examine its handiwork. Kyrill had only come to the village recently, from some distant city in the north. He had hoped for a simple rural life here. Now he was dead.

The monster stopped suddenly, sniffed the air around it, and howled once more. Then it turned its head, slowly, deliberately, and looked me right in the eyes.

It cast Kyrill's corpse aside and began advancing upon us, gibbering and snarling, each step causing me to wince. Lleyden collapsed into a whimpering ball at my feet.

Every fibre of my being wanted to run, but I stepped over the boy and, both hands clasped with white knuckles, raised Lleyden's stick—his enchanted sword—in front of me.

The monster reached me and stooped down, its face inches from mine, my weapon pressed against its throat.

I could barely breathe—overpowered by its wretched breath, and the stench of its unwashed hide and blood-soaked clothing.

It let out a slow growling laugh that gradually built up into a manic cackling, and before long the beast roared with heaving hysterics. I stood before it, eyes wide and unblinking, the pathetic stick still aloft in front of me.

When the dog-headed creature eventually calmed, it leaned in again so that its face was unbearably close to my own, and its cloudy white eyes bored into my very core.

And to my utter surprise, it spoke:

"Little Bare-Skin pup. Your head matches drying blood, and your age is as it should be. Do you wish to run? Or have I found she who is brave enough to stand and face the weave of the Vyshivka, as was promised?"

But it wasn't bravery that kept me rooted there, it was desperation. Or perhaps it was simply foolish, childish defiance.

Whatever the cause though, I wouldn't let this horrific thing take Lleyden. I would die to protect him. And, as hard as I could, I thrust his sword towards my foe's cloudy white eye.

But quicker than anything I'd ever seen move, the monster caught my weapon in a giant clawed hand. It crushed the magic sword to splinters, and loomed over me, menace burning within its pale eyes.

"Ah! So you choose to fight…" the beast whispered. "You have the Spirit of the warrior within you—the Spirit of the Mother herself. At last I have found you, and you shall be my own."

Then it struck me across the temple.

ii.

I awoke in an uncaring darkness. Cold, bruised and sore, I hung from metal manacles—my bare feet just able to touch the floor beneath me.

I could hear the sound of rain hitting stone, but little else.

I wasn't even sure how long it had been since the world had last flickered briefly back to me. I knew that I'd been carried in a caged wooden cart with several strangers. Pulled by braying, emaciated mules, and flanked by the vile dog-beasts that had assaulted us—before passing again into dreamless nothing. Other than that, I was lost.

Where was I? What had become of my family? Had my mother and father escaped? What of my baby sister? Lleyden?

I focused my hearing as best I could over the sound of the pouring rain, and blinked away the tears that welled in my eyes, then squinted into the gloom around me. As scared as I was, crying pitifully would help nothing.

There were others in here with me; smallish shapes and the soft breathing of women and children, or perhaps something else.

It wouldn't be too long before I could make out my surroundings.

Even as my eyes adjusted, there was a break in the downpour, and the light of a low-hanging full moon—momentarily no longer obscured by clouds—shone through a barred porthole in the wall to my left.

There were four others strung up alongside me. All children, though not from my village, and perhaps not all Kimori either. Two women lay curled in the straw that was piled in the corner, their ankles shackled to thick chains pinned to the wall beside them. One of them looked to be a Kimora—skin much paler than mine and my people's however, and her ears seemed to have been cut short. Her reddish-blonde hair was matted with congealed blood and filth. The other was much larger than our people. She had cropped hair, and was covered from head to toe in some sort of paint or clay.

I turned my head to eye up the children next to me. There was a girl strung up to my right, she stood on both feet, and leaned against the wall, her weight hanging on the manacles that restrained her. She was quite noticeably larger than I—a little chubby, even—and looked decidedly foreign. Her long auburn hair hung in braids on either side of her dirty, tear streaked face, her skin was pale and almost mossy, and her ears were small and round. She shivered with each breath she took, but otherwise made no sound or movement.

"Psst…" I hissed, attempting to catch her attention. "Hey, girl."

She ignored me, maybe unable to understand my language.

On my left side were three other children, so I turned my focus toward them instead. Immediately next to me, and nearly close enough to touch, was a boy. He was shorter than me by almost a whole head, but his chains were longer than mine, so he was able to crouch beside me with his unusually large feet flat on the grimy stone. At first, I thought the copious hair that covered his body was clothing, but the boy wore nothing but a ragged loincloth, and a sack over his head.

The other children beyond him were girls. Both a fair few summers older than I, and almost adult by the looks. I knew neither of the two, though they were both similarly freckled and tanned, and bore inked designs on their skin—much like the people of my village. Both of them dangled limply from their bonds, and neither appeared conscious.

I turned once again to the hairy little sack-headed boy beside me.

"Hey boy. Can you hear me? Are you awake?" I whispered. He was still breathing, so at least I knew he wasn't dead, but he didn't stir. I waited a few seconds before trying again. This time, barely whispering.

"Hairy boy, where are we? What is this place?" I asked, tentatively reaching a foot out to prod him softly.

The boy twitched—his chains rattling against the stone wall as he spasmed, and I recoiled in surprise. He jerked his head around, like a bird of some sort, and he mumbled something unintelligible through the sack in alarm.

"I can't understand you with that sack on your head," I told him. "Move closer and I'll try to grab it with my foot."

The boy didn't move that much closer, but turned towards me, and made a muffled attempt at replying—still twitching his head bizarrely, maybe to try to hear me better—so I stretched my left foot toward him as far as I could, waiting for the moment that his chicken-like twitching would bring his sack within my reach.

Sure enough, seconds later, I managed to grab hold of the corner of the boy's burlap helmet between my toes, and tugged sharply.

The filthy sack came away from his head as I stumbled backwards slightly, and I swung from my chains awkwardly. I righted myself, regained my balance on the tips of my toes, then turned to look at the boy I had unmasked. Only, there was no boy.

He was a miniature man; fully grown, but a foot or so shorter than me. He sported a hearty set of sideburns, and a chin covered with stubble. Large green eyes stared back at me, surrounded by crow's feet and purplish bruising. He smiled at me reassuringly in the gloom, and I felt strangely safer—for he had a kind and weathered face.

Then he said something in a language I didn't understand.

I squinted at him.

"I don't understand you," I said. "Do you speak Kimorin?"

"Old Kimorin? Aye, enough to get by. Haven't used it in quite some time. Although, simple Solent Fae is much the same and 'tis easier on my tongue. Like as not you understand me now?" he replied, slowly and with a thick accent, which sounded almost musical.

"Yes, I do. Where are we?" I asked.

He glanced around at the prison then back at me, before shaking his head and shrugging.

"I don't know for sure yet. But 'tis definitely a dungeon."

"I'd figured that much for myself. But in any case, I must be free," I told the little man. "I must find my family, my village."

He nodded and bit his lower lip, looking up the wall—along the length of the chains that I hung from, then back down to the manacles that held my wrists. His brow furrowed in thought.

"You are, most assuredly, one *very* brave child," he informed me, as he examined his own manacles in turn. "And do you have a name?"

"Zyntael," I replied. "Zyntael Fairwinter."

For a split second I forgot that I was chained to a wall, and made an attempt to reach out and shake the small man's hand. But upon realising my folly I merely bowed my head politely instead.

"Well, I'm pleased to meet you Zyntael Fairwinter. My name is Phobos Lend," the man said, and shot me a quick smile before returning his attention to his iron cuffs. "Now. I need you to help me with something, and for it, we may both be free in time."

I nodded my head eagerly. "What do you want me to do?"

Phobos Lend, the hairy little man, sucked air sharply through his teeth, and looked at me with a frank expression across his kindly features.

"I need you to help me break my hand."

"What?" I asked, puzzled. "Did you misspeak?"

"No, no child, I want you to swing on your chains there, and kick my hand. Right on the thumb," he replied, eyebrows raised over reassuring eyes. "You're going to need to put *all* your strength into it, you understand?"

I nodded, still confused, but willing to do anything to get myself free of this place.

"Okay then," Phobos sighed. Then he held his left hand against the wall above him, and pulled the manacle away from his wrist with his right hand.

"Maybe swing a few times at the wall to get a feel for it, and then when you are ready, kick right there. As hard as you possibly can." He tapped the first knuckle on his left thumb with a finger.

I gripped the chain above me, and hauled myself up the damp stone wall, a little unsure of how exactly I was going to swing sideways along the stone and manage to kick the man's hand hard enough to break it. After a few attempts, however, I found that I was able to jump away from the wall, and swing across sideways, using my body weight to propel me like a pendulum.

"Good, good," Phobos said, watching my progress. "Ready when you are."

I glanced at his hand—pressed against the wall, slightly below me and to my right. I glanced at his face—battered and weathered, but with nary a shred of fear to be found amongst its many creases. Then I pushed away from the slick stone with all my strength.

I arced through the air, and gritting my teeth and squeezing my eyes closed tight, as though it were to be my bones obliterated, I planted my heel as accurately as I could, on my new friend's hand.

He let out a gasp of pain and recoiled slightly, rattling the chains that bound him. I had missed the thumb joint, merely crushing his index finger and a bit of his palm. I was endlessly glad that it was him and not me, but I felt terrible all the same.

"All the Fae!" he cursed. "Try again Little Zyntael—quickly!"

I didn't hesitate. I pushed off the wall near him, bounced from side to side a few times to build up momentum again, then kicked him squarely in the hand a second time.

This time, I heard something in his hand pop—felt it through my heel. Phobos let out a stream of curses, in many languages by the sound of it, and he thrashed his left hand around in pain.

To my surprise, his unusual plan worked, and his hand slid through the diameter of the shackle he wore. His thumb folded inward enough by the impact of my foot that it cleared the thick iron bracelet. He clutched his battered hand against his chest, and the chain that had held it was drawn upward through the loop in the wall above him, when he brought his right hand down to nurse the injury.

Phobos stopped swearing long enough to drag the rest of the chain down through the loop, and drop to his knees on the slime-covered stone floor, where he cradled his wounded hand in his lap. Then, with a few deep breaths to prepare himself, he wrenched his crooked thumb back to where it belonged.

I hung from my chains, wide-eyed, observing the small man and impressed by his fortitude, though afraid that he may expect the same from me. That fear grew rapidly when it occurred that the chains that I was affixed to didn't run through a central loop in the wall, but rather, they were pinned into the stone individually—if I were to escape my manacles in the same fashion, I'd have to dislocate both of my thumbs.

I waited in tense silence as Phobos dragged himself to his feet and, still grimacing and occasionally shaking his injured hand, approached me. He began examining my shackles. The man muttered to himself and stroked the stubble on his chin, as his green eyes darted back and forth between the metal cuffs that held my wrists, and the anchors that pinned them to the wall above and behind me.

"Well?" I asked fearfully, the dread overcoming my patience. "Must I break my hands also?"

He looked at me with a furrowed brow, sucking air between his teeth as he had earlier, before finally breaking into a smile, and shaking his head.

"No, no little Zyntael. We shan't be harming your lovely hands. And besides which, I couldn't reach up to kick them into paste, without all manner of acrobatics anyway."

He reached out his undamaged hand and patted me on my shoulder. His large palm was rough and warm, like that of a carpenter or craftsman. Or a father.

"But worry not, I will have you freed. I am no stranger to these sorts of bonds and contraptions," he added with a wry smile, then turned away and began scanning the room quietly for something— trailing his chain behind him as he went.

He searched the chamber for what felt like an hour, his movements unnaturally quiet and stealthy. Eventually, just as a fear that the little man had abandoned me to my fate began to well up within my mind, he returned with a battered old wooden bucket, and something clutched in his fist.

The bucket had been used as a chamber pot judging by the stench, but the wood that made up the sides of it had warped and split, leaving the container useless. Phobos set the filthy thing down beside me, untroubled by the rank smell emanating from it (and now himself). Then he stepped up onto the creaking makeshift stool.

The small man revealed to me what he held in his palm. Two old nails; one bent, and one straight—both rusted and thin.

Like he must have already done with his own now-absent manacle, he set about picking the locks on the shackles around my wrists, tongue darting from the corner of his mouth, and his face scrunched in focus. He mumbled to himself as he worked, in a language I didn't understand. It really did sound like music.

"What tongue is that?" I asked him, momentarily breaking the little man's focus.

"That is the speech of my people." He glanced quickly at me as I watched him work.

"There are more like you?" I asked, and immediately felt my cheeks flush, as it occurred to me that my assumption that he was some sort of freak or mutant was probably very rude indeed.

"Sorry, I mean to say; I have never seen anyone like you before," I tried to clarify.

"It is fine; I take no offense—I imagine many are surprised the first time they encounter an individual from a separate peoples," he responded—at this point holding one of the nails between his teeth, entirely unfazed by how disgusting that was.

"And in answer to your query, Zyntael: Yes, there are many of us. The larger folk call us 'Gnomes' and 'Pixies.' Often 'Ratlings' too. And we have both villages of our own, and also make our homes in the cities of such other folk as they."

"Ratlings…" I repeated. "Is that not an insult?"

Phobos chuckled.

"There may have been condescension in the name at one point, but it has been what they call us for so long, that now it is but a name. Just as the other Fae and we, call your folk 'Brownies' or 'Kikimora,' even though I suppose that you may have a name for yourselves in your own language."

"Well we are brown, but I've not been called a Brownie. And it's just 'Kimori' to us. I think it's the only name we have for ourselves," I replied. "Well, besides our family names, of course. Maybe the other peoples just use our word because we were the first of the Fae to use language."

"Hah! You should tell that to the Vodyanoi," Phobos said with a snort.

"Vodyanoi?" I asked.

"You mean to tell me you have never met a Vodnik?" He looked at me quizzically. "Short, stocky, skin like the swamp creatures they live amongst. They like gold, gems and other precious things—song too."

"So are they like your people?"

"Oh child, no not at all. They mostly live deep in the marshlands, but if ever you visit a city, they will often be the first smiths and merchants you will find. Provided it rains enough, or a river runs nearby."

He seemed surprised that I had never encountered one of these people. Though to be fair, until now, I had never really left the vicinity of our village.

"Well, I wasn't old enough to accompany my father's traders on their expeditions, I have only seen ten summers," I informed him. "I mean, I've heard that there are other Fae-folk, but I don't know their names or anything. We have some quilts, pottery and treasures that were brought back from other towns, but I don't know if my father's people met with other folk than Kimori."

Then I realised that those treasures, those objects that we had traded for, were likely either taken or burned by the creatures that had raided our settlement—alongside those who had collected them for us. I fell into quiet and sombre reflection, whilst the little man softly whistled a tune, and worked his makeshift lock picks.

My morose mood didn't last long however, as my thoughts were interrupted by a sequence of loud metallic clicks from above me. First one manacle, then the other were released, and the full weight of my body bore me to the filthy stone at my feet.

"Aha! There we go little Zyntael. Free at last!" Phobos beamed, and helped me to my feet. "Apologies for the delay. I haven't had to work with an injured hand in a long while!"

I rubbed my tender wrists, glad to be free of the manacles.

"Thank you Phobos. Where did you learn to open locks like that?"

He tapped the side of his nose, and winked at me.

"Just a little something I picked up over the years," he told me, then looked around the cell. "Now, we need to escape this dungeon. Perhaps some of these others may enjoy the prospect of freedom, though the more of us there are, the more the likelihood of raising alarm and bringing attention."

"We could find a way out, then come back for the others," I suggested, glancing at the other girls strung up along the wall—none of whom appeared to pay us any regard.

A small part of me wanted to tell Phobos that we should leave them—that I only cared about finding my family and escaping this wretched place, but I suppressed the thought. For all the times he had claimed it was so, Lleyden was wrong; I was no monster.

iii.

"See anything?" I asked.

Phobos glanced away from the porthole he was peering out of, and the manacles he was hanging from swayed precariously.

"Rain," came his response—dryer than anything else in the dungeon. In a different situation, I would have laughed

"Can you make out where we might be? Is there anyone out there?" I pressed him, eager to hear anything that might lend a clue to the nature of our imprisonment.

"Nay, there is but a rain-streaked keep a few yards away from us. Fires burning inside a few of the windows, but beyond that I see only the storm. Sorry child," he told me, then dropped to the ground with a rattling of rusted chains. He made an effort to brush himself off with his hands, but was successful in merely spreading more filth over his hairy, brown skin.

"I don't know for sure, but the design of the keep, and the hue of the rock does make me think…" he trailed off. "No matter, we will soon be rid of this place, you and I."

He approached the door that stood between us and the unknown. I stood watching, shivering and feeling useless as he pored over it, until I could no longer bear the silence.

The door was made from grimy and knotted planks of wood, framed in rusted iron and with a small barred window too high up for me to peer through. There didn't appear to be any locking mechanism on this side, and my heart sank somewhat at the realisation that my new friend would not be able to make use of his particular skill set— and rusted nails.

"Is there no way through?" I asked.

"Zyntael. There is always a way through. That is what I choose to believe," he responded, turning to flash me a smile.

Phobos looked over the hinges before tapping gently on the wood a few times and in a few different places.

"Come hither Zyntael, I will hoist you upon my shoulders that you may spy what lies beyond." He beckoned me over then squatted before the door.

I approached and clambered up onto his shoulders, bracing myself against the door to retain my balance. He stood up and lifted me enough that I could reach the barred window. I gripped the rusted iron and pulled myself up to peer through.

On the other side there was a corridor. I couldn't make out much in the gloom, but at the far end, noticed that there was a soft golden light spilling from behind another door. The light glinted off something metal every ten or so feet along the corridor on both sides; but not enough that I could see exactly what was there.

"Is there anything lurking beyond?" Phobos asked in a hushed tone.

"No. It's dark but at the other end is a door and beyond that there is a light," I told him.

"The other end of what child? A room? Corridor?" he asked. "Can you see anything on the other side of this door itself? A bar or latch?"

"There is a corridor. I think maybe fifty feet along." I looked down at the other face of the door as best I could. I could make out what might have been a wooden plank, barring our escape. "Yes. There is a bar I think. Maybe wood," I informed Phobos.

"Well come on down. I will catch you when you are ready," he replied.

I began to lower myself down, holding onto the metal bars and sliding my feet down the slick wood. Then before I knew it, I was tumbling downward through empty space, no time to even scream.

Phobos caught me in his rough hands and sighed in relief as he set me back on my feet.

I realised that I held something awfully heavy in my hand, and raised it up to see that I had pulled the entire barred window from the door.

"Aha! Zyntael—you beautiful beast!" Phobos proclaimed. "You may have just found us our way through!"

I looked from the window frame to Phobos. Then realised what he meant and set the heavy rusted metal down. I looked up at the hole

17

that remained in the door. Definitely large enough to squeeze through.

"You or I?" I asked Phobos.

"Well do you think you could lift me up there?" he asked in reply.

"No, I suppose not. Oh well. Lift me up again then," I told him.

After a moment, I was clambering through the gap left in the door, having hauled myself awkwardly up the slick wood. More difficult a task without the aid of the metal bars to grip.

I pushed my torso through the door then spun myself around so that I sat on the filthy wood, the surface cold and uncomfortable on my exposed thighs. I paid no heed to my discomfort and briefly planned my next move. From this position I could reach up to grasp the iron frame above the door.

Hoping desperately that the decaying metal would hold, I hauled my lower half out of the door and dangled my feet below me, grasping in the darkness for some purchase. I found it in the form of the bar that sat halfway up the door and lowered myself carefully down onto it. From there I was able to quietly drop to the grimy stone below.

It took considerable effort to lift the wooden bar up and off the metal hooks that carried it. The beam was sodden and heavy from the damp. I struggled with my task for some time and made far more noise than I had hoped.

I had almost lifted the bar from its perch when I was startled by a voice that came from the darkness behind me.

I spun to face the source of the speech and saw only an arm, pale and sickly, covered in sores and scabs and protruding from between the black iron bars of a cell that was recessed into the wall of the corridor. I figured that barred cells ran the length of the corridor and were what I had noticed reflecting the soft light that issued from the gaps around the door at the far end.

"Hello?" I asked, scared at what might respond, and in an odd way, glad for the metal bars between it and me. "Who is there?"

My reply came in the form of a wheezing coughing fit and whatever lurked in the prison spat a wad of phlegm across the corridor.

I tentatively approached the cell, wary of the distance between myself and the grasping limb that reached out toward me.

I caught sight of the creature within and recoiled in horror at its decrepit visage.

It was a man of some sort, maybe a Kimora. But the sickly state of him made it hard to be sure. His face was covered in weeping sores, large pustules and boils that forced one eye closed. The other was an odd milky hue. His skin pallid and somewhat translucent, exposing thick blackish veins that pulsed close to the surface.

The rotten man wheezed again and attempted to speak once more. His words were hoarse and broken, and in a language that I had never before heard.

"Do you speak Kimorin?" I asked slowly, keeping my distance as the man twitched and shuddered, jerking his head around to eye me up.

His response was once again in the language I couldn't make sense of so I backed away and returned my focus to raising the bar off its stays and letting Phobos through to deal with the prisoner.

"Are you alright Zyntael?" Phobos asked from beyond the door.

"I am," I grunted as I heaved the plank of soggy wood up onto a shoulder. "There is a man here. In a cell. I think he may be sick from a plague," I told him.

"I expect there will be several others around," he said. "Don't approach anyone until I am there with you. We cannot be sure who any of them may be, and I do not wish to risk losing my new friend so soon after meeting her."

Enthused by his kind words, I redoubled my efforts at freeing Phobos and before too long I had lifted one end of the wooden bar from the door and laid the end down on the stone. Then with a tremendous struggle, I managed to haul the other down from its hook and it dropped to the ground with a damp thud.

The door creaked open and Phobos stepped out into the corridor. Tired as I was from the effort, I immediately felt safer and reinvigourated in the presence of this diminutive but brave Gnome.

Phobos ushered me to stay behind him and cautiously approached the mysterious and sickly figure in the cell. The man caught sight of my friend and wheezed out something in his strange tongue.

Phobos nodded and crouched by the bars of the cell.

They communicated briefly in that alien language and I watched, fascinated, as Phobos quietly headed back to our original cell then returned shortly after with a shallow wooden saucer filled with water.

He passed it through the black Iron bars to the pale man who drank its contents quickly and desperately, then reached out and patted Phobos on the shoulder. They continued to communicate and at one point Phobos gestured towards me.

I stepped slightly forward and at this point noticed that the figure in the cell was missing both a leg and half of one arm. Where the limbs were absent, there remained gnarled and knotted scar tissue, deep purple in the gloom of his cell. He looked to be very old. What little hair remained on his head was but rank silvery wire, and his body looked as though it were a swollen sack of rotted flour—wrinkled and sagging, yet bloated and lumpy around his belly. Despite the swelling, his ribcage was exposed through his putrid skin and protruded horribly as he took each heaving breath.

"What happened to him?" I asked Phobos, a hand resting on his back, reassuring myself that he would keep me safe.

"Our captors took him as a slave, worked him until an accident claimed his limbs then left him here to rot once he fell ill. They wouldn't risk eating his flesh in this state. By their nature they do devour the corpses of the slain, though not those who have died of sickness or plague," he told me, his green eyes reflecting the soft light—showing sadness perhaps.

"There is little we can do for this man," he sighed. "It may be some small mercy to return and end his suffering, but our pressing issue is to secure our own escape from this prison fortress."

"Our captors. They are the beast headed creatures, yes?" I asked. "They took me from my village. Killed my friends and neighbours. I don't know if they took my family, but I need to find out."

Phobos nodded.

"I shan't leave here until I know for sure," I told him.

"I understand, Zyntael," he reassured me. "We shall search for them as we make our exit."

He motioned me to follow him and we made our way down the corridor toward the door ahead. I peered into the gloom in each cell that we passed, though regretted doing so as most held only decaying corpses that were suspended from rusted chains and barbed hooks. I shuddered to think that those I loved had faced this fate and bit back tears as I followed quietly behind my companion.

The door out of the prison was slightly ajar, the flickering glow of a fire burned beyond, and the quiet was occasionally punctuated by a low, rhythmic growling.

"Stay here," Phobos whispered to me, then silently slipped through the gap in the door frame and disappeared from view.

I stood there, alone and cold in the darkness, straining my ears to hear anything I could. There was the distant rumble of the rain, the occasional wheezing from the imprisoned old man and the creaking of the dangling chains—beside the constant soft dripping of water in the oppressive gloom.

My thoughts wandered to grim places—I worried for Lleyden, for my mother and father, and for my infant sister, Zachya. I worried that they may have met some unimaginably horrific fate at the hands of the savage beasts that had taken me.

I silently told myself to remain strong; to overcome the constant deep dread that swirled like an inky vortex within me. Dread that was reaching out slimy black tendrils of doubt and worry to grope and probe at my resolve.

To take my mind off my fears, I imagined the bravery of the warriors and hunters from my village. The Wardens. Those indomitable men and women who had prowled the woods around us, protecting our people from all manner of foul beasts that had threatened us.

They never showed fear, and though scarred from many battles with the denizens of the forest, they were always the pillar of strength that we had depended on. I had always imagined myself amongst their ranks when I was older, even if Lleyden had always thought I was too idle and dumb. And I steeled myself to wear their mantle now. Only I could rescue him and everyone I loved from this place.

So, to that end, I decided to no longer remain idle. And I set off to find and assist my new companion—and to rescue myself first, and then Lleyden. Even if the plan probably *was* pretty dumb.

iv.

I squeezed through the doorway and found myself in another corridor. This one headed off to either side of me. Torches burned a short distance down the path that curved away to my right, and a staircase spiralled upward to my left. The rhythmic growling sound had ceased, but I decided to head toward the lit torches—careful to dart from shadow to shadow as stealthily as I could, as I proceeded nervously onward.

Before long, I came upon a wooden table with an assortment of junk and oddities piled upon it in two heaps. It was flanked by rickety looking stools that lay on their sides. Along the edge of each side of the table lay some sort of playing cards, some of which were scattered over the floor and around the upturned seating.

I approached the scene cautiously, and after a few tentative paces, noticed that the wet ground beneath me was no longer cold but rather, it was warm—and a little sticky. I looked at my feet to see that I was treading in pools of syrupy crimson liquid.

Blood.

The dark fluid was splattered across the filthy stone floor and was smeared in two streaking trails that led around a corner and out of sight. I carefully and quietly followed the blood around the bend and saw that both trails converged and disappeared under a closed wooden door.

Creeping up to it, I pressed my ear to the splintered wood and listened for sounds of life. I could hear a subtle scraping sound, and the faintest of metallic rattling softly echoing from the other side of the barricade. With a trembling hand, I cautiously reached up to turn the doorknob, took a calming breath, and gently pushed the door ajar.

It was a storeroom of sorts. A high wood-beamed ceiling hung above me, and the walls that supported it were lined with shelves, barrels and crates—leaving only a narrow space between them.

In that space, bathed in the soft amber glow of a single lantern, lay the unmoving bodies of two of the creatures that had taken me. These ones were much smaller than those that had assaulted our village and neither carried any weapons or wore any armour. Their fur was matted with blood, and the trails of the stuff terminated where they lay.

Crouched beside them, now dressed in a scavenged woollen tunic, and busying himself with adjusting the leather straps of some sort of metal panelled overcoat, was Phobos Lend. He looked up at me, eyes wide and alert as I poked my head around the door.

"Zyntael. I told you to wait," he whispered, a stern expression on his face.

But then his features softened, and he beckoned me over to him.

"Close that door behind you, and help me with these straps, would you?"

I did as the Ratling asked, and within a few minutes he was outfitted in a makeshift suit of armour.

"Do you know how to handle a weapon of any sort?" he asked, tucking a pair of curved knives into his belt, once he was suitably dressed.

"I have hit a rabbit or two with rocks from a sling, and have thrown javelins for sport, but I haven't yet held a real sword or axe," I told him. "Nor have I used a real spear, either."

"Well perhaps we can find something that you might carry with you, to ensure your safety aye?" he said, and began quietly rummaging through a pile of weapons and work implements.

Soon Phobos produced a short blade, with a handle bound with a green leather cord. The ragged metal blade was only a few inches long, and was battered and rusted, but it was sharpened on both sides and ended in a needle-like point. It was better than nothing, by a long shot.

"A makeshift stiletto. This will be useful as a last resort," he declared, handing me the weapon.

It was heavy and awkward in my hand, though simply holding the blade made me feel somehow more capable; less vulnerable.

"Now, if anything should make an attempt at you, aim for its eyes or throat, and stab repeatedly with all your strength, understand?" Phobos asked, and I nodded. "We will make a fighter of you yet."

Then he retrieved a belt from one of the many crates of junk, and, after cutting off a decent length of the leather and poking new eyelets into the remaining material, he wrapped it around my waist and fastened the buckle. I slid my new weapon into its home on my left hip, and looked down at where it was tucked—the metal cold against my body through the itchy dampness of my ruined dress.

I turned back to Phobos, and motioned at the two slain creatures. Their bodies smelled damp, sweaty, and rancid, and although they hardly looked as fearsome as their kind had before, they were still intimidating nonetheless.

"How did you do this?" I asked my friend, who smirked at me, and then squinted at the corpses.

"They were asleep," he told me. "I took a knife from the table that they slept upon, and slew them both before they awoke."

He dusted his hands off ambivalently as he spoke—as if discussing some mundane chore, and not murder.

"Moving them into this room was more difficult a task than killing the cursed things," he sighed, and then added; "And you never can quite get the stench of Vulkar from your skin."

"Vulkar?" I asked. "Is that the name for these... beasts?"

"Indeed it is," he said. "Blasted two-legged plains-hounds, really. Cruel, brutish, and merciless. Scavengers and raiders. One is a Vulkar, more are Vulkari—and in any number, they are a blight upon the land."

I didn't know what a plains-hound was though, so his explanation didn't tell me much more about the foul creatures than I had already encountered first-hand.

"These ones are definitely smaller than those that took me away," I told him.

"These were males," he replied. "Vulkar females are larger, meaner, and far stronger than the males. Their society is flipped around the other way, when compared to other folk."

Despite many of the hunters from our village being women, if there was ever to be a battle, the men would be the ones to do the fighting. I was surprised that these creatures lived in the opposite manner. Then again, I was surprised that these creatures existed in the first place.

"What of their young? Do the females carry them into battle? Or can the males...nurse?" I asked, though I wasn't entirely sure why I wanted to know, and may have merely been putting off leaving the relative safety of the storeroom.

24

"I honestly couldn't tell you," Phobos admitted, then to my disappointment, began to move towards the exit. "The hallway outside must have been one of the lights that I saw from our cell window. There was another a few floors above us, so we can assume that there will be more Vulkari lurking there."

He pulled the door open and scanned the hallway, then beckoned me to follow him.

"We should scout the rest of this corridor, then perhaps head up the staircase back that way." He motioned back down the hallway. "There may be more prisons down here, so with luck we will find your family. Your people."

The prospect filled me with a peculiar mixture of hope and worry.

I gripped the handle of my new weapon in a somewhat futile effort to calm myself, and followed Phobos as we made our way down the hallway of the Vulkar fort.

We moved down the stone corridor slowly and cautiously, Phobos glancing back at me every now and again. If it was to ensure I still followed, it was a pointless exercise since I maintained only a few feet distance from the little man as we crept from shadow to shadow.

If I followed too closely, or made too much noise as we travelled, he made no mention of it to me—perhaps aware that my proximity to him brought me comfort and security in such a frightening and hostile place.

I focused on his movements; lithe and silent. I made every attempt to emulate his footwork and his posture, but I was far clumsier than he. I winced each time I carelessly scuffed my feet or stepped in puddles of grimy water, sending what felt like deafening blasts of sound echoing along the dank stone path before us. Surely I was going to get us caught.

In no time at all, and thankfully un-caught, we had followed the curving passage as far as we could. But my heart dropped to see that before us, completely blocking the way ahead, lay a huge pile of mossy rubble. Broken wooden beams protruded from the slick stone, like the decaying skeleton of some rotting grey beast, and rain lashed the rock and filth. It ran in green and brown rivulets into the darkness beyond, but we couldn't follow it.

The collapse looked to be ages old. Nothing had passed through this way in a long while, and the knowledge that my family and friends were not in this direction filled me with an aching fear that they had met some much worse fate at the hands of the Vulkari.

"Well. No prison this way, young Zyntael," Phobos sighed. "Worry not though, child, we shall find your loved ones. Perhaps there are more cells elsewhere above."

"I hope so," I replied, and blinked back the stinging tears of frustration and worry that welled in the corners of my eyes.

"Come, let us leave this place, and ascend further into grave peril," Phobos said, turning to look back the way we came.

"What of the other prisoners? The sickly man?" I asked.

He glanced at me, an odd look on his face, before answering.

"We should not tarry any longer than is necessary. But if you wish to, we could make an attempt at freeing them." He paused and looked at me sincerely, his face close to mine. "Each moment we waste down here though, is a moment more that your loved ones must wait. A moment that might well be their last."

I thought of the Vulkar that had taken me, and of the man who had been practically carved in half, like a sapling beneath the creature's mighty blade. Poor Kyrill. Not a family friend, but I had spoken to him on several occasions—been given a sweet roll more than once even. And that Vulkar had cleaved through him with no regard whatsoever.

I thought of those creatures, the large ones, the females. Thought of what they could do to my mother and father, to my baby sister. And decided to heed my new companion's advice.

"We should leave them," I told him quietly, voice quaking even as I tried to steady it. "We should find my family and Lleyden."

"Good choice, Zyntael," Phobos reassured me, with a gentle hand on my shoulder. "Those who choose inaction have unchosen fates to meet. And the decisive should not wait to share them too."

Then the little man began creeping ahead. Though I was somewhat unsure what he meant, I didn't waste time pondering his words, and instead, followed him back down the hallway—my hand resting on the leather bound hilt of my dagger, ready for that peril.

It didn't take us long to retrace our steps back to the stone staircase that curved upward into the bowels of the keep. I kept my gaze on Phobos' form the entire time, not brave enough to glance back towards the prison cells as we passed by.

I felt a peculiar mixture of guilt, and of resolve. I would choose my own fate, but I couldn't quite shake the sense that those others may have been denied the chance to do the same, by my decision to press onward.

I left those thoughts at the bottom of the stairs, however. My mind was drawn instead to a gnawing fear, and a growing sense of apprehension, that rose as we did; cold stone step after cold stone step. Toward grave peril indeed.

V.

Phobos urged caution, and silently motioned me to fall in behind him as we crept along the dim passageway that curved away before us.

The second floor of the fortress was just as decrepit and filthy as the floor below. This one however, showed signs of use. Footprints, like those of a massive dog, trailed through the grime underfoot, and a brief examination of the tracks had given Phobos reason to believe that they were fresh. Maybe hours old at the longest.

The rain outside had subsided, yet the air still felt cold and damp. It carried the scent of sweat soaked fur, filth, and decay. I tried my best to focus my senses on Phobos, but the further we progressed, the more the foul odour of the place permeated the gloom around us.

We passed several rooms, and Phobos checked each in order. But none held captives, and were instead either storage for loot or for reeking waste.

Eventually we came upon the end of the corridor. Like below, this one had caved in—only here we could see out into the night. To the left of the rubble and fallen masonry was a pair of large wooden doors. Both were closed, though the footprints led beyond them, and a soft orange glow emanated through both the keyholes, and the cracks around the frames.

"Options Zyntael. There are always options," Phobos whispered, barely audible. "We could clamber out and upward, even down to potential freedom. Or we could proceed beyond."

He pointed his injured thumb at the opening in the stone before us, where the roof had given way, then at the doors in turn.

"I don't know which way to go," I told him honestly.

"Neither of us do. And when that is the case, any choice is a good one," he replied, and rested a calming hand on my shoulder again.

"We are in a very dangerous place, my girl, and any path we take is like to be fraught with danger. But now is a chance for you to make your own fate." He tapped a finger on the hilt of my dagger. "And you and I are not without the means to claim that fate—if pressed."

I looked from the closed doors, to the pile of slick stone before me, trying to imagine what lay beyond each. Then I turned to examine the tracks that led beneath the doors.

There were long, smooth gouges out of the muddy filth, as though something had been dragged through it. I had no idea if whatever had been hauled along had come or gone, but thought that if it had been somebody I knew that had been taken from our cell, then I needed to find out. My mind was made up.

"The doors," I whispered to my companion.

"Alright. Let us listen and look then. Perhaps we shall gauge what we may face afore us," Phobos said, then crept to a rusted metal keyhole in the wooden surface, and pressed a cupped hand to it. He smiled at me, and then squinted in focus as he listened at the door. I quickly followed suit.

On the other side of the damp wooden door, I could hear muffled sounds of some kind of animals—a few constant soft yapping sounds, and the occasional growl.

Phobos caught my attention and pointed to his eye and then the iron keyholes, so I leaned over and peered through, whilst he did the same.

From what I could make out, on the other side of the door there lay a large room. Wooden tables and benches stood in rows along the length and width of it. There were piles of detritus, as well as barrels and crates taking up much of the space between each table. The source of the flickering light was off to the right—too far for me to spy through the keyhole, but it cast tall inky shadows upon the stone wall at the far side of the hall.

I couldn't make out any movement or other signs of life, though I couldn't be sure whether the shapes around some of the tables were mounds of waste and filth or some sort of creature.

I looked from the keyhole to Phobos who turned to speak to me.

"I say we quietly skirt around the outside of the room. No doubt about it; there lie Vulkari, or their fell pets within. But we have the advantage of small size, light steps, and the shadows," he whispered, and I nodded as he continued. "If our attempt fails, we may need to fight. Do you understand?"

"Yes," I told him. But I had absolutely no idea how to fight, and no desire whatsoever to learn by engaging a creature at least five times my size, and so easily capable of the brutality that I had borne witness to.

"Good," he whispered.

Then, slowly and carefully, he turned its thick iron handle and pushed the door open.

vi.

I had never felt such a powerful surge of fear and excitement. Even the attack on our village, though truly terrifying, had carried with it a kind of numb shock that dulled my senses.

Creeping carefully now, from shadow to shadow, cast by what I discovered were the forms of my numerous slumbering captors, I felt every sensation more intensely than ever before.

Each grunt or shifting movement that the monstrous beasts made sent my heart into a frenzy, and it pounded in my chest with such ferocity that I could hear the blood rushing around within me.

Each scent in the warm and acrid air found its place in my awareness, and that smoky warmth, issuing from what I had soon noticed was a roaring fire pit, brought on an uncomfortable sweat. It dripped, stinging, into my wide eyes, and covered every inch of my trembling body as I followed Phobos as cautiously as I could manage.

My hand clutched the handle of my simple knife, knuckles white with urgent dread. I blinked away the burning sweat and focused on the shape of my guide; his small body blended almost unnaturally into the charcoal black shadows, and his footfalls were completely silent, as he stalked from cover to cover as though a feline.

He turned every few paces to gauge my progress, occasionally motioning me to remain still as a particularly close shape stirred slightly, or sniffed the burnt air around it, or growled menacingly.

I counted at least twenty of the monsters, as we circled the perimeter of the feast hall. Some lay between tables, some slumped on the benches, and yet more lay on the tables themselves—often in living piles of three or more.

Mixed in with the sweaty stench of their unwashed hides and overcooked food, was the unmistakable bitter sharpness of spoiled cider. We passed carefully between large casks and barrels, marked with a lively painting of an apple tree on each. It would have been almost comically out of place, if all humour hadn't left me.

"Icespire Orchard. Expensive stuff," Phobos had almost silently mouthed to me, pointing at the ornate script written above each painting.

I could not read, and knew not what this referred to, so merely nodded and glanced around nervously as the small man squeezed himself between a cluster of barrels, and scanned the way ahead.

We pressed on, circling the hall, and giving a wide berth to the many sleeping Vulkari where possible. At one point we were forced to crawl, bellies down in stinking filth, rancid spilt cider, and food scraps, underneath a row of tables—upon and around which five or so of the creatures lay. Phobos smiled reassuringly at me periodically, or turned back to steady me with a gentle hand on my shaking, sweat-drenched shoulder. Each time spurring me onward, further into danger. Into grave peril that I had chosen.

What must have, in reality, taken minutes, felt like an hours-long journey to the other end of the hall. Each step and every small movement fraught with the risk of awakening the hostile beasts all around us.

Finally, we made it to an archway that led from the hall. It must once have carried large doors, but nothing of them remained besides the pitted iron hinges that jutted from the stone on either side of us.

Before us, a wide set of steps ascended longer than they were high, the remains of a once-regal carpet that covered them, rotted, soggy, and mournful underfoot.

We followed those steps upward and forward, each footfall noisily squelching, and impossible for me to quiet—fuelling the burning fear within my heart that I was working on borrowed time, and at any moment would be beset upon by a rabid, snarling Vulkar.

The shallow staircase led us up into another great hall. This one must have been the entrance to a fortress that, in its original form, would have been splendorous. Far to our right there was a set of reinforced doors, towering into the shadows above. To our left, a stone staircase that branched off to either side at the first landing, and curled around to skirt the huge hall as a balcony.

We entered the imposing space through another doorless archway, roughly halfway along its length. Opposite us, a similar opening held nothing but threatening darkness beyond it.

The hall was lined with crude metal braziers, hanging from where I imagined something much more regal would have once been. Most were empty, although a few held smouldering embers that dripped hissing trails of glowing pitch, and cast their soft amber light around them in flickering pools.

Beneath these, reflecting the dim fires, stood the remains of once-formidable suits of armour. Most were missing plates and parts—looted or defaced. Some were emblazoned with alien writing and bar-baric emblems, as though they had been marked for ownership or even decorated, rather than mindlessly defaced.

I stood in the shadow cast beneath the archway, taking in the ru-ined glory of the vast hall, waiting for some direction from my friend, and was just about to ask him his opinion when he grabbed me, hand over my mouth, and pushed me up against the cold stone of the arch-way.

He let go as quickly as he had taken hold of me, and pressed a silencing finger to his lips, then pointed across to the opposite side of the carpeted hall.

From within the darkness ahead, a group of three armoured Vulkari strode. They were carrying ugly barbed weapons, and were holding back two hulking dog-like beasts, on thick chains and cords of black leather.

The Vulkari gibbered and snarled, speaking amongst themselves in their violent and unusual tongue as they swaggered into view—their leashed animals braying and snapping at one another ahead of them, constantly straining against their bonds.

These monsters were far larger than those that Phobos had slain. They were almost as tall as the one that had taken me. Their fur was spotted and mottled, dull brownish shades in the weak light cast from above. They had bristling crests of darker hair that ran from their heads down along their spines, between their large, rounded ears. Their jagged maws dripped and frothed as they cackled at one an-other.

One Vulkar appeared to be the leader of the three, and was wear-ing a particularly intimidating set of armour. Each piece of the suit, originally built for people, had been repurposed and attached piece-meal to a purple quilted blanket, and wrapped in fraying and filthy linen and leather.

From the armour, protruded rusted and twisted spikes of black iron, as though the bristling thorns of a blackberry thicket. A roughly stitched leather hood covered much of the Vulkar's reddish-furred head, leaving only its horrible wild eyes visible from within round holes in the material.

That monster held no mewling hound-creature of its own, rather, it carried a hooked polearm that it leaned on as a kind of walking staff as it moved, flanked by the other two. The beast had a pronounced limp, but seemed not to pay much heed to whatever injury it bore, and carried itself in as dignified a manner as such a savage looking monster could muster.

I watched in terror and awe as the small group of Vulkari entered the great hall, and hoping with all of my being, I silently begged any spirit or god that would hear me, to let their patrol take them in a different direction.

My desperate prayers were apparently answered, when the band made a left turn and began to approach the massive double doors at the end of the hall—still oblivious to our presence.

I let out a sigh of relief and felt my tense muscles relax a little.

But my solace was misplaced. One of the leashed creatures turned suddenly in our direction. The huge animal began snarling and howling at the darkness within which we lurked, drawing the attention, first of the other hound, and then of the Vulkari.

The larger of the three barked something in their savage tongue, and the other two loosened their grips on the restraints that held their pets, and raised their weapons.

I didn't wait to see the Vulkari release their animals. By that point, I was already running as fast as my legs would carry me—back down the staircase, and into the feasting hall.

vii.

I ducked under the first table I came upon, slid painfully in the slime beneath it, then sprang back to my feet and ran between two rows of benches.

In a flurry of movement to my left, Phobos launched himself over a stack of wooden crates, and threw the pile down over the pursuing beast behind him. I tried as best I could to keep him in my view as I weaved between a head-high pile of rubbish and a prone Vulkar—jumping over the creature's outstretched limbs as I ran.

I leapt up onto a bench, and scrambled onto the tabletop, slipping and scurrying over scraps of food, and wood slick with spilt cider, and worse. I heard the beast snapping its slavering jaws behind me, but dared not look back.

As deftly as I could manage, I flung myself through the choking smoky air and landed on a table in the opposite row. But I flew too fast—arms flailing desperately as I overshot the target surface—and skidded painfully into the hunched mass of a wiry and ragged looking Vulkar. The creature jerked upright as I impacted its body and sent the both of us tumbling over into the aisle behind it.

The Vulkar snarled and yelped, dragged itself to its feet, then turned to see what had collided with it. I stared up at its hideous face, and backed away, my hands groping behind me for the edge of the bench. The emaciated Vulkar cocked its head almost quizzically when it saw me before it—its attention firmly distracted from the massive hound-like form that soared through the air in pursuit of me.

Their collision knocked them both to the floor, and I ran.

I used the ensuing chaos to put as much distance between myself and the snarling beast as I could—sure that the brawl that unfolded in my stead would not keep the creatures from continuing the chase for long.

I had lost all sight of Phobos though, and panic set in. My vision narrowed to a pulsing spot before me, and I paid no heed to the direction in which I was now heading.

I sprinted along another set of tables, scattering stolen cutlery, broken ceramics, and gnawed chunks of bone in my wake. Then I dropped back into the next gap in the furniture—this time rolling sideways, to emerge in a relatively clear space.

I wasn't entirely sure if I was heading back to the door that we had originally entered the mess hall through, but knew that I had to gain as much lead on the creature that pursued me as I possibly could, so I kept going as fast as I could.

Just as I reached the end of the row, another Vulkar emerged. The feral beast towered over me ahead, this one fully aware of my approach. But as the monster made an attempt to grab at me with its outstretched claws, I ducked off to my left—into a gap in the soot smeared stone wall.

From both exhaustion and the searing heat of the small chamber I found myself in, my entire body was slick with sweat. Another, much smaller Vulkar that had been oblivious to the commotion, was taken utterly by surprise at my sudden entrance into the kitchen room.

I tried to stop my trajectory, but my damp feet slipped on the hot flagstones of the kitchen floor. Utterly unable to correct my course or halt my momentum, I tumbled headlong into the grasping Vulkar. The ladle it carried clattered against the wall, and the foul smelling creature stumbled back and let out an ear-piercing cry. The sound of sizzling meat and the unmistakable smell of burning hair and seared flesh met my senses, and the Vulkar recoiled to nurse the hand that it had just embedded in the burning coal fire.

I kicked out at its face as the monster made another attempt at grappling me in place. The combination of my sweat-soaked skin, the beast's wounded hand, and the repeated frenzied kicking I delivered to its ravenous face, saw me able to free myself of the Vulkar's grip and scuttle away on the charred stone floor.

I frantically scrambled and clawed to gain purchase, and managed to haul myself upright, just as the massive bulk of one of the dog-beasts slid through the doorway in front of me. I was caught between a Vulkar and one of their hunting pets, certain to meet my fate in the sweltering kitchen of this forsaken fortress. Here was where I died— far from my home, and the people I loved. Alone and terrified.

I didn't have time to prepare myself to meet my end. Didn't have time to accept that I would be more than likely ripped to shreds by the hound in front of me. I didn't even have time to hope that my death would be painless and quick.

A dark shape sailed through the air above the animal, a flash of shining metal glinting in the light of the fire pit. The hunting beast before me righted itself, and turned slightly to face me, with a murderous craving in its black eyes. Then there was a hissing spray of thick, hot fluid that coated my face and chest, and splattered over the glowing coals beside me. And with a gurgling yelp, the animal collapsed.

Before I could even comprehend what was happening to me, I was being dragged over the carcass of the beast, slipping and sliding in its freshly sprayed blood. A rough, warm hand clutching my arm, and a familiar, bruised but kindly face eying me up and down—checking me for wounds.

"Quick! Behind me! Get into the scullery, make your way through as quickly as you can. There will likely be a servants' entrance to this place that we may escape through," Phobos commanded me, his voice hoarse. "Go child, hurry!"

Then before I had taken a single step towards the battered swinging doors that hung behind us, Phobos ran up the corpse of the fallen beast, and threw himself upon the burnt Vulkar, sharp blades hacking and stabbing at the creature as it tried desperately to fend him off and retreat from the room.

I turned and ran, pushed my way through the barriers, and sprinted between piles of decaying foodstuffs and swinging carcasses. I threw myself against the scullery exit, heaved the wooden lock bar up and onto my shoulder, and then with a final, panicked effort, pushed the heavy plank up and away from the frame. I shoved open the doors just as Phobos hurried up behind me.

"Run Zyntael!" he yelled.

And I did.

viii.

We fled through the fortress courtyard, slipping and scrambling in the filth.

The Vulkari and their war hound made chase across the wide, rain-lashed expanse of mud, and towards the towering bastion that housed the portcullis.

I barely had time to think as I sprinted through the puddles and muck. I dared not look back, and focused only on keeping my footing, and pushing myself along as fast as I possibly could. My breath burned in my chest, despite the cold air of the outside world. A thick curtain of drizzle stung my face and blinded me as we pushed on.

To my dismay, the massive metal gate ahead was lowered, blocking our exit. To the right of it though, a decaying wooden staircase led up to a rickety looking platform that ran along the fortress wall behind the crenulations that lined it.

"Up there!" Phobos yelled to me.

I could barely hear him over the snarls and cackling of the beasts at our heels, the pounding of the blood in my ears, and the rush of the wind and rain as I streaked along beside him.

"I see it," I managed to say, and steered myself towards the wooden structure.

Phobos reached the platform first, and leapt upwards to haul himself onto the support beams, then extended a hand to pull me up.

I jumped, missed, and landed in a painful heap—with a faceful of foul-tasting dirt.

I pushed myself to my feet, and glanced quickly back, to see that our pursuers were a mere dozen or so paces away from me. They were flanked by their hound and led by the large, armoured Vulkar that we had run from earlier. The hulking monster gibbered and howled, its eyes wide with bloodlust, and its limp all but forgotten as it closed the distance between us.

Without any hesitation, I scrambled up and around the treacherous stairs. They groaned and creaked with each panicked step I took, but held out. My companion ushered me in front of him, and hurried me along the platform when I reached the top.

We sprinted along the slimy walkway—the planks, discoloured and green and threatening to collapse at any moment. The rotted ropes that held the structure aloft were frayed and mangled. They seemed barely able to support the weight of the sodden wood.

"Run and jump to the roof ahead, little Zyntael, I shall buy us more time!" Phobos called out, and pointed ahead to a slate roof that was backed against the exterior side of the wall a short distance from me. Then he turned, and began hacking away at a set of ropes that stretched taut from the stone wall to the wood beneath our feet.

A javelin hissed through the rain and cracked against the stone behind him, and Phobos cursed in several languages as he worked to dismantle the anchor lines.

The Vulkari had made it to the top of the staircase, but left their dog-like beast snarling and snapping at us from the muddy ground below.

I vaulted over the wall, sending a cascade of crumbling stone and loose slate in my wake.

The largest of the Vulkari bellowed something whilst pointing a clawed hand at Phobos, and I turned to see him gesture back at them. Then to my complete and utter surprise, he yelled back at the creature in its own tongue. I could only make out one word—"Azuur."

Whatever it was that he said, it must have touched a nerve.

The other two Vulkari that flanked the larger beast began snarling maniacally, and surged forward, brandishing their cruel blades—just as Phobos hacked through the last of the ropes.

With an ear splitting racket, the platform gave way beneath their stampeding feet, showering the muddy courtyard below in splintered wood and chunks of rock. The braying hound was buried in a torrent of rotted timber and stone—silencing its howls for good.

The larger Vulkar flung its polearm away and leapt sideways. It managed to grab onto the stone wall and scratched at the slippery rock with its dog-like feet, trying to pull its weight up.

The other two weren't so quick, and plummeted to a violent end below.

Phobos had managed to leap to safety, and caught up with me as I skidded and slid down the slanted roof on the loose and slippery tiles. The drop from the roof was still quite far and I nervously peered below.

"Hang and then drop," Phobos said, and I lay down on my belly and slid over the edge, feet-first.

I lowered myself down, and looked back the way we came, in time to see the Vulkar drag itself up and over the crenulations. Wild fury glinted in its eyes, as they met my own.

I dangled from the creaking gutter, easily eight feet from the dirt below, and hoped that the earth had soaked up enough rain to cushion my fall. It barely registered that I was falling before I hit the ground. My legs gave way beneath me and I sat, dazed and bruised, in a puddle of stinking rancid filth—my hope fulfilled, at least.

Phobos landed beside me on firmer soil, and rolled to his feet gracefully. He turned to me and rested a hand gently under my armpit, ready to hoist me up.

"Are you hurt, little Zyntael?" he asked.

I shook my head and blinked away my stunned state, then steadied myself on Phobos as I stood.

"Let us make haste then. That hag is sure to follow, and she is not a foe I wish to tangle with," he told me, wiping the muck from my face.

I nodded.

"Okay."

Still sore and battered, I ran after the Ratling as he weaved between brambles and thickets, down the overgrown hillside. The constant drumming of the rain soon gave way to a thunderous roaring.

Ahead of us and far below, a violent river surged—the water white and foaming, as the rains swelled the flowing moat. We scrambled down the slope, fighting through bracken, and tripping on ferns and roots as we went, until we reached the rocky precipice where the winding river had long ago carved out its path.

"Can you swim?" Phobos asked me, yelling over the roar of the rapids below.

He didn't give me time to respond before he took my hand in his and dragged me with him. We ran and jumped into the void. I closed my eyes and anticipated the plunge into icy waters.

But it never came.

Instead, searing pain burst through my body, as though I were being torn in half—my left knee felt like it had disconnected at the joint, and my arm threatened to do the same.

Phobos dangled below me, and the massive clawed hand of the cackling Vulkar gripped my ankle. My heart pounded in my throat, head pulsed with flashing pain, and my eyes swam with tears that flowed freely, and dropped down to join the river below.

"Your blade, Zyntael!" Phobos cried out, clutching my right hand tightly.

His voice snapped me back into the present, and I scrambled to draw the all but forgotten weapon from my belt. I desperately slashed at the Vulkar that held me, even as the beast began to haul both Phobos and I back up towards it. Small as he was, with the entire weight of my friend hanging from me, my arm was being torn from its socket. I couldn't reach anywhere close to the Vulkar's hand—let alone its body, or its snarling, slavering face. I almost gave up, almost let the Vulkar claim its prize, and then it struck me; I knew what I had to do—I knew what destiny, what path, I would choose for myself.

I looked back at Phobos, looked directly into his kindly emerald eyes. For a moment they remained wide with panic, then his features softened and his brow furrowed as it must have occurred to him what I was about to do. In that split second, I wanted to thank him for saving me time and again—ask him to find my village and my family. But there wasn't time, and the words were gone from me anyway.

All but one:

"Sorry."

Before he had a chance to tighten his grip on me, I jabbed the dagger into his flesh. His hand recoiled from mine, and Phobos Lend fell—his arm outstretched, and eyes still locked on my own, even as he disappeared beneath the surface of the surging torrent.

THE SECOND STITCH

SERVITUDE

i.

The stench of their damp hides and rancid breath made me gag, and brought water to my eyes. I told myself that this was why my vision swam and my cheeks were wet, but I was simply afraid. No matter how much I tried to choke back the fear, to abate the flow of tears, and to still my trembling limbs, I could not.

I was dragged roughly along by the massive limping monster that had caught me—through the mud-slick courtyard, and past the wreckage of the fallen platform that had claimed a few of our pursuers earlier. The monster didn't return through the larder, however, but instead, made its way around the fortress—to a huge set of wooden gates that bristled with twisting spikes and barbs of rusted metal. There, it shouted some kind of command in its gibbering tongue to a smaller Vulkar on the wall above, who repeated it to an unseen listener.

Before long, the gates swung open, and I was hefted onto a shoulder and carried helplessly back into the gloomy bastion. Past howling groups of the furred beast-people and their snarling hounds, we made our way into the imposing hall where I had first been spotted by the Vulkar that now carried me.

At the far end of the hall, at the foot of the stone steps that led to the balconies above, there was some sort of throne. I hadn't noticed it in the gloom before, but now it was unmistakable—lit as it was now by two tall braziers that cast their flickering light upon a large, grinning figure.

Surrounded by a handful of chattering bodyguards, sat the towering dark-furred Vulkar. The Vulkar that had taken me from my village, and claimed me as her property.

I tried as best I could to hide my fear, but it was no good. I was terrified, and nothing I could do would change that.

I was dumped unceremoniously and painfully before her like a sack of grain, and the huge beast cackled and rubbed her clawed hands together eagerly. She gestured for me to stand up and I did so, upon sore and quaking legs.

"You caught me. Why don't you just kill me then?" I wanted to ask her, defiantly. I wanted to at least show her that I was not afraid. But instead, I merely whimpered pathetically—unable to find any words, nor force them from my trembling lips.

I had always thought myself to be brave, perhaps simply to make up for Lleyden being afraid of everything—but there in that hall, surrounded by the wretched and cruel beasts, I felt as though that brave spirit was in short supply. It took all of my resolve just to stand before the giant, just to hold her unsettling white gaze. And the time before she spoke felt like an age.

"Lend," she growled, leaning forward even as I recoiled from her. "Where is the Ratling swine?"

Her Kimorin was brutal and oddly pronounced, but Kimorin nonetheless.

"H-he is gone," I stammered.

"Where?"

"Into the water."

"Did he leave you? Abandon you to save his own hide?" The Vulkar looked around at the grinning faces of her underlings, who giggled at her words. "How delightfully appropriate a turn of ev—"

"No!" I cut her off. Phobos was no coward. Of that I was sure.

"No?" She genuinely seemed surprised, or at least I guessed that she did, since the smile she had worn abruptly straightened into a sort of frown, and she cocked her ugly head to one side.

"I dropped him into the water. It was my choice."

"So… You sacrificed yourself to save the scoundrel? How noble," she said, then with a vile smirk. "Or is it that you felt the need to unburden yourself of such a parasite?"

"I don't understand," I told the monster. "Why are you asking me about Phobos?"

The Vulkar nodded slightly as she continued. "Wretched vermin, so bold as to retrieve you from my chambers whilst I was elsewhere— would he be so brave, were it that I remained here?"

"We escaped from the same dungeon. He unlocked the chains that…"

She silenced me with a gesture, and glanced around once more at her fellow monsters. This time they didn't grin, but rather avoided eye contact and bowed their heads.

All except for the one that had caught me. The one with the limp.

The dark-furred leader hissed something at the limping Vulkar. Her tone sounded threatening, even if her words were garbled nonsense. Then the big Vulkar turned back to me and began to question me again.

"I wish to know. Where is he heading? Where did he plan to steal you off to?" She frowned and said a word I didn't quite catch. 'Legion' perhaps?

"He never told me. I just wanted to find my family. And Lleyden."

The thought of them at the mercy of this foul animal almost brought the tears back to the edges of my eyes, but I blinked them away.

"You would not find them here," she snorted. "I had no need of them at all. And least of all some pathetic whelp. But, should you attempt another escape, then I shall see them suffer indeed. I shall return to your village, eat your family, and pluck the innards from your little friend. Whilst he still lives."

"Why me then? What do you need me for? To eat?" I asked, but the Vulkar simply laughed.

She spoke something in her own guttural language and the others joined her in laughter once again.

I glanced nervously around at them as they leered at me. There were maybe ten or so; all large and ferocious looking, with different shades of fur, and different markings on their bodies. I guessed that they were all female.

Some wore armour, some only simple clothing made from cloth and strips of hide. All were decorated with beads, trinkets and charms throughout their crested or braided manes, and all had intricate lines of thread embroidered upon their various garments. A few had brightly coloured paint that was smeared in patterns upon their bodies, matting the fur beneath it, but it didn't make them any less horrifying to look at.

"When the rain breaks—a ten-day at the most—we go east. You shall accompany me. You shall serve me, listen, watch and learn," the Vulkar began, and I looked back at her—the ugliest of the lot. "I would see to it that you come to value my favour, when we reach our destination. Such that you do not soon forget it, in the time to come."

I stared at the monster, overwhelmed by the crushing, helpless feeling of my future being dragged from before me—replaced with only torment.

The Vulkar tapped a claw against the side of her throne.

"For now, you shall remain here—in my chambers and at my side, this time," she said, as though it were a threat to the Vulkari around her.

Almost immediately I was shunted over to her flank, where one of her guards held a leather collar that awaited its place around my neck. I was stripped of my dagger belt, and chained to the monster's throne. Then another Vulkar threw a blanket upon me.

I curled into a ball and wept, squeezing my eyes closed and covering my ears with my hands, in a vain attempt to block out the gibbering and the snarling of the terrible creatures as they resumed their business.

I just wanted to go home. I wanted to wake from this terrible fever-dream, and await the spring harvest festivals with my mother, father, Zachya, and with Lleyden.

I just wanted it to end, but my ordeal—my chosen path—had only just begun.

❈　❈　❈

Not unlike the four-legged hounds that the Vulkari kept, I too was kept by the leader of the monsters—shackled by my throat to a length of sturdy chain.

When she wandered around the crumbling keep to command her raiders and examine their spoils, I was dragged alongside her. When she made her way to the feasting hall to eat, I was brought along too.

There I was fed scraps of unknown meat, stale bread, stagnant water, and spoilt cider. The worst was the strange black liquor, which smelt of mushrooms and earth. It burned as it went down, and set my head spinning. But I drank it, because the monster told me to. I drank it for the sake of my family.

It went on like this until the rains finally broke. Each day was spent in the shadow of that cruel and savage beast, dragged and prodded along on weary legs and filthy feet, doing everything she bid of me, for fear that she might turn her wrath to those I loved.

Night-time brought with it only fitful and feverish dreams and no promise of any rest, but instead the anticipation of another day wherein the misery would begin anew.

Only on the final night of my stay in that dreary and foul place did I finally sleep for longer than a few hours. Perhaps due to sheer exhaustion, perhaps because of the foul mushroom concoction that I had been forced to drink by the jeering and cackling Vulkari—until I had vomited and nearly passed out.

On that night, despite the terror of what the new daybreak would bring with it, I fell into a welcome blackness. I fell into a blackness that claimed me until the early hours.

Shortly before the sun rose, wrapped in a bundle of blankets beside the nesting place of the Vulkar Warlord, my exhausted mind began to form a dream:

Red sky and burning, and a pale green moon.
A desperate chase, only I was the pursuer.
I felt something calling me. Something dark and violent, and wholly internal.
There was bloodshed. By my hand. Done or still to be, for the sake of a child.
And I forced myself to wake.

❊　❊　❊

The morning sun hurt my eyes, and the bonds that held me hurt my wrists. It was not to be a pleasant day—but I was hardly surprised.

Lashed to a pole that jutted vertically from the front corner of the war chief's wagon, like a sort of primitive trophy, I watched as the Vulkari assembled their force.

As the morning passed and the beasts made their way from the black stone keep and into the courtyard, I realised just how many of them there were. I couldn't count high enough to keep track of the small army that set out.

There were at least thirty of the large female Vulkari, and each commanded a retinue of smaller, subservient males—or maybe just younger females. The larger creatures bullied and harassed their underlings, who served to haul carts and carry items where their non-Vulkar slaves and beasts of burden could not.

Those beasts of burden were massive oxen. Oxen whose formidable horns trailed crimson and black fabric, which fluttered in the breeze as we travelled.

It would have very nearly been a wonderful sight to behold, were it not for the nature of the convoy, and the savage monsters that drove it eastward. Were it not for the way I was displayed upon the front of the leading wagon.

Thankfully, around noon on that first day, my captor had me taken down from the pole. But it was hardly a relief. It meant the beginning of true servitude.

"Kikimora. You shall make yourself useful. I shall have you tend to my whims," the Vulkar said, and pointed out a large wooden locker near where she sat. "Count the soaps and oils, see to it that I have sufficient supply. You can count, I hope?"

I nodded.

"Then for what do you wait?" the monster growled. "Begin."

So, for the rest of that afternoon, as our cart slowly rumbled along, I counted and sorted the soaps and oils that were stored in the monster's locker. If her intent was to cleanse herself with them, then she was sorely lacking.

Next, the Vulkar had me tidy the caravan in which she lounged upon a luxuriously pillowed crib. The room was quite large, with enough space for her nest-like bed and an assortment of chests, as well as an old wooden table—upon which there rested all manner of maps, charts, and scrawled notes. I was to sleep on a pile of blankets and furs in the corner.

On the steadily rocking walls of the ox-drawn vehicle hung various grisly trophies; skulls of unrecognised beasts, hewn pieces of armour, and broken weapons—perhaps claimed in duels and battle. I was made to wipe the dust from each.

Later, as the sun began to set behind us, and the shadows of our convoy grew long on the rough ground ahead of us, I was sent to fetch food for the monster.

I walked, head down and eyes ahead of me, between carts and wagons and Vulkari that snapped at me and jeered as I went, searching for the blue-painted wagon that housed the food stores.

It didn't take a whole lot of time to find the cart I sought. Laden with barrels and crates and hauled by a team of snorting beasts, the massive vehicle rolled along, around five or six wagons back.

Beneath a flapping canopy, a particularly scrawny Vulkar sat at the helm. It regarded me with a squinting stare as I approached, but seemed far less hostile than any of the others had been.

I wasn't really sure what I was to do, nor how I was to board the slowly moving wagon without being crushed beneath its giant wheels—let alone ask for the salted lamb I had been ordered to fetch.

"Karthak?" the Vulkar said, leaning down a little.

I had no clue what that word meant, but had already heard it spoken more than a few times.

Nervously I met the creature's gaze and tried to tell it why I was there.

"I have to fetch some salted…"

"Sheep-flesh." It nodded. "For Karthak. Her favourite."

Without halting the trundling cart, the Vulkar clambered over the rear of the driving seat, and began to shift sacks and crates around. Then, without warning, a haunch of meat wrapped in rough sackcloth arced through the air towards me.

I caught it awkwardly, stumbling under the surprising weight.

The Vulkar returned to its seat, a bottle of liquor in one hand, a pear in the other.

"Closer," it said. "Wine for Karthak."

I walked along beside the blue wagon, as close as I could safely get, and the creature passed me down the bottle and the fruit.

"Fruit for you. Cannot eat only meat. Shall hurt stomach," it told me, then it grinned, and shooed me away with a casual flick of its wrist.

I trudged back to the leading wagon, my moving prison. And once there, I sat and ate my pear in silence. My captor—'Karthak' apparently—spoke the entire time she ate.

Whether it was because she spoke in her own tongue, or with her mouth full, I could hardly understand her. Except for the last thing she told me.

That, I did understand. I understood it when she told me, but I would come to understand it so much more as we travelled into the east. For the entire journey, it would become the simple truth by which I lived.

"That I have chosen you as my own shall not spare you the righting of wrongs," Karthak said. "And so, Pup, if you misbehave, you shall be beaten."

ii.

We trekked eastward for what must have been, at the very least, a half-dozen weeks. Sometimes we passed settlements—either abandoned, or if not, shortly raided by small groups of marauders.

These bands would return with food, equipment, working beasts, and always more captives.

A few of the captured villagers were killed—especially those who attempted escape. The rest had no such luck.

I had never been so exhausted, never felt so lost, alone, and miserable as I did during those first weeks that we travelled east. But I was the luckiest of my kind.

The others who had shared my cell were forced to march somewhere in the middle of the motley column of beasts, carts, and wagons winding its way over hills and through the valleys that led down from the highlands. The women and girls were cruelly whipped and prodded along by the Vulkari. They were mercilessly heckled, and occasionally outright beaten, with far more ferocity than I faced.

Some didn't make it.

The chubby girl with the auburn hair slipped on a loose stone when navigating a muddy river bank. Her twisted ankle meant that she would need to be carried. The Vulkari preferred her as food.

Another captive died of exhaustion; her emaciated body barely served to slake the war-hounds' ravenous hunger.

I avoided any such fate. Unsure of whether I was truly thankful for it though, for in place of death, there was only labour, to ensure the Warlord's every whim was met to her satisfaction. When I failed to fetch the right liquor, or misplaced a trinket, took too long to relay a message or even if Karthak just felt like it, I was hit, thrown, or kicked. And I was sometimes even lashed to the pole again—often because I was simply in the way.

I stayed up there, shivering despite the warming weather, and with the cords that held me, digging uncomfortably into my skin. Of course, that was until the cruel Vulkar Warlord needed something fetched, cleaned, or prepared for her again.

Each night I fled; slavering hounds at my heels as I ran from my captors. But come the dawn I woke where I'd laid my head the night before, cursing my cowardice—cursing my inability to carry out those fantasies.

Each day I scanned the ridges, at times spotting the odd rock or stump that in my beleaguered mind appeared as a small figure, who crouched low in the undergrowth and spied upon our passing. But for every day that passed, my hopes for a rescue, and the fire that burned with a desire to escape grew dimmer still.

I wasn't getting out of this. I wasn't deviating from this miserable path. But at least my family still lived.

And so it went, as the spring gave way to a sweltering summer—a summer that seemed to grow fiercer and brighter all the while our company travelled further and further from the western highlands.

We travelled over rolling hills, through creaking overgrown woods, and across wide plains that were home only to swaying grass. Occasionally, when the Vulkari set up camp the Warlord would chat to me conversationally in broken Kimorin or more often than not in her own tongue, whilst I simply sat, terrified before the hulking monster.

After visits and reports from what I guessed were high-ranking lieutenants or other such leaders, she would repeat to me what they had told her or muse over information.

I did not understand her to begin with, though over the time that the terrifying beast spent speaking to me in her cackling and gibbering language and her heavily accented attempt at my own, I learnt to recognise simple words and phrases—strangely, many seemed almost based upon the words that Kimori used.

After some time, another band of Vulkari joined us. These were smaller and had lighter fur than Karthak's warriors and they decorated their pelts with brightly coloured baubles and seashells. Although they too embroidered their clothing, theirs bore designs that evoked flowing water, sewn with thread of various blues and greens.

They were led by a wiry Vulkar with unnervingly pale yellow eyes.

Through all of the trinkets, it was difficult to tell exactly what colour the fur that covered its body was—a dirty yellow, or a pale ochre perhaps. Either way, the creature's hide was speckled with darker spots, and seemed to thin out to an almost charcoal velvet as it reached the ends of its limbs.

That same dark colour surrounded the Vulkar's face and the tip of its tail, as well as the thick mane that followed the curve of its spine. The mane was braided and decorated with beads as it crested the monster's head, between large, rounded ears, and spilled down around its face. It did almost look nice—or as nice as the hound-like face would allow.

The creature's eyes were wide and wild, they glittered with mischief and darted from place to place as if searching for prey or something to amuse the Vulkar. As ever it seemed amused.

Those eyes spotted me, and the beast regarded me with some surprise, but no hostility when it entered the Warlord's carriage.

Then, once it had concluded its business with Karthak, it came and sat next to me on the edge of the chieftain's giant cart.

"Star-Star," the Vulkar said simply, holding its clawed hand to its own chest.

I stared at the monster, unsure of what it expected. It smelt of salt and earth—almost pleasant.

"Star-Star," it said again, then extended a finger toward me.

"Zyntael," I told it.

The monster nodded and leaned closer to me.

"Star-Star shall not harm you."

I doubted that very much.

"Star-Star shall calm Karthak as well."

I doubted that too, but somehow, it did just that.

❈   ❈   ❈

More than a month since leaving the rain soaked fortress we finally reached our destination—A walled city near a dried out riverbed.

It was a particularly hot and sunny day. The sapphire sky was absent of clouds, and the sun burned large overhead. The cloth over the carts cast short shadows, under which the Vulkari lounged. I was free of my bonds and had been manhandled onto the lap of the massive Vulkar Warlord.

Karthak idly played with my hair and sang to herself in her own language. The yapping and howling of the Vulkari speech was ill-suited to song, but I dared not tell her so, the many times she asked me what I thought of her tune.

Her fur was damp with perspiration, and smelt sharp and unpleasant even though I had scrubbed it that morning. The cleansing was only one of the many odd tasks that Karthak had entrusted me with more recently. The others included braiding her mane, oiling her armour, and clipping the claws on her feet.

I wasn't sure if I preferred these new tasks to those I had originally been given though—at least the latter had allowed me a break from the monster's company. Now, the only time to myself that I was allowed was when the smaller Vulkar, Star-Star, spent the night with the Warlord, and I was made to sleep elsewhere.

True to its word though, the salty Vulkar did seem to have had a calming effect on Karthak over the last few weeks, and it had been some time since I was last struck by the monster. But still I feared her, and what might befall my family should I fail to live up to whatever it was she wanted of me.

The Vulkar force was at a standstill for most of that day, and the creatures sheltered themselves in whatever shade they could find. For the most part they idly waited, batting away flies and chatting with one another. One or two were busy sharpening their cleavers and spearheads, and beating out the dents in their armour that they had received during the last raid.

A dishevelled and gangly Vulkar, one I'd never seen before, approached the wagon upon which the chieftain and I sat. The strange Vulkar was flanked by two armoured people, both wearing suits of polished black maille, carrying spears, and holding large, round shields emblazoned with a black fist over crimson paint. The armoured figures marched in unison, apparently impervious to the intense heat of the midday sun—heat that I was sure was enough to boil them alive in their suits.

They approached the wagon and stopped a short distance away. The Vulkar bodyguards nearby regarded them with neither surprise nor hostility, and returned to whatever they were doing. They must have had many deallings with them in the past.

"Greetings Karthak," the wiry Vulkar said in their own tongue.

It bowed deeply before stepping up onto the wooden running board of the wagon and leaning on the pole (that I had thankfully not been tied to for some time now).

"Greetings Vellik," Karthak responded in Vulkar-speak as well, and the two began conversing.

Though I couldn't follow the entire exchange, there was mention of food and drink as well as slaves—or maybe prisoners. Some form of bartering was to be done.

I did not need to catch it all, as Karthak turned to me and spoke in Kimorin anyway:

"What say you, my pup? Do you think that we have gathered enough to retire, rich as any Bare-Skin king might be?" she asked.

"I don't know," I replied, and cast my eye back along the column of wagons. "You certainly stole a lot of things, so it must be worth a lot. Do you sell the people you took as well?"

"We sell all we do not use. They fetch a good price at times. But do not mistakenly call these naked cattle 'people.'"

She registered the confusion in my expression, lifted me down from her lap, and set me at her feet. Then she stood and pointed back at the horde of Vulkari.

"We have many strong raiders, and our numbers swell. Each must be fed and armoured. Not all things can be taken, and the best things can only be bought."

The massive Vulkar reached down and rustled my hair in what she must have meant to be a reassuring gesture, however she almost twisted my head clean off. I winced through the pain, and tried my best to hide it as she continued her lecture.

"Worry not my pet child, you shall not go to market. But the Bare-Skin males shall be workers. The females, whores and chattel—and all shall fund our expansion, and our future."

I didn't know either word she had used for the women, but could guess whatever their fate, neither the men nor the women would face a good life ahead.

"Well there are at least twenty people that you have taken, so if you add that to all of the stuff…" I began.

"Again. People? Hah!" She broke into a scornful cackle. "Oh, but they are not worthy to be called such."

The massive Vulkar crouched down, her face inches from mine.

Her breath was at least not so unpleasant now, since I had scrubbed her sharp teeth with crushed resin and peppermint oil during her morning grooming.

"They are not people," Karthak growled, her eyes squinting intensely. "*We* are people. We are strong."

I took a small step back, trying as best I could not to cower, but then the Vulkar burst into a manic laughter again. She grasped my face with both of her massive hands, squeezing my cheeks roughly.

"Oh Kimor-pup, you may be one of us yet. You show more bravery than most of the menfolk around here. Cowards and wretches, unfit for the rut. If they could not read and count so well, I would hardly tolerate them—even as provisioners."

Yet again I didn't quite understand her words, but was glad for the sudden upturn in her mood.

"What about Star-Star? You tolerate him," I asked.

The Warlord threw her head back and roared with laughter.

"Garok? Him?" she cackled. "Him? Oh pup… Garok is no male."

She shook her head, grinning.

"Speaking of craven males though…" she began, and turned back to the scraggly Vulkar before her.

It was scratching its ragged ear, fishing around for wax or scabs that it hastily devoured. I grimaced, and the creature winked at me—its face twisted into a permanent grin. Karthak re-joined conversation with the scrawny beast and I turned my attention to the armoured figures before us.

They stood statue still, their faces obscured by shining black helms that reflected the beating sun and forced me to squint. Beneath the helmets, and the veils of black chain attached to them, the soldiers looked to have ruddy brownish skin. It was darker than my own, and had an odd green hue.

From what little of their features that I could make out, they did not appear to be Kimori, or if they were, then they were far larger and scarier than any I had ever seen. I had no idea who or what they were, but I did not feel comfortable near them. Even more so than any Vulkar in the camp, these figures radiated a sense of menace, and a cold and brutal purpose that the dog-beasts lacked.

I glanced over to Star-Star. She sat in the shade, running a sparking whetstone down the ragged edge of a long knife. She paused to shovel dried nuts and fruit into her mouth, and noticed me looking at her. The Vulkar cocked her head.

"What?" she spoke in her own language, and narrowed her unnervingly pale eyes at me.

"Who is that?" I asked her, pointing at the two soldiers and hoping that I had spoken correctly.

The Vulkar's ears pricked up and she stopped sharpening her weapon then grinned at me, chewing.

"It finally speaks a little Vulk-tongue? Does Zyntael listen to Star-Star's conversations at night?"

She sat regarding me, waiting for a response. I nodded then pointed again at the figures nearby.

"What are they?" I asked, wondering if my intention was properly conveyed.

The Vulkar looked over to the strangers, then back at me, and slowly and nonchalantly poured another handful of food into her mouth.

"Hogd Gogdlins," she said, spitting crumbs.

The words didn't sound as though they belonged in the Vulkari language. The sounds were different and didn't suit the way Vulkar mouths moved as they spoke, and it didn't help that she had her mouth full.

"Hogd Gogdlins?" I repeated back at her.

She shook her head.

"Hod Godlins?"

She shook her head again, grinning more widely than before and said it again:

"Hogd Gogdlins."

I kept repeating the words back to her, changing them slightly each time, and apparently much to the Vulkar's amusement. Until eventually she enthusiastically nodded her bestial head and clapped.

"Hobgoblins? Right? Hobgoblins!" I told her triumphantly, laughing nervously with the Vulkar warrior, at our little game.

Then one of the Hobgoblins turned its head and stared at me, its eyes glinting in the shadow of its helm.

So I shut up.

iii.

Our entourage mobilised and made its way down a rocky path and onto the overgrown remains of a once grand road.

Initially, the flagstones were cracked and broken, making for a bumpy and uncomfortable ride. Gradually though, as we passed by the surrounding farms and moved into the outskirts of the vast walled city that loomed ahead, the road became noticeably smoother. Karthak told me snippets of the violent history that the place had, as our carts and wagons trundled along.

Known as the Solent, it was once a Kimorin settlement, a massive trading port of some importance. However, the river that was used to ferry trade-goods had long since been diverted by Vodnik-run mining companies. She claimed that when the water dried up, the original inhabitants had dispersed.

The place was then used as a bandit stronghold, to be fought over by many different groups, until the Hobgoblin force had marched in from far off to the east, and massacred the criminal rabble to claim the walled city as their own.

Despite the presence of a leader in this fortress, there was an even more powerful Emperor who dwelt in the east, and commanded thousands upon thousands more of the Hobgoblins. Karthak cautioned me to treat them with respect, for even a mighty Vulkar Warlord such as she knew that to contest authority with these foreigners was to invite swift and certain retribution.

I stared in awe as our wagon passed beneath the huge stone archway that allowed entrance to the dusty maze of houses and other buildings.

Towering stone blocks had been placed around as guard towers, lashed with ropes and wooden walkways that zig-zagged overhead.

Each was populated with groups of uniformed Hobgoblins that held bows and spears, and regarded our force coolly as we passed beneath.

Leaving all but Karthak's wagon and another couple, which carried a hoard of looted goods between them, we followed the road along and up a slight incline. Within the city, any disrepair looked to have been fixed by the new occupants, though both the road and the many small houses we passed still showed the scars of past skirmishes.

There were ashen smears around windows where new wood had been used to replace the burnt remains of what was there before, leaving only violent memory painted upon the stone. Rusting arrows and broken spear heads jutted from whatever wood and thatch had not been burnt and replaced, and roughly plastered gouges dotted the stone walls. I guessed that the damage must have been the aftermath of the siege engines used to conquer the city, and that the repairs were an ongoing labour.

I marvelled at it all as we travelled up the hill, away from the homes of the common-folk, through wealthier and much more impressive districts, and finally towards a massive bastion that overlooked most of the city from its perch on the crest of the hill.

Beyond an arched gatehouse, and behind a wall of its own, the mighty stone castle stood about five or six storeys high—proudly bearing the scars of numerous battles, and draped in an array of banners and flags. Each banner bore the same black fist, and they varied only in the text that surrounded the sigil—none of which I could read.

"The Legion Commander, Manox Threydon, makes this his home. He executes the orders of their 'God-Emperor' in these frontier lands, whilst the Goblin leader has turned his gaze westward beyond the Wastes. Their empire seeks to claim our Ancient Wilds, and we can do little to slow them, and less still to halt their progress.

Threydon is the right fist of the Hobgoblin war machine—something we would rather have filled with tribute, than clasped around our throats," Karthak informed me, pointing to the fluttering flags ahead.

I stood and stared. Stunned by the majesty of it all.

"You shall accompany me when I soon greet him. You shall address him as I do, and show respect. Do you understand, Kimorpup?" she asked, idly stroking my head as I gazed upon the keep in awe.

I nodded. Fear bubbled away inside me, but I dared not show it. I swallowed nervously then answered. "I understand."

"You shall make me proud. That is why I chose you," she said. Then she leaned over to scoop me from the rug beside her throne and hold me up before her frightful face.

"Now fetch your War-Mother's armour and blade. She must look the part for this audience."

She set me down and I scurried over to the large, ornately carved wooden locker within which the Vulkar chieftain stowed her black-plated armour.

It was a tiring struggle, but I made no complaints as I paced back and forth, carrying as much of her massive suit of armour as I could each time.

The task took a good while. I draped a quilted crimson undercoat over the Vulkar's thick hide, then fastened it with leather straps. The material looked to have been originally made to cover a warhorse, but had been adjusted to fit the Warlord's form.

Over the cloth, I fastened the many plates and spiked sheets of heavy iron, then finally, I adorned the Vulkar with a harness, to which she affixed her gargantuan black blade.

Karthak looked imposing, bedecked in her war-plate and carrying her savage cleaver—the hooked blade easily a head taller than I was.

"You must also be clothed," she informed me.

I stood awkwardly on the stationary wagon as a Vulkar whelp roughly pulled a strip of crimson cloth over me. It was little more than a large scarf with a hole barely big enough for my head, cut in the centre. To secure it, the Vulkar wrapped a thick leather collar (that had previously been worn by a war hound) around my waist, and forcefully buckled it up.

Over my chest, a short vest of bone strips was hung, and around each wrist and ankle, I wore bracelets of wood and woven cord. Then to finish the outfit, the male produced a necklace of deep red beads, punctuated by a single bead of onyx. He casually fastened the expensive looking trinket around my neck, and stood back to admire his handiwork.

"It looks good," was all I understood of his assessment so I nodded sheepishly and thanked him in his own tongue, then clambered down from the wagon to stand beside the Warlord.

"My pup, you are now fit to meet the Goblin King," Karthak informed me, and shoved me into step before her.

※　※　※

We marched together, surrounded by a mob of Vulkari, who bristled with barbed plate, and carried spiked and hooked weapons. And we were led through the gated entrance and across a tidy cobbled courtyard by a small escort of Hobgoblins who, despite the lack of spikes on their gear and their comparatively small size, still somehow cut a much more imposing figure than those Vulkari.

There was a terrifying sense of order and purpose to the movements of every Hobgoblin I saw. Where they marched, they did so perfectly in step, as though a contingent of dread ants labouring under a singular vision.

The interior of their fortress was a far cry from the decrepit chaos of the Blackfort—the unimaginative but appropriate name that I had learned was given to the Vulkar keep. Instead, everything looked to be perfectly maintained, and carefully positioned to maximise the troop's mobility, or to serve some strategic purpose.

The Hobgoblins remained silent as they escorted us up a set of wide steps to the massive gilded doors that barred our path inside.

The lead soldier saluted the sentry who guarded the entrance, and a command was shouted in their unfamiliar language. It was the first time I had heard one of the strangers speak, and his voice was deep and harsh.

Seconds later the massive doors swung open, and we crossed the threshold into the Hobgoblin fortress of Manox Threydon.

I had never seen such a magnificent building in all my summers. I didn't even know such places could exist.

The grand entrance hall was of a similar layout to that of the Blackfort, but where that dismal place had been neglected and outright vandalised, this building was well-kept and spotlessly clean. An ornately woven carpet lay wide across the ground, the flagstones beneath, polished to a dull lustre.

There were suits of armour too, lining the hall between massive onyx pillars. Each suit sparkled in the flickering light of the spectacular chandeliers, which hung from the lofty ceiling on thick metal cords.

We were halfway through the wide hall when I realised that the armoured suits were in fact being worn by Hobgoblins—each carrying a long spear and bearing a shield that was emblazoned with the black fist.

I had passed by at least six of the figures before I noticed that one to my left followed me with its gaze, its armoured head turning slightly as I nervously walked in front of Karthak.

I averted my eyes and stared instead at the floor before me.

The carpet that we walked upon was stitched with swirling patterns in silver thread that glinted and twinkled in the light cast from overhead. There were fantastical beasts and scenes of glorious battle woven into the deep red material, and I followed the images with my eyes, marvelling at the exquisite craftsmanship.

It kept me distracted from the reality that I was marching along with the very monsters that had laid waste to my home, held me captive, and now had taken me as some bizarre sort of servant.

We reached the throne room of the resident Hobgoblin lord, in time to catch the tail-end of a heated exchange.

Seated on a towering black throne was Manox Threydon. A Hobgoblin who, whilst much smaller in size, almost rivalled Karthak in presence. The impressively muscular man, clothed in a simple black tunic of beaten leather, and wearing a circlet of dark shiny metal over his flowing black hair, sat and listened as another Hobgoblin ranted before him. His face was set as though chiseled stone, whilst the other Goblin spoke.

This one looked quite like the other in both build and appearance, though he was dressed for battle. He wore a purple coat of padded cloth, covered with strips of metal, and similar in design to the suit that Phobos had taken from the Blackfort's storeroom, and upon his back, the Goblin carried an ornate sword that was almost as tall as he was.

He was flanked on either side by guards who wore armoured overcoats, and carried long hammers and triangular shields. Those shields bore an unusual curling design, which resembled an octopus at first glance and, in the strangest way, made my head hurt when I looked at them. I blinked away some of my discomfort, and looked back at the two Hobgoblins.

The imposing lord on the throne waited calmly and patiently for his visitor to finish each barked sentence, before coldly offering his replies. His voice was husky, and every word he spoke sounded terse and deliberate.

Another, smaller Hobgoblin who leant on the side of his stone chair occasionally interjected. It seemed as though the youth was mediating between the larger Goblins, though perhaps being his aide or squire, he clearly favoured Manox Threydon.

Despite the efforts of the Hobgoblin boy though, it was an audience that didn't seem to have gone well, and didn't look like it was going to change course any time soon.

"And you expect forgiveness, Manox Thrinax? Or perhaps you fail to see why you might need it, and it was your intent to persuade me so. Which is it?" the Goblin king asked.

The visitor held his helmet in his hand and used it to point at the lord sitting before him whilst he responded with questions of his own. It seemed like this wasn't the first time the pair had danced this dance, given the young mediator's rolled eyes, heavy sigh, and almost comically exaggerated shrug of exasperation.

"So you wish to remain blinded by your self-pity, Threydon? I come before you, with an offer that you know to be in your interest, and you would spurn it simply out of spite? Out of pettiness? It is far from befitting the Legion Commander of the Black-Skulls," the warrior Goblin said, his voice just shy of a shout. "You know that I seek neither your forgiveness, nor to convince you that my part in the affair was right. But this opportunity is far too important to be cast aside simply because of our past."

Manox Threydon leaned forward in his seat, menacingly.

"Do not presume that it is our past that dictates my rejection, Thrinax. But you really must take me for a greater fool than I would have guessed, if you think for a moment that I would turn my back on the Obsidian Throne," the lord said. "Your Consortium deceives you, and gives naught but false promises. Your eyes are not opened. You are not awakened. You are blinded by the glint of gold unearned and undeserved, and I refuse to even consider your offer."

But then the lord glanced at his aide, and his tone changed slightly. Softened perhaps.

"Though for the sake of the boy, I extend an offer of my own: cast off the purple and return. I shall not pursue that which I am due. I shall take neither your head, nor hers. It is a mercy that I do not owe, but one which I shall endure. Indeed, for the sake of our past."

At those words, spoken more reservedly or not, the visiting warrior looked as though he was about to hurl his helmet at the lord. But the Goblin aide held his hands up in a calming gesture. The purple-clad warrior looked at the boy, then blinked away his rage and turned his attention back to Lord Threydon—shaking his helmet at the king, and near crushing the metal in his fist.

"Then I refuse your offer in turn, Threydon. Know that this was *your* choice, but know too that I shall endure no such mercy on my part. That, I promise you," he hissed, and stood there, staring at Manox Threydon with a seething malice in his dark eyes.

The lord stared back, and the chamber felt full of a silent burning fury, which made me shrink in fear.

Finally and thankfully, the angry Hobgoblin suddenly bowed, and his bodyguards followed suit, before the delegation turned on their heels and marched from the hall.

Karthak gently put a hand on me and pulled me close to her as they passed us by, almost shielding me from the procession. Her uncharacteristically protective gesture rendered me confused, whilst I stood there watching the troops march calmly out of the room, their leader's face glowering and flushed despite its greenish hue.

Once the strange Hobgoblins had left the hall, the lord beckoned our group towards him.

He spoke first in accented Kimorin, then surprisingly, in the language of the Vulkari.

Karthak and he exchanged greetings, then she bowed awkwardly before them. Each Vulkar in our procession followed suit, and spoke in Kimorin, in their tongue, and in some other that I didn't know. I copied them as best I could. Neither Goblin bowed to Karthak.

With greetings given, the Vulkar Warlord presented both Hobgoblins with gifts. To the lord, she offered a hair clasp of silver, decorated with a large ruby. To the boy, a simple pendant of a beautiful onyx rock, in the shape of a teardrop.

Then they began to speak of their business. I understood a small portion of the conversation that took place. They spoke of an exchange to be made, and repeatedly used a word that I had come to understand meant either 'Kimori' or maybe just 'captives'—having been referred to thusly on many occasions.

Their talk was brief and, by my best guess, to the point. But about mid-way through, the Hobgoblin leader stood up out of his obsidian throne. He stretched his knotted and tanned greenish arms out above him and rolled his head from side to side, the bones in his neck cracking sharply as he did. It seemed like the topic had moved on to war or conflict. But I couldn't really be sure, so bad was my grasp of the Vulkar's horrible speech.

He paced back and forth before his seat, pausing briefly before each statement he made or question he asked. It was bizarre; the man looked entirely at ease despite being outnumbered by fully-armed Vulkari—the largest and most vicious of the warband—and his throne room absent of any guards. He also spoke their language fluently.

The smaller Hobgoblin eyed us up during the exchange. He looked to be only a few summers older than I, but had a sort of confidence about him that I lacked. He wore simple trousers, and a rather fancy shirt of pale silk, and he carried only a small dagger in a scabbard at his hip, yet he too looked not to be intimidated by the vicious band of armed Vulkari present.

If I'd cared to at the time, I would have described him as halfway between handsome and not. Unlike Lleyden, this boy had a ruggedness about him, and looked as though he could probably use the dagger he carried. He had angular features, not dissimilar to a Kimora's, but the shape of his brow and the angle of his nose made him look almost arrogant. Though that might well have been attributed to the expression he wore.

Occasionally, during the audience, the small Hobgoblin's purplish gaze fell upon me, but when I looked at him, he looked away with a haughtiness so exaggerated that it made me smirk. Once or twice, the lord turned to me also, but his gaze inspired only fear.

I stood quietly at the side of the Vulkar chieftain, trying as best I could to hide it, but worried that my constant nervous shaking would betray the absolute terror that held me captive. One of the Vulkar warriors must have noticed, perhaps able to smell the emotion on me, and she hissed at me with a finger held in front of her maw.

Thankfully the audience was not a long one, and shortly I was shoved once more to the front of the group as we made our way from the throne room of Manox Threydon. He returned to his seat at the black throne and watched us leave.

I stole one more look back at him as we departed, and could have sworn that he flashed a smile at me before resuming conversation with his young aide, who pretended that he hadn't just been staring at me.

We made our way back to the waiting warband, once more flanked by a Hobgoblin escort, and past soldiers who were carrying out military drills. And I spied for the first time in the city, people who were neither Hobgoblins nor Vulkari.

A group of surprisingly well-dressed and healthy looking Kimori worked to carry foodstuffs in crates and barrels from a horse-drawn wagon and into a cellar door. They looked well at ease amongst the Hobgoblins—as though they weren't captives, but rather, fellows, or at the very least, paid labourers.

One of the workers, a tall and rather overweight man with bushy silver whiskers, stopped and waved in greeting as I hurried past. I quickly looked back at the dusty earth at my feet as I struggled to keep pace in front of the striding Vulkari, who now openly and excitedly chattered amongst themselves.

"You shall be stationed here for a time. You shall work to earn your keep and shall rejoin the pack when you are strong enough to wield a blade," Karthak told me as we left the confines of the castle courtyard. She seemed a little annoyed, and perhaps a little worried.

I nodded, grateful for the chance to be freed from the company of the savage and unruly Vulkari, but somewhat apprehensive of the ominous threat of return—and especially of wielding a blade.

"It should not be too long a time... though I wager one of two things shall occur to threaten that fact," Karthak said. "One; you shall be kept by the Goblins for as long as they believe you important to me. They are never undesirous of leverage. And two; I shall be kept away by the weave of the Vyshivka."

I nodded as she spoke, even though I didn't know what she was talking about in the slightest. She continued talking all the same, as we strolled back to her wagon and I prepared to remove her armour from her hulking frame.

"There is much that I must accomplish over the seasons hence, and I anticipate there shall be interference—especially given the exchange we were just privy to. I feel the brewing of a storm in the east. There is a wildness in the air, a danger. It is war, and it is not our war. There is hope that we can benefit, but the pieces must be tipped in just such a way, Pup."

The mighty Vulkar grinned her terrifying grin, and I hurried to undress her and free myself from her presence. But before I could finish, Star-Star clambered up onto the wagon.

Thankfully she relieved me of my duty, and helped Karthak out of the rest of her armour, then rummaged about in the Warlord's furniture for some liquor. Before I could retreat though, she poured some of the brown liquid into a small cup made from half of a nut shell, then handed it to me.

"So our pup is to stay with the Goblins. Star-Star must confess that she shall miss the evening company," the Vulkar said with a toothy grin, and stared at me with her pale amber eyes whilst she poured out liquor for herself and Karthak.

I sipped the bitter drink, then smiled back at her. It was a nice sentiment, and she had been the kindest of all the Vulkari, barring perhaps the male who kept the provisions in his blue wagon. Still, she terrified me. She was a monster like the rest of them.

"Star-Star shall also miss the cleaning and the scrubbing that you give Karthak," she laughed. "But she shall miss most of all, the scented oils that you rub into Karthak's pelt."

Karthak laughed too.

"Nothing prevents you from applying the same oils to my hide, Garok," she told the smaller raider and Star-Star shrugged.

"Perhaps we must find another good pup, until this one is ready to train for the raid…"

I had no desire to be forced into service as a Vulkar raider, but was glad that at least thus far, I had managed to avoid an excess of brutal treatment and violence. If I could make it through this new ordeal, I could perhaps find a way to get back to my family. I had to know that they were fine, and I was sure that they would be worried sick about me.

I pushed those worries as deep inside me as they would go, and tried my best to enjoy the strange warmth that Karthak's liquor spread into my cheeks and the tips of my ears. It didn't make my head spin, nor my thoughts fuzzy though, and in place of worries for my family, I found them drifting constantly into worries about the Goblins, and what I would face in their custody.

⁂

I would soon find out that working under the yoke of the Hobgoblin Legion, whilst at least not as harsh or dangerous as being kept as a Vulkar trophy and pet, would bring with it an entirely new set of hardships.

The work was not easy, and began soon after a retinue of Hobgoblin soldiers marched into the midst of the Vulkar convoy, set about constructing tents and digging latrines, then allocated space for their visitors to establish an encampment.

The Hobgoblins then rounded up a collection of captives and working beasts, and marched them off into various buildings. They also took with them several carts filled with looted tools, weapons, and trade goods, and finally, they came for me.

It was the strangest feeling.

I was being torn between the desperate desire to leave the captivity of the monsters that had raided us, slain my friends and neighbours, and taken me from my family, and the fear of being taken by a whole new set of captors—this one completely unknown and unfamiliar.

Despite the cruelty, the savagery, and the danger, there was a small sense of comfort that had begun to grow in me in the company of Karthak, the terrifying beast that had for reasons known only to her, taken a sort of liking to me. And particularly when Star-Star was around as well, I felt for the first time a wish—small but still present—to stay with the Vulkar horde.

I would have no say in the matter anyway, and decided that it would serve my best interests to comply with the orders of the soldiers who took me.

After being bid farewell by Karthak and Star-Star, both Vulkari simply rustling my hair and telling me to be strong, to learn from the Goblins, and to await their return, I was jostled and shoved into the middle of a small patrol of Hobgoblins, their marching pace relentless.

They escorted me to a cart full of construction tools—saws, mallets, chisels and the like, and in a strange dialect of Kimorin, informed me that I was to unload the cart and carry its contents into a thatch-roofed stone shed next to a smithy.

That proved to be only the first task of the day, and I worked tirelessly until the sun began to set, blazing orange in a hazy pink sky.

My work was interrupted and I was shunted, sweating, trembling, and sore, into a large barn-like structure. Perhaps originally a stable, now instead used as servants' quarters, it would be a better home than Karthak's wagon had been—even if just for the smell.

I was taken into the custody of the whiskered man whom I had passed by earlier. He bowed to the soldiers and spoke to them in a foreign language. They merely grunted replies, but bowed to him in return, before they left the building, and barred the exit with a large wooden plank and rattling metal chains.

"You are safe here," the man said, in accented Kimorin. "Old Grunwald, be looking after you here on forth. Be sure to keep yourself to yourself, and I'm sure you will be free from any trouble."

I was given water to bathe in, a simple vegetable gruel to eat, and a blanketed bunk to rest in. And for that night, I slept soundly and without dreams—exhausted from the day, and from the arduous journey that I had taken to arrive at the fortress.

I slept soundly, for I did not fully realise that the next morning would mark the beginning of many long months of tireless service to an army, and to my new captor and master—Manox Threydon; the Legion Commander of the Eastern Frontiers, Lord of the Solent, and right fist of the Hobgoblin war machine.

iv.

'Sacharr.'

I liked the sound of the word, though I did not know what it meant in the Hobgoblin tongue—except that it was where they were from, perhaps.

The surly creatures called themselves the Sacharri Legion, though it was a struggle to learn any more than that initially—due to a combination of constant work with little time for talking, and the Hobgoblins' tendency to outright ignore my presence whenever I tried.

I also discovered that they didn't call themselves Hobgoblins all that much either. In their own tongue, they were Domovoi. But the word sounded far too homely—evoking hearths and sculleries, not conquering warriors and their weapons of war.

Whatever name they had, in many ways they were vastly different from the Vulkari—a few of whom still roamed the city streets even after Karthak and her warband had left to return west. However, there were some terrifying similarities.

I came to learn that what my new hosts lacked in outright savagery, they replaced with ruthless efficiency. The primary unifying feature of the two groups though, was their capacity for violence.

I would be demonstrated the almost casual ease with which the Hobgoblin Legionnaires meted out quick reprisal for dissent or disobedience, only a few weeks into my service in their city. The first punishment that I witnessed was a whipping, which was dished out impersonally and coolly by some sort of officer, upon a middle aged Kimorin man who had fallen asleep on a job, and then apparently tried to escape his captivity.

Only three or four lashes into the punishment, the slave managed to wriggle free of the rope bonds holding him, and attempted to run, but this escape was halted swiftly by three black-feathered arrows to the back.

Following that display, I wouldn't dare entertain the fantasies of escape, which occupied my dreams each night. And I made every effort to show up to any task that was allocated to me—at least a little early. I also tried as best I could to comply with my orders to the letter, despite the struggle with communication in the earlier months—before I could fully make sense of the thick Hobgoblin accent.

But despite this, I wouldn't go without my own share of punishment; some of which were deserved. One in particular, not so much.

The trouble began late one muggy summer evening, after a day spent hauling vegetables into the larder under the kind (but stern) supervision of Grunwald.

The barn that the slaves and paid staff slept in was divided into sections by wide wooden walkways—each separate part lined with bunks and blanketed sleeping cots, made from empty crates and the like. Generally, we slept in a group according to which tasks we had been assigned over any given week, meaning that we frequently moved throughout the place as our assignments changed.

Grunwald recently had other ideas, and would sometimes move my bedding to the small and separate room that he occupied at the far end of the building.

He would spend each evening telling me tales and teaching me the subtleties of the common tongue of Solent Fae—of which, apparently, Kimorin was simply a regional dialect.

That particular evening, I was carrying a small tray of supper along the wooden planked path between the various rows of bunks, heading to the stuffy little chamber where my friend and tutor waited. I squeezed between two chatting slave girls; one was a Kimora, the other looked to be the offspring of a Hobgoblin and a boar, or perhaps something even uglier.

As I passed between them, careful not to spill my meagre allocation of food and water, my foot caught on something, and before I knew it, both myself and my supper were tumbling to the floor.

"Eating off the ground like the savage you are, aye?" the stocky pig-faced girl said, and the two of them laughed.

I picked myself up and turned to confront them.

She still had the foot she had tripped me with placed across the path, and her ugly face radiated a smugness that did nothing but provoke my ire.

"What did you do that for!?" I demanded, advancing on the pair, fists clenched at my sides.

I'd never even interacted with either of the two, let alone given them reason enough to hate me, so I couldn't understand what had prompted the girl's malice.

The Kimora girl, a few summers older than me, and about a foot taller, stepped in front of her shorter friend, and shoved me roughly in the chest.

"What are you going to do about it? Call on your Beastfolk friends to save you?" they laughed again as I staggered back a few steps to regain my balance.

"What is your grudge with me?" I demanded. "I never did anything to you!"

"Really? Tell that to my village, you little Vulkar cur!"

The blonde Kimora spat at my feet to punctuate her insult.

"What?" I asked, confused as to what they thought I was. "Are your eyes dim? Do I look like a Vulkar to you?"

"You certainly reek of one, you rabid Psoglav breeding thrall!" the half-person chimed in.

"Who breeding what? I don't even know what you just said! And you are both simpletons if you think I ever wanted to be taken by anyone, let alone Vulkari," I said, and turned away from the confrontation to scoop up my scattered food.

It wasn't worth my effort, and I couldn't be bothered staying to figure out what it was they were trying to call me. I couldn't account for whatever Hobgoblin-thing the ugly girl was, but I didn't know a thing about breeding. I was barely eleven summers old.

I had managed to salvage some of my bread from the ground when I was shoved from behind. I slid face first on the hard wooden floor. My chin impacted the splintered planks and I bit my lip.

The iron taste of blood filled my mouth, and I felt a burning heat well up inside me. My hands began to tingle and go numb as I lay prone on the ground, fists clenched in front of me.

I spat a mouthful of crimson spittle onto the wood, and slowly dragged myself to my feet, the burning anger clouding my thoughts and surging through my veins.

"You filthy pig-faced mongrel," I growled as I slowly turned to face the pair. "You pathetic weakling scum."

I wished I knew more curse words, but that would have to suffice.

The two girls still grinned before me.

"What was that, Vulkar-beast?" the Kimora asked, puffing out her scrawny chest, and cockily beckoning at me to face her.

"You heard me, you worthless piece of filth!" I shouted, and charged forward—set to wipe the grin from her smarmy face.

I had never actually fought anyone before, having only tumbled around with Lleyden in mock battles as a young child, but I swung a fist towards the girl's mouth all the same.

She ducked to the side, and the force of my punch carried me past her and right into the fist of the ugly mongrel girl.

The blow caught me just beneath the sternum, winding me slightly, but in no way quelling the violent fury that spurred me on.

I twisted away from the impact, gulping in warm air, and lashed out. I caught the girl on the side of her face. But she shrugged off the punch, and advanced on me, pummelling me with a flurry of blows from her club-like hands. I held up my arms to protect my head as best I could.

I tried to maintain my distance, waiting for an opportunity to strike back, but the opportunity never came. Instead, the back of my knee was kicked from beneath me, and I pitched backward into the grip of the Kimora.

The girl locked her arms up beneath my armpits and in front of my shoulders, pinning me against her and leaving me helpless to defend against the other's onslaught.

The half-breed struck me three or four times in the stomach before I was able to kick her away from me. At the same time, I threw my head backwards and felt my skull collide with the Kimora's mouth. The girl cried out and her grip on me loosened, so I kicked at the advancing brute once more.

My foot connected with her chest, and it threw both her and the girl that held me off balance. All three of us tumbled to the floor in an angry, winded heap.

I lay crumpled on the ground, heaving and retching from the blows to my stomach, trying to recover quickly enough that I could fight back.

By this point, a small crowd of other slaves and servants had gathered to watch the spectacle, but I barely registered their presence as I staggered to my feet and delivered a savage kick to the Kimora girl's already bleeding face—just as she tried to get back up. She crumpled.

"I'll kill you—you pathetic runt!" I shouted at her, elated by my apparent victory, but once again too eager.

A sudden, painful blow struck me on the back of my head. A metallic ringing burst in my ears.

Dazed, I turned to face my attacker, but my vision blurred and I started to fall.

The last thing I saw before I blacked out, was the hideous green-skinned girl brandishing my supper tray and gloating—totally unaware of the three angry looking Hobgoblins, rushing up behind her.

※　※　※

All three of us were dragged into a chamber off the side of the castle's main hall.

The room was empty except for a plain wooden desk with piles of scrolls and paperwork laid out over much of it.

Behind the cluttered desk and sitting in a tall backed chair was the Hobgoblin official who oversaw the allocation of workers to their tasks.

He was tall and quite thin by comparison to all of the other soldiers I had seen, and he reminded me of some type of predatory insect.

The lanky Hobgoblin had thin and pointed features, a high forehead, and long black hair that was streaked with grey and tied up with a strip of red leather.

He leaned forward in his seat to peer ominously down at us with deep-set bloodshot eyes.

"So. Trouble in the servants' quarters." He spoke slowly, and with a gravelly tone.

I didn't say a thing, still groggy from the blow to my head.

Instead I glanced at the two older girls next to me, contemplating both why they would have decided to pick on me and how I could make them pay for it.

I was proud of the wounds that I had inflicted on the Kimora. Her otherwise pretty face was now swollen and still bloodied but I was a little disappointed that her smug and hideous friend didn't share the damage.

"Do you know what the most important part of the entire Sacharri Legion is?" the spindly official asked, slowly and deliberately, but without allowing any time for an answer. "Is it the generals? Is it the soldiers? Is it maybe the workforce behind them?"

He shuffled some papers and then rested his bony chin on his hands as he continued.

"Many scholars agree that the Imperial might of Sacharr is some sort of self-perpetuating machine. However, one must understand that the machine has many parts. Just as the battering ram has the mighty head that crushes and demolishes any barrier in its way, the Imperial Legion has its Legionnaires. Its soldiers trained and prepared to execute the God-Emperor's will in these savage frontiers.

"Think though, consider: What use is a battering ram without a frame to swing the shaft from? Without sturdy chains to connect the two? Without mighty wheels to carry it to its destination?"

He licked his thin lips, eyes almost closed as he weaved his metaphor and described the Hobgoblin war machine.

"You must ask yourselves, are you the bronze head of the ram? Are you the shaft? No. You are one of the simple iron nuts that fastens the wheel to its hub, a single nail that holds a beam in the sturdy frame, one single link in the mighty chain.

"The ram would fail if any one of its necessary parts were removed. It would cease to be the machine that it was intended to be."

I followed so far.

"You are an integral part of the Sacharri Legion, all. You *are* the Sacharri Legion. The sword is not a sword without its blade, hilt and pommel. The ram is but a pile of lumber and metal without each tiny part. Individually these are just that, parts. But together they are the ram. They are the sword. You are the Legion. All parts of one whole."

I already grasped his point and my thoughts began to drift. I wondered if the old Hobgoblin was just belabouring the message for the sake of his own benefit. Or perhaps he had noticed the vacant look that the ugly girl to my left wore on her flat, piggy face and was really trying to get it through her idiot skull.

He waffled for a while and I stopped listening.

"Diligence!"

The Hobgoblin suddenly shouted, causing all three of us to jump.

I stared at him, instantly and completely awake—eyes wide and heart racing. I missed whatever rhetorical question it was that the word was an answer to but nodded attentively all the same.

He leaned across the desk and regarded the ugly girl.

"What say you? What was your part in the... disruption?"

The squat little beast stuttered and stumbled over her words as she spoke.

"I'm sorry sir, it was the Beast girl, the Brownie. Sh-she said we were weak and pathetic slaves. She attacked my friend. Said she was a pampered princess."

Filthy liar. I listened to her devious excuses, her husky voice bent into a fake stammering mimicry of innocence.

"I had to hit her with a tray, she was going to kill Mellia."

The Hobgoblin nodded and looked to the Kimora girl, Mellia apparently. It was a stupid name.

"And you. What have you to say?"

"It's all true sir, Vorsa saved me from her. I think she was going to kill me. She said as much. And she wouldn't stop hitting me. I thought I would die!" she said emphatically, really getting into the lie, letting tears flow freely.

The official waited for her to finish speaking, and when she broke down, blubbering pathetically, showed not a shred of pity. Instead, he calmly turned to me.

"What do you have to say for yourself, Brownie? So-called 'Beast girl?'" he asked me.

"They are lying. They started it. They shoved me and called me cruel names."

I protested the two girls' completely fabricated version of events, almost by instinct. It was as though I were denying some (probably very true) claim that I'd bullied Lleyden, back in my home—so far away, and seemingly so long ago, that it was hard to recall much more than the feeling of indignation over the fact that I might be in trouble for something so stupid.

Why did I care about what some stupid girls thought of me? It should have been the least of my concerns. But I *did* care, even though I was still unsure of what it actually was that the girls had been trying to imply with their insults.

"Well, at least I *think* they were cruel; I uhh… I didn't actually understand them," I added.

"Is it as these girls claim? Did you throw the first punch?" the thin Hobgoblin regarded me coolly, hunched over his desk, his long fingers locked together beneath his chin.

"Well, yes, but that was after…" I tried to explain, but I figured he'd had enough of the stories. "Oh who cares? It was a fight. All I wanted to do was go and talk to Grunwald, and these two idiots stopped me, they shoved me so I threw a punch and then we fought."

He nodded. Almost looked impressed at my honesty even. But quickly, a stern expression returned to his features.

"Then you are all equally to blame. We will not tolerate such behaviour amongst our… staff. As such, you shall all be punished. Now, what are your ages?" the spidery Hobgoblin unfurled his hands and pointed a long finger at each of us in turn.

We each told him, the two girls were both thirteen, and I guessed that it was close enough to the middle of summer to count this as my eleventh.

"You will receive lashes, upon your backs and your rumps. One blow per year of your age," the supervisor told us sternly.

And I regretted counting the extra summer.

❊ ❊ ❊

The whipping, whilst certainly painful, was far from the worst treatment I had received so far. The Hobgoblin officer that carried out our punishment in the middle of the castle courtyard and in full view of the gathered servants, at least stopped when he reached eleven lashes.

Oddly enough, despite the stinging raw feeling on my back and behind, and the discomfort it brought when I tried to sleep that night, the worst part of the entire ordeal was the humiliation of the public spectacle. Or that the other girls weren't at least twice their ages.

It seemed that the Hobgoblin Legion made a point of carrying out their justice in the central courtyard, halting work and gathering the servants and slaves to witness the affair, in what I figured was a warning gesture to dissuade any potential disobedience.

I did not protest as I was marched into the sunny square on the morning of my flogging, nor complain as my hands were trussed by ropes that dangled from a pine frame near where the troops usually practiced their swordplay and spearcraft.

I tried to block out the stares and the hushed whispers from the gathered crowd, hearing only certain words from the hum of voices, 'Vulkar' being the most numerous spoken.

I couldn't stop my thoughts from focussing on the nails that held the wooden beams together, thinking that in the eyes of the Hobgoblins, that was all I was.

The first two or maybe three strokes of the thin wooden stick took me by surprise, I twisted and squirmed against my bonds after each blow marked my bare skin and I gritted my teeth and fought back tears.

By the fifth, I was dangling limply from the ropes, shuddering as my sweat seeped into the thin grazes left by the punishment.

My breathing was ragged and shallow but my eyes were still dry.

I was barely present throughout the remaining flogging, despite the shouts of the Hobgoblin marshal counting down each swing that he made.

I was thinking about the other girls. Hoping that this was the first such beating that they were to receive, remembering the feeling of powerlessness and terror that came with the first time. Remembering the way the Vulkari did it.

In an odd way it amused me that those two, so smug and haughty the previous night, were now strung up next to me, stripped naked and sobbing as they awaited their turn.

I was proud that no tears flowed from my own eyes; that instead of fear I felt only rage and spite.

The best thing about it was that I had gone first.

I wondered if it would have been more terrifying for the other girls if I had made a spectacle, if I had acted as though the whipping was actually the worst thing I had suffered, but my pride told me otherwise and I remained stoic right up until I was taken down from the post and marched back through the crowd towards the sleeping quarters.

My legs shook and I felt dizzy and lightheaded for hours after the punishment, even as Grunwald fussed over my mild wounds and applied some sort of herbal poultice to reduce the welts and seal the minor cuts.

I later heard that only half way into her lashings, the short ugly girl Vorsa had wet herself, and for once I was glad for the Sacharri Legion's harsh military justice.

My smugness would only last until I was put back to work the following day, to replace broken paving tiles under the relentless sun. I was stationed with a group of Goblins and Kimori, both men and women who avoided eye contact and conversation with me, and sat in small groups away from me when we stopped to eat.

It was only then that the ordeal affected me. The whipping I could take, the stinging from the sweat and the sun also. The whispers however, they hurt more than the thin slashes on my back and thighs did.

Knowing that so many of my fellow captives thought that it was by my own choice that I had travelled with Karthak, learning from their hushed conversations, that the other slaves who had been brought here with me resented the freedom that the Vulkar chieftain's favour had afforded me, and thought that I had desired it—any of it—left deeper scars than a mere eleven lashes with a thin wooden rod ever could.

V.

"Phobos d'you say his name were?"

"Yes. His name was Phobos Lend," I replied.

"That sounds like a right good moniker. I wonder who he stole it from."

My companion smirked as he continued peeling potatoes and throwing them into the bubbling stew.

"See round 'ere. The little man were known as the Darkrunner. He were a right murdering, sociopathic whoreson. And you make no mistake about it. He had no friends, but only people he hadn't wronged or betrayed yet," the grizzled man said, and looked at me sharply.

I didn't know what those other things he'd called Phobos meant, but alongside murder, I could guess they weren't fond names.

I thought back to how easily the Ratling had dispatched the Vulkari back at the Blackfort, how effortlessly he sneaked around, and how he had picked the locks to my bonds. It almost made sense if he were a villain of some sort, though his other actions did not.

"He was kind to me. And a few others too," I said, remembering the gift of water that he had given the sick man in the dungeon.

"Aye, but that's just how such a miscreant remains alive for so long. His kind's like to betray your trust and revoke any kindness bestowed in the blink of an eye, if it means he could save his own sorry hide."

"I don't know. I liked him. He needn't have helped me if he's as you say; some kind of 'Murdering Sausage-path Horse's son' or whatever it was," I told Grunwald.

"*Sociopathic whoreson.* And believe what you will lass, but the Ratling is a blackheart through and through."

The man sighed, and turned his attention to stirring the huge iron cauldron of meaty brown sludge. The scent of the rich gravy filled the small kitchen, making my stomach rumble with hunger as I sliced the odd root vegetables I had been tasked with preparing.

"Why was he here?" I asked. "I mean, before being strung up in a Vulkar dungeon that is."

"Well he did business with our hosts. More than a year back," Grunwald leaned in to lend an air of mystery and intrigue to his words. "He were a spy or assassin of some sort, they say. Also worked with the Vulkari of these parts."

"But they kept him in the cell where they first held me," I told him.

"Vulkari are quick to ire, and the little villain must've ired the wrong Vulkar in just the right way, and wound up a prisoner," he said. "You should pay no mind to the fate of the Ratling. You've your own path ahead, and for now should keep your focus on getting through each day without pissing on anyone's patch."

"Pissing on their patch?" I asked.

"You aren't really so clueless are you girl? Don't piss on anyone else's patch. Don't put your nose where it don't belong. Keep your fingers and eyes to yourself. Keep your head down and your mouth shut. Understand any of this?"

Grunwald turned to face me, hands on hips, ladle dripping brown liquid onto the side of his apron, and the wooden floor beneath him.

"I suppose I do," I told him.

After the punishment I had already faced, I certainly had no plan to piss on anyone's patch. Or their nose, or my fingers, or whatever it was that he said about my eyes and my head. I wasn't really listening, but rather thinking about Phobos Lend; The Darkrunner. Why would he have ever bothered to save me from the Blackfort, were he truly such an evil man?

For the first time in a long while I was thinking about where he might be, whether he, my family and my friends were safe. Whether they thought the same of me, so many months since my capture.

I pictured Phobos' face as I let him go, as he tumbled into the rapids and disappeared below. The look he had given me—that wasn't the face of a murdering assassin. I felt, in some sure way, it had been a look of genuine concern.

Our conversation meandered away from the topic of Phobos and back to Grunwald's past.

According to his vibrant boasts and surely exaggerated tales, the old man was once a warlord or baron of some renown himself, but when the Solent river dried up, his trading income dried up with it. He turned his focus and his force to brigandry and had been the ruler of the keep when the first Hobgoblins arrived.

Apparently he had avoided the slaughter of those who stood against the Hobgoblin Legion, claiming that to begin with, he and his men had managed to fend off the attempts to claim the place. But soon after the first few Hobgoblin assaults had been repelled, a massive force, much larger than the one currently stationed in the city, had marched in and laid waste to all who stood in their path.

"I were out on some dalliance with a local farmer's daughter—or some other mischief at the time, lass!" Grunwald told me, stroking his long white moustache and grinning, his eyes twinkling beneath his bushy brow.

"Then how did you end up here as a servant?" I asked, still unsure why our masters would have kept the enemy baron as a kitchen hand and labourer—and even paid him for the work.

"Well you see, I were a crafty bastard, right from my first breath. So once I saw the city were aflame, I ditched my weapons and ditched my hauberk, stole a peasant's utensils and pots, and posed as but a simple cook and merchant." He winked at me and waved a hand toward the stew that threatened to boil over at any moment. "I've always had a knack for this sort of thing. For cooking. For baking pies, and brewing mead. So I offered my services to the new inhabitants. Best way to save my own hide, if you ask me. Good food brings all folk together in the end."

It was an odd story and I was certain it had been different last time he told it, but did enjoy his way of telling his tales, so asked him to continue as I fetched another crate of herbs and vegetables.

"So these Domovoi. The Hobgoblins. They aren't such bad types to toil under. Tough and rather high strung, sure, but they do bring with them a lot of order and structure." Grunwald shrugged and gestured at the room around us. "They fix a lot of stuff. It isn't all bloodshed and slaughter."

"But both you and Karthak told me they killed all of the people who lived here," I told him.

"Aye, that they did!" the old man said. "But be sure that the previous occupants were criminal rabble, mind."

"Wait, weren't you their leader?" I asked, mildly confused.

"Aye. Hence I can assure you of their nature!" he laughed, then began another tale about his time with them, and then with the Legion.

I listened absently as we carried on working, preparing the evening meal for the higher ranking soldiers and officers. Grunwald informed me of all of the positive changes that the Easterners had instituted. Though I suspected that the overwhelming majority of work had been carried out by people in our, or at least, *my* position, and not the black-clad Legionnaires who oversaw our duties.

"So there you have it. Manox Threydon may be a cold son of a bitch, but he is no tyrant. He is a military man, and I can respect that."

Grunwald nodded sternly.

"Well, it does sound a lot like you haven't much choice," I told him.

"Oh but there's the secret little Zyntael; you *always* have a choice. Even if one of the options be your own outright murder—that is still one of the options!" he laughed, and we continued working for a while longer, before he suddenly turned to me and cleared his throat.

"So... I only really needed the help for a few days, but kept you here for a few longer for the sake of having a good ear for my tales. You were meant to spend time with the lordling, but instead you'll be going to the smithy on the morrow. To my old pal Feldspar. That dour old git; face like an arse with a lemon up it, that one," The old man chuckled. "You'll likely be put to work carrying things, but perhaps Zentar'd be like to teach you a little smithing too. He's a softer touch than he looks."

I was dismayed. I didn't want to spend my days carrying things. I'd done enough of that when I was working with the slaves who were fixing the road that led westward from the city. I told Grunwald as much, and he shook his head.

"Ah well, all of that is good in the long run. All the boring, heavy stuff has its place." He reached over and pinched my arm between finger and thumb. "Builds muscle it does. And muscle'd be an important thing to have in this world. Vagabonds and scoundrels abound; from Azure to the Icespire, from the swamps of Quaresh, to the obsidian throne of Sacharr. And most only respond to a bit of the old bloodshed!"

I didn't look up from the salt I was crushing.

"I don't know where any of those places are, you know. I mean, I can guess Sacharr perhaps. But the others..."

"Are far from here. You'll likely see them in time. On your... What'd you call it? Chosen path?"

I could tell he was pulling a stupid face, even without looking.

"Yeah. Doesn't feel like I'm doing much choosing lately though."

"What'd I just tell you about choices? I sometimes wonder why I bother." He sighed and set down his knife. "You lack patience. You're young. What, eleven? Twelve? When I was your age I was just as impetuous and eager, sure. But when you last as long as I have, you find that the lightning in your bones fades away somewhat."

"That sounds sad."

Grunwald cocked his hairy head to one side for a moment, seemingly captured by a temporary thought.

"Not really," he began. "The quieter life has its own perks. I've certainly done my share of reading since I've gone grey. Swapped the blade for the books, lass. Thought I'd seize the moment before my eyes give out, and since my body did already."

"Would you teach me to read?"

He nodded. "If we have time after your shifts I suppose I could. 'Tis is a useful thing, to make words on a page become sounds on a tongue and thoughts in a head. Useful indeed—fetch that parsley would you? Anyway, enough chatter. This stew's practically ready, and may be my best yet."

He dipped a finger into the brown liquid and then licked it clean, smacking his lips loudly for effect.

"Perhaps a little spice to season, and a sprinkle of parsley on the top. Your thoughts?" he concluded and then dunked a spoon in and handed it to me for my appraisal.

I slurped down the thick fluid, barely pausing to blow on it.

It was delicious. I had no idea if it needed salt or spice or anything for that matter, having subsisted mostly on a diet of watery gruel and flavourless jerky, for the last three or so months. It had been a trying time; worked to exhaustion each day on various labouring tasks, and locked up in the shared slave quarters every night.

It was approaching the end of summer, or so I guessed by the cooling weather and gradual increase in the number of soldiers I saw wearing fur-trimmed cloaks and thick gloves when patrolling in the early morning.

After a long stint serving as a general labourer, I had only spent the last week and a half working in the kitchens with Grunwald, since the previous girl had been sold to someone from far off. Each night for months, I'd stayed up late, talking with him regardless of where I was stationed—longer than I probably should have given every day's workload.

I wasn't looking forward to working in the smithy, or doing more heavy lifting and tiring labour. Nor did I really want to spend time with some young lord—likely Threydon's aide. I wanted to stretch my time spent with Grunwald, preparing food for the commanders, for as long as I could. But the last stew I'd help to cook with the old man seemed to be done and for some reason, this time I was going to help him serve it to the Sacharri leadership.

We carried our delicious creation in a large trolley, specifically designed to accommodate the cauldron as well as whatever utensils and bowls were needed.

I kept quiet as Grunwald heaved the handcart down the service corridors, and held the door for him as the food was trundled into the officers' dining hall.

They sat along a large dark wood table that was polished to a glossy sheen, and draped with a regal black and gold cloth. There were already platters and trays of fruit and meats as well as many pitchers of wine and mead.

I set simple wooden bowls filled with the hearty stew before each of the nine Hobgoblins, then fetched a pitcher of wine and set about topping up each goblet.

As I held the ceramic pitcher, poised to pour the strong smelling wine into the vessel before Manox Threydon, the mighty Goblin reached out and stayed my hand. His powerful grip held my forearm in place, hovering over his drink. I looked at his face, wide-eyed and afraid, but he was smiling.

As far as the creatures went, he was actually reasonably handsome. His thick and jet black hair was swept back and fastened with the small ruby and silver clasp that Karthak had gifted him. It was cropped short about the sides, and formed tidy, waxed sideburns that framed his rugged face. He had a square jaw, prominent just as all Hobgoblins' were, but with a masculine cleft in the centre, and a thin dusting of black stubble that spread up his greenish skin to join those perfectly trimmed sideburns.

His nose was less pig-like than many of the other Hobgoblins, and the bridge sat proud of his chiselled face—between two hawkish purple eyes and beneath a furrowed and heavy brow.

The mighty leader leaned close to me and sniffed.

"Under-Commander Valishar Sakorm tells me that you still smell like the Vulkar horde. And he would certainly know." He stared into my eyes as he spoke, glancing away only to flash a mocking grin at his lieutenant, then he sniffed again. "Truth be told, I smell only garlic, and the sweat of keep well-earned."

I tried to force a smile, though in my nervous state, managed only a pathetic grimace.

"So Kimor-child. You have stayed on, worked hard and with nary a complaint, done as was bid of you, and stepped out of line far less than one would expect from a supposed 'Brownie' it would seem." He glanced over to Grunwald, who watched on in silence, but appeared to nod softly at the notice.

"Karthak may have been right to favour you after all."

He let go of my arm and I filled his cup—quaking with fear, but desperate not to spill any of the probably very expensive wine.

"We were expecting the return of your owner, before the close of summer. However, it would seem her fate has been, as she would say, stitched in a different pattern. She will return to collect you; she has promised as much. My aide will have you dressed appropriately and presented back to her when the time comes."

My heart skipped a beat at his words. I could not return to the company of the Vulkari. Not now. Manox Threydon must have noticed my fear at the prospect—though not exactly a difficult task—and smiled to reassure me.

"Of course, by the sounds of it, that time shall not come for nigh on ten moons hence. I might see to it that you aren't kept long by the beast also, or that we might claim you back... for safe keeping," he said, watching my body relax slightly as he spoke. "It is strange. Though you may feel no love for the Wolf-men, I have not yet encountered a slave enquired about as much as you have been, or even at all. Curiously, it is almost as though Karthak Azuur really does feel some maternal instinct towards you, even if she might be kept from you by her Spirits, the Kimorin fates, or the will of the God-Emperor himself."

The other Hobgoblins at the table chuckled at the commander's words.

'Wolf-man' seemed to be a common term for the Vulkari, and one which conveyed little in the way of affection. The word after Karthak—*Azuur*—wasn't one I knew. It sounded familiar, and definitely sounded like it was a Vulkar word, but I had never heard any Vulkari speak it. I pushed the thought from my mind as the Hobgoblin continued to speak to me.

"For the time being, you shall have a three-day rest. Then you will begin to assist in the barracks until your Warlord returns, so that if the Wolf-Mother asks, we can at least inform her that your work here is useful to her. I shudder to imagine her rage, should it be limited to labouring and kitchen-work, and other 'Bare-Skinned' pursuits. And especially since I have changed my mind where her proposed bond between us is concerned. The Crimson Star's rage can burn itself out for all the power she has in that regard. You shall not be spending time with Anra."

He grinned, along with his officers. They seemed to enjoy making fun of Karthak—entirely unafraid of her as they were.

I nodded, unsure of whether to respond or how I should address him if I did, let alone who 'Anra' was, and what bond he was speaking of.

"Now you may leave us. Return to your lodgings and rest well," he said.

"Yes, Lord Threydon," I croaked, placing the jug back on the table.

I turned to leave but stopped when the Hobgoblin Leader called out to me.

"Oh, and one more thing," he said, as I reached the door. "You sup upon this fine stew tonight; I shall have another bring you a share. Your friend and tutor makes stew almost better than my own grandmother did. And you have earned it."

Although I would never meet Manox Threydon's grandmother, nor taste her cooking, I doubted that any other living creature ever made a stew as good as that one tasted that night.

vi.

With an aching back and trembling arms, I hefted the last crate of stained leather straps onto the shelf.

"So why all the crimson? Are there no other dyes or paints?"

"Zyntael, for a savage Vulkar slave, you sure do ask a lot of questions," Zentar replied, then stopped hammering the bent sword that he was working on, and set aside his tools and thick leather gloves.

"How can I put this?" the Hobgoblin blacksmith sighed. "Look. There are some things, known by my superiors, that I am not meant to know. And in turn, some things that I know, but you cannot."

"Sure, but the reason why there's so much crimson, is that really privileged information? I mean, it's not just the Sacharri, but Karthak's Vulkari too." I frowned at his frustratingly blank expression. "I'm beginning to think that there are no other colours around here!"

The master smith finally broke into a broad smile.

"Well, I shall let you in on a little secret then," he told me, and beckoned me in close.

"Some say that the crimson represents the power and strength of the Legion. They think it is a regal colour fit for our kind. But the truth is more pragmatic really..." He paused to look around in mock fear then cupped a hand beside his mouth as he whispered to me. "It hides the blood."

"Really?" I looked at him quizzically. "The soldiers' or their enemies' blood?"

He shrugged and began to put his gloves back on. "Maybe both. Anyway, since you are done there, I believe that Feldspar may have some more work for you. Perhaps take a short rest, have some water, then find him in the barracks."

Feldspar. Wonderful. If it wasn't to be Zentar, then why couldn't it have been Urd?

Whereas Zentar was generally good natured, eager to teach and share a tale or two, Feldspar was the exact opposite. It wasn't just in attitude and demeanour that the two smiths differed, but in physical appearance as well.

Zentar, a broad shouldered and burly Hobgoblin with a wide, stubble-spiked chin, and eyes that sparkled with humour and wit, stood at least a shaggy haired head-and-a-half shorter than his Kimorin colleague.

Feldspar was wiry and lean, with a corded and sinewy strength in his long limbs, and a permanent scowl upon his sallow features. Just as Grunwald had said; a face as though an arse, with a lemon up it. I didn't much like the man, and it was a feeling that he had made it more than apparent was mutual.

The third smith rounding out the trio, who ran the armoury in shifts, was a squat, bald, and stony-skinned Hobgoblin brute named simply Urd.

Apparently possessed of Vodnik lineage, he appeared to be something of a simpleton in terms of communication and desire, though was a brilliant craftsman—easily capable of transforming the rustiest and most damaged arms and armour into shining works of military art.

In all the time I had spent working the bellows or fetching quenching oils and water as he hammered away at the forge, he had been the calmest, and the most patient. Urd was happy to have me simply stand and observe how he beat out dents in pauldrons and breastplates, or returned an edge to a dull blade. Thus, I looked forward to each shift that I spent with him. Mostly so I could slack off.

No such luck though; it would be an uncomfortable and unpleasant afternoon, I expected.

"Brownie," Feldspar grunted, not looking up from the maille that he was repairing by bending small rings of black steel, then looping and riveting them together to form a sheet. "Fetch me another set of coils."

I nodded and set off to the storage room, where components and materials were carefully laid out in their designated homes.

After only a few minutes of rummaging, I had located the coils of thick black wire, each wrapped at least fifty times around a metal rod and ready to be clipped into the rings that made up every suit of maille.

I lugged the heavy wooden crate back to where Feldspar was hunched at his workbench, and coughed to alert him to my presence.

"Where would you like me to put them?" I asked.

"Set them on the bench there." He pointed to the empty work station beside him. "You will be cutting the rings today."

It wasn't too difficult, but it was a repetitive and somewhat boring job. I had to clip each ring with a pair of cutting pliers, then flatten and file down the edges to make them smooth enough that they wouldn't catch on the woollen tunics that the elite Hobgoblin guard wore under their maille. Crimson tunics of course.

I much preferred forging weapons, and I'd almost made a serviceable dagger—after a dozen or so failed attempts. But realistically, and as boring as it was, this sort of task was more appropriate for me.

A few hours of clipping wire passed in silence before Feldspar suddenly set his work down and turned to me.

"Brownie. What do you know of the Combine?" he asked bluntly.

I stared at him vacantly, I had no idea what the Combine was.

"Uhh… Nothing?" I replied.

"Well. I shall tell you something of a story then."

He sat for a few moments, staring into the space between us, before clearing his throat and continuing.

"I wasn't born in these parts, you know, but far off to the east, and a little north instead. In a land that was squeezed between the Empire of Sacharr to the south, and the Merchant's Combine to the north. My land was once part of a league of free and independent principalities that came about after the fall of the great Kimorin Reach. But over time, each sided with either of the two major powers in the region."

I listened quietly whilst the man spoke, mildly surprised that he would suddenly decide to talk to me, and especially about his own past, after almost a full season of only grunts, insults, and barked commands.

"My city, Kirkeport, is a trading hub on the coast. Not exactly a capital, but nothing to sneeze at all the same. Anyway, before long, it was the last remaining bastion of independent thought left in an ocean of oppressive… well, bullshit really.

"As a young lad, I apprenticed under one of the smiths adjoining a massive library. There were many great halls in my city, filled with tomes and scholars—as dusty and leather-bound as each other. They collected knowledge from all over the land. Writings on cultures, beasts, heroes, and everything in between."

The man looked almost sad as he told me of the faraway land in which he had lived.

"The Combine burned it all."

"Why would they do that?" I asked.

"Well, they hold a particular world-view, not shared by many other nations. Unfortunately, the powers that be sold our people out to them when the time came to pick a side, and our scholars didn't fit their belief system. So all that knowledge, all that wisdom, was put to the torch once the Combine took over the city. Any that contradicted their way, that is."

"But why?" I asked, struggling to understand how burning tomes would help anyone.

"Knowledge can be a dangerous weapon, in the right hands. A dissenting idea or revolutionary thought can be far more deadly than a spear. An educated public is the bane of the great dragon that is a ruling elite—a critical mind, the stout blade, which slays the beast of bureaucracy."

I didn't really understand what he was talking about, having lived in a village where decisions were made by a council of mere bakers, woodsmen, and hunters.

Even the Vulkari shared gossip, ideas, and tales freely. And I struggled to imagine what good it would do for Karthak to withhold knowledge from her lieutenants and warriors, if it was knowledge that would serve to strengthen the warband.

"Zentar told me that there is a lot that he doesn't get told, that his superiors won't tell him what they don't think he needs to know. Was it like that? Like why the gambesons are crimson?" I asked, trying as best I could to draw a parallel that I could understand.

"No, no. That's a fairly standard military hierarchy, and Zentar told you it was to hide the blood, didn't he?"

Feldspar sighed and rolled his eyes.

"Crimson is just the cheapest dye in Sacharr, they get it from the rusted earth near Redclay Bend. I expect the Vulkari get it through trading," he told me, shaking his head. "Anyway, the Combine is different regarding heirarchy. See, the Merchant Lords, they believe that society should be simpler than say, the Sacharri, or even the Vulkari do."

Feldspar tapped a finger on the table, his brow furrowed in thought, before he continued; "Here, the Hobgoblins and their allies are united under the belief that the God-Emperor is the rightful heir to the World-Throne. And they believe that, beneath him, every decent man has their place, which best suits his own proclivities—and can change as he does.

"For the Legion, each member should work for what is best for the whole, and to strive to elevate the less advanced or..." he paused. "Eliminate the waste."

I raised an eyebrow at that, but Feldspar ignored it.

"Now the Combine, they also put the many afore the few. But they do it differently. They believe that beneath the ruling merchant class and their trade consortia, all should be equal, all should be the same effectively. I mean, it's far more complicated than that, but there is supposed to be no hierarchy."

It didn't seem so bad, until Feldspar continued.

"Now you'd think that maybe that would mean everyone was free to do as they please right?

"Wrong. In the Combine, nobody is free. Sure, there are soldiers, there are smiths and so forth, but one is not allowed to choose the role that best suits his want. Rather, he is assigned a role and can never decide that he'd rather be a fisherman than a miller—if that doesn't produce more wealth for the merchant lords.

"All wealth is reallocated based on special auditors, who essentially steal from the common man and redistribute to where the Combine leadership require it be—which I suspect, is their own coffers."

He sighed.

"I was young when our lord decided that we should join the Merchant's Combine. At that point they had already purchased much of the land and the businesses in my country so he didn't really have much of a choice.

"That's how they did it, you see—trade agreements that favoured their people and their ways.

"At first they produced things with slave labour and shoddy workmanship that was too cheap for neighbours *not* to buy, then they used the wealth they had amassed to buy out their competition. Then all of the freehold land. And finally, to bribe away local government who might have resisted their influence. Or perhaps that came first.

"Either way, when the real takeover happened, and their purple banner was hauled up over our lord's keep, I wasn't the best smith at the time. So, of course, I was designated another role.

"I was pressed into service as a soldier, and marched off to war against the Sacharri, without even knowing what I was fighting them for. It wasn't a good feeling; having my freedoms taken from me that way—much less to then have to spill the blood of my former countrymen over someone else's ideological dispute."

I didn't know if he had meant to insult me, but felt that he surely couldn't have overlooked the irony of telling this fact to someone who was essentially a slave, owned by his current employers.

"I know a thing or two about that, Feldspar," I told him, unable to hide the irritation in my tone.

"I know," he said simply. "Hence my decision to tell you this. Perhaps to help you realise that there's hope for you yet."

I was even more confused than before. The man had never treated me with anything more than contempt, but was now deciding to reassure me. It was uncomfortable, and I wasn't doing a very good job of hiding that.

"So how did you wind up here?" I asked, hoping to at least hear out his story before he noticed my puzzled expression.

"Well, I was a worse soldier than I was a smith. And in our very first skirmish with the Legion, was wounded and captured. After the company smith found a spear through his throat, the regiment that held me needed the horses of an elite cavalry unit desperately re-shod. So I volunteered." He looked proud as he told me.

"The regiment commander was impressed with my work, so had me kept on. Paid even. After a time, I was allowed to leave—since the two empires negotiated a truce. I chose to stay with the military, and have been with the regiment ever since. And that commander now holds this very castle."

"Manox Threydon?" I asked.

"Yes. He is far more decent and reasonable a leader than any I served under the Combine," he replied.

"So the Combine. What are they exactly? Kimori? Hobgoblins?" I asked.

"Yes, both and more. The Combine is no race, but almost a religion I would say. They spread their world-view and absorb other empires. The only real power that they faced back then was the Legion, but now I have heard rumour that there is a third—that the Kimorin Reach may rise once more. Perhaps that's the reason for the truce. Or perhaps wishful thinking from an old Kimora." Feldspar turned the maille sheet over in his hands. "I know that there was a Combine delegate here, around the time of your arrival. An interesting situation."

"There was a Hobgoblin in purple. Was that it?"

"Sounds like it. That Combine emissary, Thrinax, used to operate out of Kirkeport. He was sent specifically to Threydon I think, maybe to broker a deal based on their history. Or perhaps, to antagonise for the same reason."

"Why would that be? I mean, they didn't look like they were getting along, Manox Threydon and the other Hobgoblin," I said.

"Well I wouldn't imagine they would," Feldspar mused. "Manox Thrinax and Manox Threydon *are* brothers, after all."

"Really? But then why would they be on opposite sides?" I asked.

"Same reason as always," he said, and looked at me with possibly the first grin I had ever seen him wear. "A woman."

⚙ ⚙ ⚙

That evening I asked Grunwald about what Feldspar had told me.

"Zyntael, you are young, and with your involvement with Vulkari, you might never come to learn how men and women normally affect one another," he told me, setting aside his book, and stretching out amongst the pillows in his den.

I stirred my gruel. "You do realise I am a Kimora right? We have mothers and fathers, and I was expecting to be betrothed around now. So I'm aware that the Vulkari are different."

I thought about that fact for a moment. If things had been different, maybe I would be learning the skills needed to be a wife and mother instead of forging maille rings and shoddy daggers. It sounded dull.

"Wait. A Kimora? You're sure? That'd be why your ears stick out so?" Grunwald chuckled then began his spiel.

"When a man feels for a woman in a certain way, it saps him of his agency. Many might think that a woman's place in the home and in so-ciety'd be the lesser, but they forget the most important thing. It's obvi-ous that all of this..." He gestured around himself. "All of these walls, all of the soldiers, all of the law. All of it were built to ensure a man's power, his legacy, no? Here's the thing though. Any man, pauper or prince, be nothing without a woman to validate him. All of his worth be wasted if he fails to find a wife, worthy of bearing those who would continue that legacy."

"Okay..." I frowned at him. "So women are only useful for bearing children and are otherwise worthless? Sounds like more of a burden than anything."

"Oh little Kimora. You are more a cynic than most."

I didn't know the word, but assumed it wasn't something I should be proud to be.

"It'd be hardly a burden to be kept safe from the front lines of war," Grunwald said. "It'd rightly be the opposite in fact, lass. Many wars were started by men over women, but can you think of one that were the other way around? If men truly thought women to be nothing of worth, why move empires to war, just for the sake of something so worthless?"

He stared at me, almost expecting an answer. But I had none. I didn't actually know about any wars, nor any real history, but for what had been told to me by Karthak and he.

"I don't know. I suppose it makes sense, but what about Lord Threydon?" I asked, trying to refocus the conversation on what I'd actually asked about in the first place.

"Well that's just it. Women have a power over men. So great be their hold—their peculiar Magick—that man will build cities and monuments—then just as soon tear them down, should he believe that a woman desires it. And our commander here, he did just that.

"He set off on a conquest, to bring glory to his name, to build himself into a man worthy of desire. But the girl that he did this all for? He left her in his village. Left his younger brother as her warden."

"And what happened? The brother take his maiden?" I asked.

"Quite the contrary! The maiden took his brother," he laughed. "Not before bearing Threydon an heir though… Which I suppose, if it were all that a man wants, doesn't explain his upset." Grunwald sighed. "What it does explain, is the fact that maybe women don't wish for the things that men think they do. Not all at the least."

"His heir. Hang on a moment. You mean the Hobgoblin boy that is always at his side?" I asked.

They did look similar now that I thought about it, and although I'd briefly spoken to the boy a few times, I'd never actually asked him about his lineage nor how he came to be Threydon's aide. He seemed haughty and snobbish, and I assumed that, given how 'savage' I supposedly was, it was why Threydon was reluctant to allow us to spend time together.

"Indeed. Anyway, you'd best be getting rest, Zyntael, it's getting late. Finish your supper and we shall continue this talk another eve," Grunwald told me. "You've a long day with the smiths tomorrow, but maybe they'll let you finish that dagger you were making."

"Which one?" I shrugged. "I tried to make a bunch. Messed it up each time. I think I'm a better help just carrying stuff around. I mean, I'd like to practice more, and I'm sure I'll help with the forge. But yeah, carrying things. That's my calling apparently."

I bid Grunwald goodnight and settled into my bunk, to dream of castles and cities built for love and war, of weddings and romance and the celebration of a new child—things that would probably ever remain the domain of others, and not of me. As long as I was kept away from all of the boys my age, of course.

vii.

It was almost six more months before the Vulkar war party arrived once more; the spring rains having come and gone. As with the time of my own arrival, many new slaves, and wagons brimming with looted goods were brought into the custody of the Hobgoblin Legion.

I spent every one of those months working in the soldiers' barracks, and in the sweltering smithy that adjoined the massive building—work that grew more unpleasant as the weather grew warmer with each passing day.

It was quite easily the hardest and most painful work that I had been commanded to carry out during my entire stay at the fortress so far. I spent most days carrying plates and bars of iron and steel, or stoking roaring fires that would be used in the forging of arms and armour.

When I wasn't assisting in the forge, I would maintain the barracks itself—repairing bunks and furniture, oiling and polishing the many spare suits of maille, and transporting newly made equipment to the various quartermasters who armed each regiment that was stationed in the fortress or nearby. I considered these jobs to be a sort of reprieve from the constant, but strangely rewarding strain of working within the smithy itself.

During my time with Zentar, Feldspar, and Urd, I also learnt rudimentary ways to cobble together parts from multiple suits of armour—a skill apparently mastered by the Vulkari—as well as which body parts should be covered in particular ways by that armour.

And over the time that I toiled, I noticed a marked improvement in my strength. Where, at the beginning of my assignment to the smithy, I struggled to carry a single sword billet, by the last day, I could easily haul four or more without breaking any more of a sweat than I constantly had due to the merciless heat of the place.

At my best guess, it had been slightly more than a year since I had left the burning buildings of my home—against my will, bound and captured by hulking beasts, whose cackling and gibbering had terrified and tormented me.

Over a year since I was abducted by savage, mewling monsters, whose every action repulsed and shocked me.

It had been four long seasons of hard labour, constant learning, and subservience to a military force that pacified and curtailed dissent through swift and efficient force, and who gradually moved out into the neighbouring lands to pacify them too.

The strangest thing was, I could barely remember what my home was like. I had become so accustomed to the daily routine of working, eating, and sleeping (and ensuring that I didn't piss on anyone's patch) under the watchful gaze of my Hobgoblin overlords, that I almost came to believe that it was my entire life.

The sudden prospect of being reunited with my initial captors brought with it shards of the original terror I'd felt when they took me. But I struggled to recall the feeling of loss that I had felt the first moment that I had gained consciousness in the dungeons of the Blackfort.

Instead, I felt a sense of sadness at the possibility of leaving behind my new friends and fellow workers, and even to some degree the Goblins, for whatever length of time that I would have to.

As usual, I would have no say in the matter, and on the late spring or early summer morning of my departure, I was roused from a fitful sleep and escorted to a lavish bathing room, by Manox Threydon's aide—his son—one Hobgoblin with whom I had only really exchanged pleasantries and small talk, up until this point.

There, in the royal chamber, I was scrubbed of the filth that coated my skin, and clad in an outfit similar to that which I had worn to my first audience with the commander.

This time however, the Hobgoblins' servants purposely created clothing for me. A gaggle of women spent an awfully long time preparing me for the day ahead, whilst the boy watched on, occasionally demanding that the girls change a thing or two.

My neck was adorned with the very same set of beads that I had previously worn on the day of my arrival to the Solent fortress. They'd been confiscated on my first day at work and kept somewhere perhaps specifically for this moment. From tiny chains affixed to the necklace, a strip of crimson silk hung front and back. It reached down to just above my knees, and was bound around my waist with a dark leather belt. This one thankfully not a reeking dog collar, but instead a two-inch-wide strip of supple leather, clasped with a silver buckle.

My face was then painted with black and crimson paint; thick lines of colour and charcoal were daubed under my eyes and a set of three black stars ran along my right cheekbone. A fourth, much larger crimson star was painted on my forehead above my right eye. They looked nice, but I had absolutely no clue what they meant.

The vest of bone was strung over my chest, and my ankles were wrapped with bracelets of cord and wood again. Instead of more bracelets, on each wrist I wore a small black iron shackle, though no lock, nor any chains were affixed. I presumed they must have held some ceremonial meaning, but did not question the servants who hurried to outfit me.

Instead, I merely gazed at my appearance in a polished silver mirror, the image hazy but impressive.

My hair was cleaned of soot and braided on either side, just in front of my ears, then the rest was cut to just above shoulder length. Three feathers, two jet black and one a deep shining red, jutted upward from a small clip at the back of my head.

I stood there nervously until the servants declared their work done, my mind swimming with thoughts of both the unpleasant past and of the uncertain future. Grunwald would of course tell me otherwise, but it didn't feel very much like I was making my own destiny, nor did it feel as though any choice I made was really mine.

"No longer a slave, but still a slave," Threydon's son said, interrupting my glum thoughts.

"What do you mean?" I asked him.

Disappointingly, it seemed he spoke in cryptic riddles like most Hobgoblins, though I didn't know why I was expecting anything else from him.

"Slaves are we all, Kimora. You, first to your bonds, and now to your duties. Me to my blood. There is no escaping it, so we must bravely face it with our best," he told me.

The way he spoke did sound a lot like his father, but there was an air of almost disdain in his speech. He sat there, fiddling with the pendant Karthak had given him, clearly no slave.

"You know, I do envy your chance to leave this dusty fortress. It gets awfully boring sitting and waiting for the order to move out," he added.

"Well I'd rather stay. It isn't so good out there," I said. "Especially with the Vulkari."

He grinned at me. "Father said that your time with them has made you strong, and that further time shall only yet make you stronger. In the long run, that's a good thing, Zyntael."

"If you say so… Hey, what's your name, anyway? Are you a prince or something?"

"Manox Anra. It is as my father's name, I suppose. And no, I'm no prince. I don't actually have a proper title. I'm only thirteen and can't attain military rank until fifteen. It's frustrating of course, but I spend most of my time learning now, what I'll need to know then. I mean, I have so much time here, so why not?" he said with a smug grin, and shrugged. "And this way, I can have an easier time of it in the future."

I smirked. It was actually a pretty clever way to do things, though I tended to lack such foresight. If it were me, I'd simply do whatever I was expected to—keep my head down and my mouth shut. And try not to piss on anyone's patch, of course.

Manox Anra picked at the edge of the cabinet he was sitting on. He looked up at me and squinted as though in thought.

"Why do you suppose the Wolf-man War-Mother took you?" he asked.

"I have no idea!" I told him honestly, a little taken aback. "I wasn't treated the same way as the other slaves. That alone has earned me nothing but hatred from the others here. But I really don't know why she took me, why she brought me here, why she did any of the things she did to me."

The thought of returning to the monster made me want to vomit.

Anra must have noticed my look of discomfort, and changed the subject with a casual shrug and a series of questions. He asked about where I was from, and what my village was like, then he told me a little about Sacharr. Apparently it was a massive land of rolling plains and wide forests.

He gave the impression that every part of the place was magnificent, but I struggled to imagine that forests, fields, rivers, and hills differed all that much from place to place. Still, he was adamant that it was a far better place than the so-called 'Solent Borderlands' and told me that if he could, he would take me there to prove it.

Finally, a knock at the door interrupted our conversation, and a servant alerted us to the arrival of Karthak, who awaited my presence down in the great hall. That old fear began to bubble away within my chest, and my palms began to sweat. Again noticing my pained expression, the boy pushed himself from the cabinet and approached me.

I was taken aback when Anra took my hand in his.

"Do Vulkari have ranks as we Domovoi do?" he asked, his dark violet eyes locked on mine, and his hands warm against my clammy skin.

"I don't really know. Maybe just the Warlord and then the raiders. I know the males are right at the bottom though." I couldn't be sure if there were titles, although they did appear to record hierarchy somehow, even outside of gender.

"Well, when next we meet—depending, of course, on the length of your stay away—perhaps we can greet one another by rank," he said. "Or at the very least, we could speak more. We didn't get much of a chance to—until now."

He released my hand and performed a small bow. It almost looked as though he was blushing, but through the green of his skin, I couldn't be sure.

"I would like that, but hopefully it is as your father said, and I won't be gone long enough to attain one!" I told him.

He shrugged again. It was a strangely endearing gesture. Then the curious Goblin boy bid me farewell, and left me with the servants.

Moments later, a group of four soldiers marched into the room and demanded that I walk ahead of them, as we descended through the castle and down into the entrance hall.

There in the centre of the room, perched on an ornate cushioned seat that was mounted upon a flat wooden platform, and carried by four slaves, sat Karthak.

The mighty Vulkar looked much the same as when last I saw her, perhaps a little thinner and certainly less clean.

She turned to regard our procession as I marched before the Hobgoblins, and she commanded the slaves to lower her kingly litter to the ground.

The Vulkar war chief smiled as I approached, tapping her overgrown claws on the base of her seat. Then she dismissed the Hobgoblin troops, and beckoned me forward.

"Do you still remember our tongue?" she first asked in Vulkar and then again in common Solent Fae.

"Only some words," I told her, nervously keeping my distance and making every attempt not to meet her intense gaze.

"Well, we shall have time to refresh your memory of the *real* language of the people," she said, leaning forward menacingly.

"There are many forms of the true language, then still more tongues that are altogether alien, and the more words you have, the more people shall listen," she said, and then looked around the hall before her gaze fell upon my new outfit.

"I see you have been kept well, and dressed as though an Imperial tribute to the attire of our people. Manox Threydon is a gracious host. Yes? Despite his little joke here." She lifted a finger towards one of my wrists and smirked at the ornamental shackle upon it.

"He is," I told her. "If I may, he told me that I was to remain here for a time after your visit. That he has need of me."

"Bah. Did he now?" the Vulkar snorted, then made an odd purring sound and spoke words in her own language that I didn't know.

"Well I shall be claiming my property, and we shall discuss business shortly. For now, come to me, Pup," she commanded.

I complied and tentatively approached her throne, the slaves stealing glances at me as I walked by.

With lightning speed, Karthak grasped me with both of her hands, pulling me uncomfortably close to her face. Her breath was once again rancid, and I struggled to breathe.

"The Hobgoblins have done a good job. You have grown much over the last four seasons. Not quite enough to join the warriors, no, but enough that you may begin training at least," she told me.

I was glad that I was still too small to become a warrior, but even being forced to commence some sort of Vulkar training worried me.

"Training?" I asked her. "What kind of training?"

"You shall see, my whelp. Now hurry back to our encampment and await me in my lounge. I have business to attend with Threydon. It is a pity that I have been kept away so long, but it shall prove to our advantage in time. We have much to discuss, you and I, but it shall require comfort… and liquor."

And with that, she shoved me away from her and barked a command at her slaves, who hoisted her mobile seat onto their shoulders and began to march toward Manox Threydon's throne room.

※　※　※

I wandered through the castle courtyard, past the smithy, and down around stone squares where the soldiers practiced their drills. I soon saw the Vulkar camp, smoke issuing from cooking pits and campfires dotted around in the field beyond the city wall.

There were hundreds of the beasts; many gathered in groups and bartered over goods traded from the city.

I had almost reached the gate when I heard my name being called.

"Zyntael! Brownie child!" came the voice from a watchtower to my left.

I looked up and saw a sharply dressed Hobgoblin and an old white-whiskered man standing together and surveying the Vulkari.

The Hobgoblin I didn't know, but the man was only ever going to be Grunwald.

"By my old eye, you look to be a miniature Vulkar warlord, yourself," he said.

I laughed. "Is that a good thing?"

"Well if all Vulkari were but a quarter as decent as you, we would all be better off," He winked, then motioned off to his right, back up the hill.

"Before you leave, I believe that Zentar were wanting a word."

I felt a bit embarrassed that I had neglected to call in, though I figured I'd be back in the sweaty company of the smiths in a handful of weeks at most.

"Alright, I'll come by this way again soon," I told my old bandit friend and hurried back up the cobbled path towards the smithy.

There were no sounds of work coming from within the building as I pushed the sooty wooden door open and wandered inside.

All three of the blacksmiths sat around chatting, but stopped and greeted me warmly upon my arrival. They remarked on my garb and fussed over me for a short while before they ushered me into the storeroom at the rear of the workshop.

There, in the middle of the room, on a bench that usually held vials of oils and chemicals, sat an old rag. It was bunched up in the centre, covering a mystery object.

"Young miss, this is the end of your apprenticeship. Usually there would be a proper ceremony but this shall suffice," Zentar stepped forward and said dramatically, waving his filthy hands around. "You have been a fastidious student of the ancient arts. Now for your final lesson. Remember that at the fore of every army there have always been great leaders. Honour those who wield the power, not simply to destroy nations and their forces, but to create the same themselves..." He finished by gesturing to Feldspar with a flourish.

The man stood forward begrudgingly, the permanent scowl he wore, still affixed to his soot covered face whilst I stood and grinned at the unusual show.

"…And behind every great army are the workers, the servants and most importantly, the smiths. Without whom, an army is but a crowd of angry men. Honour those who toil to outfit the troops, to mend the broken blades, to shoe the horses for war…" he grumbled and looked sideways at Urd.

The squat Hobgoblin stepped forward. Opened his mouth and frowned.

He stood like that for a minute or two, opening and closing his mouth, staring blankly, before finally speaking.

"Small Brownie, one day, you both. Not sword or horse though, worker and…"

"Yes, what Urd means to say is that you have the capacity to fulfil both roles; the leader and the worker. Honour those who embody all parts of the whole. Now, ordinarily an actual apprenticeship would last for longer than a year, but we heard from Grunwald that you were to leave us. So as a token of goodwill, and in the hopes that what you've learnt here might keep you safe in the time to come, we present to you a small gift," Zentar said, still gesticulating flamboyantly.

At the conclusion of his compatriot's speech, Urd enthusiastically tore the cloth away from the table, flinging the object that it had hidden across the room.

The gift skittered along on the stone floor and bumped against the bottom of a wooden storage shelf.

"Oh. Sorry," Urd said and recovered the object, dusted it off on his filthy tunic, and held it out towards me in his massive palm.

It was a dagger.

The hilt was bound in crimson leather; the broad blade housed in a black scabbard, and the pommel fashioned into the shape of a fist.

The second dagger I had been gifted, and easily the most impressive I had ever seen—the smiths had taken one of my scrapped attempts at forging a weapon, and perfected the blade.

My eyes widened at the sight of it, and overwhelmed by the kind gesture and the generosity of the trio, I reached a trembling hand up and took the gift.

I unsheathed the short blade and held it up to my face.

It was forged with black steel, and along the length of each side there was beautifully inlaid silver writing.

I stared at the small weapon, eyes watering, before looking up at the three blacksmiths.

I didn't quite have the heart to tell them that I couldn't read so had no idea what the inscription said, but Feldspar must have noticed my absent stare and told me what was written there.

"It says: 'Anything can be slain with a stout blade,' then on the other side; 'And a stouter heart.'"

Then the man uncharacteristically chuckled.

"A little something I always like to remember."

"Thank you. I don't know what to say," I told them honestly, then embraced each one tightly in turn.

Though the months in the barracks and the smithy had almost broken my body, it would remain one of the most satisfying periods during my stay, and the prospect of leaving the place to return to the company of Karthak and her Vulkar raiders filled me with dread.

I had no idea how long I would be required to stay in their company and clung to the hope that it would be as Manox Threydon had told me; a short stay before returning to familiar work, regular food, and safe bedding.

Once farewells had been exchanged, I left the smithy and headed back down the path toward the Vulkar camp.

Grunwald was still where I'd left him and he called out to me as I approached.

"Those craftsmen bestowed a gift upon you I see. It suits you well," he said.

I held the dagger up towards him.

"It's so beautiful, I could only dream of making something like this myself. I hope one day to learn," I told him. "I shall be sure to practice when I return."

He frowned briefly, then broke into a smile once more.

"Well—let us hope you do not need its use. All the same, be careful Zyntael, and remember that there are always options."

"I know. I remember," I told him. "I will only be gone a short time anyway."

"I hope so," he replied. "I surely hope so."

I waved him goodbye for now, and for the first time in about a year, passed beyond the gateway and into the midst of the Vulkar rabble.

And, as afraid as I was, I'd do as the kind Hobgoblin boy, Manox Anra, had said:

I'd bravely face it with my best.

viii.

My fears at the prospect of remaining with Karthak and her warband would prove to be well placed. Whatever the negotiations that were held after I left the castle, they must have soured, for, within an hour of my arrival, the chieftain returned to the camp as well.

She dismounted her regal seat, and strode into the tent that housed her highest ranking fighters. And she remained there for the rest of the morning. By noon, the order had been issued to complete any trading and prepare to mobilise. And by dusk we had left.

Before Karthak returned, however, I wandered up to her wagon— as was bid of me. The pole that had carried me so long ago still jutted upward from the corner. An unpleasant reminder of the beginnings of my journey east.

I decided to check on the contents of the supply locker within the luxurious room, where the Warlord rested at the rear of her large wagon.

Alongside looted odds and ends, and nestled beneath a curious golden statuette of a nursing Vulkar hound, which was wrapped in crumpled greased paper, there was a small amount of perfumed oil and soap left. I made a mental note to locate some mint as well. If I was to be kept in the company of the massive brute, then at least I would see to it that my death wouldn't come as a result of asphyxiation—due to either her breath, or reeking hide.

I briefly examined the statue before I placed it carefully back, as well. It looked to be very old—the surface of the metal covered in nicks, scratches and a film of greenish filth.

It would have originally stood around four inches tall, but whatever young the mother was nursing had mostly broken off at some point, and only part of its face and head were left of it. Its oddly Ki-morin features ended in a delicately sculpted mouth that remained locked on its mother's teat. The remaining ear was dangerously sharp—and judging by the browned dried blood that was smeared over the little child's hair, someone had pricked themselves upon it some time ago.

I wrapped the unusually artful treasure back in its brown paper covering and closed the storage locker, then idly paced around the lounge. I examined the various trophies and trinkets that had been claimed since the last time I had seen the place. Most were various skulls, and other grisly parts of creatures, presumably slain by Karthak herself. A few were broken remains of what I guessed were ritual or shamanistic relics.

Whilst I skulked around in the lounge, a Vulkar warrior stepped up onto the platform behind me—every second footfall accompanied by the striking of metal on wood.

I froze in place, poised next to the war chief's lushly blanketed bed, and wheeled around to face the limping monster.

The creature pushed her hideous face through the curtain that covered the doorway, and grinned at me from beneath her leather hood. She snarled something that I didn't understand at me in its own speech then laughed.

"The scion still lives, and now returns, dressed as though she actually belongs," she said, in Solent Fae.

I nodded, and began to explain that my appearance was not my own choice, but the beast cut me off.

"The favourite pup. I have come to regret not allowing you to drown with your little Ratling friend. I had hoped you might remain a slave to the Goblin whelps. But I had to venture here to see for myself that the rumour was true. That you were to be reclaimed," she said, voice a low rumble. "To confirm my regret."

I frowned in confusion.

"Chosen Pup, do not think that you are so lucky. We shall see what becomes of you in time. Karthak is old. She may just be losing touch. Her gambit is made upon faith in a Bare-Skinned animal, and an empire who cannot see beyond the reach of their iron.

"She shall see the folly in clinging to her old ways—hopefully before our lives have been bartered. If it is to be those who deny us our Magicks, with whom we must ally, then I bid the frost take them all. And if it is to be you with whom our future lies, then I shall *ensure* that it takes you first!"

None of her words made sense to me, but I didn't doubt for a second that they were meant as some sort of threat.

The Vulkar hissed at me and I recoiled in fright. Then she let out a high pitched cackle, and hobbled away—leaving me there in the cushioned nest of the Vulkar Warlord, my heart hammering away at my ribcage.

※　※　※

When Karthak returned from her talks with the other Vulkar leaders, I tried to tell her about the visit from her limping warrior. But she was in no mood for conversation. She merely ordered me to sit on a plush cushion, and listen quietly, whilst she gibbered and muttered to herself in her own speech, occasionally demanding that I top up the massive goblet that she drank her foul-smelling spirits from.

Her mood barely improved over the next few days, as the warband made its way back towards the western foothills, crawling slowly across the wide expanse of the grassy plains, before halting at a ruined river crossing to allow time for bridges to be rebuilt.

It was there that Karthak first decided to talk to me for any length of time. The extent of our communication thus far having been only demands to fetch more alcohol and food, or to occasionally relay commands to her officers.

"Did you know, small Vulkar…" she said, drunkenly slurring her words and lounging on her throne in the gentle sunlight.

It was the first time that she had ever referred to me as such, and I turned to her, confused, as I sat cross legged on the rug at her feet, and carved meat from a lamb haunch with my exquisite dagger.

"Did you know that we used to roam these plains?" she asked, and not paying any regard to my response, carried on drunkenly babbling.

"We were once as our hounds are, they say. Simple animals with no care but for eating and breeding."

She extended an arm and gestured at the wide grassy expanse before us.

"We roamed these plains, hunting and mating. That is all we did. And the whole land was ours."

"What happened?" I asked. "You walk upright, and you speak. No other animal does that."

"Well yes, you see. It was…" She leaned toward me conspiratorially and whispered; "Magick."

"Magick? But there's no such thing!" I told her.

"Hah! What would you know? Your weakling Bare-Skinned brethren are too concerned with their tools and their treachery now to ever bother with the truth. They cannot know the true way of the world, whilst they keep their eyes so closed." She slouched back in her chair and let out a long sigh. "There is Magick in all things. It changes things, it grows things, it even destroys things."

"Like time?" I asked.

"Yes, like… What? No! Not like time, stupid whelp! What have those Hobgoblin knaves been filling your head with?" She shot me a frown and continued. "The ancient Magicks of this land found our people when they walked on four legs and could not speak. When they were but simple beasts. That is of course except for Yanghar."

"'Yanghar?' What does that mean?"

"It is a name—you simpleton!" Karthak snapped at me. "By the Spirits! If you stopped interrupting me, then maybe you would find out!"

With wide eyes, I sat and listened, trying to hold in the many questions that boiled within me as her tale drunkenly unfolded.

"Yanghar was a clever beast. The only one who knew how to listen to the Spirits of the trees, the grass, and the sky. She knew that the time had come to move on from a simple existence. She understood that the lands were under threat from the many other creatures that swarmed from the east, carrying weapons and fire, hunting her kind for sport or food.

"She knew that if her mute and simple fellows were to survive, that they would have to be able to do the same or become even stronger. So one night, under the light of a blood moon, she ventured up onto a craggy peak and called to the Spirits, to the Magick within the lands."

Karthak drained her chalice and held it out to me absently, waiting as I refilled the vessel from a small cask of sickly dark liquor, before she continued dramatically.

"The Spirits took pity on Yanghar. Or maybe they were impressed by her cleverness. They granted her a single pup. It was born shortly after. A female who walked upright, and one with ideas in her mind and words on her tongue. The first Vulkar."

My mind swirled with images of Vulkar children, small and frail, guarded and nurtured by the hulking war hounds.

Parents they now kept as pets.

"Poor Yanghar. She was the mother of all Vulkari. But that primal duty, that special gift, was to be her sacrifice—for her Vulkar pup killed her in its birth.

"Some of the hounds in Yanghar's pack sensed the importance of the pup and raised her to be strong. To hunt and to fight. Their work was rewarded by the Spirits, and in time they too learned to speak, and to walk as we do now. The males who did their part were gifted as well. They became the breeding whelps that began our people." Karthak sighed. "Some of the others did not feel the same, and could not overcome their animal nature. They did all they could to slay the child—to neglect her or to bully her.

"Those foolish beasts now serve us on leashes. Nothing but pets and guards. A fitting punishment would you not agree?"

A small part of me, a brave or perhaps very foolish part, wanted to tell her that she was wrong, and that the world would be better for it had those beasts ended the Vulkari before they began. I looked away and nodded in agreement; I knew better than to provoke the temper of the Vulkar Warlord, particularly in such a drunken and unpredictable state.

"I see your thoughts. Your little red head is like a hollowing rotted fruit to me, and your mushy thinking oozes from your long ears like thick pulp," she told me, smiling.

I stared at the chunk of roasted meat before me, afraid to confirm her suspicion.

"You are thinking that your life would be better, had Yanghar the Beginner's pup perished early on. But I can assure you that you are wrong. I have given you the chance to be as that pup was. To begin something great. You shall see," she told me cryptically, and before I had time to query her words, the massive Vulkar had slid lower in her throne and fallen asleep—her goblet still clutched in her clawed grip, spilling her drink as she snored heavily.

I spent the rest of that day pondering her words whilst I tidied up the many empty barrels and bottles of drink that the Warlord had finished. Then, once her lodgings were sufficiently clean, I stretched out in the shade and sipped a small cup of leftover liquor. And I thought about my time ahead.

I would be once more subjected to the depravity of the multitude of feral beasts that made up the convoy, the results of the raids, the fighting and the cruelty that they so frequently engaged in—and so I quietly sat, trying to enjoy the strong and sweet drink that I had scavenged.

The sparse bushes nearby were alive with the hum of innumerable insects, and the sound was soothing, despite the well of fear within me. I watched a bee dance from flower to flower, lazily enjoying its freedom amongst the spring blooms.

And as my head began to swim, I wished only to be as the bee; busy, and sure of its purpose—and entirely free from the horrors of the impending unknown.

ix.

I had assumed that we were returning to the Blackfort. But I was wrong.

After several weeks of practically uninterrupted travelling westward, and with the foothills that sheltered the Blackfort in their midst still mere hazy bumps in the distance, the warband halted.

This time it was not to make a raid on some unfortunate village. Instead, Karthak held a meeting with several of her top lieutenants, and she brought me along, rather than relegating me to the lead wagon to await her return—as was usually the case.

I was told to sit on a small and quite uncomfortable stool, carved haphazardly from a single stout log, and remained there in silence whilst the Warlord held council.

My grasp of the Vulkar tongue was still rusty, so understanding what was discussed in anything more than the most rudimentary capacity was all but impossible. But still I listened on intently as the discussion became more and more heated.

Before long, the tent was a cacophony of yapping, snarling, and cackling, as the massive creatures argued.

I could still manage to understand the occasional words, but the full cause for anger was lost on me.

One Vulkar, a smaller one that seemed to be more outspoken than the others, appeared to be accusing Karthak of some misdeed or another. There was repeat mention of what I understood to mean 'glory' as well as something that translated roughly into 'theft.'

The limping hooded Vulkar looked to be using the dissent amongst the high ranking warriors to drum up support in favour of her as leader, and appeared to be somewhat successful in forcing a schism in their ranks.

Frequently throughout the row, she pointed at me whilst snarling and frothing, spewing what I barely understood to be insults, and claiming that I was some sort of evidence of Karthak being unfit for rule.

I had, up until this point, assumed that the Warlord was as she was through force or strength, maybe even birthright. But I was now beginning to think that the Vulkari elected their leaders—and were set to elect a new one presently.

The creatures were seated in the spacious tent in a loose circle, as though children telling stories of frightful monsters around a campfire. Only, in place of the campfire, there stood whichever frightful monster stepped forward to make its case or weigh in on a matter raised previously.

The entire scene was surreal and terrifying. I expected that the debate would, at any moment, erupt into bloodshed and outright slaughter, and kept my eyes on the Vulkari that appeared not to approve of my presence there.

I wondered if Manox Threydon's suspicions about Karthak having some maternal instinct for me might extend as far as protecting me from harm, should it come to that. Then I remembered the constant cruelty with which she had treated me over the time I had spent in her company on the journey east, and reconsidered my reliance on her goodwill towards me.

I nervously fingered the pommel of my black dagger as I sat and waited for the worst.

The worst however, never actually came. Despite the ferocity with which they argued, the group of twenty odd creatures never resorted to blows and within a few hours a resolution was met.

From what I understood, the limping Vulkar would take with her a group of the others and leave the warband to return to the Blackfort, whilst Karthak and her retinue would head north along the foothills for some purpose that I didn't grasp.

A part of me was somewhat disappointed at the rather anticlimactic outcome, hoping in some way that if the beasts had begun to tear each other to pieces, then perhaps I could have used the ensuing chaos to make an escape.

I pushed those thoughts from my mind, knowing full well that I had absolutely no idea where I actually was in relation to my home and that I lacked the skills to maintain my own survival in the wilds alone.

I returned with Karthak, flanked by two of her most intimidating and loyal warriors. One was an older, veteran Vulkar, with an unusually shaggy grey pelt, and one eye. She had large patches where, in place of her mottled fur, there ran terrible pink scars—burns or perhaps vicious wounds that had never quite healed properly.

Despite this, the warrior walked with a spring in her step and held her ugly head high as we made our way back to the front of the convoy. It occurred to me that I had never seen this particular warrior wearing any armour, and she certainly made no attempt to hide her raggedy appearance. Rather, she appeared proud of the marks and scars, and the various bald patches.

The other Vulkar was Karthak's occasional bed-mate, Star-Star— the small bodyguard who had taught me the name for the Hobgoblins.

"Stick with us," Star-Star told me. "We travel north into the Wilds, to lose the dead-weight. And Star-Star would not like to lose you along with them. These lands are hostile to the unprepared."

Although I'd have far preferred to be anywhere else than with Vulkari, Star-Star really was the best of them. So I stuck with her.

Soon, we travelled north, just as she said. Within days, the terrain began to grow rougher, and the roads that had once dissected the lands were, more often than not, slippery clay-lined ruts (or simply missing entirely). Here, the hills and dales really did feel hostile.

The dissenting warriors took a small share of the wagons, slaves, and beasts of burden, and broke away from the main group. They carried on westward—ascending into the misty and humid foothills where the Blackfort awaited.

I was glad to avoid returning to that horrible place, but remained apprehensive of what our new direction would bring.

Happily, Karthak's dire mood cleared up with the departure of the others, and she once more began giving me spirited lectures about her peoples, and the strange and ancient lands that we travelled.

For the first time in perhaps ever, I actually began to somewhat enjoy the company of the Vulkari. Between the gradual increase in my confidence in speaking with them, and the gentler nature by which the warband leaders began to treat me, I no longer felt as though I was one wrong move away from being devoured.

Of course, that was before I began my training.

THE THIRD STITCH

TRANSFORMATION

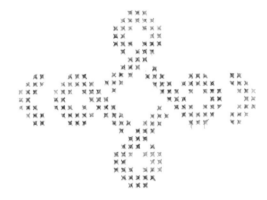

i.

"Star-Star is sick of your pathetic excuses!"

She turned to the mud-covered Vulkar pup, fury in her pale yellow eyes, and spittle frothing at the corners of her sneering maw.

"Star-Star shall rip your spine out through your throat if you so much as *think* about giving up again!"

The small and filthy Vulkar was shaking, her short tail curved beneath her haunches, as she stared at the ground in shame and fear.

I wanted to feel pity for the mongrel, but was glad that, for once, it wasn't me who was being lectured and abused. For once, it wasn't me who was the slowest, the weakest, and the worst.

Our task had been to run down brightly-painted hares. They'd been captured and held in a small cage for the entire day, awaiting their demise. Though I suspected that mine—a runty and pathetic beast, which had been coloured with a splash of blue along its body—was already half-dead by the time the hunt began.

All the same, I had chased the creature into the undergrowth a few hundred yards from our small camp, and then waited. I circled around the scrub and crouched down, hoping that the animal would move on to a better hiding spot.

As soon as it did, I hurled my javelin. It skewered the squealing hare.

I lacked the advantage of the strong sense of smell that the others had, but had hunted rabbits on the outskirts of our village as a child, and so knew that the animals were both impatient and stupid.

Apparently the scrawny Vulkar who was being berated by Star-Star, didn't share this knowledge, and for whatever reason, her quarry had escaped. It was at that point that the pup decided to call it quits, and had made an attempt to set off on her own—to find a way back to the main camp of Karthak's warband.

Star-Star had caught up to the young warrior-to-be, and nearly drowned the creature in a shallow muddy stream, before hauling her back to where the rest of us waited—each clutching our dead prey.

"I could not do it; the t-task was too hard," the pup stammered.

"And Star-Star should care, why? Is this the attitude that shall bring glory to our people? That shall ensure that your fellow raiders return after a hunt?"

The veteran raider gestured at the six other young Vulkari and then lingered on me.

"Each of these miserable animals brought back their prey. And this soft little freckled Kikimora did so without a strong nose and fast legs."

She glared at me, perhaps disappointed that I had actually succeeded at something for once, and so no-longer served as an example to the others of what *not* to do. Then she returned her attention to the filthy, quaking failure before her.

"After many moons of training, you have been beaten by a hairless, toothless, clawless little Kikimora. What do you think Star-Star should do with you?"

"I... I... I do not know..." the beast-child muttered, and gazed at the grass at her feet.

"You are all dismissed. You may return to the camp and prepare your catches for your dinner tonight. You, whelp..." She leaned in close and grasped the muddy Vulkar by the throat. "You shall *not* fail us tomorrow!"

I was mildly surprised at how light the punishment for failure was that day—especially given that there was an attempt to leave the group. I'd been given far harsher treatment for much smaller transgressions, and had never once outright given up. Even if I had certainly considered it on more than a few occasions.

Each beating I received, each time I had been thrown to the ground, spat on, kicked, or worse, I had considered running, considered even taking to the elder warrior in her sleep.

I had thought about whether I was even capable of slitting the monster's throat. I would hold my Legion dagger each night, bitterly contemplating just how I would go about doing it as I drifted off to sleep. Then, each morning, I would rise again to begin some other new torture in earnest. To fail again and again.

It actually surprised me that since my return to the warband, and despite my unguarded proximity to the Vulkar chieftain, at no point had I been disarmed.

In fact, many times even, the fearsome raiders had complimented me on my tiny weapon, or offered to trade it for some ludicrously oversized and primitively fashioned blade of their own. Or some spear or blade, stolen from the very barracks I'd toiled in.

The Vulkari consistently managed to surprise me with their odd sense of honour. Despite how much they stole from others, I had never once witnessed theft amongst the warriors. And, more often than not, disputes were handled through bartering and trade of both possessions and tasks—instead of violence.

For all their outward savagery, they did have some contrary civility toward those they saw as equals. The day following our hunt, however, would unfortunately not be one such time. After all, I, and all the other pups, were *far* from equal to the raiders.

❈ ❈ ❈

I slept uncomfortably. There must have been a root or a stick underneath my bedroll, and I awoke with a sore back.

Still groggy, I took my pack with a change of clothes and made my way through the dew-soaked overgrown grass, and down to the small creek, where I washed the sleep from my eyes with icy mountain water.

The other young raider hopefuls were still asleep in the semicircle of tents laid out around the smouldering remains of the campfire, as I quietly dressed myself for the day in a thin woollen tunic and a belt to carry my dagger.

When I was done, I took a moment to look around at my peaceful surroundings, taking in the crisp morning air. The hills that crept upwards to the north and the west, dark silhouettes against a pale morning sky.

There were still a few stars visible in the clear sky above, though the sun was sure to begin cresting the other side of the shallow valley within the hour.

I stretched out, trying to get my backbone to click into a comfortable position, but to no avail, so I staggered back to the campsite, rubbing the small of my back as I walked.

Star-Star was awake by the time I arrived.

She sat on a mushroom-covered old log, and had begun to stoke up the glowing embers in the fire pit, rustling around in the flaked ashes with a long pointed stick, and casting bundles of dried twigs on top.

She nodded at me as I approached then sat down beside her on the log.

"It shall be a hot day," she told me as she stared into the slowly kindling fire.

"I imagine so," I replied, and began to fish around in my rucksack for some sort of breakfast food.

"You need not find food there. Star-Star has been on the prowl. She has a nice surprise," She grinned at me, and pointed to a cloth bundle that sat in the flattened grass beside her.

I went and retrieved the wrapped package and then returned to my position, carefully unfolding the soft woollen cloth to reveal her surprise.

There were a dozen mottled eggs, some brown and some a very pale blue, each no larger than a hen's egg.

"There are eight of us and you though. Should I search for more?" I asked her, covering the delicate eggs up, and placing the bundle beside the log.

"You need not worry, there is more to come. This is all that Star-Star collected. But she was not the only one who went a-searching for food."

The Vulkar winked at me, and placed a small log on the crackling fire.

"The others should arrive any moment now. In the meantime, this warrior would like to ask you something." She looked at me sincerely, for once there was no manic grin upon her face.

"Okay, ask away," I said, wondering what it could possibly be that could make a Vulkar cease its constant smirking.

"Karthak, she is old, yes? She has put a lot of faith in you, yet you were not born as one of us. You are weaker, smaller and frailer than any other youngling. But still she chose you."

I nodded.

"Do you know why this is?" she asked.

"No. I have wondered, sure, but I never felt it a good idea to ask," I told the warrior honestly.

"It is not Star-Star's place to say, and they are our leader's reasons to give when she deems it necessary. For now, though; another question." She shifted in on the log and leaned towards me, speaking quietly.

"Do you promise Star-Star that you shall not fail, that you shall not give up?"

I hesitated. I wasn't entirely sure that it was even something that I *could* promise.

"I promise I will try not to, but I can't guarantee my success," I told her.

The warrior laughed, her grin once again stretched across her monstrous face.

"Well today, Pup of Karthak of the Crimson Star, you shall be truly put to the test. For now, warm yourself and prepare."

"Prepare for what?"

Star-Star cackled, waking the other Vulkar pups. Then she looked me in the eyes, the flickering fire reflecting in her deep pupils, her expression wild and menacing.

She leaned in close again and spoke softly, unblinking eyes locked on mine.

"Prepare for battle!"

"Wait, what?" I asked, bewildered.

Star-Star resumed her cackling and ignored my further questions. And, before long, the other young trainee warriors had gathered around the now merrily crackling breakfast fire.

Our fearsome tutor told each of the others as they arrived that they needn't prepare breakfast, and I wondered how she intended to stretch a dozen eggs between seven hungry, growing Vulkari and myself. Especially since, by the time the lot of us were roused and ready to eat, no other egg-hunters had shown up.

Thankfully, we didn't have to wait long. Within half an hour or so, three other adult Vulkari strode into our small camp; other trainers who had alternately coached us on throwing spears, selecting and donning armour, as well as fist-fighting, over the past months.

They brought an entire pig, which swung beneath a long wooden pole that two carried on their muscular shoulders, as well as various other foodstuffs in backpacks, satchels, and sacks.

The group set down the breakfast bounty and greeted, first Star-Star, and then each of the young Vulkari and me in turn.

That morning, we ate a rich and hearty breakfast of pork, what I learned were quail and mountain hen eggs, and some type of kippered fish that one of the adult warriors had made herself.

It was the finest morning meal that I had eaten in an awfully long time, but with every bite of succulent pork crackling or salted fish and scrambled eggs on bread, I couldn't help wondering if it was because it may have been our last.

If Star-Star was to be believed, and we were to fight in some sort of battle, then given how badly we had managed many of our tasks over the last few months, there was a good chance we might not survive the day.

Even so, as far as good candidates for last meals went, that breakfast may have been a second choice only to Grunwald's amazing stew.

ii.

It was the first time that I had seen Vulkar young. It felt strange to call them as the adults did—pups. But that was what they were.

Safely hidden away from the dangers of the world in a magnificent ancient temple, guarded by a group of fearsome warriors, the infants were held by towering wet nurses—as wide as they were tall.

I hadn't even considered the possibility that a Vulkar could be fat, but there, on massive and ornate thrones, sat four of the largest, most overweight creatures I had ever seen. Each was easily bigger than even the mightiest wild bear, and was nursing two tiny swaddled Vulkar pups from swollen bosoms that seemed to grow from midway up their torsos.

The immense females were bedecked in layers of opulent jewellery and gold—bangles, necklaces, beads, charms, and one even wore a ceremonial breastplate, clearly made for a smaller creature so barely able to cover the Vulkar's bulging stomach.

I had actually pondered whether it was the males that carried out the duty of rearing the young, though I'd never felt particularly comfortable asking about the subject.

Now I knew that it wasn't the case. The males really were only used as breeding stock and labourers; the females carried out almost everything else of worth.

Each Vulkar in Karthak's retinue greeted the nursing behemoths as 'Mother' when the warband delegation entered the vast and intricately carved stone hall in the centre of the temple, intending to claim those pups that were old enough to begin their training for warriorhood.

The mighty raiders treated the flabby wet nurses with the utmost respect, stooping to touch and kiss their bellies, or squeeze their hands briefly as the retinue passed through the ancient stone chambers to where the seven young Vulkari waited. There was an almost mystical sense of reverence paid to the four wet nurses and I felt both a warmth, and at the same time, a distance from the creatures. I could not fully comprehend their unusual ways—awe inspiring and oddly beautiful though they were, and even despite the length of time I had by now spent in Vulkar company.

"Each Mother is to begin with, a proud and successful war chief. When she has gained sufficient status, she casts aside her spear and her blade, shrugs off her armour and her glory, and stitches a new Vyshivka to tell her new story. She takes a new name and ascends to the throne of the purest of all Vulkari," Karthak whispered to me as we waited in the hallowed chamber, its stone walls carved with reliefs that depicted Vulkari raiding and pillaging.

"Each Mother is Yanghar. Every Vulkar that produces offspring shall bring them to this temple, where they shall be judged. If the young is deemed fit to keep, then it shall remain here, raised and nurtured by Yanghar, as should have been the first of our people."

It was fascinating and completely alien.

"Do you know the name of that first pup, little brown Kikimora?" she asked, before I could question her on what happened to the unfit pups.

"No, sorry, you never told me."

"It was Vulkar," She grinned. "That is why we are thus. Our name, our language, our thoughts even. All are Vulkar. And before Vulkar, there is always Yanghar." She held an open hand out to the four hulking Mothers, and turned to see that I followed her explanation.

I nodded, and watched the small, dark-furred Vulkar babies suckle.

They would grow to become raiders, warriors, and destroyers. It almost seemed sad that, as they were then, mouths locked on a teat each, not snarling, not cackling, not gibbering or cursing, they were completely innocent of what their futures would shape them to become.

Each and every one of the small Vulkari that were in training with me had spent their childhood in that ancient stone temple, playing, learning, running around in the hallowed stone halls, climbing up and down the mossy stairs, and being nurtured and raised by former war chiefs.

I was soft, pathetic, and weak by comparison. But now, standing over Sarga, one such Vulk-pup, I was about to prove that it wasn't the physique or the upbringing that mattered. Rather, it was the driving fury, and the relentless rage that would not abide failure.

I had suffered so much. I had been beaten, enslaved, tortured, worked to the bone, and I'd be damned if I was going to let some Vulkar whelp, raised safely in a mystical ruin in the middle of nowhere, stand in my way.

I knelt on the whimpering beast's chest and pelted her with blow after blow of savage, furious punches to any russet furred flesh I could connect with.

I didn't even realise that I was screaming, as I beat the bedraggled Vulkar child to unconsciousness.

One of the adult raiders dragged me off the fallen wretch, but I continued kicking, thrashing and frothing at the mouth, my entire world blood red—each and every part of my being focused on destroying the poor creature that stood between me and my place in the warband.

The place that I had earned in blood, sweat and tears.

Afterwards, I sat quietly on my own in the long grass near the camp, tufts of seed floating softly around me in the gentle breeze, my wounds bandaged and sore, but satisfied that I had let neither Karthak, nor Star-Star down in my trial by combat.

※　※　※

The day hadn't actually started off so badly. The breakfast that we shared was fantastic and filling.

After the feast we had been split into pairs, each then taken to be prepared by an adult warrior.

Star-Star had taken me, along with the useless rabbit hunter whose actual name, it occurred to me I didn't even know, since the other Vulkari called her only 'Runt' or 'Smallest'.

She led us into the shade of a dishevelled tree and laid out a selection of equipment.

We were to be adorned in some sort of tribal armour, none of which seemed to be designed for actual protection, nor any other body shape than that of a small Vulkar.

And whilst the Vulkar girl looked quite impressive, bedecked in strips of bone that were lashed together into a sturdy chest protector, and with rings of black and crimson encircling her short tail and backwards dog-like legs, I felt somewhat inadequate.

I had to wear the stone tail bands around my ankles and wrists, and the vest of bone and wooden sticks dangled uselessly over my otherwise exposed chest.

Around my waist, I had several strings of stone beads and a soft cloth sash wrapped. The cloth hung short in front of me, between my legs, and although it did look quite purposeful, it annoyed me as it flapped against my thighs when I moved.

What was worse, was that there wasn't any good way for me to affix my dagger.

Whilst we prepared, Star-Star told us both that we would be representing her in the skirmish to come, and that we would do well to make her proud, or she would see to it that we would be marched into the wilderness and abandoned there.

I wasn't sure if her and the other three adults that had each tutored us on various difficult tasks over the last two or so months had drawn straws and she had ended up with the shortest, but I decided not to push my luck so didn't ask.

I did find it odd though, that one of Karthak's top ranking warriors would have the two lowliest trainee raiders as her representatives in whatever 'battle' was to come.

Before long, once she was satisfied that we looked the part, she led us back to where the trial would take place.

One of the adult warriors began to explain what was expected of us.

Eight, or maybe nine weeks of gruelling training would culminate in a fight. Each pair was to choose weapons, and attempt to best one of the adult Vulkari in combat.

It almost seemed silly, and as I stood awkwardly next to my partner it occurred to me just how much the odds were stacked against me.

We were presented a selection of weapons, which were laid out on a woven rug in front of us. There were several swords, more like cleavers really, and a range of spears, cudgels, and other barbaric implements.

All of them had been blunted and wrapped in linen and rope, or ragged animal hide. I guessed that it was not meant to be a fight to the death, though that assumption did very little to slow my pounding heart and still my shaking hands.

I began to regret eating so much earlier—there wasn't enough room in my belly for that morning's meal *and* the cloud of butterflies that had begun to swarm within me—and I felt as though I might vomit.

From the collection of blades and other tools of war, I chose a short spear. It was little more than a wooden shaft, and in its blunted and wrapped state seemed the best option, being both longer and lighter than the swords and curved knives that some of the others collected.

I hoped that the reach it would afford me could in some way compensate for my own lack of size.

Our opponent was the fearsome fighter Kovvik-Shar, easily seven feet tall with gnarled muscular arms covered in grey spotted fur in contrast to her ugly pinkish scars, a tall crest of a mane running from her head to her tail, and one eye missing. In the scarred socket she had placed a red bead which lent her a terrifying and rabid look about her at all times.

Despite her imposing size and hideous features, the Vulkar veteran actually seemed somewhat less brutal in her dealings with us previously. She had been the one to teach us how to stitch wounds, prepare herbal ointments to assist in staving off infections, and also on one particularly crisp autumn day, had called off lessons altogether to show our group how to catch fish from the frigid stream—a hobby that she was particularly good at, judging by the kippered fish that now threatened to find its way back out of my stomach.

Even so, the realisation that myself and the runt were now to tackle the behemoth in combat was a dreadful one.

I wasn't the only one to feel that way and noticed that all seven of the other trainees were fidgeting and glancing around nervously.

The trial began with a sharp howl from each of the adult warriors.

We maintained our distance to begin with, circling clumsily around the unarmed but still fearsome foe.

The failed rabbit-chaser made the first move. She rushed suddenly forwards whilst the raider focused her attention briefly on me. With almost supernatural quickness, Kovvik-Shar weaved out of the way of the arcing club swing, batting the small Vulkar off balance with the back of a hand.

I took the opportunity to move into range and jabbed sharply at the adult's midriff with my spear.

The blow connected but did nothing.

The one-eyed warrior snarled at me and made a swipe at my weapon, perhaps attempting to pull it from my grasp, or worse, drag me towards her and into range of her massive clawed hands.

I leapt backwards just in time to avoid a follow-up swipe from her, and waited—circling slowly as I did—for my partner to stagger to her feet.

Our second attempt at a coordinated assault did not see us fare much better to begin with. This time, I stepped forward too eagerly, baited by the massive creature when she looked to be making a move towards my teammate.

She whirled around, clipping me on the shoulder with a hefty fist.

I crumpled beneath the glancing blow, and she followed it up with a foot to my stomach.

My spear disappeared off into the undergrowth somewhere, and my entire body was catapulted through the air from the force of her painful kick.

I looked up from where I landed, dazed and winded, in a scrubby bush, to see that the little Vulkar had managed to leap upon the larger foe's back.

"Get up Kikimora!" she cried. "Help me!"

I forced myself to my feet and rushed to help her, just in time for the entire bulk of the towering Vulkar to fall upon the small fighter.

I wasn't sure if she was dead or unconscious, crushed beneath the weight of a seven-foot behemoth, but I didn't hesitate to check. I scooped up her short metal club, and with all my strength, hefted the weapon over my shoulder.

I scurried into range of the flailing beast, and swung the weapon as forcefully as I possibly could down into the side of the warrior's face. The red bead that had been her eye flew several feet away from us.

The massive Vulkar snarled and rolled over, freeing the battered and broken child from beneath her back, and swung a clawed hand at me.

I didn't move fast enough, still off kilter from the momentum of my swing, and was knocked sideways onto the flattened grass and loose dirt.

I tried to haul myself to my feet, but Kovvik-Shar had caught me by the leg.

I kicked out, but connected with nothing but air.

In seconds, I was hauled upside down, held aloft by the huge Vulkar who cackled menacingly as I dangled before her.

"Is this the best you can muster? Would you be better suited to stew? Or a filling for my pelmeni?" She leered, prodding me as I squirmed and struggled in her grip.

I still clutched the heavy club in my sweaty palms, and didn't want to become the filling for Vulkar dumplings, so with as much strength I had remaining in me, I swung it upwards towards the Vulkar's smiling face.

She blocked the blow, caught the club, and wrenched it from my grip, then cast it to the ground beside her.

It was a mistake.

The limping and wheezing little Vulkar whom she had foolishly discounted, collected the metal cudgel from the dirt at her feet, and with a feral snarl, swung it viciously at the warrior's knee.

There was a loud crack as the metal impacted with the adult's leg—maybe even doing some real damage. The huge beast dropped me to the ground and keeled over in pain.

Then the two of us proceeded to kick and punch the fallen giant, until she raised a clawed hand and yielded.

I was still shaking. My ordeal was over, and I was glad that I had survived.

I retrieved the tutor's bead eye and handed it back to her, appreciative of the fact that she seemed to hold absolutely no ill will towards me for the blow to her face.

She smiled, as the Vulkari practically always did, and nodded in thanks, then told the both of us to wait in the shade for the outcome of the other fights.

We sat and waited, drinking cool refreshing water, and attempting to calm ourselves with idle chatter about the tasks we had faced thus far. And I discovered that the small Vulkar beside me was actually called Mazgar.

"Does it have any meaning?" I asked.

"It is from Ar-Mazgari. They are little flowers that grow in the icy mountains," she informed me.

So she was named for some type of flower, and alongside Star-Star, it seemed odd that such fearsome and warlike creatures would choose or be given such un-intimidating names.

"That's very... pretty," I said. "So are all of you named in such ways?"

"Well there is me, and Yinnik. Both names are from flowers. Sarga is a type of bird that used to hunt the lands. I do not know if there are any left though. Otrek does not really have any meaning to her name, I do not even think it is a Vulkar name."

She cocked her head, and counted the other pups on clawed fingers.

"Then there is Ar-Tarak—Icy Wind. You know, that is just the actual words we use for a cold wind. But because it is a name, you stress the first part. It is the same as mine and any other," she explained.

I hadn't actually noticed that, despite now realising that there were a few Vulkari whose names were clearly just their words for things such as bears, rivers, and more—merely pronounced in a different way.

"What about Uya and Oya?" I asked, of the twins. "It sounds like one and two."

"That is because it is," she replied with a shrug. "So what does Zyntael Fairwinter mean then?"

She stumbled over the pronunciation.

I tried to explain to Mazgar, that my name was not of Vulkar origin, and that it consisted of a first name and a family name, but she couldn't quite grasp the concept—arguing that there was no use for a family name when all were raised by the holy Mother, Yanghar.

It was odd speaking with a creature that had such a different idea of what it meant to belong to a group. Someone who couldn't understand that within my village there had been many families, and that although the mothers would often raise their children together, they were still unmistakably their own.

Our chatter was cut short by a chorus of howling from the adults. The three other groups had finished their tests and I was genuinely surprised at how long it had taken them.

As far as her name would imply, Kovvik-Shar was the 'killer of great beasts'— so perhaps she had simply gone easy on us.

It turned out that one pair of young hopefuls hadn't managed to beat their opponent. They limped and hobbled into the shade, looking dejected.

We waited there quietly, all eight of us, whilst the adults conferred. Then within a few minutes they too joined us in the shade cast by the sprawling branches of the old tree.

"You have each fought bravely. Not all cleverly, and not all successfully. But you have fought bravely, to be sure," Star-Star told us.

Otrek, a very dark-furred Vulkar pup, and one half of a pair who had successfully beaten their older opponent into submission as well, spoke up.

"What does it mean? Are we fit to become raiders and fighters now?"

The elders laughed.

"No. Far from it," the one eyed Vulkar told her. "You have beaten unarmed and outnumbered foes. Foes that have gone easy on you." She grinned, menace radiating from her. "Now you must see how you fare when the tables are turned."

I glanced around at the others to see if they shared my puzzlement and worry. As far as I could tell, they all did.

"Rest now, and later in the day you shall once more be tested in combat. You shall fight one another for one of six places in the warband. The two who do not succeed shall be returned to the temple," one of the other adults said. "I do not know what shall come next for she who is not strong enough to stand with our people."

My heart sank.

I was at least a foot shorter than even the scrawniest and weakest of the Vulkar young. I had no claws and was no feral monster, bred for warfare and pillaging. As far as I could tell, I did not stand a chance.

Or so I thought.

╳ ╳ ╳

Early that afternoon we were taken back to the dusty clearing, this time given only short sticks to fight with.

Within minutes of the brawl beginning, one of the twins, Uya, had been knocked unconscious. I had no idea how our teachers were to decide who was a winner, but the remaining seven of us clawed, punched, kicked and head-butted one another for the better part of an hour.

I was exhausted. It looked as though I would not be part of the warband after all.

The largest pup, Sarga, singled me out after tussling with two others for some time. I had managed to avoid most of the attacks thrown my way up until that point, and had the advantage of a small frame and a lack of fur to grab hold of. But the young Vulkar girl clearly decided that she need only knock me out of the fight, in order to secure a place for the other five and herself.

She came at me with a relentless assault—her claws cutting and scraping skin from my bare arms. I kicked her squarely in the chest and rolled away, desperate to locate a weapon that might have been discarded or lost in the preceding melee.

I found only a fist-sized rock and so waited until the creature was almost upon me, then lashed out with it.

The stone connected with skull, but still she kept attacking me. Before long I was pummelled to the ground, bleeding from a cut above my eye and barely able to focus through the pain.

I wasn't sure if it was the blood in my eyes or something else entirely, but as the Vulkar stood over me, taunting me for my weakness and the fact that I did not belong, something changed.

The entire world went a shade of red. All noise became a hollow echo, punctuated by a high-pitched squealing that almost seemed to come from within my head.

Before I could fully comprehend what I was doing, I had swung a fist at the Vulkar's shin. Then, as she buckled, I followed it up with another to her throat.

The young fighter dropped to the ground, gurgling and gasping for breath, spittle streaming from her dark snout.

I didn't gloat. I didn't hesitate. I hit her as hard as I could, everywhere I could.

There was nothing that could stand in my way, as I beat the choking creature half to death.

iii.

It was pretty much for nothing, as far as I was concerned.

No young Vulkar was marched into the wilderness and left to die, and nobody was sent back to the temple where they came from.

All eight of us eventually re-joined the main warband. Bruised, battered, some with broken bones or stitched wounds, but all of us still present, nonetheless.

It had been some sort of ruse perhaps; a convincing reason given to us to spur us to bloodshed. Or maybe the whole ordeal was for the adults' amusement and nothing more. I had thought I was beginning to understand the way that the Vulkar warriors thought, but they had no difficulty in constantly surprising me—consistently keeping me guessing as to their motives.

Star-Star had given me back my dagger, after having me patched up and bandaged by the bead-eyed Vulkar.

She gently wrapped the belt around my waist and over my as-yet unembroidered Vulkar sash, then fastened it up.

"You now look as though you should. Perhaps the best of both them and us," she told me, and sent me back to the camp to await the others.

I sat with my back against a knotted old tree, sipping cool water, watching the dandelion seeds float in the gentle breeze and reflecting on the training and the fighting that I had miraculously survived.

It would not be the last. I was sure of it. Strangely I hoped for more.

Something had happened to me that day. I had let go of a part of me that still wanted normality, and given into a rage that both terrified and excited me.

Perhaps I was becoming like them. Like the Vulkari who surrounded me.

A bee danced by and landed on a flower beside me. I flicked it into the grass.

Our small group stayed one last week in that picturesque valley, surrounded by gnarled old trees and low scrubby bushes. It was the only plant life that seemed to flourish in the cool foothills of the northern mountains—of course, besides the long rugged grass that spread out over every flat stretch of land for miles around.

The area around us was wild and primal. I could imagine the Vulkar hounds crying out in the evenings, Yanghar the Mother whispering to the Spirits in the chill wind that rustled the grasses and carried the autumn leaves from their trees.

I imagined the winds whispering back. What ancient secrets they told her. What knowledge they imparted.

I stayed up relatively late on the final night in the valley, listening to the lonely shrieks of some solitary bird of prey, the gentle trickle of pure mountain water in the creek that ran down from the snow-capped peaks of the mountains looming in the distance to the north.

The Stormhills westward of our camp cast dark and imposing silhouettes against a pale purple sky, heavy with thick and ominous grey clouds, and gradually darkening.

I was glad that we were leaving this place, we had been lucky to enjoy hot and clear weather but the chill rains that gave these hills their name looked due to set in over the next few days and I didn't anticipate the prospect of camping and training whilst soggy, cold and miserable. Let alone having to put up with the choking, wretched stench of wet and filthy fur that followed the Vulkar pack in such climates.

"Take thread and cloth and mark the beginning of your Vyshivka. The first prick of the needle, the first loop of the thread marks the first step on your journey towards adulthood. Towards womanhood. Towards Vulkarhood.

"Stitch the first lines of your Vyshiv little Vulk-lings, then stow them in a safe place and prepare yourselves for the journey back to the warband—and the feasting that shall follow our return," Star-Star had said, passing us each a needle and producing a pile of coloured threads.

I'd agonised over the colour to pick, but a pale blue somehow seemed like the right choice—even over the obvious crimson.

All of the Vulkari enjoyed embroidering cloth in their spare time, and the pups had been eager to teach me the skill early on in our training; but to stitch one's very own Vyshivka sash was an important part of growing up apparently.

I was sitting on a stump a few yards away from the campsite, my back towards the resting Vulkari and my needle and thread working its way through my Vyshivka, when I heard a twig snap in the darkness to my left.

I turned to peer into the gloom but couldn't see the source of the sound—hearing only the rustling of someone or something approaching instead.

"Hello?" I called out to the night, tense and apprehensive.

The rustling shifted closer and Mazgar skulked into view.

"What pattern do you stitch?" she asked. "My first line is a line of points. Like the teeth of Yanghar—protecting me from harm."

I was just stitching triangles and straight edged spirals because they were easy and it was relaxing. I showed her, and she nodded as if the pattern meant something.

"What were you doing out there?" I asked her as she sat on a mossy rock opposite me.

"I was watching you," Mazgar said. "You are not like the rest of us, you know."

"Obviously," I said, wondering if the beatings of the trials had addled her mind. "I am aware that I am no Vulkar."

She almost looked embarrassed and picked at the moss and lichen on her seat as she spoke.

"But you are as Vulkar as I am. Perhaps more. You may be weaker in your arms and your back, you may not be able to catch scent on the wind. But you are stronger than me and all of them." She waved a hand towards the camp.

"What do you mean?"

"Well, I was nursed by Yanghar, I was born to join the raid. But you, you were..." She frowned. "Where are you from?"

"I am from a village. I don't actually know where it is from here." It still felt strange to speak to a Vulkar about it.

"I had a mother and a father, and a sister too. I told you about her, my mother raised us both. Maybe from your perspective she was my Yanghar," I sighed. "You know; I don't even know if they are alive."

"And you were taken, yes? In a raid?" the small sandy furred Vulkar asked.

"Yes. By Karthak herself."

"And yet you stay. Do you feel grateful?"

"Well I suppose I do in some way," I admitted for the first time to a Vulkar. "The alternative looked to be death. I don't feel any love for Karthak or what she has put me through, but I haven't really stopped to think about everything, and I'm really just glad to be alive."

"Yes, see? I was born for the raid, but you were not. So you are strong."

"I don't see how you think that is strong," I protested. "I haven't had a choice really. I wouldn't survive out there, and I don't even know what Karthak and the other warriors would do if I tried to run."

She shifted on her rock and sighed.

"You are both strong and lucky. You have seen the raid despite not being the blood of Yanghar."

"What? Lucky?" I asked, confused and almost a little insulted. "It was my village they raided. I didn't want to be taken!"

"You saw the War-Mother! You saw the raiders!" she seemed genuinely excited about the prospect and I began to realise that she had no concept of what it could be like to be the victim of true Vulkar brutality. To her it was such an impressive thing; raiding, pillaging— she had been raised on tales of its glory, I assumed. I didn't think she even could empathise with anyone on the receiving end of that.

"Look, it wasn't fun. People I knew were killed, I don't even know if my family survived." I hadn't really thought about it for some time, having been too busy striving to be accepted by monsters, and I felt a strange mix of both sadness and guilt.

Guilt mostly because I could barely remember what life was like before the Vulkari came.

"But Karthak chose you. A Kikimora. You are very lucky," she told me.

"I don't think you understand what I am trying to say," I clarified. "I was happy in my village. I had family, I had friends. Since Karthak and her raiders came and burned our buildings and killed our people, since they stole me from my home—my life has been nothing but a struggle."

Mazgar nodded.

"Yes, so you are strong. You were not bred for this purpose, you were claimed, by our leader herself." She looked impressed at the thought of my miserable fate. "You were chosen; no other slave or prize was. I was told by some of the older warriors that they had orders not to harm you. That is very special, so there, lucky too."

"Well they mustn't have listened very well." I replied, bitterly re-calling the months of mistreatment at their hands.

I hadn't really spent much time dwelling on my situation, and only with the reminder from an almost envious young Vulkar, was I realis-ing just how much I actually resented the warband. Karthak most of all.

"I don't know how I can make you understand. Karthak took me against my will. She beat me, chained me to her throne and tied me to a pole on her wagon."

"Yes. But it is you that does not understand; it was Karthak. And she also took you down, she taught you our words, she claimed you as her own. Karthak herself. That is an honour that no other pup can claim," she told me.

I wasn't sure why Mazgar was bringing this up, nor how I could ever convince her that it wasn't an honour, but rather torture.

"You told me you had a family name. Do you still want to keep it? Now that we have beaten our trial?" she asked.

"Well yes, of course I do. I will have it for my entire life, I will always be Zyntael Fairwinter." I was a little perplexed as to how she still couldn't grasp the concept.

"But you have a new family. And if you stay with us, if we survive our first raid and become sisters in battle, should you not have a new family name?"

"That's not how it works. And besides which, who is to say that I even want to stay?" I asked her.

"Well you have stayed so far. You always could have left," she said.

"No, I told you—I would never survive."

"But you never tried." She glanced up at me from her focus on the rock that she sat on. "I think you belong, and I shall gladly fight be-side the chosen pup of Karthak."

"Well, I appreciate the thought, I really do, but this was never my choice," I told her, feeling almost ashamed of my previous burning desire to prove myself to the warriors and to be a part of the Vulkari warband.

"Was birth?" she asked simply, and shrugged.

"Well, no but…" I tried to counter her point but she cut me off.

"Exactly. Nobody chooses where they start, but only where they go."

They were surprisingly wise words from a young, savage Vulkar—something Phobos might have said. It still amazed me that despite being towering, fur covered, animal-faced monsters, they held quite a few thoughts and beliefs that seemed far more complex than their appearance would suggest. At times, they weren't all that different from my own people.

"What is all this about, Mazgar? Did you come over here just to remind me of what I have lost?" I asked.

"No! Of course not!" she protested, raising her hands defensively. "If anything, it was to tell you what you have gained."

It was quite a touching sentiment.

I sat quietly opposite her, considering the unusual mixture of feelings swirling inside me.

"How many seasons have you seen?" she asked after a while.

"Well, I don't know, let me think." I counted on my fingers.

"More than forty. Maybe fifty?" I had never been particularly good with numbers. "I think I have seen, perhaps, twelve summers. Kimori count summers, even though I was born at the beginning of winter," I informed her.

Mazgar's amber eyes widened. "Twelve?" she asked, sounding surprised. "You are very old then, but so small!"

"What do you mean? I might be a little short for my age, sure, but not by much," I said.

"I have seen only fifteen seasons. I have seen only four summers!" she declared.

"What? But you are bigger than me. And you speak well." I thought that maybe she was even worse with numbers than I was, but she explained.

"We suckle at the teat of Yanghar for but two or maybe three seasons. By our fifth we are walking and beginning to learn many words."

"So you grow much quicker than we do then, how long do you live for?" I asked.

"I think… not long," she said. "I think most of us shall die in battle, so maybe one hundred seasons. And more if we survive."

She was so earnest. I shook my head in amusement as I took a minute to work it out.

"That is what? Twenty-five summers? It doesn't seem all that long."

"I have heard that Karthak herself has lived double that though—maybe even triple, despite so many battles. They say that the Spirits have blessed her with old age, and shield her from harm!" Her amber eyes were aglow at the prospect.

"Still though, that is an awfully short time to be alive," I told her.

Mazgar shrugged and gazed up at the stars—stragglers that were slowly being consumed by dark clouds.

"You know, if we survive battle and raiding then we may still die in another forty seasons. Most of us do not live through the birth of a female pup."

"That is horrible," I said.

"No, it is not. The mother shall pass her strength on to her daughter, who shall need it more than she," she said, clenching a fist in front of her dark snout. "We hope to die in combat or in birth. No exceptions."

"What about males?" I asked.

"Ha! What about them?" she sniggered quietly.

"Well, what if the pup is a boy?"

She smirked at me and began twirling a stalk of grass as she replied; "If the pup is a boy, then the mother shall keep her own strength and spirit, and save it for when she is blessed with a girl. Simple!"

"So wouldn't she be at just as much risk of dying though?" I asked, unsure of how it all worked, but enjoying the explanation.

"Well no, I mean, sometimes yes—if the warrior is unlucky." She squinted at the grass that she fiddled with. "Males are small and pathetic, remember? Not like with your kind right? I remember you said it was the opposite with Kimora males."

"Yes that's right," I said.

"Weird." She made an odd sort of grimace, then carried on.

"So when the pup is a male, if there is need of another, then the mother shall pass him on to the other males to raise and teach him to serve. She shall not be disgraced; the Spirits know that we do need the males of course," she said, nodding as she spoke.

"But there is always hope for another warrior, a potential war chief or raiding leader. You can tell from how fat the mother's belly is. I think."

She snapped the blade of grass and looked up at me.

"You are the smallest pup yet though, barely more of a bump in a Vulkar belly than if she ate more than usual that day!"

"Thanks, I guess…"

"You are very brave. Even though you are small, I saw what you did to Sarga!" She leaned in and lowered her voice. "I thought you were going to kill her. And I was excited."

"I think I might actually feel the same," I admitted and we both laughed.

"Zyntael Fairwinter. You are a good sister," she told me, once our giggles had subsided. "I think we shall always be best friends."

I was a little taken aback, I had only recently begun speaking with her, and had been too caught up in surviving our training without failing too badly to consider actually befriending the young Vulkari. I assumed it was just that I had been paired with her in our trial, but perhaps even the small interest I had paid towards her was more than she would find from other Vulkari; pups who had been bred to compete with her.

"Thank you, and likewise, Mazgar." I told her, despite the feeling that in doing so, I was making some sort of promise that I'd come to regret. "So uhh… What do you think comes next? Did they prepare you for this stuff, in the temple?"

"I suppose so," she replied. "I grew up with many gruesome tales of the challenges and tasks. I think I was expecting worse."

"Well this could be just the beginning." I looked up at the sky above us, a vast and cold expanse dotted with uncountable stars and gradually being swallowed up by the heavy storm clouds moving in from the west, it seemed to reflect how I felt inside.

"Do you really want to become a raider Mazgar?" I asked. "Do you want to go out and kill people? Kidnap slaves?"

"Of course." Mazgar plucked another blade of grass from the ground and crushed it in her clawed fist. "I shall destroy the weak, take what I can—by the right of my strength and the strength of our warband."

"So you would have murdered me? My family?" I asked, alarmed that someone could be raised to lack any empathy.

"If they were weak, and if you did not fight back and earn life, then yes. But you did fight, you stood against the mightiest war chief of all time with a stick—or so I heard. So here you are," she replied.

"Mazgar, I don't think I could ever make you understand how I see the world, and I think that it's a real shame," I sighed.

"Maybe, but I think that you are beginning to see things my way. Maybe that is what matters. I suppose we could ask Sarga."

We laughed again.

In a way, I was beginning to suspect that the small Vulkar was right. It felt good to be the victor, to take what I deserved by the strength of my own determination and grit. Perhaps those Sacharri slaves were right to treat me as an outsider—something vile and violent and not at all like them. Something dangerous.

Perhaps it would explain, then, how easily I let the tragedy of my past slip away from my memory, over the following summers spent in the wild and exciting company of those monsters.

And perhaps it would explain how *I* became a monster too.

iv.

A fire raged on, both inside and out. It sent glowing hot embers swirling into the inky night sky, and to the furthest reaches of both my body and my mind.

We danced and capered around the roaring inferno. Howling, cackling, and chanting.

Faster and faster we went, whipping the ashen smoke and sparks of flaming dust into a tornado that surged upward with howling fury.

Glistening with sweat, my skin painted with swirling red and black patterns, and the beads, bangles, and bone jewellery that decorated me clattering as I moved—I danced the Vulkar Khorovod feverishly with my fellow young warriors, well into the night.

This night was different than any in the months since we had re-joined the warband, for before the frenzied merriment reached a crescendo, each of us was led in turn by chanting warriors to where Karthak sat upon her carved throne.

There we were anointed with poultices, and smeared with un-known substances. Then, for several hours, we were fed potions and brews that had been carefully prepared by the older, veteran Vulkari. They chanted and sang throughout the whole ritual, scattered sparkling dust over us, and breathed pungent smoke in our faces as the eight of us stood in a semicircle, beneath a great and ancient tree.

I coughed and choked on the foul tasting liquid that we drank, as it caught in my throat and burned within my belly. And I coughed and choked on the acrid smoke that we breathed, as it surrounded us and blurred the night air with the haze of a thousand burning herbs and reagents.

Karthak the Warlord leered before my face. An orange inferno flickered in the pupils of the massive monster, and her jagged ivory teeth glinted in the wide grin she wore.

My vision swam. The scarred and hideous face of the great warrior took on twisting, alien shapes, her features sliding and shifting on her bestial visage.

I felt as though I was going to fall, but the earth beneath my feet reached up clawing tendrils that rooted me in place.

My sweat began to boil, and became hissing and moaning Spirits that dissipated into the smoke of the bonfire, joining the vortex of liquid obsidian that slowly swirled around us.

"Breathe it in deep, war-child," Karthak spoke. But it was not with her own voice. It was instead the low rumble of mountain stone, grinding and grating over millennia. It was instead the dry and hollow creaking of the ancient oaks, and the thunder of a wrathful hailstorm that rolled overhead. It was instead all the Spirits of the Ancient Wilds.

The voice filled my ears, wormed its way inside my mind, and then grew from within me. It became a deafening chorus of sounds that didn't so much speak the words, as allow me to simply feel their intent.

"Breathe deep the world. Breathe deep the Magick that gives all life. Breathe deep the strength of the warrior."

I sucked air in through gritted teeth. Cold air, like that of the frigid glacier. Cold air that twisted and changed to the dry and dusty air of the mighty sweeping desert—even as it passed my tongue. I had no time to be confused, no presence of mind to do anything but heed the wishes of the Spirits who commanded me.

Karthak slid away from the space before me. Her form was replaced with a heaving mound of bubbling flesh, the surface of which constantly folded in on itself—exposing jagged bones, broken spear shafts, and rusted blades that disappeared as quickly as they emerged.

But I wasn't afraid.

I merely watched as the colossal oozing mass grew and shifted before my unblinking eyes, then spilled from the Warlord's mighty seat to pool onto the dirt below. Faces briefly formed on the skin of the shapeless entity—each wide-eyed and afraid, but quickly swallowed up and replaced with grasping limbs or flailing tentacles of glistening flesh.

"Witness the echoes of a thousand defeated foes. This is the legacy of the despoiler."

The cacophony roared within me.

"Witness your destiny, Scion of the free."

I forced my gaze from the horror that shuddered and spasmed in the dirt before me and looked down at my own body—at my up-turned palms.

Within each one, blood began to pool, syrupy and crimson. I clenched my fists, and the hot liquid pumped from between each finger, flowing in hissing rivulets to the blackened and charred soil at my feet.

I glanced around, hoping to catch sight of the other pups, and I wondered briefly how Mazgar was handling the sensory assault. I wondered if the rituals would have a different effect on Vulkar young. Perhaps my own state was as a result of herbs and potions not made for my kind to imbibe.

I couldn't see through the swirling fog—unsure of whether it was the smoke or was something behind my eyes that blurred and twisted my vision. My thoughts of the others were soon forgotten.

My breathing quickened, and I could taste nothing but the foul ichor that had coated my mouth and tongue. I tried to speak, tried to question my failing grasp on reality, but my voice was lost, and I croaked like a dying frog instead.

Gradually though, the burning within me gave way to a sparkling warmth that spread from the core of my being to the tips of each finger and toe, and filled my entire body with energy and excitement. I felt alive and powerful.

There seemed to be trails of luminous light that danced around me. Slivers of energy arced from my outstretched hands to the ground, trailing glittering dust and wisps that evaporated into the night.

My chest heaved and my limbs trembled as I tried to fight the ocean of sensation that swallowed my consciousness—but I was wracked with shuddering spasms, and my eyes rolled back in my skull.

I finally let go of the struggle and slipped into the welcoming embrace of oblivion.

※　※　※

I dragged myself to my feet, head heavy and pounding, and looked around at the scenes of chaos. The sky was awash with a red glow. The village beneath it, consumed by a roaring inferno. I felt a surge of excitement that carried with it the remembrance of why I was here; a singular desire, a violent driving purpose—this was it. This was the raid.

"Tonight we destroy! Tonight we kill! Tonight we burn everything in sight!" I cried out to my cheering and cackling vanguard, my voice hoarse, and somewhat alien to me.

The young Vulkar raiders, each bedecked in their black iron plate and scavenged armour, spread out amongst the buildings. They cast pitch soaked torches upon any hovel that wasn't already ablaze, tore down heraldry and trampled the purple banners of the Combine into the muck.

One or two of them occupied themselves with leading panicked mules away from a collapsing barn. It was good thinking, we needed more working beasts. I would be sure to commend them once we returned to camp.

I watched the destruction unfold around me—proud, excited, and aching for more.

A movement ahead of me caught my eye, and through a cloud of thick, choking smoke, and the rippling haze of the flames, I made out a figure.

It was no Vulkar.

A straggler, some brave fool perhaps, unable or unwilling to flee deeper into the village with his fellow militia.

I was glad I noticed the villager when I did. Soon enough to call out to Mazgar, and for her to duck the crossbow bolt that streaked towards her and embedded in the frame of the village well—sending swirling eddies of smoke and glowing embers spiralling in its wake.

The second bolt glanced off the ragged steel of my scuffed and battered breastplate.

The peasant soldier hastily began to ratchet the wire of his weapon back, trying to load a third bolt.

But he was too slow, and within seconds I was upon him, with Mazgar on my trail.

I crashed through a pile of small barrels and crates, spilling apples over the muddy ground, and leapt towards the man, my heavy blade poised to strike.

He twisted as I lunged at him, catching the jagged metal across the shoulder.

The man cast his bow aside and tugged a dagger from his belt; one hand pressed over the bleeding wound I had opened in his flesh, and the wild panic of a cornered animal in his gaze.

"Zyntael!" Mazgar called out. "Duck!" And with no pause for contemplation, I did as she bid.

A black javelin arced overhead and thudded home in the villager's chest.

He gasped and gurgled, dropping his weapon and falling to his knees, still clawing at the shaft protruding from beside his sternum as the life left his eyes.

"Good throw Sister!" I told my hulking friend, as she rushed up and wrenched her weapon from bone. "I was going to kill that one myself though."

"Then you should have been quicker!" Mazgar cackled. "You and me Zyntael, Let us kill them all! The next one is yours!"

"Yes it is!" I agreed, and we set off further into the chaos together, hunting for prey.

We wound our way through the village, between burning hovels, working our way further into the settlement. The cries of the panicked peasants and the garrison alike reached my ears, and I followed them—leading Mazgar, Sarga, and two rookie warriors toward the carnage.

Perhaps spooked from his hiding spot by our approach, an adolescent boy scurried from the shadows to my right and tried to run, his bare feet sending a spray of mud into the air.

I let out a howl and sprinted after him, eager to spill the blood of the pathetic Combine animal.

The chase led me along meandering paths and narrow alleys, sodden with mud and filth, and steaming from the heat of the blazing buildings that flanked them. I was slower than I felt I should have been, for a strange weight in my belly seemed to sap my strength and stamina, but I pressed on—unwilling to allow the escape of my quarry.

Blood rushing in my ears, and heart pounding in my chest, I finally caught up with the villager half way along a path that led to an open square. I lashed out with my blade. The iron clipped his calf, and sent him sprawling into the muck.

A woman cried out in horror nearby as I brought my weapon down on the prone boy—quieting his whimpering, and putting a brutal end to his writhing.

I looked up to see the female villager, who stood frozen, in the doorway of her as-yet unburned home. She clutched a babe to her bosom in an attempt to shield it from the violence. She pleaded and begged in some foreign tongue, whilst the other Vulkari rounded the corner—weapons readied.

A group of purple-clad men rushed from the other end of the alley. They had simple tools gripped tightly as weapons, and each man mewled and yelled unintelligibly.

Heroes in their minds perhaps; they would pose no real threat though.

The Combine rabble charged.

It was barely a skirmish. The mud soaked with crimson, severed limbs and spilled innards spread about the place only seconds after the men reached us.

The woman still stood—transfixed by the scene before her.

"Take this one," I told my raiders, judging by her physique, she would fetch a decent price as a slave—to be sold to the Hobgoblin brothels or taverns.

"And the infant whelp?" Mazgar asked, striding forward to claim her prize, sharp maw dripping in anticipation.

"We have no need of leeching Combine offspring. It may as well find some good use," I told her. "It is yours, share the meat if there is meat to spare."

The woman screamed. Shrill and piercing. The sound bored into the very core of my being, and scratched at some long-dormant part of me that was not of this place—not of this life.

Soon, all I could hear was the high pitched squeal, echoing inside my skull and burning my consciousness away.

I awoke.

※　※　※

I was drenched in sweat, and coated in layers of war paint, filth, and foul-smelling ointments. My hair, matted across my face and obscuring my vision, reeked of smoke and herbs.

Despite the beginnings of a headache, I felt giddy and elated. My heart was pounding in my chest, but began to slow as my senses returned to me once more.

My whole body felt uncomfortable, though not sore at all. It felt as though it were an outfit that fit oddly—too small in some places, and too large in others. I wriggled my fingers and toes, trying to shake the feeling that something was slightly off, and as I did so, small pulses of tingling warmth spread throughout my limbs.

Gradually, the feeling of excitement gave way to confusion—and a peculiar sense of guilt and shame—though I couldn't quite recall what I had done wrong.

The low murmuring of hushed Vulkar voices and slumbering beasts met my ears, and I forced myself to sit upright and look around.

I was in a spacious tent, stitched together from the hides of a variety of animals, and decorated with strings of hanging bone and colourful beads. From the curved wooden poles that supported the hide, bundles of flowers and odd roots swung gently in the cool smoky breeze that found its way through gaps and seams in the structure.

Around me lay the sleeping bodies of seven young Vulkari. They were painted gaudily, and decorated with bangles, beads, and feathers, as well as scraps of ceremonial armour, and their unique Vyshivka.

One or two of the pups occasionally twitched or whimpered, and I assumed that whatever phantoms they were facing in their slumber were probably not dissimilar to those that I had encountered. Strangely though, the specifics of what I had experienced in that vision or dream were slipping rapidly from my mind. I could only picture the burning of a village, and feel a distant but ever-present thrill at the prospect of battle and bloodshed.

I rubbed my eyes and forced myself to my feet, keen to seek out the adults and get some answers to my questions—to put my confused mind at rest.

I pushed aside the flap of tanned hide that served as a door, and was immediately blinded by the morning light. Filtered through a silvery mist, the glow of the new day's sun lent the area an otherworldly and ethereal appearance. It also annihilated my eyesight.

Wincing and holding a filthy, painted hand up to shade my face, I made my way through the foggy camp. The earth at my feet had been compacted into a solid clay by the innumerable footfalls of the Vulkari, who had danced feverishly through the thick smoke of the bonfire. That strong smelling smoke now mingled with the cold fog that blanketed the entire encampment. It shrouded the many tents, wagons and awnings—around and within which, Vulkari still slept off the previous night's festivities.

I passed a group of raiders who were playing some sort of game using small bone tokens and dice. They looked up from their entertainment and grinned at me as I went.

"Kimor-pup!" Tan-Shar, the closest of the three, hailed me. I turned back to the raiders.

"Do you know where Karthak is?" I asked, and pointed towards the smouldering bonfire in the clearing at the centre of the encampment, where her cart had been situated for the last few days. "Still in her wagon?"

"She is gone for now. Set off at the break of dawn to seek counsel from the Shaman of these parts." I didn't know what that meant.

"The Shaman? What is that?"

"Surely you have learned of the one who communes with the Spirits!" one Vulkar exclaimed. "No matter youngling, Garok awaits in our Warlord's lodgings. She can explain if she wishes." Then the warrior gestured at the game before her. "So, should I raise, lucky Kikimora?"

I had no idea what their game was or why she would think me lucky.

"Sure, why not?" I said with a shrug, then waved them goodbye and headed to where Star-Star waited. Shortly after, the sound of cheering and laughter erupted behind me, and the other Vulkari who played the game, began accusing the winner of using Kimorin witchcraft and hexes. I smirked, and carried on. Perhaps I really was lucky—but I was sure the losing players might not agree.

Karthak's wagon was still in the same place. It was nestled between a large boulder that had been scraped of all its moss then painted with jagged glyphs and symbols, and a mighty tree that towered over the camp—a creaking wooden sentinel that loomed ominously out of the fog. From the branches of the ancient plant, dangled bone charms and other curious decorations—for the most part identical to those that had been strung up in the tent where I had awoken.

In the eerie morning light, they took on a macabre and haunting nature, and I averted my eyes as I clambered up onto the oversized wagon.

The pole that I had once spent the better part of a month or so lashed to, had been painted in spirals of alternating red and black, and was wreathed in twine that held brightly sparkling beads and trinkets.

Dangling limply from the pole was a straw-stuffed figure, not unlike something the farmers had used to ward hungry birds from their crops—maybe in the Hobgoblin stronghold, or perhaps even in my village that I had left so long ago. I struggled to remember anything else about the place.

My memories were fleeting and unfocused, behind a fog that was thicker than the one that surrounded our camp.

The unusual figure was painted with war paint the same as I wore, and upon its poorly made head—over a thick mane of painted red straw—sat a crown of braided white flowers. Similar plants lay at the foot of the pole, along with crudely carved figurines of Vulkar war hounds and other animals.

It seemed almost to be some kind of shrine, though to what purpose I could only guess.

"Zyntael!" A hoarse voice called out as I stood, examining the sight before me. "You survived the night in good health. Star-Star is proud... and a little envious."

"I'm sorry?" I asked, turning to face the warrior, who staggered out of the war chief's cushioned lounge, with one hand pressed against her forehead, and a beleaguered look upon her animal features.

"What Star-Star would not give to contain, once more, the spirit of youth. Now she suffers greatly, the morn after such celebration."

"Are you hurt?" I asked her, unsure of what she was getting at.

"Only where pride is concerned." She shook her head. "Star-Star thought it fun to attempt to out-drink some of the youthful hunters. Now she feels only regret and the pounding of a Hobgoblin anvil within her stupid skull."

The Vulkar staggered past me and sat down heavily on the wooden planks of the wagon.

"Come, sit." She beckoned me towards her.

I sat down a few feet away but within seconds she reached out and pulled me into an embrace. Where I once would have been terrified, now I felt utterly at ease as she held my back to her warm body and gently began to stroke my head.

"Our small warrior," she said, running her clawed fingertips along the length of my ears, idly pinching the tips between a finger and thumb. "Fierce and brave yet so naked and frail. Who would have expected that the Spirits would deliver such a contradictory creature to us?"

In the recent months that I had spent in mock skirmishes with the other young fighters, stalking and hunting wild game, and passing each night with dance, drink, and ritual, the adult Vulkari had begun to display more and more gentle behaviours to us. At first, it had seemed contrary to their violent ways, but by now, it was the norm.

Many evenings were spent decorating one another with beads and flowers, plaiting fur and the Vulkari's shaggy crested manes, or painting the warriors' claws with coatings made from crushed insects and coloured oils. Last night had begun with many such preparations— and whilst their adornments for the raid were generally savage and brutish, the Vulkari took great pleasure in assembling a variety of outfits, and decorating themselves for any occasion.

"Uhh... Star-Star? Some of the other warriors said that Karthak has gone to consult the Spirits, and you and she always mention that stuff when you talk about me," I sighed, gesturing towards the straw figure. "But nobody ever wants to tell me what's going on!"

She chuckled and rustled my hair.

"As Star-Star has told you, it is truly not her place to explain these things. But know that all shall be revealed to you in time." The warrior stretched out in a loud yawn. "Suffice it to say, there is a belief shared amongst many that you have been provided to us by the Spirits themselves. It is not as though this means that you should be given special treatment, though Star-Star does on occasion find it difficult to remember this fact."

She chuckled.

"Star-Star finds herself enamoured with your freckled hairless skin and short limbs. She wonders often how you manage to get by despite such a lacking body."

I feigned outrage.

"How could you say such things? What I lack in fur and claws, I make up for in other ways!" I exclaimed.

"Like what?" Star-Star asked.

"I don't know, perhaps Sarga could tell you."

"Still wringing worth from that, are you? How many moons now past?" she said, and rolled her eyes. "In truth, many of the fighters were impressed by that display, even Sarga herself. She now looks up to you, as does your runt friend Mazgar. Despite both now easily outmatching you in physical prowess."

The raider paused whilst she picked pieces of grit and twigs from my filthy hair.

"It is not just strength of body that makes a leader. You must remember that the other pups shall look to you that way because of your tenacity and your attitude, they shall see past your physical form in their innocence. They have no prejudices based on experience raiding and fighting Bare-Skinned creatures," she told me.

I was amused by the way she spoke of non-Vulkari, and a long-unmentioned thought occurred to me:

"Star-Star, how is it that you are fine with eating other people? I know Karthak doesn't think of them as such, but like me, they have thoughts and minds. I don't know how comfortable I am with thinking of them as food."

"Star-Star had wondered how you would feel about that. She has a question for you." She rested her mighty hands on both of my shoulders. "Do you have the same qualms about eating pigs? Rabbits? Sheep?"

"Well no, but they are dumb animals, I don't think they are the same."

"Why not? Can you be sure that they do not have hopes and thoughts? Simply because they cannot express them in a way that you understand? They might well, yet you happily consume their flesh since you gain strength from their Spirit.

"And is it not true that the mightier the beast, the more strength you partake of? The rabbit may stave off hunger, but the ox shall help grow muscle, build your body into that of the warrior. It is the same with the animals that walk upright."

I hadn't really considered it. I still felt queasy about the idea of eating another person though. And now, if anything, I felt worse about other animals.

"No matter, strength flows upward from beast to beast. Just as the sheep gives no thought to the grass she eats, so does this Kikimora believe the sheep thinks not." she chuckled. "The Bare-Skin is but a sheep or pasture to us."

It made me wonder if the 'lamb' I had eaten in the company of the Vulkari was actually truly from a sheep.

I put the thought to rest and changed the subject.

"Why did you keep Phobos Lend in your dungeon at the Black-fort? A man in the Legion kitchens told me he had wronged the Vulkari, but that he also worked for you."

"Ah the Ratling—the Darkrunner, yes? He betrayed the trust of Karthak. You see, she puts great stock in the whispers of the Spirits, and there are those who believe her to be mistaken. Misguided perhaps."

"Like that limping warrior?" I asked, remembering the vile creature's threats and insults.

"Yes, like Urga. She is a moron, but a worrying one. Has aspirations to unite our folk with the empire of the purple fools—the Combine." She hissed the name. "Indeed, as vile and delusional as they may be, they promise status and comfort for Vulkari. Karthak believes it to be a false promise at best—a trick to rob us of our freedoms, more like."

I nodded as she continued.

"Anyway, as much as Star-Star likes him, the little man *is* dangerous. He served many purposes, but mostly himself.

Karthak used him to reclaim something of great spiritual significance. But he tried to renege on the deal they made—much to the satisfaction of Urga and her non-believers. Funny thing is, to Star-Star anyway, if not for him and his work, we would not have found you."

I was surprised, unsure how I was connected to whatever Phobos had done.

"How so?" I asked, sitting up and turning to face the Vulkar, who still nursed her head and looked exhausted.

"Do you not wonder how and why we came upon your village? That was no mere raid—for it was well out of our way, and within enemy custody," she said. "But too much has been said already. You take advantage of Star-Star's poorly state."

"Wait a moment, what are you saying? Phobos gave you our village's location? But why?"

It made no sense, I couldn't imagine what anyone would stand to gain from attacking a village of peaceful Kimori. Slaves, sure, but they were in no short supply—and as far as I could tell, I was the only one taken. Or at least the only one of my people that I had seen in Vulkar company, so far.

And that it had something to do with Phobos made me most confused. I couldn't quite rectify why the Ratling would have sent the Vulkar raiders to us, and how it could possibly benefit him to do so. More so, why Karthak would have him thrown in a dungeon with the very same captive that they had taken.

"Star-Star, none of that makes any sense. Why would Karthak have come to my village, taken only me as far as I know, then kept me as she did? If I'm somehow special, and she went to so much trouble to take me from my home, then why did she treat me so badly? Why did she give me to the Sacharri Legion?" I asked.

"What little it is Star-Star's place to tell, has mostly been told. You should consult Karthak upon her return, if you wish to understand the machinations of the Spirits that have led to your present position in the world," she said. "Star-Star knows that the little Bare-Skinned man caused much mischief with his words, and that the raiding of your village meant trouble for Manox and his Hobgoblin horde. Trouble that needed to be set right. Karthak was willing to risk whatever the terms set out by the commander, if it meant fulfilling the desires of the Spirits of the Ancient Wild."

"Well I shall ask her. Where is it that she has gone?" I enquired.

"You wish to know her location, that you may follow her into the frosty hills? You think yourself ready to face the dangers that lie outside the protection of the warband?" she grinned, a wry twinkle in her eyes.

"I guess so. If it means that I can finally understand why I'm even here, then I suppose it's worth it. Besides, I can't imagine there are worse things lurking out there than what I've faced so far," I told her resolutely.

The Vulkar cackled with amusement.

"Is that so, brave pup? You think that we are such monsters still? Star-Star finds it hard to ignore the fire in your eyes at mention of your brawls with the other pups—and the raids to come. Do not presume that you are not as much a Vulkar as any other. Furred-skin or no." She cocked her head then leaned a bit closer and added with a whisper. "In the wild lands we currently occupy though, there are far more monstrous beasts than any Vulkar ever aspired to be. Star-Star would suggest taking with you a friend or two, if you intend to face them."

I nodded. I supposed I would find out if her words were true. I had to know what Karthak's Spirits had in store for me, and do something about it. I couldn't allow inaction to force an unchosen fate upon me.

I would forge my own destiny.

V.

Clutching my Legion dagger in one hand, I scrambled up over the crumbling ridge—dragging my bruised and battered body over grasping brambles as I went.

Mazgar and Sarga bounded up the muddy incline almost effortlessly on their backwards hound-like legs, and I envied their strength and stamina.

"Behold Sisters! We have not long to journey!" Sarga called out, extending an arm to point across the thickly forested valley before us.

I estimated half of a day's travel ahead of us to reach the other side—provided of course that the trek was no more treacherous than it had been to reach the top of this craggy outcrop.

I was beginning to think that inaction wouldn't have been such a bad choice after all.

"Should we stop to eat? I feel a hunger growing within me," Mazgar said, though I wondered if there was truth to her words, or whether it was out of pity for my miserable state.

"I can push on. Don't worry about me. Perhaps there is a stream below that we could draw water from," I told the two expectant Vulkari.

I wasn't so sure of the truth in my own words, but had resolved not to let my physical limitations slow our pace too much.

We had made surprisingly good progress, all told—having left the Vulkar camp at mid-morning. The other two had remained in the ritual tent, apparently dreaming of battle and carnage, and after leaving Star-Star to her suffering, I had roused them both and told them of my plans to seek out Karthak.

From what I had gathered, she was somewhere to the north of our camp, beyond the forested valley and seeking counsel from a Spirit-Guide that dwelt in a place called the Whispering Cavern.

The caves within which this reclusive Shaman made her home were visible from where we stood, as though the gaping maw of some gigantic creature that had been swallowed up in the rocky hills. Stalagmites and stalactites lined the ominous entrance, visible from miles away—the teeth of the beast. From our vantage point I could see a thin wisp of dark smoke, lazily drifting from the cave.

We had taken a small collection of supplies. Each Vulkar carried with them a few javelins, and between us we had enough food and equipment to camp out for at least a few days.

Star-Star had warned us of dangers that lurked in the wilderness around, but we had so far encountered only a few ravens, three hares and a solitary deer. All of which had escaped into the undergrowth at our approach.

I couldn't shake the constant feeling of subtle fear, however, that blended with an excitement at being out in the world. It formed an intoxicating mixture of urgency and energy.

The two Vulkari must have felt it too, for they constantly chattered, and excitedly gazed around. They sniffed the air and cackled with laughter as we travelled.

"Have you heard tales of these parts?" I asked them. "From the Mothers, that is."

"Not a lot," Sarga said. "Though we heard many stories of the beginning times. When Yanghar and her pack hunted the mighty stag-bears of the forest."

"Stag-bears?" I asked, having never heard of such beasts.

"Do they not roam the woods where you are from?" Mazgar asked.

"No. I mean, there are certainly bears. A lot of stags too, but I don't know that I have ever heard of a mixture of the two," I told them, beginning to worry about the possibility of running into any type of bear for that matter.

"I heard that they are easily twice the size of even Karthak herself!" Mazgar exclaimed, apparently excited at the prospect of such beasts residing in the shady wooded valley below.

"Oh Zyntael, do not look so afraid, they eat honey and berries, not Vulkari!" Sarga laughed. "Or Kikimori... I think," she added and the two Vulkari set about giggling.

"Well that's comforting, but Star-Star did mention dangerous monsters that hunted these parts, so we must be careful," I told them. "Anyway, I suppose we should descend into the forest down there, and find out for ourselves what horrors await."

I pointed to the dark green foliage far below us, and for a split second, could almost make out a dark shape—a shadowy creature that darted into the cover of the trees.

A stag-bear perhaps. I certainly hoped they ate only honey and berries.

❈   ❈   ❈

We slowly but surely wound our way down the rocky hillside. My legs were more suited for the downward slope, and my companions awkwardly scurried, often on all fours, beside me.

The steep ground was slippery and damp, and the many goat trails and channels served to make our progress difficult. There had been a good deal of rainfall lately, with only the last week sparing us the deluge.

In place of the constant showers though, there had crept in a chill fog—barely burned away by the watery sun. It layered the ground with a coat of glistening dew that remained until mid-afternoon most days.

Winter was slowly stretching its icy claws out across the land, and each rainless morning I had woken to cloudy breath, and a world white with frost.

We reached the bottom of the valley and crashed through ferns and bracken, sending ground fowl into the air in panicked flight.

The sound of gently running water met my ears. The frigid waters of a brook danced over a pebbled bed somewhere in the brush to my left. Before me, an ominous forest loomed.

The trees here were ancient and gnarled. They were swaying ever so slightly in the breeze, creaking and groaning, perhaps warding us away and back to the safety of our warband.

There looked to be an old path that disappeared into the shade of the forest, well-worn at some point I imagined, though now long overgrown and disused. A wooden post jutted from a bed of weeds and barbed thorny bushes near the entrance to the forest proper—a ragged signpost, eroded by weather, and its directions erased by time and rot.

It would not have helped in any case, for between the three of us, nobody could read.

"I suppose this is the trail by which Karthak travelled," I said, pointing ahead into the gloom.

"Should we stop to rest and eat, or push on to avoid wasting the light?" Sarga asked me.

It appeared as though such decisions would fall upon me, having been the one to instigate our journey.

"I don't think much light reaches the forest trail by the looks of things anyway," I told her. "Perhaps it would be best to take a rest here, then push on with torches lit."

And so we rested, refilled our water skins from the nearby stream, and ate morsels of jerky and dried fish as the shadows of the trees began to stretch out, long and thin under the weak glow of the early afternoon sun.

Eventually we set off once more, striking tinder to light up pitch soaked torches, and casting a flickering orange light around us. The amber glow danced off mushroom covered roots, knotted and gnarled trunks, and whispering leaves that were heavy with moisture from the constant damp fog that crept across the uneven ground at our feet.

The alien howls, shrieks and chattering that echoed through the woods from all around us set my skin crawling and my nerves on edge.

At times the sounds came as though attempts at language. There were calls for help, or odd sentences—that it was chillingly obvious, did not originate from any actual speaking thing. I did my best to ignore them, and kept looking to my companions to reassure myself.

My nose was filled with a mossy earthen scent—that of damp, rotted wood, and lichen covered stones—ancient and unwelcoming.

"Why would anyone choose such a place to make their home?" I asked my companions with a hushed whisper. "I can't imagine that passing through these woods is something anyone could get used to."

"They say the Shaman of these parts is an odd sort," Mazgar said quietly. Her ears were pricked and her eyes constantly scanned the undergrowth around us as we went. "Who knows what inclinations dwell within one who holds counsel with the Spirits."

We pressed on deeper into the forest, our meandering path lit only by our torches and the occasional shaft of light from above, that breached the green canopy and hung in the foggy air in hazy columns.

Before long, the earthen scent of the forest air gave way to an un-usual metallic smell. It was alien and inexplicable, and it stuck in the back of my throat as I breathed—like the taste of blood. The strange odour was accompanied by an increasing feeling of being watched by something malevolent.

Each sudden cry or movement in the gradually thickening dark-ness gave cause for us to crouch low—awaiting the appearance of some unknown horror. It was slow going.

Slower than I had hoped, and beginning to worry me that we would be caught somewhere in the dense foliage come nightfall.

A few hours of travel saw those fears allayed however. Our trek along the path led us over a short rise, where the trees began to thin, and before long we breached the clawing undergrowth to emerge in a wide and flat clearing that was unlit by the setting sun. The strange coppery taste dissipated as we entered the clearing, though the sense of being observed by some unknown sentinel did not.

Off to one side of the glade there sprang from the damp grass, a circle of bright red toadstools. They stood, as though in reverence, around an obelisk of hewn black stone.

The dark slab had runic symbols carved into its curiously smooth surface, and was so far the only object I had seen in the entire forest that was not covered in a layer of lichen and moss.

"That looks to be some sort of beacon, or marker," I whispered to the others. "A signpost perhaps?"

"Be cautious Sister." Mazgar spoke in a low growl. "I feel uneasy."

"Like we are being watched," Sarga added with a hiss, her round ears flat against her head, and her eyes darting from tree to tree.

"I have felt it for a while now," I told them, and both Vulkari ad-mitted the same.

I glanced nervously around at the encircling forest, though could make out no sight of movement or life, and whether because of the Vulkari words or because of some real threat, I began to feel a fearful chill well up within me.

"Perhaps building a camp, with fire and food may bring us com-fort," I suggested. My hand rested on the hilt of my blade as I scanned the treeline. "I would rather stay here than press on in com-plete darkness."

So we set about constructing a camp on the opposite side of the clearing to the mysterious onyx stone. Sarga fetched armfuls of small logs and branches to burn, whilst Mazgar constructed an ox-hide lean-to for us to sleep beneath. I prepared food to be cooked upon the campfire and started by slicing some vegetables and meat that I had wrapped in sackcloth and stashed in a satchel.

Once the simple stew was bubbling away above a merrily crackling fire, my bravery began to return to me. It washed away the feeling of cold unease that had been holding my mind hostage.

I approached the obelisk—still cautious, but without the fear that I had felt before.

From up close, I could make out tiny carvings all over the stone. There were small stars arranged as though plotting a map of constellations. Every so often, the stars converged on a larger shape. Some were carved animals—a horse, a hound, others were not—instead being weapons and even a skull. I pondered their meaning and circled around the stone to examine the other sides, careful not to disturb the ring of fungi at its base.

On one side there was writing—long passages in some unknown script and maybe a language I could speak, for all I knew.

Without being entirely sure why, I laid a hand on the strange stone structure. The surface was cold to the touch. Unnaturally cold, even given the frosty weather.

Unable to make heads nor tails of the obelisk and its curious carvings, I started walking back to where the two Vulkari were sitting, poking the campfire with sticks, and chatting.

I had only taken a few steps when off to my left, beyond the edge of the treeline, a stick snapped. The sound was sharp and clear against the otherwise unusually quiet forest. It stopped me in my tracks, and I wheeled around to face the source of it—hand clutching the hilt of my knife.

For a split second, in the darkness between two ancient trees, it looked as though there stood a figure. It was roughly my own height, perhaps shorter. It was hard to be certain since as soon as my eyes registered that they had indeed seen something, it was gone.

I rushed back to the others, and in a hushed whisper, I informed them of what I had seen.

Both young warriors leapt to their feet and scooped up their weapons. Mazgar took a torch in one hand and thrust the wrapped end into the fire to set it alight.

Then, together we edged cautiously to where I was certain the figure had been.

To my confusion and dismay, despite the earth being moist and soft, it was undisturbed. There wasn't a single track on the leaf strewn ground.

"Zyntael, our tales of stag-bears has you spooked and seeing phantoms!" Sarga said after a while of staring fruitlessly into the gloom. Both she and Mazgar laughed, but their mirth did little to shatter my unease.

I had seen someone or something, standing and watching me from the shadows of the treeline. I was sure of it.

Nevertheless, I returned with the two laughing Vulkari to our little camp, where we sat and ate hearty stew, and chatted around our flickering fire in an effort to keep the oppressive evening chill and the constant sense of dread at bay.

Had we known any better, had we actually had any real experience out in the wilds, or paid better attention to the teachings of the older warriors, we might have kept watch.

Perhaps, if we had not been so naive, we wouldn't have been taken so utterly by surprise when the Kobaloi attacked.

vi.

They poured from the undergrowth; a tide of screeching and whooping marauders. Wearing strips of hide and bone, and hauberks woven from reeds and flax, they brandished daggers, hatchets and picks.

Their ugly faces opened beneath flat noses to display rows of jagged teeth as they bellowed and yelled—large, luminous eyes alight with malice.

The Vulkari reacted quicker than I did. Perhaps their stronger senses alerted them to the danger even as I slumbered, nestled between their warm furred bodies.

Their movements jolted me to waking action and, still confused and bleary, I managed to stagger out from beneath our simple lean-to and draw my Hobgoblin dagger from its sheath just as one of the attackers reached me.

I had never been in a proper melee outside of training with my Vulkar sisters, and barely had time to register what was happening. Even so, I instinctively blocked a swing from a short stone-tipped cudgel.

The clash of weapons sent sparks dancing along the edge of my black steel dagger.

I defended myself as best I could, backing away to keep distance from my attacker—and the others that closed in alongside it.

Sarga let out a cackling roar and ploughed headlong into the oncoming group of the tawny skinned creatures. She jabbed at them with a spear in one hand and brandished a burning branch in the other. The latter of which exploded into showers of dazzling orange with each blow she rained upon her foes.

To my other flank, Mazgar was kneeling. By the looks of it, she had been struck by an errant arrow. With an enraged snarl, she wrenched the small wooden shaft from her chest, and then hurled her own javelin back at the creatures before charging forward, blade in hand.

Mazgar and Sarga were far better fighters than I was—both Vulkari having grown a lot quicker than me over the last three months. Mazgar was now over five feet in height and possessed of a strength and fighting instinct that I seemed to lack. Sarga was larger and fiercer still. They waded forward into the teeming mass of flailing limbs, jagged blades, and brutal clubs—shrugging off blows and responding with violence unmatched by anything I was as yet capable of.

It astounded me that they had so quickly become fearsome warriors, having only several seasons prior, been roughly my own size and not that much more formidable than I.

Now however, the two Vulkari would have easily torn me limb from limb, and I was glad for the bond of friendship and sisterhood growing between us.

Despite my physical shortcomings, I resolved not to let them down, planted my feet and steadied myself. The creature before me hunched low, ready to spring once more to the attack, but this time I was ready. I dodged to the side as the shrieking foe came, and brought my weapon upward, driving it all the way up to the hilt in the monster's abdomen.

It let out a gurgling shriek and the full weight of its body dragged me off balance. It was a good thing it did, as an arrow whistled by overhead, aimed to hit me where I had stood.

I was mildly surprised at how easily I had killed the thing, and although I was no stranger to death and violence by now, it was still the first life that I had taken in actual combat.

I had no time to reflect upon it however, as the fight raged on around me.

I wrenched my weapon free of the creature and let the body slump to the damp grass. Then I advanced on the others, murderous intent burning within me.

Two more of the feral creatures rushed past the congestion caused by my companions' onslaught; the first leapt at me—a curved blade held overhead.

As it brought the weapon down to strike me, I launched myself forward, inside the reach of the attack. I collided with the monster, too slow to bring my dagger around and slash at it, and both of us tumbled to the earth.

I landed on top of my attacker, pinning it down and causing it to let go of its short sword, which landed a few feet away from the monster's grasp.

Before it had a chance to grapple me or shove me off, I managed to manoeuvre my dagger between us, and with the full weight of my body, drove the blade home into the creature.

It writhed and spasmed but I didn't relent, stabbing it again and again between its protruding ribs.

The wounded creature's ally approached to assist it and I lashed out at its legs, cutting deep into the flesh just above its ankle.

That attacker also dropped to the ground, this time kneeling to clutch the terrible wound.

Inky blood pumped out over the grass.

I forced myself off the dying foe beneath me, and turned to face the one that knelt. Before it could react or recover enough to defend itself, and driven by some unrelenting fire within me, I hacked its throat open. Then I kicked it to the ground.

"Mazgar! Sarga!" I cried out, scanning the fray for sight of the two warriors.

In the weak light cast by the dying campfire, I could only make out the slightest detail. The smaller attackers looked to be retreating before the two rampaging Vulkari. I caught glimpses of their towering silhouettes, flashes of slick, blood-soaked blades and manic, frenzied grins as they moved about the clearing, dealing out death and dismemberment with almost casual ease.

I hurried towards the closest of them, bounding over crumpled corpses of our mystery foes, dodging the grasping limbs of the defeated but not quite dead.

I reached Sarga. She caught sight of me and let out a howl of joy.

"Zyntael! I knew you'd be fine! Look Sister, look how they cower and run before us!" she was holding one of the savage little creatures by its throat with one hand, then to illustrate her point, threw it at its brethren, who stood just out of her reach. They brandished their weapons threateningly, but were no longer advancing to attack.

True to her words, a handful of the creatures turned tail and scarpered into the cover of the woods, whilst the rest backed away slowly.

"Are you hurt?" Sarga asked me, wiping blood from her own face; crimson, so definitely her own.

"No, I don't think so," I told her, and looked over to where Mazgar was single-handedly driving another assault back into the forest.

"We should help Mazgar!" I said, and motioned for Sarga to follow, before rushing towards the other Vulkar.

I was glad I reached her when I did, for she looked to be in a far worse condition than Sarga. Two or three spears had pierced her, and she was bleeding profusely from her mouth and nose. Still though, the smaller Vulkar fought on with a feverish aggression; her weapons abandoned or lost, claws and teeth making violent and effective substitutes.

I arrived beside her in time to wrench one of the attackers from her back. I threw it to the ground and stabbed downwards repeatedly, until its clawing hands no longer groped at me.

Sarga delivered a kick to the face of another of the creatures, and sent it sprawling to the ground at the feet of its allies.

Within a few moments we had successfully driven the bulk of the monsters back into the cover of the treeline.

We waited, expecting a counter attack but none came.

The forest clearing was filled with the moans of the broken and wounded, and as the weak morning sun began to pierce the damp fog, my companions set about finishing them off.

Mazgar and Sarga worked efficiently—crushing windpipes underfoot, and rending flesh with their powerful claws.

They left only two of the creatures alive, trussed them with rope and the reeds that had been their own armour, and laid them before the campfire.

I spent those early hours of daylight dragging the multitude of corpses into a pile at the opposite side of the glade. Where I went, the bodies left trails of thick obsidian blood across the flattened grass.

We then spent some time trying to communicate with our captives.

Neither would speak to us, and out of frustration, Mazgar freed one of them of its head, with her bare hands. The other merely cowered, before eventually succumbing to its wounds and finding itself added to the pile of its brethren.

Afterwards, I sat and tended to the wounds that covered my companions. Mazgar had received the vast majority, although she barely registered the pain whilst I stitched the gashes left by spears and arrows. Once done, I bandaged her as best I could.

"That was glorious, do you not agree Sisters?" she asked, gesturing at the considerable pile of the defeated attackers—their sandy skin smeared with blackish blood; their large dark eyes staring vacantly into the afterlife.

"Indeed, we are not so weak as to fall to such pathetic foes. Even attacking us in such numbers!" Sarga laughed. "What do you suppose they were?"

I looked at the two of them and shrugged. "I would have thought you might know. Star-Star told me there were horrors amongst these trees, but these didn't seem all that formidable."

"All in all, they disappoint. They fight like weaklings, they could tell us nothing, and worse still—their flesh tastes vile and acidic, so we cannot even make food of them!"

Both Vulkari laughed.

So did I.

It was my first proper taste of bloodshed, and it felt good.

Despite the elation that our victory brought with it though, we were anxious to move on—worried that our trek through the forest would take us through trapped territory, or into ambushes. The cloying undergrowth would be much more difficult for the Vulkari to fight in, and I was afraid that I might not be able to contend with an assault by myself, should another begin.

Mazgar and Sarga smeared themselves with the inky blood of our defeated attackers, and stared at me expectantly until I followed suit, then together we scavenged whatever useful pieces of armour and weaponry we could.

Finally, once we were suitably outfitted and prepared to move out, we cautiously continued along the dark and twisting forest trail—constantly alert and prepared for further attacks or sudden ambushes.

No attack came, however, and I wasn't sure if it was disappointment or relief that I felt when we eventually found ourselves climbing up and out of the valley—towards the looming cave above.

⌗   ⌗   ⌗

The Whispering Cavern. The place was named appropriately, for whether because of the wind or something much more unnatural, my ears were filled with the soft sound of hushed voices. They spoke in a multitude of languages, none of which I could make sense of. Though all the same, I felt watched, judged, and on edge as we weaved between the jutting stone teeth of the cavern's spiked maw.

"Do you hear it?" I asked the Vulkari.

"Likely better than you do!" Mazgar whispered in reply, then turned her eyes upon my ears. "Though I wonder; why else do you have such long ears, if not to hear things better?"

"You know, that might be the first time anyone has asked why my ears are as they are." I considered the thought, treading softly as I led the way further into the damp cavern. "I think I might hear better than a Hobgoblin would, but perhaps not as well as Vulkari do."

"What?" Mazgar asked, and we all sniggered.

"I hope Karthak is near. I am really not fond of the feeling that this place stirs within me," I said, nervously peering into the gloom of the mossy, dripping tunnel ahead.

"Who is this Spirit-talker, do you think?" Sarga whispered. "A Vulkar? Something else?"

"I have not heard anyone speak of her as anything other than a Shaman and a witch. Nobody has given mention of what form she takes," Mazgar said. "Though we were told of forest hags that could take the form of the beasts—so as to speak with them, use them as spies. Remember?" she looked at Sarga who nodded and continued gazing into the shadows.

"Yes, but many of those tales that the Mothers told were deliberately grim, I think. Warnings and such, to teach pups not to venture into the woods alone. I doubt a forest beast is as threatening as a forest beast who may be a mystic hag in disguise."

"Still though, who knows? Anybody who would choose to live all the way out here, beyond a forest full of stag-bears and those... things—might hold all manner of strange powers." I said.

We continued on, pressing deeper into the damp cavern, our footfalls muted by the dripping ichor and softly glowing fungi that lined the smooth stone walls.

We had not travelled far before the passage split; one path seemed to descend further into the mountainside, the other curved off to the right.

"Which way?" I asked the others.

Mazgar approached the stone ahead of us and wiped a hand across the slimy surface.

"There is writing here," she said. "Spirits only know what it says, but there is an arrow that points that way." She gestured toward the left passage that sloped deeper into the earth.

"Are there tracks or anything? Any sign of passage? Surely Karthak must have left traces in this muck," Sarga suggested.

We searched for footprints or anything else that might hint at the Warlord having travelled this way.

There were indeed tracks in the soft earth that lined the floor of the caves, though surprisingly they appeared not to belong to a Vulkar, rather they were left by a single pair of booted feet and led off in the same direction that the writing indicated.

"I guess we should follow them; the Spirit-talker may be a Hobgoblin or a Kimora even," I said with a shrug. "Can either of you smell anything useful?"

"Only the scent of the earth, and a hint of metal or blood," Mazgar replied. Sarga agreed.

It was strange. Since they mentioned it, I noticed a hint of the same odd metallic scent as before—this time very faint, and without the taste that had accompanied it.

We ventured on, chatting softly as we went.

"So do either of you know the sorts of things that Karthak learns from the Spirits? I wonder if you are told, or hear things that are kept from me," I asked.

"Not much, I have heard that Karthak spoke to the Spirits about the Goblins, I heard it from one of the older warriors," Sarga said. "Something about there being a war brewing. But I do not know who it is supposed to be between. Maybe the Legion are splitting apart."

"There are more than just the Legion you know," I told her.

"I thought they were all the same. Hobgoblins that is. Do they not all share the same beliefs and behaviours?"

"No, that's not how it works. The Legion is run by Hobgoblins, and only they can wield any real power, but it isn't made up of just Hobgoblins. It has Kimori too, maybe other creatures. They aren't like the Vulkari." I said.

"How so?" Mazgar asked.

"Well it's hard to explain, but there are different groups amongst the Fae. It's not like those different groups are made up of only Kimori, or only of Goblins either," I began, stumbling over what I was trying to express. "They might be ruled by one people or other, but they have other peoples amongst their number..."

"So it is like how you are one of us, but have naked skin?" Sarga asked.

"Well sort of, but in the Legion, there are all manner of peoples, and what makes them the same is their belief in the Legion way of life. Same goes for the other Hobgoblins and Kimori and whatever they are that belong to the Combine—at least, that's what I was told,"

I said. "Whereas with us, I think I'm the only Kimora who isn't a slave. I think it might be a bit different."

"I think you are a Vulkar. A small, hairless, short-armed, long-eared, backwards-legged, and kind-of-weak Vulkar. But just as fearsome as any one of us—and certainly more so than any Kikimora," Sarga told me.

I wasn't sure if I should be flattered or insulted, but chose to express the former.

"Uhh, thank you."

"I still find it somewhat funny that despite your size, you are many seasons older than us," Mazgar added, and both Vulkari turned the conversation towards making fun of me.

It carried on whilst we walked for the next few minutes.

"Wait, wait. You might be bigger and stronger and kept warm by your fur, but at least I don't have fleas!" I protested.

"That is true Zyntael, it is torture at times. As are the knots." Mazgar laughed. "Anyway, what was your question again? Oh yes, the Spirits and their advice?"

"Yeah, so you've not heard anything about how and why I was taken into the warband?" I asked.

"Well no, not really," Sarga admitted. "After our trials, I was maybe embarrassed, but mostly impressed. I asked Garok why we had a Bare-Skinned creature in our midst. She told me that it was the will of the Spirits that you be treated no differently than the rest of us."

"I was told the same. Though I heard that Karthak herself chose you for your bravery," Mazgar added.

"Yes, you told me that," I said. "I suppose I really just wanted to know why Karthak decided to take me. You know? It is odd that I am the only Kimora amongst our warband." I looked at my feet as we trudged along in the gloomy cave.

"You want to know the strangest thing?" I said after a while. "I can't actually remember what being a Kimora is really like. I don't know where the 'me' from before all this ends, and the Vulkar 'me' begins."

Mazgar laughed. "Perhaps that is because there is only the one Zyntael."

The Vulkar looked me in the eyes, her features softened by the flicker of her torch. "What did you think about? What were your dreams? When you were in your Kikimora village, I mean," she asked.

"I can't remember. I think I just wanted to explore the forest. Eat berries, that sort of thing."

"Well we have done both of those things just today!" Sarga interjected. "Kikimori goals are so easily fulfilled!" And she let out a sharp cackle of laughter.

"Yeah, maybe they are," I agreed, realising that I now wanted so much more—The thrill of the raid, the challenge of combat, but above all, answers.

So we trudged on, in pursuit of those answers. The cool and damp tunnel meandered through the rock of the mountain, as though the burrow of some vast and ancient worm.

At uneven intervals, the footprints that we followed seemed to stop and face either wall and on closer inspection there were more of the same unintelligible markings.

I found it odd that there were no Vulkar tracks, and began to feel a nagging doubt that Karthak had even ventured this way. Worse still, that this was not even the abode of the supposed Shaman, but someplace else entirely.

As we ventured, the coppery scent grew stronger, and eventually became accompanied by a strange pulsing buzz that drowned out the whispers of the wind and made my head feel heavy and full of fog.

The others noticed it as well, though neither made any complaint as we ventured into the depths. Rather, their manes bristled, their ears lay flat against their skulls and they repeatedly sniffed the air, grimacing.

After what must have been nigh on an hour of the travel that bore us deep into the bowels of the mountain, we reached the end of the passage.

The stone walls converged on a simple wooden door, constructed of dark and grimy planks, and sporting neither handle nor keyhole.

My Vulkar companions stood on either side of me, eyes fixed on the barrier as though it were some terrifying and alien sight to them.

I reached for the slime-covered wood in an effort to push the door open and Mazgar held a hand out to stop me.

"Caution Zyntael, I cannot explain it and do not know why you are not feeling this as well, but something here is…"

"Evil." Sarga finished her sentence with a dry whisper.

"Do you not smell the blood? It is burning and the smoke is filling my thoughts," she said slowly.

I certainly felt unknown eyes upon me, and a pervasive sense of mounting unease, but nothing that I would outright call evil.

"Well I'll look beyond, if you wish to remain here. I will call out and let you know what awaits us," I told them.

"Brave and strong," Mazgar murmured and the two young warriors glanced knowingly at one another.

"Alright Sisters. Here goes nothing," I said, and pushed the sodden wood aside.

vii.

"You are no Kimora!" I told the creature. "Why then do you wear the naked skin of one? Where is Karthak?"

It laughed—a grating and unnerving sound that bounced from the walls of the domed stone chamber.

"Naked skin? You speak as though a Vulkar. Wouldst that it be kinder on your eyes for us to wear their shape, we could do so."

The thing before me spoke in an odd form of the Fae tongue. It was absolutely unnatural, each sound not quite blending into the next and giving the impression that it was not so much language, but a rough mimicry of it—as though made by a raven or some other animal.

"Why do you speak so? And refer to yourself as many?" I asked, eyes scanning the beautiful features of the Not-Kimora woman before me.

Even its masquerade was slightly off. I couldn't quite place it, but the thing's subtle expressions, the movements of its eyes, brow and mouth as it spoke; they were all wrong somehow.

"We do as we have always, and become as we must to commune with those who call. This flesh is but the trappings of your world, not ours. Canst you see beyond? We know you are able." It made a sound like a hacking cough.

"So you wore this... Kimora, because you knew that I looked this way?"

"Indeed, we felt only your touch upon our calling stone, we knew not that you are as we are, and not the skin you wear."

"That black marker in the clearing? You felt me through that?" I asked.

"We did." The creature, whatever it was, turned and shuffled towards the small bed in the corner of the chamber, passing briefly through a pool of shadow, cast by a hanging stalactite.

It emerged a Vulkar.

I didn't even notice the change, one moment there moved a beautiful Kimorin woman, clad in fine robes of rich greens and browns, the next, a Vulkar—smaller than Mazgar even, but outfitted as though a warrior of the raid.

"How..." I stood there staring. "How did you do that?"

"Magick," was the creature's simple answer. And at this point, I really didn't doubt it.

"You avoided my question before. Do you know where Karthak is?" I asked.

"She came and went. Though we did not commune within these caverns, last day."

That would explain the lack of Vulkar tracks.

The 'Vulkar' sat down on the side of the bed and beckoned me closer, but I remained planted where I was. There was no way I was going to approach whatever it was that sat before me, wearing the grin of a Vulkar on its false face.

"So did she say where she was going? We didn't run into her on her return journey."

"No. But tell us, these are not the questions that you truly wish to ask, are they?" it croaked.

"I have many questions, but first I want to know—how can you expect me to trust your words, when even your form is so deceiving?" I asked the creature, examining it, noticing small details that belied its attempt at a disguise.

"We do not deceive, but rather promise no truth wrought of stone. For if there is no immutable truth, then what canst you claim is the lie?"

I struggled to grasp the creature's point.

"So are you saying that you only offer your opinion? What kind of Spirit-Guide are you then? Why would anyone heed your advice?" it seemed that this may have all been a big waste of time and effort. If anything, I felt disappointed that Karthak would put so much stock in the words of whatever this thing was.

"Impatient. Impertinent." It coughed out each syllable. "You are as Vulkar as any other."

"So I keep being told," I sighed. "Well I would really rather return to my companions and find my way back to our camp if all I'm going to get from you, whatever you might be, are guesses, opinions, and riddles."

"If that is to be your wish, then we canst do naught to stay you. But perhaps we may enlighten you to those whispers that we whispered to the ears of your Warlord." The false Vulkar pushed itself to its feet and approached me.

The pervasive scent of burnt copper made me feel nauseous, but I remained where I was.

I supposed that I might as well hear out whatever it was that had guided the actions of Karthak. At least then, I might be able to make sense of all that she had put me through.

"Best to rest here and listen to our words than to venture out and face more of the Kobaloi yes?" it asked, in a mockery of a comforting tone.

"Kobaloi? Those little brown forest-creatures?" I shrugged. "They posed barely a threat to my sisters and I, but fine. I will hear you out. Though I would rather the others be present."

"Certainly," the creature said, and extended a furred arm awkwardly toward the door.

I retreated from the cramped chamber to find the two Vulkari sitting side by side, their backs against the wall of the tunnel.

They were playing a game, their hands clasped together, wrestling one another with thumbs only.

Mazgar looked up as I entered the corridor, and Sarga took the opportunity to beat her by pinning her thumb. I had never seen Mazgar win a round.

"Distracted is defeated!" Sarga proclaimed then turned to me also. "Well Sister, what lies beyond that feeble wood?"

"Something. I couldn't tell you what it truly is, it was a Kimora before but right now it is a Vulkar," I admitted.

"A shapeshifter then? Maybe a Mavka," Mazgar said, nodding her head in thought. "What did it say? Is Karthak present?"

"No, she was never here. But it said that it would tell me whatever it told her. I elected to fetch you first though, that creature makes my skin crawl."

The Vulkari looked at one another and back to me, eyes wide. Sarga spoke first.

"No, sorry Zyntael," she said.

"Indeed, I am not venturing into the den of some skin-stealing forest Spirit," Mazgar affirmed.

"Fine then, you wretched flea-ridden cowards!" I exclaimed. "I will be sure to call out to you if I am killed and eaten then. I hope I don't interrupt your game though!"

I laughed at the shocked expression that they both wore, before waving them a potential final goodbye and turning back toward the mysterious creature's room.

"Brave and strong?" I heard Mazgar ask.

"Maybe just stupid," Sarga told her, and the two giggled and returned to their game.

❈ ❈ ❈

"You return alone. Your friends share the superstitions of their kind. Perhaps your ignorance insulates you from the same," the creature said as I pushed the flimsy wooden door closed behind me.

It stood with its back to me, and wore armour, but was unmistakably a Kimora once again—its skin a rich freckled brown, just as mine was, its hair a similar crimson shade and by the looks, worn in a similar fashion to my own.

"Why do you look as I do?" I asked it. "I know that it is just a disguise. What is the point? Why not show your true form?"

"We wear not your form as you are, but as you are to be. At the intent of others that would see your path be theirs." The mimic turned to face me and I gasped, stumbling back a few paces.

It didn't just resemble me, it was me.

Though not me as I was at that moment, but rather older by a dozen seasons, maybe more.

She—it—stood before me, clad proudly in the rugged and mismatched armour, and adornment of the Vulkari. Each piece of blackened plate and strap of leather was wrapped over a well-built and muscular body, marked with war paint and scars.

Upon each leg my older twin wore quilted crimson cloth that stopped a few inches above armoured knees and was held up by straps of black leather, wrapped around powerful thighs. Her feet were protected by expensive looking boots, over which were affixed plates of scuffed metal—with vicious vertical points over the toes.

The rest of the armour was piecemeal—the pauldrons mismatched, the gauntlets, simple chunks of beaten plate bound by cord and leather to roughly patched gloves.

I stood and stared. If this was me, as I was to be in the future, then I was truly formidable to behold.

The doppelganger wore a set of three feathers in her hair, just as I had when dressed by the Legion, and around her right eye there were the same stars—this time etched into the creature's, or rather, my future skin.

She wore the upper part of a damaged breastplate, which seemed more for show than protection.

Over her belly she wore no armour, but instead there dangled strings of beads, teeth, and stone tokens. And the belly was what my eyes were drawn toward.

This future presentation of myself, this Kimorin Vulkar warlord, was heavy and swollen with child.

The pregnant Zyntael, whilst only maybe five or so feet tall, still cut an impressive figure, leaning on the handle of a mighty, black, hook-bladed cleaver. Karthak's cleaver.

"Witness who it is that you are to become," it said, the voice still only a rough approximation of real speech.

"What? But how?" I stared, transfixed by the bulging stomach with its smooth and freckled skin—a deep earthen brown, almost aglow in the flickering light of the candles that dotted the chamber.

My eyes followed the swirling patterns of blue and purple Vulkar war paint that encircled the slightly protruding belly-button. I could swear that I caught a glimpse of movement. The being within shifted and pushed against its cocoon as if maybe to reach for the world around it.

"Is this not a future you desire? To achieve all that it is to be a Vulkar? The Warlord, the Despoiler, the Conqueror and Destroyer?"

The Zyntael before me looked down at her own endowed midriff with a tender smile, and cradled the bulge with a gloved hand. Her eyes flicked upward to meet my own.

"The Creator? The Mother?"

I looked into her eyes—the yellowed green of the dry summer field; the yellowed green of my own.

"I don't know," I admitted. Though within the potential future that stood opposite there lay a completeness that I couldn't deny—I still had no wish to be a playing piece in another's idea of destiny.

"Why this future? Why with child?" I asked it. "I am sure that's my place eventually, as it is with all girls. But why is this so important to others? To Karthak?"

The simulacrum cocked her head and continued to idly stroke her belly as she stared back at me.

"Is this what she wishes of me? That I bear children?" I asked.

"Children? No. But a single child is all that is required. You shall carry the future of your people." It pointed at my stomach then back to its own. "You are to be their Mother. Their Yanghar."

I looked away and shook my head in disbelief.

So this was the great plan of the Warlord? That I birth a child? I could achieve that without having been taken as a slave, sent to work for the Legion, trained to fight as a Vulkar raider. And in any case, I was twelve, nearing thirteen summers old, hardly of any age to bear young anyway.

"I still don't understand," I said, eyeing up the mimic's belly once more. "What would Karthak possibly gain from me becoming a mother? It would be no Vulkar child. They cannot breed with Kimori." I stopped.

"Wait, they can't, can they?"

My mind was instantly flooded with terrible thoughts. They lingered on the image of some half-Vulkar, half-Kimora abomination, either possessed of the shape of a Vulkar, but hairless and frail, or hulking and furred, but with the physique of a Kimora. Neither was particularly endearing, nor any child that I would want.

The creature seemed amused by my fear and laughed once more— a hollow and broken choking sound.

"We can assure you that this is not the case, and pity you the thoughts you must now harbour."

"Well, that *is* a relief!"

I was no fool, and by now understood the mechanics involved in the creation of new life thanks to the rather forthright way that Vulkari spoke of such things.

Thankfully there was no danger of Karthak expecting that horror from me. Although, if not a Vulkar pup, then I could see no reason why she would desire that I bore any child at all.

"Still though, surely she could have left me with my village if pregnancy is all she wished for my future," I told the shapeshifter.

It regarded me with some interest at mention of my village so I decided to ask it of their fate.

"My family. If you see things beyond what I can, please tell me, are they safe?" I implored the thing.

"Do you truly wish to know? Have you ever asked your Warlord?" it asked.

Each question I posed to the creature had thus far been met by questions of its own, and I was growing weary of it—especially now, regarding this subject.

"Of course I wish to know!" I said, my calm demeanour slipping as my patience ran dry. "I've had enough of your riddles and games. Please, just tell me of my family and my friends."

It smiled a false smile, unnerving as before but made worse so by the face it currently wore.

"How long have you been in the company of Vulkari, yet you did not ask after the fate of your village? Your family? Is it because you assumed them dead? Or that you needed them to be, to give you reason to stay? To mask what you truly desired?" it said.

I clenched my teeth, the rage once more bubbling to the surface of my being.

"How dare you…" I began, but it cut me off with a raised palm.

"Calm yourself, child. We canst but tell you that which concerns your path. As hard as it may be to hear, but of your family, we see naught." It paused, a single twitch briefly visible in one of its eyes. "Of your friends, we see only the realisation of a truth of sorts. This is not knowledge that can be told in the now, but we warn you this: when you finally face the Betrayer, do not allow ire and retribution to stoke the furnace to an inferno, for only destruction and ruin follow."

I spat. "What's *that* supposed to mean? Tell me, curse you!"

"We shall not. All shall come to you whence it must. For now though, know that you shall be safe on your return to the camp."

My pregnant clone ran her gloved fingers over the Vyshivka that encircled her hips. She lifted the fully embroidered end and her eyes followed the stitching—reading the story it told.

"We like you child, and shall relent. Remember this one small instruction, and know that when the frost grips your sixteenth eastern sun; beware the violet scourge. Make haste on that morn, with the three parts of who you are, to the Fortress of the Fist. There you shall find your deliverance—and find your true path to greatness."

"What? I don't know what any of that means," I admitted.

"You shall. When the moonlight reveals the truth, you shall," the warrior Zyntael said then looked over my shoulder at the door behind me. "Your companions await. Eager to return."

I turned to see the two Vulkari peering into the room, confused expressions on their faces.

"Wait…" I began to say, looking back at the pregnant copy, but there was only empty space where she had been.

"Zyntael?" Mazgar ventured. "What are you doing?"

"Talking to an empty room by the looks of it," Sarga told her.

And apparently so I was.

viii.

"Hobgoblin scum! Interfering Imperial swine!" Karthak bellowed, scattering the carved stone figurines from their positions on the ancient map that was stretched across a stump in the centre of the command tent.

She slammed a fist onto the surface of the makeshift table, sending more figurines—as well as a jug of rich wine—earthward.

"I ask you," she snarled to the warriors present. "Why must Threydon and his squat, hairless, pig-faced ilk push us from every inch of territory they can? If it is to resist the Merchant Lords, then why did the whelp turn his nose up at my proposal for a lasting bond between us? *That* would have served his kind far better than mere land shall."

She stared at me as she said the last part, and I looked up at her in silence. I had seen her furious on many an occasion, but this time I wondered if the copious quantities of wine and spirits that she usually drank would calm her, or further fuel her rage.

Around the cluster of Vulkari lay at least a dozen pitchers, bottles and goblets, each drained of its contents, and the pile was sure to grow rapidly over the course of the evening given the mood in the war chief's tent.

Star-Star noticed my expression and flashed a quick grin at me before casting her eyes upon the near-empty goblet she held. I figured I should probably make myself useful and scurried off to fetch more wine.

I learned that the wild lands we roamed, the vast plains of grass and scrub, rolling hills and meandering brooks punctuated occasionally by easily raided villages and farmsteads, were but a small fraction of the territory that was soon to belong to the Legion.

Their so-called 'God-Emperor' had cast his insatiable gaze westward of the fort that had been my temporary home, and throughout the months that our warband roved, the frequency with which we would encounter Legionnaire scout parties steadily increased.

This vexed Karthak and her senior lieutenants more so than anything I had seen so far—the Vulkar raiders averse to the likelihood that such easily plundered settlements would soon fly the banners of the untouchable black fist, and thereby no longer stand as a source of food and slaves, ripe for the taking.

The meeting the senior warriors now held, was the third such occasion in as many moons, and the rate at which they drank themselves into a rage, combined with the lack of raiding possible, meant that our liquor supplies were rapidly running dry.

A young male stood in the supply tent when I arrived, writing something on a scrap of parchment and mumbling under his breath. He jumped in fright as I pushed open the ox-hide flap and strolled inside.

"More wine?" he asked, then paused and looked at my stomach with a grin on his lean face. "Should one drink when they are with child? I have heard tell that the young shall come out addled and weak!"

"Well that explains you then Narod, you mangy whelp!" I retorted.

Every time. Every damned time I fetched wine, the scrawny wretch made the same joke. I regretted telling Mazgar and Sarga how the Spirit-Guide had appeared to me, though I couldn't be sure which of those loose-lipped blabber-mouths had spread the tale throughout the camp.

"You humble me with your quick wit as always, older Sister," Narod said with a bow of his head, probably hoping that flattery would somehow benefit him. I wasn't entirely sure why the males treated me with deference, since I never really acted with the demanding hostility displayed by my sister Vulkari. Even so, the many that tended the warband constantly worked to gain my favour with compliments and strange acts of kindness.

Both Mazgar and Sarga thought it was hilarious, Mazgar at one point even suggesting that the whelps all thought that they may be chosen as a mate by me, given the tale of our adventure into the Whispering Cavern.

In a way, I enjoyed the treatment and so neglected to tell them that Vulkari and Kimori could produce no young together, and that they would all find themselves disappointed. Furthermore, whilst my two friends were rapidly reaching maturity, I probably still had a few summers to wait.

"Narod, what is the feeling amongst the male-folk?" I asked the scrawny Vulkar. "We have had slim pickings of late."

He sighed and flipped through the bundle of parchments that he clutched in his grasp.

"There are not many supplies, nor slaves to tend. This leaves many absent of things to do." He looked up at me from his scrawled notes. "A bored Vulkar is a wasteful Vulkar. I pray to Yanghar that we come upon a decent settlement soon, otherwise we might as well disperse."

I had learned from Karthak that often the Vulkari would roam the lands in much smaller bands, coming together as one usually only in the springtime, when they marched upon the Legion fortress to trade spoils.

It had been her command that the force remain together for some time now, perhaps out of a fear of reprisal from an expanding Legion presence in the region, perhaps something else entirely.

"What about the Blackfort? Heard anything from the Vulkari there?" I enquired.

"Nothing for a month or two. I had expected a messenger to bring news of their inventory and requests for resupply, but perhaps they have taken their own lasting spoils. Urga is a shrewd Vulkar."

"Perhaps, but I'm glad to be rid of her presence in the camp. She gives me the creeps," I told him.

I hadn't seen that horrible Vulkar for some time now. After the disagreement between Karthak and she, and the resultant meeting, I'd hoped never to have to cross paths with the monster again. Unfortunately, I'd had no such luck, and she'd ventured from her grim bastion in the Stormhills, to visit the warband a few times since.

She'd come to inspect the pups after we first collected them, and she had come to discuss some sort of deal that had existed for some time apparently; Karthak and her Vulkari would supply the Blackfort with food, but I really wasn't sure what they'd get in return. Sometimes she would bring alcohol, or herbs and mushrooms. But it didn't seem worth it.

Every time Urga had come to treat with Karthak, I made sure I avoided her. Sarga and Mazgar thought it was funny, since she didn't strike them as particularly scary—despite being second only to Karthak in size, and radiating a sort of cruel menace that no other Vulkar did, no matter how drunk and angry they were.

I remembered why I'd come down, and pushed that ugly rust-furred villain from my thoughts.

"Well, I should return with this wine," I said, then hefted the small handcart, and began dragging it out of the tent. "Be well, Narod."

"Blessings of the Mother be upon you and your pup," he replied with a smirk, and chuckled to himself as I went.

"Alright horse-son," I said out of his earshot.

"What was that word?" a voice asked, from between two tents ahead. It was Sarga, though why she was lurking around the supply tents was beyond me.

"Horse-son. Like the son of a dumb old horse. It's some kind of insult in the Legion," I told her. "What are you doing here anyway? Not with the others?"

"No, I came to find you. Horse-son... That is a great insult. Though I would consider oxen and sheep to be more stupid," she mused.

"My thoughts exactly. The Legion have some strange ideas. Now why were you looking for me?" I asked. "I have been observing the meeting of Karthak and her warriors. It's pretty interesting—even if I don't understand much of what they say and do in there. I mostly just sit and watch, occasionally fetch more for them to drink."

"Sounds to me like you are set to learn the skills of the leader. Do you also practice your pointless angry shouting over how much you hate the Legion?" she asked with a snigger. I rolled my eyes.

"Anyway, Mazgar, Yinnik, and some of the others were preparing for the next raid, apparently we are to finally join the warriors. They wanted to know what weapons you would like to use. They want to make sure we do not carry the same, but cover all of the tactical possibilities."

"That's very clever," I told her. "I think I'll carry my Legion blade at the very least. Maybe a spear, but I don't really know. What do you think?"

She pondered the question then began listing the options—clubs, cleavers, javelins, and more—as we wheeled the cart full of wine back to Karthak's tent. It amused me that amongst the listed tools of slaughter, bows didn't have a place. Apparently, they were seen as a coward's weapon in actual combat, and so were only used for hunting.

I wondered what the Legion would think of that, given the long ebony bows that their scouts and lookouts carried. And I wondered what that boy, Anra, would think of it. Perhaps, if we met again, I'd have that rank he'd spoken of—once we'd embarked on our first raid.

But, as the days slowly passed, and spring began to warm the earth in earnest, I began to lose hope that there would even be a raid.

We still awaited our first chance as young warriors, and I certainly didn't want to have to spend yet more months travelling around in search of unclaimed territory.

The many nights spent in ritual—drinking foul tasting liquids and inducing vivid, violent dreams by breathing in the smoke from strange and mysterious herbs—had been fun for a while, but I craved real action.

Our skirmish with the Kobaloi had been invigorating and, whilst somewhat exaggerated, its retelling had inspired awe and no small portion of envy in the other young Vulkari. As such, we all shared the desire to finally strike out and raid one of the countless hamlets that dotted the landscape.

Far to the southwest of Threydon's fortress, our desire would end up fulfilled somewhat.

When the time finally came to embark on our first real raid, though, many of the young Vulkari were stricken by an illness that spread throughout the camp.

As a result, we were relegated to the rear of the raiding party, un-likely to see any real combat. I was especially disappointed by this, having been lucky enough to be spared the stomach cramps and con-stant need for latrine use that plagued my fellow rookies.

"I shit three times today. Water, each and every one," Mazgar whispered to me with a sickly grin, as we equipped ourselves for the raid. "I do worry about an urgent need to relieve my bowels in the middle of combat though."

"I very much doubt there will be any combat, what with you all being dribbling wrecks," I replied, focused on buckling a plate of metal over my wrist.

I sat back and extended an arm in front of me to examine the dented armour. I wished I'd listened to Urd more than I had.

"Are you nervous?" I asked the Vulkar.

"Of course! I have waited my entire life for this!" She paused and sighed. "Only, I did not expect that we would be in such a state. I rather thought it would be a glorious occasion."

"Still might be…" Sarga added hopefully, though judging by the look of her, she was feeling anything but glorious.

"What about you, Sister?" Mazgar asked me, turning away from the vest of leather and bone that she was fumbling with.

"I am both terrified and excited. I don't know what to expect of myself," I told them.

I wasn't entirely sure what I felt, but I knew that it was an odd feeling all the same—as though my life, or what I could remember of it, was coming full-circle.

I distracted myself from my uncertainty by helping Mazgar equip herself with her armour. Then we sat and joked amongst ourselves in an attempt to ease our nervous excitement, until Kovvik-Shar, the one-eyed warrior, came to let us know it was time to move out.

We marched from our makeshift camp towards an isolated farming hamlet, before spreading out and creeping across fields of swaying wheat. The smoke from the chimneys drifted lazily into the evening sky—a beacon to us, as we moved.

The farmers and peasants who dwelt within the village, all unaware of their approaching doom.

When we were mere yards away, masked by the approaching dusk, and crouched amongst the springtime crops, the signal was given for the first group of warriors to attack.

And so our first raid began.

ix.

If Mazgar truly was going to shit herself during the raid, now would be the perfect time.

It was terrifying.

My senses were overwhelmed—by the cacophony of the melee and the ceaseless shrill ringing of a warning bell, by the billowing, noxious smoke that surrounded and choked me, and by the sprawling chaos that had erupted in the village square.

"You two pups!" a raider yelled, as she rushed past us and towards the fray. "Cease that racket. Quiet the alarm bell!"

Mazgar and I caught each other's glances and nodded.

I turned towards the source of the noise.

A single unarmed peasant was feverishly tugging on a rope under the awning of the hall that overlooked the hamlet.

Their militia had already come, and were locked in combat with a heavily outnumbered (and completely surprised) group of Vulkar warriors—but still the ringing went on.

I shifted my grip on my short spear and began to jog in the direction of the panicked villager.

"Wait Zyntael! We must avoid the soldiers, Sister!" Mazgar shouted, pointing out an alley between two rows of burning buildings.

She was right; we would be no match for the armoured troops who had poured into the village square once the townsfolk realised that they were under attack.

I shouted back my agreement, and followed Mazgar's advice.

Whilst the two of us weaved between shabby wooden houses, dashing from cover to cover behind piles of crates and barrels, jutting corners, and low fences, I wondered where Sarga and the other pups had gone.

When the chaos began, they'd set off in pursuit of a farmer who had tried to lead his livestock to safety. I hoped that they had avoided the well-equipped soldiers who had sprung from seemingly every building, as though prepared and expecting our attack.

There was scarcely time for worry though, as Mazgar skidded to a halt in the alley in front of me.

"Down. Down," she hissed.

A group of soldiers rushed past the end of the alley in front of us.

From the little I could make out, they were all Kimora or Hobgoblin. Dressed in maille and carrying torches, spears, and shields, their arms and armour rattled with each hurried footfall as they went by.

We waited a moment to ensure that we would not be spotted, before proceeding up the sloping path between the buildings.

"There!" I pointed across a small stretch of open ground, at the large building ahead of us. "That's the town hall."

We had managed to flank the building, and now approached it from the east. The bell-ringer made their racket from the southern face of the wooden hall—we had the element of surprise.

My hands were sweaty and trembling, my mouth dry, as we crept as cautiously as possible through a well-kept garden of flowers, and along the east wall of the building.

"On one. We rush him and stick him," I whispered to my companion. "Are you ready?"

She nodded.

I swallowed dryly, and counted down.

"Treyt..."

"Oyk..."

"Ut!"

The bell-ringer didn't even see us coming, so absorbed was he in his frantic task.

For some reason though, I hesitated as I thrust my weapon, and he turned. It wasn't quite enough to fully face us, and so the sharpened blade of my short spear buried itself in his right flank.

He didn't even scream. That surprised me, and for the briefest moment I thought that I might have somehow missed. The hot blood that splattered my face and stung my eyes confirmed the hit, however, and the boy crumpled before me.

He let out a low, animal, whining sound.

The weight of his body wrenched the spear from my slippery hands, and I stood back a pace, unsure of what to do next as he squirmed around in the dirt and moaned.

He wouldn't stop moaning.

"Mazgar. What should I...?"

Mazgar leapt forward and finished him off with her blade. She didn't even flinch as she slit his throat to drain him of his blood.

It was strange. There was something different about it all. It felt almost surreal, and not at all the way our combat with the Kobaloi had been. I had killed a fair few of those forest creatures, and hadn't really felt anything but excitement. But watching a Kimora boy clutch at his throat, his life pouring from the wound to pool around him, I felt somehow a little dirty.

That feeling wouldn't last long however—the seeds of neither pity nor guilt would have time to germinate.

"Zyntael, we must move," Mazgar hissed, rousing me from my brief stupor.

I retrieved my spear, and we scurried back down towards the melee in the village square below. We had only just made it half way when we ran into another group of Vulkar pups.

Oya was dragging her twin away from a violent brawl at the mouth of an alley. It looked as though Uya had been struck by something heavy and solid, and her left arm dangled at an unnatural angle. She was unconscious, and blood issued from a gash above her left eye.

Oya looked up at us as we hurried towards them.

"I think she is dead!" she cried out. "Help! Please help her!"

Beyond the twins there were two other young Vulkari and one older raider locked in battle with a handful of militiamen.

It didn't look anything like what I had imagined armed fighting to be. They didn't fight gracefully, or trade blows with swords and spears. Rather, they wrestled desperately on the ground, and against the walls of the hovels.

The adult threw one of the men away from her and into a pile of barrels, then grabbed another by the face.

It didn't look as though she had a weapon, though she was hardly struggling. The same couldn't be said for Yinnik and Sarga—who were both occupied by one soldier, and merely held him at bay with blade and cudgel.

"Bind her wound to stem the bleeding, then leave her for now—we must help!" I shouted at Oya, and charged into the fray to fight alongside my sisters.

Amidst the smouldering ruins and scattered corpses, I shook uncontrollably.

From excitement, from relief, from the residue of nervous fear that had gripped me, and from a rushing elation that numbed the scrapes and cuts covering my battered body.

No matter the cause, I was near-overwhelmed by the feeling, and by the looks of Sarga and Mazgar, I was not alone.

Both of them were filthy; their hair was matted and coated in blood, their equipment beaten and ragged, but they wore wide grins nonetheless.

"We yet live!" Sarga cried hoarsely. "We are raiders now!"

And the two filthy Vulkari embraced in celebration.

I stood before them, grinning madly myself, before one of them reached out and dragged me into the celebratory embrace.

I was honestly surprised that we had survived. Our first raid had become a pitched battle. A chaotic melee between the two dozen Vulkari and a garrison of armed soldiers, clad in purple and armed with more than mere peasant farming implements.

Why Merchant Combine military men had been encamped in a remote farming village, nobody seemed to know.

The surprise encounter had downed at least two of the adults, before Karthak had rallied her warriors and mounted a more coordinated offence.

Luckily, none of the injured Vulkari had been killed, with the worst of it being Uya's broken arm and head wound, but the whole ordeal had been harrowing nonetheless.

It turned out that soldiers were far more dangerous than the Kobaloi.

Sometime after our fight in the alleyway, I had been struck by maybe two arrows—both luckily doing no real harm—and at one point in the subsequent chaos, had even narrowly avoided being skewered by a spear.

My stature, and the fact that I didn't resemble my fellow raiders, had been a blessing; the soldiers perhaps thought I was a stray villager.

Whatever the reasons, I had survived—and despite being only a season shy of thirteen summers old (and half their size) as far as the Vulkari were concerned, I had attained the only rank I would ever need—I was now an adult. A raider. A woman.

I was now a Vulkar.

THE FOURTH STITCH

GROWTH

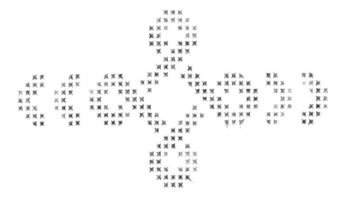

i.

Womanhood was harder than I thought it would be though. Over the following summers, as if to match the status bestowed upon me by my fellow raiders, my body began to change. It wasn't just in the collection of scars that marked my skin—each a reminder of the wounds I had received (and the lessons I had thus learned) from every new raid we embarked upon.

In the final few days of my fifteenth summer I fell ill with a fever and, wracked with terrible pains that grew from within my belly, I was practically bedridden as our warband made its way slowly south—towards a place called Azure.

The others set off on another short raid without me this time, leaving me only the company of Narod, the mangy provisioner, when the bleeding began.

Even though I knew that with adulthood came bleeding, and so the ability to birth a child, I hadn't really been prepared for such things. Worse, nobody had ever told me that it was also to be a regular thing.

Nor, for that matter, that it would be so painful and debilitating.

Narod fetched me soothing concoctions of his own design and shared wisdom on my predicament—though since Vulkari themselves didn't share the same experience, I got the feeling that he was making things up as he went.

The scrawny Vulkar told me that my body was expelling my childhood. That, since blood was the essence of life (and indeed where the spirit of oneself truly resided) the child who I was before had died, and so was flowing from within me.

His words did little to comfort me, though the alcohol that I suspected he had brewed into his potions certainly dulled the uncomfortable pains, which sapped my strength and soured my mood.

Upon their return, Sarga and Mazgar visited me to regale me with tales of their raid, and so Narod retreated once more to his place amongst the warband's food stores.

"We did not even need to kill anything. It was disappointing," Sarga said, and glanced sideways at Mazgar, who was staring intently at my belly. "You really did not miss much."

"Oh don't pretend for my sake," I told her. "I don't mind. Narod told me that I will be well again within a day or two, and that this is only a passing thing, so I will be able to come next time."

"So you bled?" Mazgar asked. "With no wound?"

"Yeah, pretty much. Not an awful lot, but it soiled the pelt I was sleeping on. I thought I was imagining it to begin with," I replied.

"That is very strange," Mazgar muttered, eyes still locked on my midriff.

"Why are you staring at me like that?" I asked her.

She looked away, a sheepish grin on her face.

"Well I wondered if maybe it had been the failed beginnings of a pup. I know you said that Vulkari and Kikimori cannot..."

"What? Of course not!" I cut her off. "That wasn't a lie, and even so, who did you think I'd mated with?"

"Well we did see Narod leave here. He seemed awfully concerned for your well-being too."

Both she and Sarga looked at one another and laughed.

"You are both addled!" I told them sternly. "Now tell me about the raid, or scram. If all you are here to do is make fun of me, then I'd prefer that you left me to my misery!"

"I was not lying for your sake, Sister. It really *was* a bit of a disappointment," Sarga said. "I would not even call it a raid, really."

"The villagers did not fight, but rather, one came out to where we set up and asked to speak with Karthak. He brought a mule—laden with salted meat and sacks of maize," Mazgar added.

"Really? That's pretty strange," I said.

"Yes it is. But what is stranger, is that Karthak did not order an attack, but rather that we accept the food and supplies that they had prepared for us, and then leave!" she replied.

"Were they under Legion protection or something?"

"Maybe. I saw no banners or troops, but like I said; it was disappointing," Sarga answered. "Well, it is nearing time for food and I guess it is to be salted beef. Are you able to walk?"

"I suppose so. I should probably eat something. I really need to regain my strength," I said, and hauled myself from the pile of furs and blankets that I had nested in. "Let us go and see what the others have prepared, and I'll tell you what Narod said about my childhood dying."

His assurance that I would be well again within days was correct, but Narod's assumption that the blood would be a one-off thing, something to do with the transition to womanhood, was not.

It turned out that around the same time every two moons, I would face the same predicament. The ache in my belly and the weakness in my legs was probably the worst of it though. At Star-Star's suggestion, I was able to bind myself with linen and moss to stem the blood flow in the same manner as we used for battlefield wounds, but I could do little but wait and suffer through the pain and discomfort.

Karthak explained to me what she understood of my problem one autumn evening, as we wound our way along the old road that led us through barren and hostile lands, and ever further south.

"It is a curse that all of the Bare-Skinned women share," she told me, pouring a goblet of strong, rich wine then handing me the drink. "You should consider yourself lucky in some regard, the Bog-folk and the Goblins bleed as often as each new moon."

I didn't envy them that.

"The first time, Narod said that it was the essence of my childhood leaving me," I told her.

"That is because he is a moron," she laughed. "Kimor-pup, you shall bleed for each chance you miss at bearing a pup of your own. Some do believe it to be the essence of a child—but that it is each child whom you miss out on having. Others, that it is merely a curse that one must abide. No different than passing food, or water. Thankfully not as frequently, mind."

"So will it ever stop?" I sighed. "I mean for good and not just temporarily."

"Yes, for a while when you carry a child, and for good when you reach an age where that is no longer possible... Should you reach it."

"Oh..." I didn't much like either prospect. "Nobody told me this would be so... annoying."

The Warlord rustled my hair affectionately. "There are many things in life that are to be so. If each was told in advance, what would you have left to find out for yourself? To be surprised by? Pleasant or no, life should be experienced first-hand where possible."

"Come now, I know that you are lying for my sake. You consult the Spirits for guidance all the time!"

My foul mood had really reduced my tolerance for platitude.

"Oh of course! But I do not always tell you what I hear, now do I?"

She had me there. The massive Vulkar had, so far, deftly avoided all of my prying and questioning about what the Spirit-guide had spoken of.

"You know that bothers me no end right?"

She answered only with a grin and an offer of more wine.

Despite her slippery answers, more cryptic than any Hobgoblin's, I did enjoy what little time I spent in her company of late. For the most part, I spent each evening playing dice or bone token games with my peers, and I lodged with them in a shared tent, so didn't spend as much time in the Warlord's presence as I used to.

"You never did tell me what it was that the shape-shifter meant, you know. Nor what she told you." I tried my luck once more.

"Nor shall I for the moment, but that what the Shaman tells, might not be the same to us both. Rather it is what is needed to be heard by each," she said with a wink.

"You sound just like her, or it I suppose," I said, then rolled over onto my back. The ceiling of Karthak's tent was decorated as though a night sky. Small silver beads hung from dark thread, against a blue-black stained hide backdrop. It was quite soothing to look at, and I had spent many nights doing so when I had first been captured. Those stresses and fears long forgotten, however.

"So what is this 'Azure' place?" I asked, hoping for a subject on which I might actually get some answers.

"Azure is a port, far to the south. Operated by the Legion. Though run neither by Hobgoblins nor even Kikimori. The inhabitants are mostly of our kind."

"Vulkari? In a port?" I couldn't really imagine Vulkari settling— nor sailing for that matter.

"Mostly male, they value different things than we do. They have abandoned the truth of Yanghar." She sounded almost sad when she said it. "But even so, they are Vulkari the same, underneath all their Imperial rubbish. And the seas are a good source of slaves and plunder."

"So why are we headed there?" I asked.

"To warn them. Threydon has thrust a war upon us, and soon we must all be ready to fight." She grinned without humour. "Or find some other reprieve…"

※　※　※

We continued south over the course of the next few months and although autumn soon gave way to winter, the further we travelled, the less it felt like it had.

The weather remained warm and comfortable and we spent many evenings sleeping beneath the stars. The sky itself somehow seemed far larger, down in the flat plains.

Frustratingly, Karthak was apparently concerned with our sluggish pace and so limited our raiding after a while. Though, despite this, over the strange and warm winter we did manage to plunder a few settlements and camps.

The majority of these were populated by people with skin almost as dark as my own, and who dressed in flowing gowns and other impractical garb.

Sarga and Mazgar called these folk 'sand people' and told me that they came from the deserts to the southwest, where they lived in cities made from glass, kept gigantic crawling insects as pets, and also ate sand—among other, more fanciful things.

The two of them said that they were mostly fat merchants or shifty smugglers, but rich or poor, they all wore useless robes and far too much perfume, and couldn't fight to spare themselves our raids.

I didn't really believe them, but when I asked Star-Star, she confirmed most of it and told me I'd see much of that for myself, once we reached Azure. She told me that I'd like the place. After all, it was possibly her own favourite place in all the world.

I'd have to see it for myself in order to make up my mind. Surely it couldn't beat the rolling hills, the wild forests, the easily raided hamlets, and the ancient and mysterious ruins of *our* lands.

ii.

I liked Azure.

Although I didn't see anybody (intentionally) eat sand, and certainly met no gigantic crawling insects, I still really liked Azure. Star-Star was right.

It was a beautiful place. Not just because of its location at the edge of the shimmering water, with its salty spray and gently foaming waves, but I liked the port city itself.

The crowded sandy streets were lined with all manner of bizarre sights; from juggling entertainers to shouting salesmen who peddled exotic oddities from their rickety stalls, crammed into every available space amongst the brightly painted and glass panelled buildings.

It was a chaotic hive of activity, and it was thrilling.

Unfortunately, my first impression was a hurried one, as I paced along at the flank of the war chief.

"Shahbaz-Gill. Are you deaf? Shahbaz-Gill! Fetch the scoundrel!" Karthak shouted at the guard who blocked our entrance to a most breathtakingly fancy home. "He should have been told to expect us!"

We had split the warband up as we entered the city through a massive set of gates that were decorated with shells and beautiful frescoes of sea creatures.

Some of the raiders had ventured down to the bazaar, to trade spoils and slaves. Many had gone straight to the taverns, and some other gaudy looking buildings that Karthak informed me were for the satiation of certain impulses. Apparently it was something about adulthood that I would one day soon come to know.

Mazgar and Sarga had opted for the latter, giggling to one another as they went.

I instead elected to remain with Karthak, and so had proceeded to a sprawling villa, situated amongst lush and beautiful gardens. It was home to the port master of the trading hub.

We were to meet with someone called Shahbaz-Gill, a name that Karthak struggled with. I wasn't sure if it was her poor pronunciation of the name or simply the guards' desire to be as difficult as possible, but for whatever reason, we had been referred to merchant after merchant—a rage building within our leader with each new person we were directed to.

Finally, just as the sun was beginning to set behind the coastal hills, the latest victim of Karthak's wrath returned with a group of others.

He walked beside a Vulkar. This one was smaller than Karthak by height, but far fatter than any in our warband. His many bangles and trinkets clattered merrily as he strode toward us through a garden of spiked plants, blooming spring flowers, and manicured paths.

"Karthak the warrior, burning star of the crimson skies!" he called out, his voice deep and heavily accented. "Vulkar-Sister! Long has it been since your band graced our joyous walls."

"Shahbaz-Gill. Should I believe your men to be truly incompetent, or were we delayed for your own amusement?" Karthak replied. There was no pleasantry in her tone.

The fat Vulkar regarded me curiously when he reached our small group.

Ar-Tarak had ventured with us, the young Vulkar with whom I probably spent the least amount of time, and who I suspected didn't really like me much. The wiry and speckled youth nudged me and whispered.

"He thinks you strange."

"Most do, I guess," I replied, and shrugged.

The port master noticed our hushed conversation and once more turned his attention to us.

"New raiders, Karthak? Would holy-Mother Yanghar be proud to call a Bare-Skin daughter?" he licked his black lips and his beady eyes darted from me to Karthak.

"Well you would certainly be the last I would assume to understand the desires of the Vulkar-Mother. You, with your Imperial opulence, false and difficult name, and your chosen company."

She laughed dryly. "A pirate once, but the lure of laziness is always too strong for male-folk, and thus you have retreated behind your painted walls and trade agreements."

The smile never left his face, but it was clear that Karthak's words insulted the fat Vulkar.

"All the same," she continued. "I did not venture all of this way to trade petty insults as though a pup. I come with a proposal. And a plea."

"A plea? Karthak, you have a strange way of warming one's desires to assist you," he said.

"It is not us who need help, but you," Karthak told him. "Let us discuss this inside though. Some words are not to be spoken lightly, nor without care as to the ears that catch them."

I made to follow the Warlord and the Merchant master, but Karthak halted me with a raised palm.

"Return to the streets below, find your sisters and enjoy yourselves. You shall run into no trouble. Of that I could not be more certain."

The last words she spoke were almost a threatening hiss, and seemed more directed at Shahbaz-Gill than me.

He nodded. "But of course! In fact, take a small token of my goodwill to you and all of Karthak's daughters. Enjoy our humble port, Bare-Skin."

And the Vulkar reached into the folds of the many billowing sashes that he wore, and retrieved a small—but laden—pouch, which he tossed into my unexpectant hands.

❉ ❉ ❉

The streets didn't sleep in Azure, and I doubted I would much either.

Ar-Tarak and I split the money we were given into shares—three coins for each of the young raiders. Then we set off into the lively mess of the place. It was as busy at night, as it had been during the day.

"I think Oya and Uya went into a tavern. I shall go and find them. I expect you shall be going to join Sarga and Smallest in the bathhouses?" my sullen companion said.

"Bath houses? It would be good to clean ourselves. But to be honest, I want to go and look at the sea. I have never been to the coast before," I told her.

"You are a simpleton. The bathhouses are not really for cleaning. There are servants and pleasure-slaves. How do you not know these things?" She laughed. "Why else do you think the others went? You know those mongrels do not wash."

That much was true.

"I don't know. I thought there were actual baths…" I felt stupid. "At least now their giggling makes sense. Anyway, you can take their share if you want and I'll come and find you later."

We parted ways and I set off to explore the port city, on my way down to the beautiful waterfront—totally unaware that I was being followed.

iii.

The inky black water lapped against the shore; a living mirror to the night sky, and the fires of the port. Countless specks of light danced and sparkled across its sighing surface, a calming mask to the infinitely threatening depths below.

I had reached down and dipped my toes in the ocean, but was afraid that I may be swallowed up by it, snatched from my perch on one of the countless jetties that protruded from the port city. So I clambered back up, and simply took in the sights instead.

Not too far away from me, a boy sat down. He carried with him a long rod and a small basket, and began affixing a set of hooks to his line.

I smiled at him and imagined that he smiled back from beneath the cloth wrap that hid his features.

Many of the people I passed on my way down here, whether beggars or merchants, men or women, seemed to adorn themselves with flowing fabric.

Just as often brightly coloured and patterned as not, the cloth was wrapped around their heads, or swept across their faces. I didn't really know why, so I resolved to ask the boy.

"Boy. Why do you dress yourself so? Is it the dress of Azure or the sea?" I waved a hand in front of my face and around my head.

The boy stopped working on his fishing gear and looked at me, then simply returned to his work.

Perhaps he didn't understand.

I shrugged and looked back out to sea.

There was something rejuvenating about it all. The salty air, and the rhythmic rushing of the waves that broke upon the beach; the cries of the strange birds that perched on the jetties and docks, and in the rigging of the many boats that creaked softly as they rocked in the harbour.

I could hear the bustle of the bazaar as well, smell the spices and smoke from the food that was sold, bought and eaten by Hobgoblins, Kimori, and Vulkari alike.

The Vulkari of Azure were vastly different to my raid-sisters. Instead of armour and Vyshivka, they too wore the flowing robes and sashes of almost all of the port city's inhabitants.

Most of the Vulkari seemed to be males too, and whilst still shorter than the females, just like Shahbaz-Gill, they were often flabby—or at least well-fed.

I even saw a group of Vulkar pups on my way down to the docks. They stared and whispered as I passed them; each one carrying an assortment of fishing equipment, as well as pails filled with the small fish they had recently caught.

I hadn't tried to speak with them, but afterwards thought it would have been interesting to ask them about the city.

If the boy, who was still struggling to bait his hooks, had been receptive to conversation, I might have asked him of the place too.

I wondered what the others were up to. After Ar-Tarak told me that Mazgar and Sarga were going to some sort of brothel or pleasure house, I understood their excitement and amusement. The two of them never shut up about such things, and were fixated upon the many differences between our bodies—as well as bodily functions in general.

It was amusing to me also, but I didn't yet share their enthusiasm for talk of mating and pleasure—perhaps because of the differences between how our bodies seemed to work, or maybe it was yet another thing that would just come to me in time.

Despite those things which set us apart however, the three of us had grown incredibly close, and spent almost all of our free time together. We watched out for one another on raids, shared spoils and burdens alike, and slept in a pile in our lodgings.

We planned to meet up later this evening and explore, but in the meantime I was enjoying the solitude.

Nearby, the boy must have finally completed his preparations. He stood up and cast his line into the water, then, whilst he waited for the fish to begin to bite, he started whistling a muffled tune.

It sounded familiar—almost nostalgic and comforting—but I couldn't place where I would have heard it.

I watched him fish, and could have sworn that he kept stealing glances at me. Though as with his response to my smile, I couldn't really tell for the cloth about his face.

From what I could make out of him, in the flickering glow cast by Azure's streets, he looked to be maybe only eight summers old. Perhaps younger, but I wasn't really too sure, having seen only a few Hobgoblin children of that age over the years, and he lacked the pointed ears of a Kimora.

He was dressed in a dark pair of cloth trousers, that were puffy and loose down to just below his knees, where they were bound with some sort of wraps. His large feet were bare, but for rings on several of the toes, that glinted and sparkled when they caught the firelight.

Around his waist he had a sash, within which he had tucked a curved knife that he used to cut his fishing line and slice up his bait fish.

Above that, he wore a loose blouse and some sort of small, buttoned tunic.

It was a curious way of dressing. I had expected the denizens of the port to dress as the Legion had in their fortress, given Karthak's assertion that this was a Legion city as well, but everyone seemed to wear similar clothing to the boy's.

It was warm in Azure, and the coastal breeze carried with it no chill. I would be happy to wander bare-skinned or with only a light cloak, but had been told by Star-Star that within strange cities, I should be sure to dress as though ready for a skirmish.

I wasn't though. I lacked many of the metal plates I would usually protect myself with, and carried only my dagger for a weapon.

I had at least taken care to paint and adorn myself as though for a raid, but I had spent less time than usual, due to having been caught up with weaving trinkets and charms into Mazgar's mane.

She always seemed to struggle with such things, but I suspected that she was just lazy.

All the same, outfitted as I was, I had been the focus of some curiosity, and could forgive the boy his stolen glances.

I pulled my needle and thread from its place in my satchel and began to stitch another row into my Vyshiv.

Embroidering during peaceful moments supposedly let the calm flow through the thread and into the Vyshivka, and I could scarcely recall a more peaceful moment than this.

Despite the fireflies that danced on the surface of the ocean however, it proved a little too dark to stitch without pricking my fingers—

so I tucked my needle and thread away, and decided to try my luck with the boy one more time.

If that proved futile as well, then I'd head back into the city streets to locate the others, and find out what all the fuss was about with brothels and bathhouses.

"Little boy. Care to speak with me?"

He stopped whistling his tune and turned his head.

"Tell me, why do you cover your face?" I asked, being sure to speak slowly, and hopefully sound friendly. "Is that flowing cloth the garb of your people?"

"It is," he replied. "And is that embroidered cloth the garb of yours?" his accented voice was a lot deeper than I was expecting, and it threw me off guard, giving me pause before I answered.

"Yes it is," I told him. "It is the way all Vulkari dress. Well, except in this place for some reason."

"So you claim you are a Vulkar. Is this not strange?" he spoke, returning his attention to his so far unsuccessful fishing.

"No. It isn't strange," I said. "I mean, sure my body is different, but in spirit I am no less Vulkar than any of my sisters."

"Sisters? The Vulkari are your sisters?"

"Yes they are. We hunt together, eat together, raid together, and share all things. Whether joy or troubles," I told the child proudly.

"And the Warlord? She is your mother then?"

"I'm not so sure," I replied. "In a way she is, but at the same time, she is an older sister, under Yanghar the Mother of all Vulkari."

"And you believe this? Truly?"

I nodded. "Truly."

The boy dropped his rod. It clattered from the wooden planks and fell into the waters below, and he didn't so much as move to stop it. Then he turned to face me fully.

He began to remove his veil and spoke—slowly and deliberately, and with no more accent:

"Then, little Zyntael Fairwinter, you truly have chosen a most unusual path—since last ours crossed."

iv.

I threw myself upon the Ratling, almost pitching us both into the water below.

"Phobos! I thought you were dead!" I cried out, almost overcome with tears of joy. "Why did you not find me? Why did you wait for so long?"

I had so many questions—so much I wanted to tell the little Gnome, but he merely held me in a quiet embrace.

After a long while, he pushed me away from himself, and rough hands upon my bare arms, held me before him as he looked me up and down.

"You have grown so much. The scrawny child, eager to escape her captors—now, almost a woman. One of those captors herself," he remarked. "How many summers now? Thirteen? Fourteen?"

"At least fifteen. I have seen so much. Done so much. I barely know where to begin!" I was excited to pour it all out, but he narrowed his eyes at me and shook his head.

"We should distance ourselves from any that may pry. Let us take a boat, and row out beyond earshot of potential lurkers in the shadows."

And we did just that—climbing unsteadily into someone's rickety wooden dinghy, then paddling a short way out into the gentle waters.

"Now, tell me what happened. After you stabbed me," he said, once we were a satisfactory distance from the pier. He rubbed the back of his hand where my borrowed blade had found its mark, as he spoke.

"Well I was taken by Urga, before Karthak and her lieutenants," I explained, my words flowing almost too quickly for me to speak them properly. "Karthak, she asked me about you. She wanted to know how I knew you, where you were heading. Lots of things."

I thought back to that time. I couldn't honestly remember all that much. It was as though a fog obscured the images, and dulled the feelings in my mind.

"We travelled east. To the Legion fortress. I remember that at first I was bound up like a trophy. But I can't recall much else of it, and I can't recall why that was," I said.

"The frontier fortress of Threydon. Yes, I recall. You spent time with the braggart and liar, Janos Grunwald. You worked the forges and the bellows."

"Yes, but how do you know?" I was taken aback by his knowledge of my time there.

"I kept a watch from afar. There was never a safe chance to reach out to you though. And truth be told, as hard as it may have been for you, it was always the safest place for you to be," he sighed. "Karthak would have sought you out, wherever you were."

It was strange to hear. She had left me there, by her own later admission, to learn from the Imperial folk, and to fulfil some deal struck with Manox Threydon.

"You could have found me. Got word to me at the very least," I said.

"And disrupt your chosen fate? No. You had set a course of your own, and it was not my place to intervene."

"You sound a lot like Karthak, you know. Everyone around me is always speaking of fate and destiny, then neglecting to tell me a damned thing! It really is quite frustrating!" I told him seriously. "Please, for once just speak honestly. I have had my fill of mystery and riddle-work."

He laughed and then gazed up at the stars.

"I shan't withhold my thoughts from you. I know that it mustn't be fun to be constantly kept in the dark. But please, continue your tale. How did you come to be, well, this way?" He gestured at my adornments.

"Well, once I returned to the warband, we ventured into the wild hills and there we collected the other pups. We eight trained for many moons, and when we were ready, we joined our first raid."

Phobos sat quietly and listened whilst I described the rituals and trials, the things we learnt, and the many raids we had embarked upon over the summers.

"A true Vulkar you are, then," he said when I finally finished my tale.

"Now it is your turn. You must tell me what happened after you were swept away by the rapids!" I told him.

"I barely survived that icy plunge. Washed up a long way down river, my first thoughts were of rescuing you. But try as I did, I was far too weak to embark upon such a quest.

"I was taken in by farming folk whilst I rested and regained my strength, and by the time I reached the Blackfort, you were long gone." He smirked. "Such is the price of dallying."

"Anyway, I tracked the warband and saw that they had made off eastward—to trade with the Legion. So I slipped within the walls of the Goblin city, and spied upon you—unseen and unnoticed."

"You said."

"Yes, so once I was sure that you were safe in the hands of that old fool, I set off to see if I could locate your family and friends."

"Did you find them? Are they safe?" I leaned forward, eager to hear news of them.

"I did. But it is not a pleasant story for me to tell you." A frown creased his brow, and Phobos shifted position before continuing.

"Your mother is no longer with the living. For that, I am eternally sorry. Though, it was not the Vulkari that slew her—merely a fever."

A long unfelt sadness briefly stirred within my heart. I hadn't spared a thought for those whom I left behind, in a long time—each passing day having further obscured the memory of them. I wasn't all that sure why really, but for whatever reason, the loss I had felt in the early months no longer troubled me in quieter moments.

"What of the others? I have an infant sister—a father too. And there was a boy. Does he yet live?" I asked quietly.

"Your father and sister do indeed survive; I spoke to both even. Of that friend of yours, I could learn nothing, for he had ventured off some time earlier.

"I reassured your father that you were safe, strong, and growing stronger each day. That one day you may return, a woman he might barely recognise. I don't know if that will be possible for now however. Those lands fly the purple banner, and unfortunately, I am unsure of their fates of late—for our meeting was many seasons ago."

I didn't really know how to process this information. Despite the smallest ache for the loss of my birth mother, I didn't feel any burning desire to seek out my village. The world somehow seemed bigger than that now.

"Thank you for finding them, Phobos Lend. You are decent after all," I told the little man.

"You know, Grunwald—Janos, did you call him? He certainly had bad things to say of you though. Star-Star too, told me that it was because of you that I was taken by the warband in the first place. You are spoken of unkindly by almost all who know you, and I am confused as to why."

"I suppose it is to be expected from those who do not understand. I make no claims that I am anything but myself. I serve no gods nor Spirits, but work where work is needed—and for whomsoever needs it done."

He stretched out and looked at me with an oddly cold expression.

"Zyntael Fairwinter. There are many things in this world that even Karthak with her Spirits, and Threydon with his advisors and spies, could only hope to know. I do as I must to ensure that the world remains as it should. This may irk those who see my loyalties as fickle, but they do not understand that my true loyalty will always be to freedom."

I rolled my eyes and sighed.

"And there are those riddles once more. At this rate, I am starting to think Mazgar and Sarga may be right to focus only on things that go in, and things that come out of people's bodies," I said, mostly to myself.

"I assure you I do not mean to be evasive, I told you I would speak honestly. My path is my own though, and like yours is with you, it is a thing that owes no explanation to any but the one walking it."

He leaned forward and brushed my cheek affectionately with his fingers.

"I do not mean to trouble you, young warrior, but I chose this time to approach you for a reason."

I looked up at his emerald eyes, kindly and warm once more, reflecting the dancing lights, just as the water around us did.

"What reason is that?" I asked.

"The threat of open war hangs over us all. I worry that you and your 'sisters' as you now call them, will be thrust into the thick of it. Two powers clash, and their collision is nothing you should want to be caught in the midst of."

He gestured back at the mansion on the hillside. "Within the walls of the harbourmaster's opulent home, your leader seeks to grow her numbers. To assure survival, within the conflict to come. Or should that fail, to at least negotiate the means for her Vulkari to escape that conflict's reach. One way or another…"

"What do you expect me to do though? Karthak follows the guidance of the Spirits, and will do what is right for us. I'm sure of it," I told him.

He raised an eyebrow. "You believe that those Spirits truly speak to her?"

"Well yes, I've spoken to them too. They showed me a future—of me, with child. A warlord myself."

"That is interesting, and quite the surprise. I had long suspected the belief of your war chief to be misguided." Phobos sat quietly in thought for a moment, stroking his chin.

"Tell me…" he said at last. "When you spoke with these Spirits, was this during one of your rituals? Had you imbibed potions brewed of fungi, and breathed the smoke of herbs?"

"No, it was in a cave. I forgot to tell you about that. My friends and I ventured into a forest and up a mountainside to find Karthak—early in the winter before our first raid. There I met a shapeshifter, who like everybody else, spoke in riddles and didn't really offer much in the way of help."

I shrugged.

The Ratling laughed. "The world is a queer place, my young friend. Spirits aside, I ask that you remember my words spoken when first we met: That you must forge your own way. For if war is to find us all, then you must be prepared to shift your loyalties and judgements—so as best to serve your own ends."

I nodded, though I didn't agree.

"Be careful that you don't blindly follow those that would lead you to doom, nor use you simply as tools to their benefit. After all, that is why I did not whisk you away from the Legion's custody. I do not want to be yet another agent who would seek to control your destiny."

He once again touched my face.

"You are growing into a fine woman, and I am sure you will continue to. Now I will return you to shore, and you can find your two scoundrel friends where they bask in the debauchery of this port." He began to row the boat back to the jetty.

Once we were again on dry land, Phobos pulled me into an embrace, the top of his wrapped head reaching only the middle of my chest. I held the little man tight against me. I didn't want to let him go again.

"I must leave to pursue my work elsewhere. If I am successful, you may find my warnings hollow. If not, then I will once again seek you out. Do not feel as though you must hide our meeting from those you trust, but be certain that such trust is well placed first."

He looked up at me with a broad and gentle smile, and his emerald eyes sparkled with affection.

"Stay safe, little Zyntael Fairwinter. Stay strong, and stay vigilant," he said. "Now go, and enjoy yourself in the bountiful port of Azure. And may moss ever cushion your footfalls."

Then we parted ways once more. This time, under far better circumstances. This time, with the knowledge that each of us was walking their chosen path.

⚔ ⚔ ⚔

I found Sarga first. Half-drunk, and covered in all manner of substances, she was relieving herself between two buildings—much to the horror of a small group of well-dressed, and wealthy looking merchants.

A guard stood nearby and watched with a grin, though did nothing to prevent her disorderly behaviour.

The burly man was equipped with a polished bronze breastplate. He carried a large round shield, a fancy looking spear, and a strange curved sword at his hip. He didn't cover his face with cloth, but rather, a carefully groomed beard of dark hair, which was shaped into a curled point.

He greeted me when I approached, prepared to have to answer for my friend's behaviour.

"Vulkar-Sister of Karthak. Our distinguished guest. Your other compatriot awaits inside, perhaps better able to tolerate the experience of our fabulous entertainment houses. She asked that I direct you to her, and keep an eye on this one."

He nodded towards Sarga.

"Thank you. You don't need to stay if you don't want to," I told him. I was sure he had better things to do than mother a drunken young raider as she made a mess of herself—and the alleyway.

The guard bowed to me, then marched away, and I approached the uncouth drunkard that was my friend.

"Zyntael! Zyntael! I am pissing on the streets of this fancy place. Nobody cares at all!" Sarga told me, her words slurred but sincere.

207

"I can see that Sister, though I suspect they've been paid not to care. Should we return to Mazgar then? You will have to tell me of your adventures, and perhaps we can go and have more together," I said, struggling to guide the bulky creature back to the entrance of the establishment.

"Ohoho! But you shall not want to leave this place! You shall not be prepared for the things you shall see!" she shouted excitedly—right in my face.

And she was right. I really wasn't prepared at all.

V.

We left the last building only a short while before the sun rose over the water, blinding and cruel where the previous day it had been so welcoming.

I had a fog in my head, could barely walk straight, and had a strange taste in my mouth, which could have been from any number of things that went down (or came back up) over the course of our drunken rampage.

Somehow, Mazgar now seemed to be in a sorrier state than Sarga, who helped her along poorly as they staggered down the street in front of me. They bumped into strangers and stalls alike as we made our way down to the water. This time, we went to a beach instead of the docks, and I looked forward to washing away whatever it was that matted my hair and made my filthy skin so sticky. How sticky I was, despite the time we'd spent in the steaming baths.

I didn't think it was possible to drink as much liquor, ale, and wine as we had, nor for me to keep up with the Vulkari. Though in fairness, they had been busy with it for a while before I found them.

At some point during the night, we ran into Star-Star and two other adults, as well as Oya and Uya. They had taught us a fun game that involved bouncing a coin around on the table, between the many pitchers and bottles that littered every establishment we visited.

It was surprising how far our coins carried us, but I didn't actually have any clue what things were worth, or how much wealth we even had.

In one place, we gambled and won another sack of the little square coins from some off-duty guards, who were far too distracted by the woman who danced around us. She was nude, and covered from head to toe with perfumed oils and shimmering paints, and she was very pretty.

In fact, much to the amusement of Sarga and Mazgar, there were an awful lot of naked people—many engaged in activities that I had always assumed were not to be carried out in view of others.

Because of such attractions, those men hadn't even noticed that neither myself nor Sarga could actually read the symbols on the cards we played, and so we were merely declaring ourselves to be winners and pouring drinks to distract them further.

We also fought with another group, and I could barely remember why, other than someone having pulled Uya's tail and Oya then flattening them with a barstool.

It was fantastic, though in the state I was in, I did little to help.

After our brawl, we had bought those battered Hobgoblin sailors some food as an offering of peace. Then together, we sat outside on a flat sandstone roof, sharing stories of raids—ours on land, theirs at sea.

"Zyntael…" Mazgar croaked, interrupting my hazy recollection. "I think I am going to be sick…"

She vomited into a tall urn, then both she and Sarga laughed pitifully.

"Honey! That tasted of honey! Do you remember the honey?" Mazgar said, turning clumsily back to face me and colliding with a shelf. Expensive looking rugs and carpets scattered upon the sandy path.

Sarga threw a handful of copper coins at the merchant, who simply stared in disbelief as we passed. I gave him a wave and a broad grin.

"The honey?" I vaguely remembered something. Maybe it would explain the stickiness.

"You spilt it upon yourself. You tried to lick it off your own chest and stomach. It was hilarious Sister! Do you not recall? Then you smeared it upon the dancing women too!" Sarga said, laughing as she spoke.

Mazgar almost collapsed with laughter at the reminder.

I could vaguely remember something like that, and it wouldn't surprise me in the least—given how utterly uncoordinated, and woefully suggestible the alcohol had rendered me.

"You spilt everything you touched!" Mazgar said between bouts of hysterical cackling.

"And you licked all manner of things too! Almost anything we told you to!" Sarga added.

It was too much for Mazgar, and the Vulkar buckled and collapsed; a heaving and shuddering wreck of uncontrollable mirth.

Sarga and I dragged her the rest of the way down the sand, to where the other Vulkari were lounging around and either reminiscing about the night's activity, or nursing their hangovers.

The warm water of the ocean was far more inviting in the light of day—a brilliant azure blue, which perhaps gave the port its name.

I bathed for some time; I lay in the shallows and let the soothing tide wash over my aching body—let it carry away trails of glittering residue and other mysterious substances that had caked my skin.

Some of the others soon joined me, and we spent a while scrubbing the filth from one another, and splashing about merrily.

I couldn't swim too well, but found that I could float easily enough in the ocean waters. It was curiously different from how I felt in the lakes and rivers of the land.

I liked Azure a lot.

I hadn't ever had fun of this sort, and wondered why more folk didn't live in such a manner. My mind drifted for a time until I suddenly recalled my meeting with Phobos Lend—all but forgotten about, once the first jug of ale ran dry.

I wondered if he had left the city by now, or if he still lurked around. I wondered if he had borne witness to last night's debauchery. I wondered if he would still recognise the little girl he had met hanging in the dungeon of the Blackfort. After all, I barely did.

※　※　※

Although the nights remained far more subdued than our first, we enjoyed Azure for a few weeks before assembling the warband, and beginning the long journey north again.

Karthak wore a necklace of seashells and pearls, gifted to her by the merchant lord, and she had embraced him warmly before we set off. She remained in a far better mood than usual, and so I guessed that her dealings with Shahbaz-Gill had gone well.

That fat Vulkar had personally seen us from his city's bounds, and had bestowed upon us fresh beasts with which to pull our carts and wagons.

The journey north went far quicker than our approach to Azure had been. This time our convoy followed one of the old roads that carved a path through the plains and hills alike, linking Azure with Threydon's fortress. When the overgrown tracks curved off to the east, we left them and went northwest instead—and by the last days of winter, we were mere leagues from the Blackfort.

Spared the usual dampness and rains, instead the weather remained in our favour as we climbed the foothills on our approach.

I was a little disappointed that we had not stopped to raid any of the villages or hamlets on our journey, despite how much that fact had vastly sped up our progress, and I yearned for the taste of combat once more.

The other young Vulkari felt the same, and occupied themselves with unnecessary preparation, and talk of raiding when we camped.

On a slightly overcast day, when the hills that enveloped the Blackfort were in sight before us, Karthak called for me to join her for a meal in her tent.

It was good to know that she hadn't forgotten about me, and as much as I enjoyed spending my time with my young sisters, I did miss our talk of the ancient knowledge that she held, and our conversations and musings on the nature of the world.

"Indeed Gill was generous to sponsor your activities in his city," Karthak told me, after I recounted our adventures—leaving out the meeting with Phobos, of course.

"He had no choice really, for he owes me much."

"Why is that?" I asked.

"Ah, that is a long tale, so I shall give you only a summary of what is important, my pup. You see, some of the male-folk of our people do not appreciate their lot in life." She grinned. "Gill was one such Vulkar, so left to find glory as a pirate in Azure."

"He was young and foolish and so was beset upon by brigands whilst travelling through the drylands that we recently did. There I came upon him, myself only a young raider tracking a group of sand dwellers with a few of my sisters. And together we liberated the sorry fool from his plight."

"So for that, he owes you? You didn't seem too fond of one another when we met him," I remarked.

"Well over the years, we have had many dealings. Being young and impressionable, I was attracted to his sense of adventure and quick mind, so for a time, took him as a mate. Though it was short lived, for I certainly believe him to be misguided, and he believes me to be overly concerned with the original ways of the Vulkari. 'Superstitious' he says." The mighty warrior almost looked wistful as she stared into her goblet—a strange thing for the usually fearsome Vulkar to portray.

"So did you carry his pup then? I have often wondered about that," I said. But instead of answering, Karthak quickly finished her drink, fetched a fresh bottle and some more meat, and promptly changed the subject.

"The Blackfort is home to Urga and her band, as was the case before I united the warbands. Did I ever tell you that? Garok was the leader of her own raiders too. Seafarers from Azure's sister port."

"No you never did," I said.

"Yes, Garok was one who saw the reason in increasing our strength through the joining of our numbers. Some, like Urga, did not feel the same way. Now though, we return to her domain and I doubt that she shall be pleased. Vulkari should not be cooped up in fortresses and cities. It runs contrary to the spirit of the wild that seethes in our blood."

She glanced up at me from the haunch of meat that she held.

"You should visit the room in which they chained you. It is good to view your past through stronger eyes. To see that it is when you are without shackles and walls around you that you are free—and so truly a Vulkar."

"I will do that," I told her. "Karthak, I have something to ask you. You just reminded me that I've never really thought about it."

"Yes?"

"Why did you really hold Phobos Lend captive? I know he worked with you, and for the Legion too. I know he was a spy or something. Star-Star once told me that he went back on a deal you made. So I ask, what happened?"

Karthak didn't answer immediately, but rather she moved over to the chest that contained her private trinkets, and the soaps and oils that I was proud that she continued to use herself.

"Let me show you something," she said, and retrieved the brown paper wrapped object that I recognised to be the little golden Vulkar hound and her unusual pup. The same trinket that I had stolen a look at, so long ago.

"This," she began, unwrapping the statuette. "This is you. It was given to me by the Pixie spy."

"I've seen that before. I found it when I returned from the Legion. I didn't mean to pry, but was searching for perfumes and soaps to use," I laughed. "I didn't want to choke on your stench, in honesty!"

She snorted. "I wonder what your past-self would say if you could smell yourself now! Anyway, I was given this. It was a message from the Spirits—that I was to seek you out."

"Okay. But why?" I asked.

"The Darkrunner, I believe the Sacharri call him, well he came to my camp one day as an envoy of his employer. He brought a request for an alliance between us and the Legion, and promised a season's work as a scout and a spy for my cause."

I listened to her as I ate.

"Previous to his arrival, the Spirits had whispered to me that he would deliver a sign of their intentions, and sure enough, as token of his goodwill, he offered this trinket."

"So how is that me? It could be any Kimora," I asked. "And why then, did you imprison him in the Blackfort?"

"I held counsel with the Vaela of the Whispering Caverns—the Shaman—and she spoke of the child as one possessed of an innate and unquenchable bravery. One of thirty or so seasons of age," Karthak told me. "So I sent the little man away to find such a Kikimora. Once the spy had advised me of the location of a village, with a Kikimorin girl-pup of the right age, I took a group of my most loyal, and sought out the little Bare-Skin promised to me."

The Warlord sighed as she recalled her frustration.

"But time and again, the Ratling failed me. And each pup we claimed, was either a pathetic coward, or too old—so fit only as a slave to be sold. Eventually, I grew tired of this, so ventured once more into the forests of the Spirit-guide. There, she told me to sit under the light of the new spring moon, holding the figurine. To call upon those same Spirits that had come to Yanghar and given her purpose."

She grinned at me, likely reading the skepticism on my face.

"Yes. They did not answer. Not in words, anyway. But rather, when I grew impatient and made to leave, cursing my faith and casting the damnable figurine into the grass, I was overcome with a profound sense of guilt.

"I had no right to demand the Spirits guide me. They would do so at their own whim. So, I retrieved the statuette, but in doing so, I pricked my finger upon the sharp ear of the little suckling Kimor-pup. And her hair became as crimson. I knew then that it was the sign I was hoping for, and knew what to search for."

"That seems an odd sort of sign though," I told her.

"And yet here you are; crimson haired daughter of Yanghar, with the body of a Kikimora." She gestured at me with a shrug. "The Ratling sought out a village within which I could find you, and so I did."

"And the reason you chained him up?"

"Well, whilst I made to claim you as my own, the Ratling had been feeding information to Threydon, and the Spirits only know who else. For when I sent an envoy of my own to the Sacharri Legion, she returned with the news that there had been no offer of peace made through the Ratling, but that the Hobgoblin was curiously aware of my every move in seeking you out.

"I had Lend imprisoned by Urga in my absence, and was set to extract the truth from the little man when you released him into the rapids."

So it really had been all because of Phobos Lend that my life had taken such an unexpected path.

"I met him in Azure," I admitted to Karthak. "He had spied on me for some time, he said. I don't really know why, though he said it was to ensure my safety."

"Bah! Did he now? Well ensure you do not pay heed to his lies, should you cross paths with him again. I hold no anger for the runt, for here you are. And I have no doubts that Manox Threydon shall do what is right—come time. For now though, we must turn our attention to those who would seek to forge bonds with the purple plague. Soon, they shall march upon these lands in no small numbers, and I would prefer that we were neither trampled beneath them, nor used as the tip of their spear."

"Do Urga and her Vulkari want to be a part of the Merchant Combine?" I asked.

"That hag has mentioned a leaning towards that option, as she greatly distrusts the Sacharri. Abiding them only insofar as they serve to be useful in the trading of spoils and slaves. I hope though, that she has reconsidered, and so we return to the Blackfort to extend a better offer. We shall know come the light of tomorrow's day."

We chatted for a while longer before the weight of the brandy started to tug on my eyelids.

I rolled myself up in the furs and blankets at the foot of Karthak's bed—just as I had years ago. This time, there was no fear that kept me from sleep, and my mind easily drifted into dreaming.

There was a red sky. Burning and inky smoke that billowed from dotted fires—maybe a village.
I hovered above the scene, disconnected from my body. Below me there stood the unmistakable silhouettes of Vulkari, they were gathered before a pedestal—no, a well—atop which there stood a smaller figure.
I tried to move closer, but couldn't get far. The charred air was like a thick oil, through which I could hardly swim.
But just those few yards closer, and I could make out that it was a woman that stood and addressed the gathered Vulkar warriors.
She held something in her hand, and to the cheers and cackling of the Vulkari that increased in their pitch and fervour, she raised it above her triumphantly.
It was a severed head.
I remained there, suspended above the mob and peering down curiously.
Then, without warning the woman turned her head and looked straight at me.
I fell, tumbling over and over, hurtling toward the blackened earth, the smoke whistling in my ears as I shot through it like a rock.

⌘   ⌘   ⌘

I woke with a start, having bashed my forehead against the wooden floor of Karthak's wagon.

Dazed, I got up and staggered out into the light of day. I headed over to the tent where my sisters slept, to see if I could find Mazgar and Sarga, but they weren't in the tent. Rather, they were gathered around the provisioner's carts, chatting excitedly with one of the scouts who was explaining something apparently very exciting, in between mouthfuls of jerky.

Just as Karthak said, this morning Urga's grim bastion had finally come into view of their party, so they had hurried back to the warband to tell Karthak—and apparently now everybody else—the news.

The Blackfort now flew the purple banner.

We were too late.

vi.

M y head hurt a little. Somewhere behind my eyes. The glyph which marked the Merchant Combine's banner still somehow unnerved me, but I couldn't help but stare at it.

From the grassy hillock a mere stone's throw from the blackened rock of the fort's border wall, I watched Urga's troops scurry around.

I wasn't entirely sure if Karthak meant to recapture the fort through violence, or still held out some hope that its inhabitants might abandon their new alliance in favour of whatever it was she was planning for us.

Even so, I had equipped myself for combat and joined the other young raiders when they decided to approach the fort for a closer look.

"It is not quite Azure is it?" Mazgar said, a look of disappointment clear on her face.

"And you were brought here? By Karthak?"

"Yeah. It looked even worse then, I think," I told her, and pointed out where barricades had been erected, and crumbling black walls were repaired.

"See there, and there? Those were just rubble. And that bit over there, near that little building thing? We actually collapsed that bit—so all of that stuff is new."

The Vulkari had been busy in the many seasons since I had been a prisoner in the grim place. There were new watch towers, walkways and scaffolds—well constructed by the looks, and Mazgar nodded as I pointed them out to her.

Urga's Vulkari had also reinforced the keep itself, at some point even repairing the massive hole that had once opened the side of the building.

"Do you think they had help? I can't see anything but Vulkari from here, and there don't look to be many of them," I asked.

"Well they have Combine flags and banners so there must be people from there. Or at least there were," Mazgar said, then paused briefly. "Where do you suppose 'there' is?"

"Feldspar told me the Combine ruled his homeland. He said they had a city called Kirke-something. But I don't know where they're from, originally. We should probably ask Karthak."

"You are her favourite, you do it," Sarga said. She had been strangely quiet for the last few days, and seemingly short tempered when I did try to talk to her.

Mazgar was still her usual self though, and rolled her eyes at Sarga.

"Well I suppose we should return to Garok. Hopefully the others are finished with whatever they were doing." Mazgar grinned. "And I am hungry."

"When are you not?" I said and took one last look at the strange and unpleasant banners that fluttered in the gentle summer breeze.

We ate fish that Yinnik and Otrek had snared in a net from one of the many icy rivers near our camp, and talked excitedly about the assault that we all hoped would begin soon.

It was a strange thing though, how eager the young Vulkari were to spill the blood of their own kind. But then again, I was sure one of the many villagers I had thrust my spear into or cut open with my dagger could have been a Kimora like me; their recognisable features hidden beneath armour or cloth.

I didn't really pay attention to that sort of thing, and in fact, I was surprised at just how little the lives I'd claimed over the recent year had actually affected me.

When I was a small child, I assumed that killing someone was a great and terrible act—an act that would weigh heavy on one's mind. I had been sure that the phantoms of those whose lives were taken, would follow the killer in their dreams.

But as it turned out, killing was both surprisingly easy to do, and surprisingly easy to accept. And no phantoms clawed at my mind as I slept. Instead, there were only dreams of more raids, fiercer combat, and richer spoils.

If anything—I resolved before re-joining the conversation—I rather enjoyed battle, and I wasn't even ashamed of that fact any more.

"Pass me the bottle Uya." I held a hand out for the brew that was being passed around.

I took a swig of the bitter drink and blinked away the tears it brought to my eyes.

"Ugh! It goes down like sand! Where did you find this one? The desert?" I coughed.

Uya cackled. "I made it. I mixed it from some other bottles!"

"You just picked the ones with the pretty labels right? Spirits only know what is in it." Oya nudged her twin "You been spending time with Narod, learning his alchemy and Magick? Zyntael shall be jealous."

I shot her a glare.

"Hey now. I think we have established that Zyntael still likes her chances with that Hobgoblin boy she told us about. The one from the Sacharri fort—what did you say his name was? Talked to him all night long, right? But that was not all you did, was it?" Mazgar said with an exaggerated wink to the others.

"Ah shut up you horse-son! I told you I only spoke to him for any length of time, what? Once or twice?" I put the cork in Uya's bottle and threw it at my friend.

"And if anyone is jealous of the many admirers I apparently have, then by Yanghar it is you! Do you not remember how desperate you were to speak to those pirates in Azure?" I mimicked her voice and pretended to swoon over imaginary Vulkar sailors,

"Oh tell me more about your sailing and your adventures! Please show me your ship!"

"Show me your mast!" Yinnik added and we fell about laughing.

Mazgar looked resolute in her defiance.

"They were exciting and had impressive scars. I think you all have bad taste," she grumbled. "Anyway, I am sure there shall be plenty of male-folk to go around once we take the Blackfort."

"Who says we are going to? Urga is not stupid," Sarga suddenly interjected, snatched the bottle from Mazgar, and downed the rest of the draft. "Or weak," she added.

"What is itching your arse?" Mazgar asked her.

"You are behaving like pups. We are not going to fight our own for no good reason. Do not be so silly," Sarga said, and scowled at each of us as she spoke. "You really think that Urga would just throw away what it means to be a Vulkar? Take on the beliefs of the Combine, whatever they might be?

"I do not think so. And anyway, who is to say that even if she did at least house them, Karthak would want to kill our sisters and take their fort? There is more to it than that. There has to be."

We all quietly sat and regarded her.

"Why do you care so much? I thought that of all of us, you were the most eager to fight?" Ar-Tarak asked her.

"Well not if it is pointless and stupid," Sarga said quietly. "But what do I care? You have your fantasies of killing our own, and you can keep them. I am going to get some air."

And with that, she cast the empty bottle onto the dirt, stood, and strode away.

Mazgar and I shared a glance, each as confused as the other. Then I sighed, and got up to follow the angry Sarga.

※　※　※

I found Sarga some distance from the camp. She sat atop a hillock that offered a view of both our forces and the Blackfort. I coughed softly to announce my presence, then joined her on the rock upon which she sulked.

"What do you want?" she asked quietly, but not looking away from the gloomy fortress ahead.

"What's wrong, Sarga?" I began. "You have been different of late. Ever since we caught wind of the Blackfort flying the purple banners. You've been quiet, angry, and haven't been yourself."

I reached out to touch her shoulder, but she shuffled away slightly. "It is fine. I am fine."

"Clearly not," I corrected her. "Otherwise I wouldn't have said so. You know I hate riddles and mystery, so please. Just tell me honestly, what has been bothering you so?"

Sarga let out a long sigh, then turned to face me. She pulled herself fully onto the rock so that she sat cross legged before me.

"Do you know much about the way new Vulkari come into this world?" she began.

I grinned, thinking it to be a joke about mating, and was about to reply with a stupid remark, but then caught her serious expression and stopped myself.

"What do you mean?" I asked. "Not... *breeding,* right?"

"No, no. Of course not. I mean, when a Vulkar pup is birthed. After that, what is done with her. Has anyone told you?"

"Well yes, Karthak said that if the pup is a female, then she is taken to the temple to be raised by Yanghar the Mother. Is that not right? I mean, I didn't really question it. And it never occurred to ask one of you."

That was embarrassingly true. For all of the time spent with the others, we really hadn't spoken much about their lives before we'd met. Well, other than to share some of the games they'd learnt, and amusing stories they had.

"Vulkari do not know their own mothers. I mean birth mothers, that is. We just have Yanghar." She scratched at the lichen that sprouted from the rock. "There are other matriarchs, guards and helpers. They teach things too. But no Vulkar who is raised right is held by their mother instead of *the* Mother."

"Okay…"

"Well, you see, I was. For a short time anyway." It seemed like this was something that Sarga was ashamed of, but I couldn't really understand why. I simply nodded as she spoke.

"My mother kept me, believing that the old ways would not teach me to be strong enough for this new world. She thought that the Vulkari were dying out because we put far too much stock in the ancient traditions. You know, Karthak and her Spirits—that sort of stuff.

"Well, she held onto me for two whole seasons. I think, hoping to raise me as her own. The same way your mother would have done."

She was almost whispering as she told me this.

"I do not know if it was by force or by choice, but she did end up sending me to the temple. It was Karthak's doing. And even though I was very young and the words I speak now were not there to describe the situation at the time, I remember the day.

"I was in a room that had a fireplace. I was pushing sticks into the burning maw of that glowing beast—imagining that I was feeding it so that it would not eat me.

"You know, that room may have been in there somewhere. In fact, I am pretty sure it was."

She pointed down at the Blackfort.

"I remember the rain, and the dark stone. I also remember the smell—sharp and bitter. If I smell it when we enter the fortress, then I shall know for certain it was my original home. Anyway, Karthak came. There was some argument, and I remember many warriors getting ready for something. Then my mother came to me and wrapped me in cloth. She bundled me into a cart, driven by a male that talked non-stop, and so I left for the temple.

"I do not really remember much else. Maybe just flashes or glimpses that I might have even dreamt instead, but I remember the other pups. They were already there in the Temple of the Mother, and I recall that they did not much like me to begin with."

Sarga turned to me and smirked. "I beat them until they did."

I laughed—unsure as to whether that was actually a joke or not.

"So do you know who your mother is then? Does she yet live?" I asked.

"Yes and yes. She certainly does live for now, though if you all have your way, then that much shall not be so."

"Urga?" I asked. The similarities in their rusty fur and dark eyes suddenly occurred to me.

"Urga is your mother?"

"Yeah." Sarga shrugged and turned back towards the fort where that mother lurked.

"Oh wow. All of this time. I didn't know, and I'm sure I've told you some awful things about her. Why didn't you say anything earlier?"

"There was no real need. I guess that before, I was happy to accept Yanghar as my Mother. I mean, I obviously still do. It's just that with how things look now, I just get the feeling that Karthak seems to be determined to separate the two of us, whichever way," Sarga said.

"Well I don't think it's personal or anything…" I began, but Sarga cut me off with a snort.

"Of course not! Do not be an oaf! The Spirits guide Karthak on her own strange path, but she has proven herself as the true Warlord. I just hope that it does not end how the others seem to want it to. My memories of Urga are fond—brief and fuzzy though they are."

I struggled to imagine any aspect of Urga that could inspire pleasant memories. She was a horrible and downright scary Vulkar.

Then again, Sarga's own fondness for violence, and her generally brutish sense of humour did make the possibility slightly more likely.

"I don't think Karthak will seek violence, when there are other options. And even though I really don't like your mother, it isn't a reflection upon you. You know that right?" I said.

Sarga smiled and took my hands in hers.

"Of course I do. I have been her daughter and your friend all of this time! I only tell you what I do because of that fact. And anyway, I have liked you since our trial. None of the others ever really stood up to me, yet you did. I mean, it obviously could not happen now, but back then I misjudged you and so you bested me. I respect that strength, and even if your body is lacking, you still carry it within you."

I may have been blushing.

"Thank you," I said, and avoided eye contact whilst Sarga resumed her frustrated fidgeting.

"You know, I don't think that the others really want to kill Urga and her warriors," I told my friend, not entirely convinced of that fact myself but hoping it would cheer her up all the same.

But Sarga was smarter than the others. She easily saw through me, and frowned in suspicion.

"You do not *really* believe that do you? We have not raided in weeks! Have not tasted blood or victory, so of course they want to fight!" She sighed. "I understand and would feel the same were it not Urga in the fort. And do you want to know what the worst thing about it is?"

Sarga hopped down from the rock and began pacing as she spoke.

"The worst thing is that I feel shame for my desire not to kill Urga, should it come to that. I feel bad that I am having those feelings because I know I should not be. My Mother is Yanghar. It is wrong to push my loyalty to the warband and our war chief aside, in favour of Urga, simply because she birthed me—no, *kept* me."

I sat quietly, watching her stride back and forth.

"She should never have kept me. That is not the Vulkar way of things. There are rules. Maybe this sort of thing is why! And now, because she broke them, I am feeling conflicted—which is stupid and weak."

"No it isn't Sarga. You just said before that you think I'm strong, but I'm conflicted about stuff all the time! I never really know what I am doing until I'm doing it, and even when I do know what to do, I doubt myself once I've done it!" I said and she stopped and looked at me, puzzled.

"What was that last bit? Say it again." A grin was slowly spreading across her face.

"I don't know, what did I say? I doubt myself after I do the things I do? Or that I don't really know what I'm doing?" I started to grin as well.

"That was the weirdest way to say that you think too much that I have ever heard. Who even speaks like that?" she said. "If that is the sort of thing that thinking too much results in, then I think I shall stop now."

"Well you and Mazgar always tell me that I do, so now you know what it's like." I shrugged.

"Yes. And it is stupid." She laughed. "Forget Urga, forget my beginnings, forget all of that stuff. Let us just do things the Vulkar way, like she should have done in the first place—let us go drink, make fun of Smallest, and try to make Uya and Oya fight each other!"

So we did just that, and to my relief Sarga seemed to be fixed.

She didn't seem to care one way or another about the outcome of the situation, nor did she want to know what was said by Urga to the messenger who was sent to the Blackfort to parley.

Sarga seemed to be back to normal, but beneath the surface, she probably wasn't. I knew all too well how to push my feelings deep inside myself, where they wouldn't show, and I suspected that Sarga was doing exactly that.

It wasn't really my place to push things though. She would work things out on her own, and until then we'd just do a little more drinking than normal. There wasn't really much else to do anyway.

Once our messenger came back from the Blackfort, Karthak kept us in suspense as to what it meant for us. She held council with Star-Star, Kovvik-Shar, and the other older warriors, and none of them would tell us what was going on.

All eight of us were bored out of our minds waiting, and so planned another adventure—like the one we had embarked upon into the Whispering Cavern.

Otrek said that she'd heard from one of the adults that apparently there was another place nearby, where Karthak would go to consult the Vaela, so we had decided to locate it.

I had a feeling that it wasn't just me who wanted answers this time, and knew for sure that we all hoped that those answers might be guarded by more Kobaloi.

We each readied ourselves for our journey, and Otrek tried to find out specifically where we should search. Once she had the rumoured location—somewhere to the northwest, beyond the Blackfort, and high in the Stormhills—we set off on our quest. Oya told a few of the older Vulkari that we were going hunting in the nearby forests, and that we would be back within a few days.

As we left camp, early in the morning and full of excitement, something that Star-Star once said to me sprung to mind:

"In the wild lands we currently occupy, there are far more monstrous beasts than any Vulkar ever aspired to be."

She had suggested travelling with a friend or two then, and for some reason, this time I had a nagging worry that even seven friends might not be enough.

vii.

It took almost a whole day just to reach the rocky mountain foothills that rose from the highlands behind the Blackfort. And it took another two, to climb those ridges that stretched northward, far beyond where we had trained in the valleys and forests as pups, so long ago.

We made every effort to skirt around the fortress, hidden by the crests of the surrounding hills and ridges, and careful to stay out of sight of Urga's guards—as well as whatever else might lurk in that black structure currently.

"Why do we need to be so secret? Karthak has been in talks with Urga, and we have spied upon her walls a few times already," Oya complained, whilst we heaved and panted, rising ever higher into the western hills.

"Because, stupid," Uya replied "If one of the lookouts sees us circling the fort and thinks it is some sneak attack being launched, then we could cause all sorts of problems for our sisters!"

I had to agree. As much as the extra care slowed us down, the last thing we needed was to accidentally cause conflict. Who knew what rage Karthak might unleash upon us if we ruined whatever plans she had? I certainly didn't want to find out.

"You think you have it bad?" I wheezed. "Your backwards legs carry you far easier than my legs do."

Ar-Tarak stopped and glared at me as I struggled up and over a stretch of loose rock. "Backwards legs? You are the one with backwards legs, and so you walk slow."

She was right and could have stopped there, but decided to carry on.

"You have no fur and so you freeze in the cold. You cannot smell, you are practically deaf, and your arms are spindly and pathetic! Backwards legs... I shall bend your legs backwards... Horse-son..." the wiry Vulkar grumbled as she walked away.

Mazgar shot me a grin and I grinned back. We'd had the same conversation countless times over, so I wasn't really fussed with Ar-Tarak's words. If anything, I was glad that my borrowed Sacharri insult had caught on—even if none of us could quite figure out its meaning.

"So Otrek, did you find out more about the Shaman than just where it lives?" I asked once I'd managed to catch up to the group of Vulkari.

"Not really. I talked to Tan-Shar. She did not really know much about the Shaman, but she did go with Karthak once." Otrek shrugged. "Waited outside a little cave that was burrowed into a big old tree, she said. Apparently Karthak went in alone. So I guess it is just you and she, who have actually met the thing."

"Well I gave these two their chance, but they wanted to play thumbs instead," I told Otrek, nodding towards Sarga and Mazgar—who were leaning against a slab of mossy rock and chatting about Kobaloi.

We joined them in their discussion, and carried on talking about those strange and wild little monsters as we walked.

Thankfully the land had flattened out somewhat, so the trek across the plateau and to the mountain forest went considerably quicker than our ascent had.

We camped out at the edge of the old forest, sure to take turns at standing watch this time. It was a spooky place. Old dead trees stood, their gnarled fingers swaying and clattering in the cold evening wind. And the sky that they clawed at was a dark grey, which denied the existence of summer as it threatened to drop rain—even if it never really committed to it for longer than a few minutes of drizzle at a time.

It made the time I spent scanning the edge of the forest and the deep pools of shadow amongst the rocks and boulders a tense and unpleasant experience.

I sat away from the crackling and hissing fire so that its light wouldn't blind me, wrapped in a rabbit-fur cloak and with my back against a tall rock.

Even though Yinnik was also awake, and would look over at me every now and then to check that everything was all clear, I felt deeply afraid that something would come stalking from the tree line—from beneath the curtain of dangling vines and cobwebs that fluttered eerily in the gloom, or from amidst the dark and cold rocks around where my sisters slept.

Those cobwebs unnerved me too—whatever made them must have been big, numerous, or both.

I distracted myself from my fear by trying to remember the details of my last visit to the Spirit-talker. I could recall its appearance as an older me, but the words it spoke were fuzzy in my mind. Something about a winter morning—some ill-omen to do with the Combine.

"Beware the scourge, on your sixteenth frost." Was that it?

I sat there trying to remember for some time, and picturing the version of myself that the creature—whatever it actually was—had appeared as.

She had been a battle-hardened warrior, by the looks of her muscled body and numerous scars. And she had been pregnant.

I didn't really know why she had seemed so beautiful to me, given that she shared my boyish face, with its flat and broad features that I wasn't particularly fond of. The belly, carried by her short but still powerful frame, had appealed to me though.

It was strange that Karthak would desire such a future for me, and stranger still that she would go to all the lengths that she had, just to ensure that I—

A rock clattered loudly down the slope to my right.

I jolted upright and fully awake—had I actually fallen asleep?

My skin tingled and the small hairs on my arms stood proud, as I stared into the gloom with wide, unseeing eyes.

Yinnik had heard it too, and leapt to her feet—weapon in hand.

"Shhh…" She pressed a finger to her black lips, just as I opened my mouth to whisper to her.

Her ears rotated, tracking some sound that I couldn't hear, and the thin Vulkar sniffed the air with a sickly grimace on her face.

"Blood," she hissed. "Blood and metal. Like rust."

"Copper and iron," I told her. I'd smelled it before, and knew exactly what it was before the scent even reached me.

"Wake the others," she told me, and I crept over to where my sleeping sisters lay.

The fire was out. I hadn't noticed it die, though I was sure that I hadn't fallen asleep. But it was out nonetheless, and dead cold too.

In the dull glow of the moonlight, I could make out the huddled shapes of the others, so moved to wake them. But I stopped in my tracks when my eyes fell on the soft earth near the fire.

There were footprints everywhere.

They weren't Vulkar, and they certainly weren't mine. They were long and thin, and they weaved a path around each sleeping figure—someone or *something* had been walking around the camp. How had we not seen them?

I looked up at Yinnik, horrified, pointing to the ground, but unable to find the words to say. She squinted at me questioningly then her eyes widened in fright.

Puzzled, I squinted back at her. Then it occurred to me, and my blood ran cold; she wasn't looking at me, she was looking *behind* me.

I whirled around to see what had frightened Yinnik, my hand moving to the hilt of my Legion blade.

There, in the darkness of the undergrowth, about fifteen feet away and partially obscured by a veil of silvery webs, stood the most horrifying creature that I'd ever seen.

It was at least as tall as a Vulkar female, though where they were hunched over so never really reached their full height, this thing stood stretched out, with the posture of a Hobgoblin.

But no Hobgoblin nor Vulkar ever looked so vile.

Its skin was as pale as chalk, its arms and legs long and thin, and its face was nothing like any creature's I'd ever seen. It didn't appear to have eyes, ears, nor any noticeable nose—only a gaping, toothless maw.

I stepped slowly backwards, away from the monstrosity—as quietly and as calmly as I could, despite the relentless drumming of hot blood inside my head. I glanced down at the unmoving Vulkari. Sarga was closest.

I looked back at the thing, and kept my eyes locked on it whilst I carefully crouched down to shake my oblivious friend. I could swear it was somehow closer now.

Sarga stirred, and I desperately tried to quiet her, pointing to the figure that stood dead still in the tree line.

I wasn't sure what Yinnik was doing. I couldn't hear her, and didn't want to take my eyes off the creature, but Sarga gripped my arm and I unintentionally met her gaze.

There was something off about her, but in the moment, I really couldn't tell what it was. Until she spoke. Her voice was almost distant—distorted somehow.

"Do not be afraid." It wasn't Sarga.

I tried to pull my arm away, and glanced quickly up at the pale figure. It had turned to face me, definitely closer than it had been. Its mouth moved, but the sounds came from my friend.

"Do not fight. Do not run. Do not be afraid. Only sleep. "

The thing could tell me that a hundred times, a thousand times, and it wouldn't change a thing.

I wasn't just afraid, I was far past that.

In a panic, I wrenched my arm free of Sarga's grip, and pushed myself away. I scrambled backwards and frantically tried to distance myself from it all.

I cried out. "Yinnik! Kill the horse-son!"

I heard her snarl, and felt the air ripple. Then my ears were filled with a terrible squealing. I clutched my head and staggered to my feet, turning to see Yinnik throw another rock. The first had hit the beast in its chest, and the second struck its skull. Almost too quickly for me to comprehend, the frightful thing dropped to all fours—its limbs bent outwards like a spider.

And it scurried away into the darkness, clicking and hissing as it went.

"Are you hurt?" Yinnik called out to me, another rock held ready.

"No, I'm fine. What was that thing? It spoke through Sarga!" I stumbled over to check on her.

She was lying on her back, panting and whimpering softly. Her eyes were half closed and her tongue lolled from between spittle covered lips.

"Zyntael," she croaked. "I saw such things. Is this real? Am I awake?"

Yinnik eventually approached, and began rousing the others.

"What happened? Are you alright? I dreamt of bizarre things," Oya said, rubbing her eyes then looking around in confusion.

"You as well? I thought I might never wake," Uya told her twin.

Within moments, Yinnik and I had helped our groggy friends to their feet, and the last of the residue from whatever strange things had filled their heads seemed to have evaporated.

"That thing. It spoke through you," I told Sarga. "It told me not to run, and not to be afraid. And it told me to sleep!"

She shook her head.

"Well it is a good thing that you did not listen. I feel so drained. Like it was feeding on my very being. And the things I saw in my dreams…" She stared into the forest.

"I think it meant to ensnare us all. Maybe to eat us while we slept."

"It already was. Eating us, I mean," Ar-Tarak whispered. Then she looked at Yinnik and I, accusation in her eyes. "What were you two doing? Why were you not keeping watch?"

"We were!" Yinnik protested. "I was over there, and Zyntael was there. We were keeping watch and did not sleep or anything."

I nodded.

"Yinnik's right. We just didn't see the... whatever that was. We heard a sound. I came to look over by the fire, and I saw the prints. They were already there, like it had walked around you."

The others looked confused and scared.

"We did not see a thing. It is as if it was invisible or something."

"Well that is not good. Why did you not tell us that there were things like that in the forest? You only told us about the little forest beasts, not some invisible horror," Uya whined.

"We never encountered anything of the sort though, how would we know about it?" Mazgar replied. "So what now? Garok was right. There really are worse things in the wild."

For the next short while, we debated whether we should continue on into the forest where the creature had gone, or just turn back.

As the sun slowly began to drag itself over the eastern hills, and its rays pierced the greyish gloom around us, it seemed to me that it brought our sense of bravery and adventure back with it.

"So that's settled then. We carry on, but with fire and blade at the ready," Sarga said definitively.

And so we did.

It was easier going. The groping webs burned away before us, and each Vulkar scanned the flickering undergrowth, as we made our way into the gnarled and knotted forest.

The path we took was scattered with old bricks and paving slabs, long cracked by twisting roots, and reclaimed by the earth, but it made me think that there had once been a road that cut through the foliage.

We weren't really sure where it must have led though, since we hadn't really noticed any signs of civilisation, no matter how old, on our way up to the plateau.

"So did Tan-Shar say how deep they went? I feel as though we have been wandering for an eternity," I asked Otrek whilst we wound our way along the side of a forested peak. The trees were thinner here, and between them, there were glimpses of a valley that dropped away towards the west.

"I know how you feel, but she said it was not even half a day's travel. I suppose they might have held a faster pace. Who kno-"

Her words were cut off by a thunderous blast, which shook the trees around us, and showered us with twigs and leaves.

We all crouched low, and looked around at one another in surprise as several smaller blasts rang out—followed by a long and low rumble.

"Spirits! What now?" Ar-Tarak groaned.

"That came from down there." Mazgar pointed down into the valley. "Let's find out what it was."

We made our way to the edge of the forest, and peered into the morning mist, which lay thick in the foothills below.

There, barely visible in the dim light of the early day, and masked by the fog, looked to be a kind of mining operation. There were numerous figures scurrying back and forth between the rock face nearest to us, and huge carts—each pulled by unusual ox-like beasts.

The creatures would have easily dwarfed the oxen that pulled many of our largest wagons though—these things were massive.

At first, I recalled tales that Grunwald had told me about Vodyanoi who made their living carving tunnels into the mountains. But then my eyes adjusted and I could finally make out the colour that many of the figures wore.

"Combine. What do you suppose they're doing down there?" I asked, to nobody in particular.

Yinnik answered.

"Maybe we could work our way down and have a look. I would rather that, than wander aimlessly in this awful forest," she said, and looked around to seek agreement.

Uya was enthusiastic, but her twin wasn't.

"Are we not supposed to be soon at war with the Combine? We have killed a fair number of their people, and have raided their villages," she said.

"Yes, but then why fear them when we already know how easily they die?" Uya countered.

They began to argue.

"Zyntael? What do you think?" Sarga asked. "I would like to know what they are doing, or at least make out their number. It may gain us favour with the older sisters to have done some scouting of our own!"

She made a good point so I nodded. "I'm convinced," I said.

"Well that settles it," Sarga declared, and watched for Ar-Tarak's expected protest at me having been the one to decide, but she simply shrugged.

"I want to go down there, stupid," she said. "Zyntael is not always wrong."

That was a first, but it was enough to get the others to stop debating.

And so we fought our way free of the cloying plant life, and began to descend towards the mysterious Combine operation below.

※　※　※

It took us a long time to reach a point where we could easily survey the workers, and perched atop a chunk of rock that had peeled away from the cliff face to sit askew, we flattened ourselves out on our bellies and watched the proceedings.

"Look there, what are those beasts?" Oya whispered, awe plainly heard in her voice.

"They are magnificent! Imagine riding into battle upon the back of one!" Uya added.

"But how would you reach your enemies to lance them? Those things are easily twenty feet tall," Oya said. "And besides, when have you ever heard of Vulkar cavalry? That is stuff for Bare-Skins."

It had begun again. The two spent the next few minutes in a whispered argument about the best use for such creatures in battle.

Sarga regarded them for a while, then shook her head and turned back to Mazgar and I.

"I would also like to know what they are, but who cares about battle? They are doing some kind of digging."

And, as if to punctuate her observation, the rock that we lay upon shuddered from the force of another blast.

We could almost make out the source of it from our lookout.

A massive cloud of black smoke and ashen dust billowed into the air, pushed upward and outward by a flash of bluish flame.

The Combine were somehow blasting a hole into the face of the cliff, as if tunnelling into the mountainside.

Still though, we had no idea why.

After each blast, groups of workers would haul chunks of some sort of material out on little carts, then pour the stuff into containers that were winched up onto the backs of the massive waiting beasts.

Oya was right—those things were very impressive.

They were similar to giant oxen, though instead of fur they were covered in a grey hide.

Where an ox would have horns, these creatures had small tube-like ears, and along the centre of their broad heads there ran a crest of bone. It almost looked as though it were an axe-head, that was growing out of their skulls.

Once a beast was fully laden with the rocky stuff that they were hauling, a horn would sound, and the hulking animal would begin to slowly trudge away. As each went, another would come and the process would begin again.

"It does not look like there are many soldiers. I think those over there are maybe guards." Mazgar pointed out a group of figures who appeared to be holding spears and shields.

"I'm glad I can't make out their symbol. Do you feel strange when you look at it?" I asked. "Like it moves?"

"I suppose so, I wonder why that is, and what it represents," Mazgar said. "I mean, the Sacharri have their fist. That makes sense I guess, but what is that squiggle supposed to be?"

"An octopus, I think," I told her.

"An octo-what?" She frowned. "Is that some Goblin thing?"

"No stupid, it's an eight-legged sea creature. Like a starfish only uglier. It wriggles and grabs stuff with its tentacles. They taste kind of good too."

She stared blankly.

"You ate them in Azure! Remember?"

"I did? Wow, that place really was crazy. I hope we can return some day." Mazgar sighed.

"For your pirate lovers?" Oya asked—her argument with her sister clearly resolved.

We all laughed, before Sarga hushed us.

"How long do you want to watch those workers? Should we head back up and try to find the Shaman once more, or return to the camp and tell the older sisters what we have witnessed?"

Another blast rang out.

"Well all this talk of octo-things has made me hungry. I say we stay a little longer, eat something, and think on it," Mazgar suggested.

"You have arse-worms, Smallest. Nobody can eat as much as you do, and yet remain a runt," Otrek said. "But I suppose I am hungry too—now that you mention it."

It occurred to me that we had eaten nothing since late the previous night, so I added my vote of agreement.

"Alright. We should probably retreat to a less easily noticed spot, and prepare some food," I said, and the others all stared at me. "Oh come on! Really?"

I sighed.

"Fine. I'll make the food. You can wait here and keep watch if you want. I told you we should have brought rations, and not just a bunch of meat and vegetables. But no, 'Make that stew again Kimor-Sister! You are such a good cook! If the Sacharri are good for one thing, it is stew!' Idiots."

I mimicked the pestering that I'd received time and again from my sisters, as I pushed myself to my feet, took the sack of ingredients from Ar-Tarak, and made my way towards a more sheltered spot. Somewhere where the smoke from a small campfire might be easily hidden.

⚬ ⚬ ⚬

I hadn't been gone all that long when I heard one of the others swear.

I dropped the parsnip that I was cutting, and hurried back to where I'd left my sisters.

They were in the same place, though were no longer lying down and spying. Instead, they were standing with their backs to the dig site—weapons held at the ready, and surrounded by a group of figures. Figures who had crossbows trained on them.

I dropped to the ground and peered through the long grass at the situation.

"I ask again. Why are you up here? Did your leader not think our agreement worth honouring?"

"Uhh… We were hunting in the forest, but heard those blasts. We just wanted to look at your beasts," Sarga told the lead figure.

His back was to me so I couldn't make out much of him, but the man was likely a Goblin, judging by his stature.

"So you would violate our agreement with your leader, just to look at our brelts?"

"Well they *are* pretty magnificent," Uya mumbled, and Oya nudged her.

"Did you not see enough of them during our visit to your fortress?"

Even from my hiding spot I could sense the suspicion.

"Sure. Sure. But we were away for most of that... On uhh... adven—"

"Business." Mazgar finished Sarga's sentence for her.

"Yes, adventure business. So we did not really get to see them."

A few of the Combine soldiers looked at one another. One of them let out a snigger, before quickly regaining his composure.

"Well then, perhaps you were absent when the terms of our arrangement were set."

The man at the front gestured for weapons to be lowered. My sisters complied hesitantly; his soldiers did so immediately.

"Your leader agreed that none of you would venture westward, that none would interrupt our operations. Yet here you are. Is it customary of Vulkari to disobey their leaders? To violate agreements and deals?"

"I suppose it sort of is," Sarga said, and the others murmured their concurrence. "We mostly just do what we want."

The strangers looked at each other again and the same man as before, fought to suppress his laughter.

"Well, we shall have to have words with your leader once more. Come. We shall escort you back to your fortress," the leader said, then turned to leave, and I ducked lower in the foliage.

My heart was racing. If they saw me then they would know that we weren't with Urga, and I really wasn't sure what they would do to us if they discovered that fact.

"It is fine. We can make our own way back. We know the way," Yinnik said. "No need to trouble yourself."

"Oh I am sure you do, but that is not the point. You see, we were assured that you would respect the terms that were agreed upon. If you cannot comply with such a simple one, then we have to wonder if any will be complied with at all."

He gestured for the Vulkari to follow, and begrudgingly they set off together, in a group that was flanked by the Combine troops.

As the men passed by my hiding spot, I could finally get a better look at them.

The lead figure was definitely Hobgoblin, though his features were broad and flat, and he squinted as if blinded by the morning sun.

At his side walked a shorter figure, maybe even a Kimora, though it was hard to be sure since his face was obscured by a hood. He didn't look to be a soldier, as he was barely armoured, and carried only a short cudgel at his hip.

The others were most definitely soldiers, though. They wore long jackets with metal panels riveted to them, and domed helmets, with chain sheets to cover their necks and faces.

Each held a bow, and carried a blade at his hip and a round shield upon his back. Their armour and gear looked to be of good quality, but worn and scuffed from constant use.

Most of them had a variety of charms and medals, which dangled from their chests and necks, and I assumed that these marked the soldiers' status as elite guards or veterans.

There was no way we were getting out of this through violence— these weren't the pathetic village militia that we'd slaughtered by the dozen.

I lay in the grass, desperately hoping for an idea to strike me. Hopefully nobody had seen me, so I might have been able to make an escape—but there was no way I was going to leave my sisters to be marched into the hands of Urga. Nothing useful sprang to mind, and I could see no good way to rescue them though, so I decided to follow the group as quietly as I could.

The leader asked the Vulkari a series of questions as they made their way down a well-hidden path, which wound its way down to the work site below.

Each one seemed to be a test, and I was unsure if the collective answers that were given by the others had the man very convinced that they were, in fact, who they said they were.

"Yeah, we talk to Urga all the time. She is a great leader." Otrek was lying poorly.

"I see. And she knows that you go on these… *adventures?*"

"Sure. We do not really have to ask for permission. We are not pups or males."

"Right. And has she spoken of the other Vulkar presence? The one that has made its way from Azure in the south?"

"Uhh…" Otrek trailed off.

"Sure. We used to travel with them," Sarga told the man. "They are our friends and Raid-Sisters."

"Raid-Sisters? Whom do you raid?" the man slowed his pace and stared at Sarga.

"Villages." She fidgeted as she spoke the word. It was odd seeing the most fearsome member of our group appear so nervous.

"Interesting. There is much about these other Vulkari that perhaps you could tell us. Urga was not forthcoming with information. Nor affection. Not at least, so much so as to call them 'sisters.'"

They resumed their steady march, and crossing a stretch of the path that had no cover, I was forced to let them gain some distance on me.

I scampered across the clearing, and hid behind a fallen log once I was sure the coast was clear. I caught up in time to hear mention of someone who could have been me.

"Almost five summers ago. She was taken to the black stone fortress, then apparently sold on to the Legion. It was reported later that she had been reclaimed by your so-called 'Raid-Sisters.'"

The speaker was the short figure in the cowl and cloth tunic.

"We had many Bare-Skinned slaves, I cannot really seem to recall a specific Kimora. Maybe she was eaten?" Yinnik suggested, then laughed cruelly. "We eat Kimori, you know."

The other Vulkari laughed too.

The figure raised his voice. "It is no laughing matter. I seek her out. But thus-far, your kind has done nothing but aggravate and misdirect. You say you travelled with the other group, then you would know of whom I speak. Now I ask again."

He drew in a frustrated breath through his nose and retried:

"What became of the red-haired Kimora girl, who was taken from a village in the southwest around five summers ago, sent to the Legion, then supposedly reclaimed by the leader of the other Vulkar group?"

Why was the Combine asking after me? And it must have been me, since everything fit. Though in honesty, I had no idea where my former village actually was.

"Oh *that* Kimora. Right," Sarga said. "She died."

Mazgar sniggered.

"Yeah. Definitely dead. Why? Did you know her?"

The figure didn't reply and the group carried on in silence for a while.

I followed them down into the valley, which had once been the bed of a river, and crouched behind a boulder whilst the leader left them. He approached another group of armed men, led by a towering Hobgoblin who reminded me of Threydon somewhat.

After some time, he returned and spoke to the group.

"So it has been decided that I am to escort you to the Blackfort myself, and I must admit, I would like to see what becomes of you once Urga finds out that Karthak of the Crimson Star has sent spies to scout our operation."

He wore a smug grin and watched the Vulkari glance at one another nervously.

"Do you truly think me so gullible as to fall for your terrible ruse?" he gloated.

"Well, most of the Combine we have met and killed were pretty hopeless. So… Kind of. Yeah," Sarga admitted.

A few of the soldiers shifted their grips on their weapons.

"Ah, but those were mere villagers. The newly awakened, but the unenlightened," he told her, still smiling. "But I don't imagine that we need to disarm you, and expect that you will comply. Is that a fair assumption?"

"Fine." Yinnik spoke up, sounding more bored and annoyed than worried. "How long is the trek? We have not eaten since last night."

The man touched the short figure on the shoulder.

"Brother, please fetch our friends some meat." Then he turned to Yinnik. "It isn't Kimora meat unfortunately, but it shall suffice. After you have fed yourselves, we shall march through the valley, then over the low hills to the east. It is but a few days' travel at most—especially on those backwards legs of yours."

I wished I could have seen Ar-Tarak's face.

The man allowed the Vulkari time to eat and drink, then they began to head off to the Blackfort.

I remained crouched behind the rock, contemplating what to do next.

The Combine had known that we were not part of Urga's band, but intended to take my sisters to her all the same. I couldn't think of any way to rescue them, but I knew roughly where I was, and which way to go in order to at least make my way back to our own camp.

Before leaving though, I decided to see just what it was that the Merchant Combine were mining from the cliff, so crept toward one of the gigantic beasts.

Inside the wooden container beside the massive brelt, there were chunks of rock. All of it was laced with black crystal.

I had no idea what it was, so hastily pocketed a chunk before I set off in pursuit of the others. But at this point, getting the others back by myself wasn't exactly a simple task. It would take an intervention by the Spirits themselves—or at least a lot of luck.

As I stalked along behind the group of soldiers and my friends, hopefully undetected, and moving mostly after dark, I tried to decide between a rescue attempt or a return to camp.

Perhaps I could urge some of the older warriors to mount a daring raid on the fort. Or maybe I wouldn't even need to—Karthak and Urga might have reached an accord by now.

Whatever my choice might have been though, I would never have to make it.

It seemed that the Spirits had made it for me after all.

viii.

I couldn't recall who said it, but it was something about being crushed under the weight of two empires. Some sort of warning about their forces clashing.

Was it the Shaman? Karthak? Or maybe Phobos?

I wished the Ratling were here now—he'd know what to do.

I was so tired. Why was I so tired? How long had I been gone?

I could remember tailing the Combine and my friends, but I'd lost them in a fog. How did I get back to camp?

My mind was a mess of thoughts, and my body trembled, as I slowly made my way towards Karthak's wagon—or what might be left of it.

I passed by the twisted and smouldering corpses of Vulkari and men alike; each body peppered with arrows or spear shafts.

Only the crows that loitered in the nearby trees, and upon the burned frames of our tents and wagons, made any sound.

I shooed them away from each Vulkar corpse that I checked—my heart racing with the fear that the body may be Star-Star or Karthak.

I recognised some of the fallen, but thankfully, none were particularly close friends of mine.

Even so, members of our warband lay dead—right beside troops dressed in purple, and others wearing crimson.

And the crimson didn't hide the blood at all, despite what someone once told me.

The ground was awash with it. It had seeped into the soil to form a sticky mud, which coated my feet and sprayed my back as I began to pick up pace.

Karthak's wagon was just ahead of me, atop a small rise.

But it was ruined as well. The timber was charred and the trophy pole fallen, and the oxen lay dead—still lashed to their harnesses.

"Karthak?" I called out, coughing from the smoke that hung in the cool air.

"Star-Star?"

Silence.

"Anyone?"

Only the carrion birds answered me.

I paced around, searching for someone who might have survived whatever massacre had occurred. But the camp was deserted.

Despite the scattered and mangled bodies, no clue led to the whereabouts of my sisters. And so I made my way, dejected and filled with worry, up to that same flat stone where I had comforted Sarga.

I needed to get to higher ground—to get a better view of the surrounding area.

I trudged up the hill, hoping against the growing fear that churned in my belly, that perhaps the Blackfort held the answers.

As I went, the haze and fog slowly dissipated. What almost looked like blurred figures, which had been present all around me prior, seemed to linger below, in the ruins of the camp. And the air was clear once more.

When I reached the top, and cast my eyes down into the valley, tears of relief began to well within their corners.

My suspicion was correct. The banners that now fluttered from atop the rugged towers were all the answer I needed:

Black fists upon a crimson fabric, proudly marking the desolate fortress as territory of the Legion. Of Manox Threydon.

I ran the rest of the way there—no care as to how that might have looked to the soldiers who manned the walls, and unable to stop despite the burning in my lungs and legs.

The Hobgoblin who saw me approach briefly raised his bow, but then he was halted by another figure; a Vulkar.

It wasn't a female, but rather was the wretched male who had greeted Karthak upon our first arrival to the Solent fortress.

"Kimor-pup!" he called out. "I had wondered if you would return!"

Vellik? Was that his name?

"Please..." I panted. "Let me..." I couldn't even finish the sentence, so merely gestured at the spiked iron gates that barred my exhausted entrance.

"Password," the mangy bastard called back.

"You horse-son! Just open the cursed gate!"

He let out a shrill cackle, the gate opened, and I stumbled into the courtyard of the Blackfort—the courtyard that I had run across in a desperate escape, nigh on five summers ago.

For all that time, I had absolutely no desire to return to the place, but now couldn't be more glad to be within its walls.

One of the older Vulkari smirked at me as I staggered towards the keep, relief no doubt painted vividly upon my grimy, tear-streaked face.

"It feels good to be home, yes?"

She rested a reassuring hand upon my shoulder, and walked me the rest of the way.

"It feels good to be home," she told me.

※　※　※

Later, when I had been fed, Star-Star found me.

She sat down on the bench opposite me, in the now much cleaner dining hall—bandages and dressings covering various recent wounds.

"Zyntael, you had us worried. You had best head up to where Karthak rests. She has been told of your return, but wanted for you to be fed and warmed first."

She picked at the wood of the tabletop.

"How is it that you went missing for so long? Where have you been?"

"I'm not sure, Star-Star. I was following a Combine officer and his men. They had captured the others, and meant to bring them here." I strained my mind, but couldn't, for the life of me, recall what had happened after the fog rolled in on the second morning of my pursuit.

"We hadn't actually gone all that far. Two or three days' travel. How long was I gone for?"

"Almost a moon. Long enough for the Legion to take this place. Long enough to miss the preceding skirmish."

I remembered the creature in the woods and the mining operation, but there was no way that a whole month had passed.

"Star-Star, that makes no sense! I can only account for a week at best!"

Then my searching thoughts seemed to fixate on an image—fuzzy and unfocused at first.

There was a gnarled tree that loomed, shrouded in mist before me.

The trunk of it was infested with crystalline growths—as though lichen—and its roots wormed their way between more of the crystal at its base. Onyx crystal, which seemed to hum and whine, and call to me with a song that resonated with sombre familiarity.

A young girl, her skin dark and freckled, and her hair a crimson red, reached out a hand and touched the pulsing trunk.

I touched the trunk.

My memory seemed as though remembered by another person entirely—some hovering observer. It flexed and waned, and I couldn't be sure that it was even a memory in the first place, and not just some half-forgotten dream.

"There was a tree. It was covered in black crystals. That's all I can remember," I finally said.

Star-Star cocked a brow and nodded slowly.

"I don't know what it was, or why I went to it. It called to me. I think the crystals did. I don't really know how to describe it," I began. But then it occurred to me that I could just show her instead.

I rummaged in my satchel, and retrieved the rock that I had taken from the dig site.

"Here. The Merchant Combine troops were digging this stuff up. That's what we spied on, and that's why they took Sarga and the rest captive. That's what was growing out of the tree I saw."

I frowned.

"Where are they? Sarga, Mazgar?"

Star-Star shrugged.

"They returned only a short while after they left. With those Combine troops you spoke of—that is what caused the chaos at the camp.

"Star-Star is confused as to how you made it through the Combine line, though. They have amassed troops in the direction of the camp, where we previously guarded the pass into their lands. Hence we have not retrieved our fallen sisters, and hence we barred your young friends from searching for you."

"What Combine line? There are none but the carrion birds there."

The warrior looked perplexed.

"This is all very mysterious to Star-Star. She does not have the best grasp on the supernatural, so you must therefore head up and report to Karthak. Her chamber is in the far tower."

Star-Star pointed in the direction of it, perhaps forgetting that I once slept there.

"It is a relief to have you back. Star-Star is glad you are not dead, even if this old sea-raider does not quite understand how that is!

"And she is but one who was concerned. Some of the Legion even enquired as to your whereabouts. In particular, a boy."

She pushed herself to her feet and rustled my hair, before making her way out of the hall with a noticeable limp.

※　※　※

I did as was bid of me, and headed through the fortress to the room where Karthak was.

It was surprising just how much tidier the Blackfort was now. The Legion obviously being unable to abide the state of disrepair and chaos that had previously been the norm.

At the top of the northeastern part of the structure there was a long hallway, with fancy looking doors along its length. I supposed that they were all lordly rooms, and remembered just faintly that I had slept in one for a time, so I made my way to that door and knocked sharply on the old wood.

"Enter," came a voice from within. It didn't sound like Karthak, and perhaps belonged to a male slave or attendant instead, but I pushed the heavy door open and peered inside the room beyond all the same.

"Oh, sorry. You aren't a servant," I stammered. "I thought this was Karthak's room."

It wasn't, and the voice definitely did belong to a male. A naked one at that.

He had been crouching in a tub of water, wearing naught but a small stone pendant around his neck. But no slave or attendant, he stood and welcomed me into his chamber when he saw me.

"Zyntael!" Manox Anra greeted me, his open arms held wide. "I had thought you to be a servant too, but I am most glad that I was wrong. You make for a far better visitor than one of the male Wolf— sorry, Vulkari."

He rinsed the suds from his olive skin, then stepped out of the bath, and gripped me by both shoulders.

"And so it is that these prisoners meet again—the inverse of how last we spoke. But you have grown much in these past... 'summers' was it you call the years?" he said. I nodded and he continued. "Can we address one another by rank, like I once hoped?"

"You have uhh... grown too," I observed. Out loud. My face felt hot. I didn't really know where to look. And I really *had* just said that out loud.

"Oh uhh… Sorry, we only really have one rank," I told him. "But I am a proper raider now, if that counts."

Was I sweating?

"Well, Raider Zyntael Fairwinter. I am now Under-officer Manox Anra!"

He stood and held me in place for an uncomfortable length of time, whilst the tips of my ears burned ever hotter. Then he finally and mercifully moved away to dress himself.

"So… You missed much."

"Yeah, a moon's worth, apparently," I agreed. "I can't honestly remember what happened. It's like I've been robbed of several weeks of time!"

"Well. We reached these parts about two weeks ago, and came upon the camp of your raiders—under attack from a Combine detachment," Anra told me. "Our vanguard came to your sisters' aid, and pushed the Merchant bastards back to the fort.

"We seized an opening, and captured the place after one of your young friends broke free of her bonds and opened the gate for us. You'll hear all about it from her. God-Emperor knows I have!"

His eyes glazed over as he recalled the events.

"Vulkari fight with such savagery! Those who sided with the Combine were a greater danger than the Domovoi at their side. You really missed something special, Brownie!"

"Yeah, I've been on many raids. I learned to fight as they do. Obviously I've never fought against them outside of training though."

I imagined that I'd die very quickly if I ever did.

"You said a friend of mine, what, escaped and helped you?" I asked. "Who was she, and what happened? Last I saw before things went strange was that my friends were being escorted here by the Combine."

Anra finished dressing himself—in simple trousers, and a black calfskin jerkin that left his muscular arms exposed. It only alleviated my sweating a little.

"It was the largest of them," he said.

"Sarga."

"Yes. She somehow convinced the Combine rats to take her with them here. Then tore a man's throat out with her teeth, before making her way to the gate house, breaking the locking mechanism, and letting us in. Of course, she took a few arrows and was subdued—but not before we were able to make use of the opportunity, and begin the assault."

"And the Vulkari who were already here? Urga, their leader? What of her?"

"She fled. Your own warchief had some rather colourful things to say about that. I recall her calling the retreat 'Bare-Skinned' and craven."

"That sounds about right. Urga should have stood and fought," I said, and caught his furrowed brow and piercing stare. "Oh, and pay no heed to the whole 'Bare-Skin' thing. They say it all the time, and about practically everything. You know, like with the Sacharri and maybe 'horse-son.'"

Anra laughed unexpectedly.

"It's *whoreson*. And it means something a little different than the son of a horse."

He saw the wide-eyed look of realisation on my face, and must have mistaken it for confusion. The poor boy began to explain.

"So some women, they—"

"I know what a whore is! I have visited the bathhouses in Azure!"

I felt a bit silly, but there was no way I'd ever admit my mistake to the other raiders. To us, being the son of a horse would forever be an insult now.

Anra looked surprised and amused. And something else. Maybe jealous even.

"You visited the bathhouses? And did you..." he trailed off and bit his lip. Avoiding eye contact whilst he fidgeted with a button on his little teardrop pendant.

"Did I what? I drank a lot. That's for sure."

"No I mean... I know the older warriors probably... I had hoped you might wait for..."

I didn't follow.

"Well, you know what those places are famous for," he sighed.

"Certainly not their baths."

I recalled all of the things that I'd seen—the things that had amused Mazgar and Sarga so much—and finally realised what he was getting at.

"Oh right. No, no I didn't mate, or lie with anyone."

It seemed odd that he'd care.

"I think some of the older sisters did. And Narod apparently paid a lot for time with two desert Vulkari. One even had white fur and pink eyes. Can you believe that?"

He shrugged. He was blushing, maybe.

"What about you? I don't remember there being those sorts of places in the Solent fortress. Or the city around it. Though to be fair, I didn't really venture into the city very much at all. And I was probably too young back then to really know what to look for—definitely too young to care."

"No!" he replied a little too quickly. "I mean, sure there are brothels. They go where armies go, I suppose. But I haven't visited any. I was waiting for…"

Anra glanced around nervously. He seemed rather uncomfortable, despite having stood naked before me not five minutes ago.

I pointed that out:

"You were just naked before and you are uhh… older. No longer a child. Why are you so nervous? Is it not something that people talk about in the Sacharri Empire? I'm pretty sure it's all the soldiers *ever* talked about! Is it different if you're of noble blood?"

"No it isn't that. It is just… Well, how to put this?" He sat on the edge of his bed and looked up at me earnestly. "Do you recall when I came to oversee your outfitting? When you were to return to the warband?"

I nodded. I'd always thought that was a bit odd.

"Well, I'd seen you a fair bit before then, working with the servant master, Janos. I wanted to talk to you more before, but couldn't because I had my duties to attend, and you always seemed shy and evasive. Anyway, that day, I asked to see that you were properly dressed. It was okay because it was sort of official duty, but really, I just wanted to talk to you."

"Alright. You probably could have just found me at any time, you know. I was evasive because I was trying not to piss on anyone's patch… something Grunwald—Janos—told me to avoid. But if I'd known you weren't horrible, I would have been happy for the company."

"Yeah I know. I put it off because I was young and afraid. And when I finally worked up the courage, my father forbade it anyway. He said it would have been playing by the rules of Karthak's game.

"Then, when I learned that she was to reclaim you, I didn't want to miss the opportunity. Forbidden or not. Luckily, my father relented. He is a fair-minded, decent man really."

"I dunno about that. Your father led me to believe that I'd only be gone a short while. Not almost four summers!" I said.

Anra smiled.

"Of course, that was meant to be the plan. But come on, it's Karthak we are talking about."

That was true.

"Well anyway, when I was watching the servants scrub the filth of hard labour, and the ash of the smithy from you, I noticed the freckles that mark your skin. Like the stars that hang above on a clear night. I think I finally noticed the colour of your eyes too. They made me think of summer, and the vast grasslands of Sacharr."

He was definitely blushing now, and I might have been as well.

"I thought you were pretty, and I wanted to spend more time with you. After you were gone, I regretted not having approached you sooner. I often dreamt of spending time with you—but in the waking world, had missed my chance due to childish fear."

It was the first time that anyone had said such a thing to me. I thought that the Hobgoblin might have been making a joke, but he looked sincere—and sincerely embarrassed.

"Thank you," I croaked.

I really had no idea what else to say to that. My first instinct was to protest it, given that I personally didn't see the appeal. I always thought that I looked like a boy—the other Kimorin girls I'd met, had delicate and pointed features, but maybe my flat face and broad nose were what passed for desirable in Hobgoblin eyes.

Manox Anra sucked air in through his teeth and looked away to the side. I fiddled with one of the beaded bracelets I wore, and kicked my feet against the rug covered floor.

"So..." he finally said. "There you have it. I was hoping that maybe you might remember me. I know we only spoke briefly, but I remembered you. Those dreams never subsided.

"When I learned that we would begin the march westward, to confront the Combine expeditionary unit, I was excited at the prospect of meeting 'Karthak's chosen pup' once more. And perhaps on more easy terms."

"Easy? Well, I think this might be the most awkward meeting I can recall," I confessed.

"Yes. And please accept my apologies for my candour."

I didn't know that word, but I didn't think he had any need to apologise for anything anyway.

"It's fine," I assured him. "I'd like to stay with you awhile, and share our tales, but I really must find Karthak and my friends. I probably should sleep too. Yanghar only knows how long it's been since I last did."

Anra nodded, then stood and led me to where Karthak's room was.

Before he departed, he awkwardly pulled me into an embrace that was part Legion handshake, and part friendly hug. I noticed that he smelled slightly of apples and peppermint, and could only imagine how foul I must have smelled to him.

I stood alone for a brief moment, before knocking on the door before me. I felt somewhat giddy, and a little excited—but mostly confused. I hadn't ever really considered the possibility that someone might be interested in me in any romantic sense, let alone a boy who I had only barely spoken with, almost four summers ago.

And then there was his strange question about what I'd done in Azure. Something about his comment bugged me, but I couldn't think of what it was, through the strange, cloudy feeling in my head.

I drew in a long breath and sighed, then rapped on the wooden door.

This time, the voice that responded was unmistakably Karthak's.

"Bastard Bare-Skinned louts. No reprieve from your demands and incessant reports. Just enter. Get it over with."

I stepped into her room and closed the door behind me. The space was dimly lit by a few flickering candles, and most of it looked to have been cluttered up with equipment from an infirmary.

Karthak lay on the bed, bandaged and battered. There were patches of fur that had been shorn away, probably to allow for stitches and dressings.

"Approach. What fresh torment do you bring me now?"

"It's me," I said.

Karthak could move quickly, I'd seen it many times, but the speed at which she tore herself from the bed and swept me up in her arms was paralysing.

"Kimor-pup! You returned to me! I thought you taken by the Combine scum, and arranged a rescue party to depart from here only a few days ago…"

She checked me up and down.

"You are unharmed, yet made it through the enemy lines?" she asked. "How? And by the Spirits, where have you been?"

Once she set me back down, I perched on her bed and began to tell her the tale of what I had thought were only the last few days. By the end of what I could remember enough to tell clearly, I was half asleep, resting my head on her side, and barely murmuring the words.

I didn't manage to finish my tale before sleep plucked my mind from my exhausted body.

A red sky, over a burning settlement.

A crowd of raiders gathered in the village square—I had seen it so many times before.

A severed head was raised before the victorious mob, by the Kimora Warlord.

"Behold, Sisters! The debt has been paid. The betrayer is dead. We must cast our Warlord into the Void, and free us all!"

I recognised the features of the disembodied head—I recognised the face.

It was the last face I'd seen, before sleep had claimed me.

ix.

Mazgar woke me. I had no idea how long I'd slept, but it did feel like it was almost long enough to make up for how exhausted I had been. Almost.

Someone had moved me into another room, and had also taken my clothes and gear from my sleeping body.

"Sister." My friend was pulling on my arm. "Sister, wake up. There are important talks being held in the great hall."

"What? Where am I? How long have I slept?" I sat up and rubbed the sleep from my eyes.

My skin was clean. So, I had been washed, as well.

"A day. Give or take. But you must rise and come too."

"Fine. Fine. Where are my things?" I looked around the room.

Next to the fireplace, hanging from the back of a stout chair, was my dagger. Everything else was missing.

Mazgar hauled me from the blankets and squeezed me against her for a moment, before shoving a simple linen shirt and some trousers into my arms.

"Quick, quick. I am most glad you are alive, Sister. But we must hurry, so the others might speak with you before the meeting takes place!"

I dressed myself and then followed along sluggishly whilst she led the way to the main hall of the keep.

Karthak was sitting in the throne, alongside Threydon, who had pulled up a simple wooden chair at her side. Before them were amassed our warband, and a fair few Hobgoblin soldiers. There were Kimori around the place too, though they were servants of course— only the Hobgoblins wore the armour of the Legion.

Manox Anra was sitting cross-legged with Ar-Tarak, Oya, Uya and Sarga. The latter of whom was wrapped around the torso in bandages, and had her left arm in a sling.

Yinnik and Otrek weren't there.

We made our way over to the group, who stood to embrace me in turn, and then we sat and whispered excitedly whilst we waited for whatever occasion this was to begin.

"Where in the name of all the Spirits did you get to?" Uya asked.

"And did you finish that stew?" added Oya.

I relayed my story to them, answering whatever questions that I could, then listened to theirs—which frankly, was the more interesting one.

"That man, the Combine lieutenant. He was in charge of some special force. They called themselves the Sons of the Frost hammer? Frost spear? I forget," Sarga told me.

"It was something like that," Mazgar said.

"Yeah. So they were going to take us to Urga, but then we ran into our own camp. I do not think they even knew that Karthak had positioned us where she did. You know, further to the west. Well anyway, some of the scouts saw our approach and came to parley I guess, but that horse-son attacked them outright—they killed three of our own, and then retreated."

"Didn't they let you keep your weapons? How did you not manage to overcome them?" I asked.

"Oh well, they disarmed us early on. You can thank these idiots for that." She nodded at Uya and Oya. "Said they were worried that these two would kill one another over some quarrel about their—what did he call them?"

"Brelts."

"Yeah, those. So the lieutenant had our weapons taken, and our hands bound behind us. None of us could really fight. Though of course we tried."

"They killed Yinnik," Ar-Tarak said. Almost casually.

"What? By Yanghar!"

"Yep. She headbutted one of them, kicked him to the ground, and stamped on his helmet until his brains came out of the eye holes." Sarga was grinning. "But then they stabbed her a bunch, and she died."

I couldn't quite believe it.

After everything that we'd survived.

"What about Otrek?" I asked.

"Well, *they* did not kill her. That happened later," Sarga said. "I shall get to that bit."

I looked around the room. There were still warriors arriving, and it looked like we had enough time for Sarga's tale.

"So at some point—cannot remember when—I had let the Combine know that Urga was my mother. They took me with them, and left these four and Otrek behind. I think that they intended to use me as a bargaining chip, or maybe thought that Urga would be grateful for my return."

"Who knows? Why would they think *you* valuable?" Oya said and Uya hushed her.

"We went to the southwest a short way, and guess what? More Combine! They had a small force there. One that was marching on our camp, by the looks of it!

"That force attacked within a few days, and while that was happening, the squinty man took me to the Blackfort. Urga ordered me to be taken to the dungeon, and when the man was taking me there, I managed to finally tear myself free."

Her eyes sparkled with menace.

"Even with his sword and armour, I overpowered him, ripped off one of his arms, and then bit his head clean off!"

She tapped the broken medal that was pinned to her bandages—a little black disc with a shattered octopus upon it.

"His rank did nothing to help him!"

I shared a smirk with Anra. It was a little different than how he had told it.

"And so you let the Legion through the gate?"

"Yep. I smashed the lock thing, and opened it up for them."

"How did you know they were coming?"

"Uhh…" Sarga looked away.

"Ha! You were just trying to escape, no doubt. It was just coincidence!" Mazgar laughed.

"Whatever. I was trying to fight off the other soldiers. There were maybe four of them. And that is before Urga's traitors came too!" Sarga shoved Mazgar weakly.

"After that, I was hit with a bunch of arrows, stabbed once or twice, and then smashed with a hammer. I think some of my guts came out even! That is about the last of what I remember, but it was pretty glorious all the same! I killed at least three or four of the Merchant Lords' best!"

"That's very glorious indeed. But what about Otrek?" I asked.

"Oh, Urga tore her in half," Sarga said.

I stared at my friend. Then Mazgar began to enthusiastically tell the tale.

"Yeah. She and I were some of the first to assault the Blackfort. We fought alongside Karthak and the older sisters, all the way up to this hall. There were arrows flying everywhere, and javelins being thrown. Urga got her. Stabbed her like this!" she said, and mimed a spear thrust, before tearing upwards with her other hand. "Then ripped her right in half."

Still I stared.

"Funny thing is; right after that, Kovvik-Shar lost her mind, and just carved a path right up to Urga and her traitors. Perhaps she birthed Otrek. Anyway, they escaped. Did you know that there is a secret exit in the dungeons? Is that how you got out back when you were a prisoner here?"

"No. I escaped through the larder. But it would have been great to know about that passage back then," I said.

I still couldn't quite come to terms with the deaths of my friends. Probably more so, how easily the others had.

I decided to ask about the Legion, to change the subject.

"How did you come to be here anyway? And with such timing?" I asked Anra.

He gave me a strange look.

"We are the Sacharri Legion. We bear the blade of the God-Emperor of the World-Throne. And in His eternal glory, He sees all," he said.

"I love the way they talk. Do you not?" Uya asked.

"Never get tired of their fancy words for stuff," her twin agreed.

Anra sighed, rolled his eyes, and shrugged.

"Spies, Zyntael. We have spies everywhere."

"Like Phobos Lend? The Darkrunner?" I asked.

"Who? I don't know who that is." And he gave me a sly wink, and tapped his nose.

We chatted for a bit longer, talking about the Combine and their mining, the weird thing that we saw in the forest, and what might come next for us. But in truth, my mind couldn't let go of images of my two dead friends.

I'd seen them grow from small, wide-eyed pups—no taller than I had been—to hulking warriors, a match for any Legion or Combine soldier.

It was what they had always wanted I supposed; death in glorious combat. But now it just seemed kind of pointless, and a waste of life. And I'd never see them again.

I didn't have too long to dwell on such thoughts though, for whatever was supposed to be happening in the hall, was finally starting to happen.

"Our fallen sisters lie outside these walls. We let them rot alongside the Sacharri who sacrificed themselves to come to our aid, and the filth who slew them," Karthak told the gathered warriors. "We sit and wait for a siege. To be starved out of the fortress."

There were murmurs and shared glances. Threydon stood up and cleared his throat.

"Messages have been dispatched to the forces in the east. These lands are Sacharr. These lands must be held. We shall not allow the Combine to push their way into the Solent heartlands, and so we must act now, to disrupt their foothold," he said, then Karthak continued.

"We shall pour from these walls and annihilate the regiment that has taken the pass. We shall fortify it, collapse the alternate pathways through the ranges, and establish a clear path for resupply—should a siege be inevitable and unavoidable.

"If the bastards approach with their full force, they shall have no choice but to attempt to retake this bastion." Karthak slammed a fist into her palm. "And we shall not allow it!"

So war was here. Phobos had predicted as much.

I wondered what became of him after our meeting in Azure. He'd spoken of an attempt to prevent all of this, but that—whatever it was—must have failed.

"We shall move out in the coming weeks, and shall disrupt as much of the enemy's operation as we can. We shall ensure that the scum are faced with chaos and harassment at every turn. Our people are the people of the wild. We do not belong behind walls.

"The Legion shall hold the Blackfort, and shall use it as a staging base to mount their offensive into the western marshes, to the waters of the Gold-Fenn."

"We anticipate that it will be approaching winter when our full force arrives, and our supply lines are established," Threydon added.

"The Solent river is to be once more directed along its original bed, and will be used to transport supplies. But this will take time, and it is the will of Sacharr that you prevent disruptions. May the God-Emperor favour you, and may your own Spirits bolster your strength.

You are the vanguard. You are the sharpened edge of the Sacharri blade."

It wasn't the first time that I'd heard such analogies. Both from the Sacharri overseer, and as a concern that Karthak expressed.

So we really were to be the tip of the spear.

I didn't relish the thought.

※　※　※

Once the customary discussions began, and older veterans began to suggest tactical movements, or ask for specifics regarding the taking of captives and slaves, I decided to leave the hall and pay my respects to my fallen sisters.

After the skirmish for the Blackfort, our warband had gathered the present dead, and burned them. The ashes were mixed with dyes and paints, then used to decorate small, flat stones—which were stacked in piles as memorials to each lost warrior. Even those who had fought for Urga were honored in such a way. All were sisters under Yanghar.

Some of the pigment was always kept, to be used to mark armour and blades with blessed sigils—so that the Spirits of our sisters would protect us and guide us in combat.

"Come Sister, we should visit Narod. The male-folk keep the paint. It would be good to honour Yinnik and Otrek upon your Sacharri blade," Mazgar suggested.

Anra had followed along, enthralled by our customs, but silent despite the many questions that must have bubbled beneath his controlled surface.

"Do you not feel a heaviness within you?" I asked Mazgar, whilst staring at the colourful rocks that were all that was left of Yinnik and Otrek. "A clawing within your heart?"

"No. I am proud that these two died in battle, as we all hopefully shall. And I am glad that they stride alongside Yanghar and Vulkar now."

Sarga agreed. "They are eternally free now, and died as warriors both. For that I feel nothing but pride. But I shall avenge Otrek. Urga may have birthed me, but she betrayed us, and killed my friend."

Before we left, I pricked my flesh with my dagger, and after marking them with blood, I placed a small flat stone upon each pile.

"May the Mother welcome you as her own. May your freedom be eternal. Goodbye Sisters." I uttered the final prayer. "Goodbye for now."

We crossed the courtyard and made our way into the larder to find Narod. It felt a little odd passing through the door in this direction, but once the rich smell of spices and curious brews met my nose, all was as normal.

I took a bone from one of the benches and tossed it to the hounds that lazed around next to the fire pit.

"Hey! I was going to use that!" Narod snapped.

I shrugged and grinned.

"Narod, it looks as though you have made yourself a home already. What are you making?"

"Yanghar only knows now. I was going to use the marrow from that bone you just wasted, to make a broth. Thanks a lot though, Sister. Why, oh why, did you have to return?" he stood there, hands on his hips for a short while, then suddenly dropped his angry facade, and held his arms wide in welcome.

I embraced the scrawny male, then sat myself upon a workbench to chat with him whilst Mazgar and Sarga began to pick through the supplies for things to snack on.

"It is good to have a proper kitchen. I can make far better food, and brew far finer ointments and poultices." He raised a hand and motioned at the many bubbling and spluttering pots and cauldrons around the room. "Though, that being said, it does mean that I must prepare so much more food. We are apparently feeding the damned Hobgoblins now."

Anra glanced at him and Narod quickly raised his hands in apology.

"I meant no disrespect by that. It is just an unexpected turn, is all."

"It's fine Vulkar, I could see to it that some of our servants make themselves useful in your aid, should that ease the burden some," Anra said, then he fetched himself an apple from a hanging bushel, and tossed me one as well.

"It would help. We have an awful lot to do, and I hear whisper that there are to be more of your kind present soon. Is this the truth?" Narod said, occupying himself with his brews.

"Well I suppose that you may need to move out with your warband soon. I'm not sure if you are going to mount raids from here, or move further west," Anra told him.

"Karthak doesn't like being walled in," I said.

"So probably the latter. Whatever the case, I'll ask that we can spare some help for you," Anra confirmed, and Narod seemed grateful.

I asked the whelp for the paint that had been mixed from the ashes of my friends, then painted each side of my Legion dagger with small dots of the colour, once he fetched the little pots of it for me.

Yinnik was a pale sky blue, and Otrek had been blended with a rich purple.

I whispered a prayer to them as I marked the blade, then set it upon the brickwork next to the fire, to harden the markings.

Once I was done, and the small brass pots were safely returned to their shelf, Narod turned to me and spoke in Vulkar.

"So is this the Hobgoblin boy whom Sarga and Smallest teased you about?"

"Yes. He is the son of their war chief."

Narod nodded knowingly.

"A political union, or a courtship then? Or perhaps he is the only Bare-Skin fool enough to have you?" he asked, grinning.

I threw my apple core at him, and the Vulkar cackled.

"Watch how she swoons, when he speaks in his fancy Legion way," Mazgar called from the pantry.

"Oh shut up. Both of you. I met him once or twice only before, and have only seen him today since arriving here." I shrugged. "He *is* quite nice to look at though."

"You are a terrible liar, Sister. I heard that you visited him last night!" Mazgar said, and poked her head from behind the doorway to wink at me.

How on earth did she know that?

The two Vulkari took turns at making fun of me, all the while Anra looked back and forth at them in silence.

After a little while, I relented and joined in, telling a fanciful (and rather lewd) story about our secret meeting. Even Sarga ceased her search for food in order to listen.

Finally, after a particularly explicit and colourfully vulgar part, Anra cleared his throat.

Then to our surprise he spoke—in broken, but still understandable Vulkar.

"I can... a little bit... understand you."

I felt my face flush hot, and my heart plummeted into the deepest pits of my stomach.

Mazgar and Narod stared at each other and then me, wide-eyed and shocked. Then they both collapsed in fits of laughter.

Their hysterical cackling was infectious, and shortly, the whole kitchen was echoing with mirth.

※　※　※

Unfortunately such mirth would be in short order in the coming weeks—the Vulkari concerned with the conflict ahead, and the Hobgoblins being Hobgoblins. Plans were made for our warband to split into raiding parties and disperse into the wilderness, to cause as much pain to the enemy as possible.

Before that, however, we would need to break through the small force that had amassed to the southwest, and was guarding the main pass through the Stormhills.

One evening, only a week before we were to move out, Karthak summoned me to her lavish solar, where she lounged around on a massive pile of cushions, in a haze of incense and pipe smoke.

"Kimor-pup. I must ask you something that has bothered me since you returned," she told me. I wasn't sure what it could be—what I'd remembered, I'd told her.

"The crystal that you took from the dig site. Does it remind you of anything?" She was holding it before her eye, and looked from the small rock to me.

"Uhh... I'm not sure. I remember that I saw a tree that was growing the stuff. It looked like it was an infection. A sickness," I offered.

"You ventured into the woods to the north, many seasons ago. Do you recall? When you told me the story, you mentioned something that you found. Before your fight against the Forest-vermin," she said.

I recalled the events.

There was a clearing, a fairy ring, and an obelisk. A carved, black obelisk. I had touched it.

"I remember the beacon, the Spirit-Talker said that I had called it when I touched the rock." Strange that the Combine would be unearthing the same rock. "Is it the same stuff? And what exactly is it?"

Karthak tossed me the stone. The crystal had been cleared of the earth that had encased it, and was icy to the touch.

"When you hold it, what do you feel?" she asked, frustratingly ignoring my previous questions.

"You mean besides the cold?" I asked.

"Close your eyes. Focus your thoughts on what it wants to tell you."

I did as Karthak bid, and at first felt a bit silly—sitting in a lordly room, holding a rock, and trying to connect my thoughts with it.

Then, subtly at first, I began to feel something. It was as though a thousand voices were shouting, screaming and crying out—but so quietly as to be a mere hum, like the surging ocean tides of Azure, or the soft drumming of rain upon a hide tent.

I couldn't make out any words, only their intent; it was malevolent.

I dropped the stone and looked into Karthak's eyes. She was staring at me intently, with the slightest smile upon her face.

"By the Spirits! What was that?" I asked her.

She laughed. "Zyntael, it *is* the Spirits. I am unsure why the Combine would seek to unearth this beaconstone, but it cannot be for any good reason. This rock channels their voice and their sight," she told me.

I prodded the rock.

"Their voice? They sounded angry!" I said.

"They are. And I suspect their anger may have been what provoked their attack upon you and the other younger sisters." She suddenly looked thoughtful, as though something was making sense to her, that was still a mystery to me.

I had pretty much given up on ever expecting a straight answer from Karthak. Usually, I'd just ask Star-Star about the same things that our leader withheld from me.

Star-Star would tell me it wasn't her place to inform me, then would inform me all the same, and so it would go after each of these cryptic conversations.

"So what does it mean then?" I decided to at least test the waters. "The rock, that beacon, the tree I saw, and that ghoul that tried to ensnare us in bizarre dreams?"

"The purple plague seeks to infect not just the living, but the dead, and all things between." She sat back and nodded to herself. "Perhaps they seek to exploit the ancient knowledge of the Spirits, or perhaps they mean to destroy them. I do not know, and to find out, we shall need to ask."

"Ask the Spirits?"

"No. Ask the Merchant Combine. Unfortunately we slaughtered most of those present when we retook our fortress. And those that did survive, refused to speak to us. Even under... *duress.*"

She sighed, then turned to me suddenly. "There is another thing, I just remembered. We must return to the temple, and claim our new young."

"We do? How will we train new pups, should we be split up and out raiding?" I asked.

"You shall take them with you of course!" Karthak replied. "The strongest weapons are forged in the hottest fires after all. Time to spend in training is a luxury we have no more. So you, and a few others shall go north to the temple, and escort them here. I shall dispatch a messenger to relay my wishes to the holy Mothers. They shall make the appropriate arrangements, and shall select the fittest of the pups.

"I would leave it to you, but then our warband would suffer runts and friendly weaklings."

She laughed at my reaction. But she was right. We couldn't all be like Mazgar and I.

"One other thing, Pup." Karthak leaned in close, and her tone softened. "The son of Threydon."

Great.

"You have spent a fair bit of time with him. I have noticed your little evening talks. Something I should worry about?"

I frowned at her.

"When do you ever worry? And yes, we talk. I like him. He feels the same way I do in a way. Bound to his path through no choice of his own. Like a slave."

Karthak snorted.

"Well he ought not to. He is the Commander's son, so no slave at all." She seemed rather amused. "Though I can see how a romantic youngster could make such an outrageous claim and yet believe it. Just be sure not to believe the same. You have more than just the Spirits to thank for your current life. And more than just me—do not give me that look, Pup."

I glanced away and nodded.

"Sure. It doesn't often feel as though I'm in control though," I admitted.

Karthak picked up a well-worn instrument from the cabinet beside her bed, began to idly pluck at its strings and stared at me for a while. Then she began to hum a tune.

The years hadn't done her singing voice any favours.

"My favourite song, this," she told me. "The words tell the tale of a young couple in love. I suppose that they do not feel in control, swayed as they are by their feelings for one another. But their fates are still their own. They do not heed the warnings of the Spirits, and their tale ends a sad one."

"Now *that's* encouraging," I said. "So what's the moral? That I should resign myself to the will of the Spirits? I don't even know what they want from me! The Shaman was confusing, cryptic and un-helpful. And frankly, you speak in riddles just as much."

Karthak still stared at me and plucked out her melody.

Finally she let out a long sigh, and set the instrument down.

"Well, allow me to tell you this clearly: You are important to me, and I would see it that you remember your duties to our people. The Sacharri have their appeal, but they are as the Merchant Combine—a force used to control. We do not belong in their world, and for now must choose the lesser evil."

"The lesser evil? I spent time in their care, remember? They were good to me—So I'd hardly consider them an evil," I told her.

"Not an evil? Tell me pup, beneath their banners would you be a raider?" there was a twinkle in her eye. "Or a wife?"

I hadn't actually thought about that. I didn't even know much about Sacharri women, other than the servants and slaves.

"I might ask Anra about their women. Do they stay back home, whilst the men fight?"

"Have you seen a single female soldier in their ranks?" Karthak asked, and I shook my head. "Well there is your answer."

"So why *is* it that we fight and the males stay behind and look after things? I mean, you told me the tale of Yanghar, but why would the Spirits make it this way around? Wouldn't it be dangerous to be with child, and yet fight in a raid?" I asked. It had perplexed me for the longest time.

"Well I could not honestly tell you why they made us as we are, but the strength passed to our young is drawn from blood spilt, to be sure," Karthak said. "It would serve none of us, for our mothers to cower in the safety of our camps and dens, now would it? With other folk, they gain their strength through their machines and their smithies. They do not have fang or claw, so make up for it with steel and fire and order of all things—so I presume there is no need for their young to be born strong

"You are a curious exception. When you bear a child, you shall mix the two traditions. I expect that it shall be a great blessing—for a wolf and a hound may birth a hybrid, as fierce and as the former, and loyal as the latter."

I didn't even bother to question her about that. She never gave a straight answer concerning the way the shapeshifter had appeared to me, and seemed to still believe it to be my destiny, even if I didn't.

But then I remembered something else about that pregnant Kimora—the weapon that she had carried.

"Karthak, tell me about your blade. Why is it so different from those carried by the others?"

Karthak looked over at the weapon.

"Pick it up. Go on, examine it. And you tell me," she said, and extended an arm towards where the great blackened cleaver leant against the wall near the fire.

I stood and approached her weapon. Now that I was much older, it didn't actually seem quite so large. The blade was maybe three and a half feet long, and the handle added another foot to its length. I suspected that I could probably heft its weight and actually use it—albeit with two hands to swing it, and probably quite clumsily.

It looked like it was forged from a single chunk of black iron, or perhaps even a slightly metallic stone. Near the handle, a notch had been cut and leather had been wrapped around the blade so that Karthak could hook the weapon to her harness.

There were faint markings along its scuffed surface, and they seemed to dance and shift in the flickering light of the hearth.

"It is made from something different. What are these symbols? Are these prayer markings?" I asked, running a finger along the etchings on the unusually warm metal.

"They are. Blessings of Yanghar. The blade was wrought of a crimson star that fell to the earth many leagues away, and many seasons ago. I took the arcing star as my banner, and with that blade, carved a path across the lands. Each warband that rallied to my call gave blessings, and so these were writ upon the surface of the meteorite cleaver."

She watched me trace the sigils with my touch.

"Who forged it?" I asked.

"A dear friend. One long since passed from the world of the living. One of the Bog-folk."

"A Vodnik?" I'd never actually met one, though I certainly had my suspicions about Urd's lineage.

"That is what the Bare-Skinned call them. But then they call us Wolf-men, Beast-men, Hound-Folk, or even Psoglav, as I understand it," she said. I'd heard those names, alongside things like 'savages' and 'monsters'—but didn't really want to mention it.

"I thought that the Combine mining may have been... Bog-folk was it? They had the most impressive beasts of burden. Unlike anything I've ever heard of." I lifted the cleaver, and tried to hold it as if ready for combat. But whilst lighter than I remembered it being, it was still large and cumbersome.

"There are many unusual beasts in the far reaches of the world, my pup. You would be impressed by the great dune-walkers of the Wastes, and the bog beasts of the Gold-Fenn. I suspect though, we may have some of those western beasts to contend with when we assault the Combine." Karthak watched my poor form. "Move your leg forward a little, there. Yes, and lean more of your weight upon it."

With her guidance I could definitely manage her cleaver with more ease. Still though, I far preferred a simple spear, and my trusty dagger.

"So what's next for us?" I asked, after returning Karthak's blade to its original place.

"You shall need to prepare for your northern trek, Pup. But in the meantime, do as you want. Enjoy your youth, and your burgeoning friendship with the boy. I have many things to attend to, then I shall lead the way into the wilderness—to raid."

It would be strange to head to the temple once more, but I was quite excited to meet new rookie pups, and maybe to actually have a proper look around the place this time.

We discussed the details briefly, until Star-Star entered the room, and joined Karthak in her nest of cushions.

We three chatted for a bit. But experience told me that privacy was in order, so I bid them both goodnight, then made my way from Karthak's room to see if I could find my friends, and perhaps find something to drink.

Drinking seemed to be something of a hobby of mine of late, and helped to relieve the constant sense of nervousness that I felt.

Things were changing around me. And just when I thought I had grasped a sliver of normalcy in my abnormal life, the fates and the Spirits turned my world on its head.

THE FIFTH STITCH

DISCOVERY

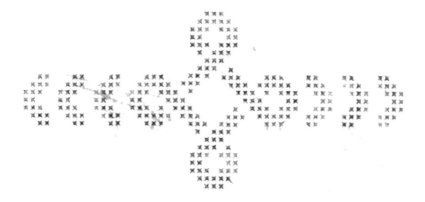

i.

"So I said to him, I said—'You are a flat-faced oaf, and your mother was a whore to pigs and cattle!' And then I smashed him in the face with a bar-stool!" Uya yelled, her face uncomfortably close to the young Hobgoblin soldier's.

"Oh, do not lie Sister! You were throwing bottles at the other Bare-Skin! I hit the captain with the chair!" her twin corrected her, pressing in on the young man's other flank.

That seemed more like how I remembered it, drunk as I was then too.

"Sometimes I forget which one of us I am," Uya admitted, and as strange a thing it was for *her* to say, she really wasn't alone in her confusion.

"Well, which one are you again?" asked the Hobgoblin, leaning as far back in his seat as he could without falling off, but avoiding neither Vulkar's invasion of his space.

"That one is Uya," Ar-Tarak explained. "You can tell because One has this one big spot here…" She reached over the table and poked Uya in the head. "And Two has these two. See?"

She tried to point out the markings on Oya's forehead, but the drunken twin was leaning on the poor soldier.

"Anyway, it looks as though we need more cider. I shall fetch Narod, so that he can fetch it!" she said, and pushed herself to her feet, before staggering off towards the kitchen.

We were spread out along one of the tables in the mess hall—appropriately named, for all of us were in a fairly messy state.

I hadn't meant to get as drunk as I was currently, but someone had found some dice to wager drinks over, and I was useless at it.

I was soon to leave the Blackfort and journey north and a little east, so probably shouldn't have been wasting time drinking, but still I drank—and not wanting to seem weak, I drank far too much.

The trek would take some time, and the weather was worsening with each passing day, so I began the process of preparing myself well ahead of my departure. It took the edge off any guilt I felt for the time I was wasting, though Karthak wouldn't agree.

Of course Sarga and Mazgar wanted to venture out with me, but none of the others seemed particularly excited about the prospect of herding young pups, and instead elected to stay with the warband and do the fun stuff—the intensive raiding on the Combine, as well as the initial assault on their surrounding force, alongside the Sacharri vanguard.

I'd heard the Imperial warriors refer to the Vulkari as 'shock-troopers' and they seemed eager to go into battle together, which must have concerned Karthak somewhat, given her reluctance to become tools of the Easterners.

Whatever the situation though, alongside preparation, I spent a fair deal of time mingling with the Sacharri garrison. In particular, with Anra. And tonight the mingling had devolved into a mess of drinking, singing, gambling, and conversation between off-duty Sacharri Legionnaires and Vulkari.

Not that Vulkari were ever really on any sort of duty.

"So Brownie…" began one young soldier as Ar-Tarak returned with another cask of fancy Icespire cider.

"Zyntael," Anra corrected him, to choirs of mockery and cooing from the Vulkari.

"Uhh… Zyntael. So do you feel strange raiding and killing others of your… uhh… physical kind?"

"Do you?" I asked in reply. What a stupid question. The Combine troopers were often Hobgoblin too.

I noticed the embarrassment on his face, and sighed. I hadn't meant to be rude, and I did understand what he'd meant, having answered countless similar questions.

"I don't think of them as my kind to be honest. I am just as much a part of the warband as these louts. In fact, I have been a part of it for longer!" I told him.

"Hey! That is actually true!" Mazgar added.

"So I just do what we do. Raiding is just the Vulkar way," I said.

The young Hobgoblin nodded, then batted away a Vulkar hand that reached for his mug.

"And there aren't any other Brownies in your warband? No Domovoi either?" he asked.

"Just some slaves. But we sell them to you. Sometimes they get eaten, if they are useless for the market. And before you ask, no, I don't eat them myself. Karthak said that cannibalism is an ill thing to do," I added when I caught the look of horror creeping across his features.

"Star-Star also once told me that when a Vulkar eats the flesh of another Vulkar, she loses her mind and turns into a gibbering and cackling wreck. She was talking about Vulkari, but I assumed the same would apply to me…" I said, and Ar-Tarak weighed in on the matter whilst she poured more drinks for us.

"To partake of your own kind for sustenance is a grave misconduct, that is suitable only for the likes of Arbour Ghouls, the truly deranged, and perhaps those Kobaloi things. Though we think that maybe Uya and Oya have had a little Vulkar snack here or there."

She pointed at the twins, who were pushing their noses together and making strange grunting sounds at one another—for some reason known only to them.

The Hobgoblin laughed, then stopped and looked thoughtful for a bit before asking:

"But if it were my flesh for instance. Would that actually be cannibalism?"

"Well we are both Bare-Skins so I think so. Karthak said that a long time ago, we were born of the same mother. All the Bare-folk," I said. I didn't really know all the answers, and I didn't much care in all honesty, since I didn't plan on eating any captives, so I decided to change the subject.

In retrospect, it might have been innuendo.

"So where were you stationed before you came to these lands? Have you ever been to Azure?" I asked.

He nodded. "I have indeed, I sailed to these frontiers and arrived in Azure. It is a wonderful place, is it not? Before here though, I was part of a scouting detachment based out of a fortress called Highwall. It is perhaps the absolute opposite of Azure, in fact. Cold, boring, as closed up and inhospitable as Azure is open and welcoming."

It sounded like the worst place in the entire world.

"So what took you to the southwestern coast besides their bar fights?" he nodded at the twins. "Selling slaves I presume?"

I shrugged.

"I don't really know. We just went there because Karthak wanted to meet her old friend. Something to do with boats. I mean, we did sell slaves and other spoils in the market, but mostly we just explored."

"And drank," Ar-Tarak said. Then she interrupted a hushed conversation between Anra and Sarga, which sounded like it might have been about me.

"Hey Sarga, tell us some more stories about Azure. Do you remember Mazgar's pirate lovers?"

Mazgar groaned.

Sarga recounted the tale of Mazgar and her hopeless swooning over a crew of pirate Vulkari, much to the group's amusement. This time though, the tale was filled with obscenity and lewd acts that I was certain were completely made up.

Either that, or at some point, I'd passed out during our adventure in Azure, and had missed all of the good bits.

"Wait, wait. You put the candle where?" Anra turned to Mazgar, his eyes wide. "Still lit?"

He looked at me, as if seeking clarification, but I simply shrugged, with a grimace.

"Savage…" Anra muttered into his goblet, then finished his beverage and looked around for more. "We are going to need more, or stronger drink, if these sorts of things happen. Best to erase all memory of the night, lest this one get her hands on any candles."

Now that he mentioned it, I wondered where Ar-Tarak went. Did she leave during Sarga's tale, to find more cider? Or was it Narod that she was hoping to find, so that he could get the cider for her?

"I think I'd better go and find Ar-Tarak. Do you reckon that she has just sneaked off and fallen asleep somewhere?" I said, and got up to follow her into the kitchen.

"Need help?" Anra asked. "I mean… uhh… to carry things."

The Vulkari once again cooed and mimicked him, and his fellow soldiers nudged one another and shared knowing looks.

"Sure," I said, then pulled an offensive gesture at my friends and his as we left.

※　※　※

We found Ar-Tarak, and she had obviously found Narod, and neither were in any way asleep.

The male grinned at me shamelessly. He pushed a bottle of liquor toward me with his foot, before I closed the pantry door and left them to their debaucherous drunken act.

"Well, the pantry is out, and this bottle won't go far. To the cellar?" I suggested, stifling my laughter.

Anra hauled open the cellar hatch, and I lit a lantern, then clambered down the wooden steps into the musty chamber.

I rested the lantern on a stack of boxes some distance into the cellar, then in the flickering glow that it cast, Anra began shifting crates around and looking for something good to bring back to the others.

Instead of helping, I sat on a barrel and watched him.

"Brandy... Brandy... More damned brandy..." he sighed. "What about this? Let me guess, brandy? No wait... This one is... Oh, yeah this is brandy too." He turned toward me, holding a bottle in each hand.

"Does anyone actually like this stuff? I suppose there's a reason it is down here and covered in dust."

I wasn't really paying attention to what he was saying, as he carried on sorting through old casks of undesirable alcohol.

I was just quietly watching him do it.

Watching the way the soft light danced upon his skin. Watching the way the muscles in his arms flexed, as he heaved each dusty box up and into the light.

I thought about how strangely he had behaved when I had first returned to the Blackfort. It was awkward, even beyond the fact that he had been naked and not at all expecting me to interrupt his bathing.

The whole conversation had been an odd one—him questioning me about my visit to Azure, then somehow confessing that he had taken a fancy to me when it was me that had bathed before him, all those summers ago in the east.

What was it he had said about my skin? Something about stars. It had been a nice comment, but the stars presently dancing in front of my eyes made it very hard to remember.

I hadn't really given him much thought other than to tell my friends about him, and how good looking I'd thought he was—for a Hobgoblin of course.

Telling them that was something I'd promptly regretted.

The others had mercilessly mocked me. Claiming that he was some secret lover of mine—even when I was of absolutely no age to even understand the idea, let alone consider it.

Now though, their mockery seemed like encouragement. Watching him search a musty basement for liquor was somehow filling my stomach with butterflies, and making me feel a little dizzy.

Or maybe that was just the cider. Either way, I was excited and terrified.

I had survived myriad skirmishes—even if it was mostly due to a combination of luck, and the ferocity of my fellow raiders—and yet here I was, defeated by my feelings, and incapable of following a clear line of thought. I was positively unsure of what I should say or do about the strange desire that I had to just reach out in the half-darkness and touch his skin...

"So do you think it's true?" he said.

I jumped to my feet, and stared at Anra's face as my own burned.

"The secret passage. Think it's really down here?" Anra asked, recognising my confusion.

Had he been talking to me the whole time?

"I... Uhh... Yeah. Sure..." I managed.

"Well let's find it then, shall we? The liquor here is rubbish, and I feel an odd desire for an adventure coming on," he said.

Then he took my hand in his, and holding the lantern, led me further into the depths of the Blackfort.

We really didn't need the lantern to light our way though, given how much my cheeks and the tips of my ears were ablaze as we wandered between the dusty stacks of crates and barrels. We didn't find a secret passage, but rather a servants' exit that led back up to the ground floor. We also only had the one bottle of liquor, so I suggested that we perhaps attempt to borrow some from Karthak's personal stash.

It would make sense that sneaking around in the Blackfort in the dark of night, might well have dragged a long-forgotten fear back into my thoughts. But, whether because of the alcohol coursing through me, or my present company, I felt a new and different kind of fear.

This fear was not born of memory, but rather, that the strange warmth that tingled within me in the company of the Legion commander's son might subside. And that getting caught this time, might mean an end to what felt like such a fresh and exciting adventure.

Hoping that she was off doing something important, we stalked along the halls of the Blackfort on our way to where Karthak usually slept, and more importantly—where she stashed her liquor.

By now, the various twists and turns of the gloomy corridors were familiar to both Anra and I, and we hastily—though probably not particularly stealthily—made our way up to the northeastern wing of the fortress.

I crouched in front of the door that led to Karthak's luxurious solar, and although I couldn't remember where I'd learnt it, knew first to listen, and then to look through the keyhole and into the room beyond.

When I cupped a hand and listened at the portal, there came not the usual grumblings and mutterings of Karthak (somewhat more of an occurrence of late,) but instead, only the crackling of a fire in the hearth, and the rhythmic drumming of the drizzle on the outside balcony.

I looked up at Anra, who was standing nearby, and fidgeting with his little pendant—a gift from Karthak of polished black stone, apparently. He was staring at me expectantly, eyebrows raised, and with a grin on his face.

I held up a finger to signal patience, and took a moment to blink the constant blur from my eyes, before leaning on the door and taking a look through the keyhole.

It looked like the coast was clear.

Luckily it was, since before I was done peeking within, Anra took the liberty of simply reaching out and opening the door.

With a squeal of surprise, I fell face-first onto one of the many rugs that covered the rough stone floor of Karthak's abode.

Anra helped me to my unsteady feet, giggling the entire time at his little prank, and when I was up, I kicked him in the shin.

He feigned agony, and hopped around the room, before falling upon Karthak's plush bed of cushions and blankets.

I tried my best to ignore him, and set about pilfering some of Karthak's various spirits. I decanted a little of each, until I had filled another bottle. That made two bottles of liquor to bring back to the others, only now that we were alone, I was beginning to hope that the purpose of our mission would be forgotten.

In time, it was.

First, we lay upon the bed together, talking about Karthak, and how she came to be the leader of my brethren. We discussed my place in the warband, and how that came to be as well—though I could scarcely remember many details by now.

Then, the conversation moved toward Anra, just as we moved to Karthak's private balcony, once the drizzle stopped and the stars began to emerge from behind the cloud cover.

We talked about Sacharr, and what it was like, as both a place, and a home. We talked about Anra's life in the Legion, and then his past before that, and eventually about his mother.

He had a fairly dim view of her—considering her to be a poor mother, and a poorer wife to his beloved father, having eloped with his uncle, Manox Thrinax. In fact, his views on women in general, as well as their place in Sacharr, seemed a little insulting. Fired up as I was by the potent mix of Karthak's liquor and his scathing words, I took it upon myself to defend my kind.

Somehow though, the conversation led to Azure. To the bathhouses and brothels, and to the strange worry he had expressed; that I had lain with some other man during my stay—absurd though I thought that was. I couldn't quite comprehend why it should matter, nor why it meant so much to him, what I had or hadn't done.

"So what? A man can whore to his heart's content, yet a woman must remain pure? That seems like a bit of a double-standard to me," I scoffed, and stood up to move inside, next to the hearth. "Sounds like you just want to control your women!"

Anra followed me inside, trying his best to make me understand what he meant.

"No. You misunderstand, Zyntael! It's an indictment of men more so than it is a desire to control women. As far as I see it, men are expendable, they're cheap. Whereas a woman's value to Sacharr is immeasurable," he explained, and sat next to me before the crackling fire. "A woman can be taught to raise a spear in times of war, she can tend a farm and raise livestock if need be—but can a man ever be taught to nurse a suckling babe?"

I took another swig from my concoction as he continued. He'd almost finished the other, and this bottle definitely wasn't going to make it back downstairs either.

"How long does the man's part in the creation of life last? He may brag that it is hours, but no matter how great a lover or a liar he may be, it is nothing compared to a woman's role. It is no nine moons to carry the babe, then countless more to raise it.

"That, Zyntael, is why a woman should always look to be better than a man. That is why she must value herself above all others. After all, if a woman lays with a lout and a whoreson and the seed takes root, then how long must she bear the burden? Who then protects and provides for her and her offspring?"

He looked proud of himself, and paused to drink.

"Hence; marriage," he said, and pushed the cork back into his bottle for emphasis.

"You know who you remind me of? Right now?" I asked, pointing an unsteady, accusatory finger at the smug bastard. "Do you remember back east, there was that magistrate? The one in charge of who worked where? Looked like an insect?"

"You mean Quaestor Baculus?" Anra asked.

"Yeah. Him. You remind me of him."

The boy looked half insulted, half confused. "What? Why that old toad?" he asked.

"Because all that nonsense you just spouted, sounded just like something he'd say. I remember once; I got in trouble for fighting," I told him. "He went on and on about some siege weapon or other. And just now, when you were talking about Sacharri women, I almost thought I was back there."

He laughed.

"Yes I suppose that is the official Sacharri explanation. It is what father used to say," he said.

"Ha! So you admit it. It is all just another Sacharri way of controlling people. I am right, and you keep your wives as slaves!" I declared triumphantly. "Well, I refuse to be some man's slave. One day I might be Yanghar to my own Vulkar, and the whelp who gave me the pup will be honoured to have been chosen for the duty. I shan't just be some property. Some stupid wife, just because a dumb law makes it mandatory."

He looked at me as though I was no longer speaking Solent Fae, then popped the cork back out of his bottle, and threw it at me.

"Who'd want to wed you anyway?"

It bounced off my forehead.

"Oh that does it!" I hissed in mock rage, and attacked the Hobgoblin.

ii.

Clumsy grasping and accidental scratching. The occasional bump of tooth against tooth. There wasn't much about the experience that even a generous person might call romantic.

Neither of us knew what to do, and were driven instead by some inexplicable instinct, and desperate youthful passion—helped along by our inebriation, of course.

It was awkward and uncomfortable to begin with, though not really painful—he first atop me, then I, him—shifting around in an attempt to find something that wouldn't numb limbs, or bring cramp to joints.

We found our confidence the further we went—pausing briefly only to scurry away to his chambers, for fear of Karthak's return.

It even began to feel good. A strange mixture of warmth, and an electric tingling began to spread through my body—not unlike the feeling caused by many of our ritual draughts.

But it was all over too soon, and Anra flopped weakly back upon the sweaty blankets, exhausted and spent.

I lay there, confused and messy, but glad for the experience we had shared, and thinking of the ways that Mazgar and Sarga would react when I told them.

They might have wondered where we had gone—whether we'd found the entrance to the secret passages that burrowed deep into every part of the Blackfort.

Or maybe they wouldn't. After all, they were as drunk as we were, and enjoying the company of the Hobgoblin soldiers a little more than the soldiers might have fancied.

"That was good," Anra panted.

I nodded, unsure whether I completely agreed.

"I suppose it was. It sort of got better, but... Oh well, maybe we need practice." I didn't want to ruin his moment of apparent glory, but was a terrible liar, so instead opted for clumsy honesty.

"I didn't hurt you, did I?" he asked suddenly.

I laughed. What a strange thing to say.

"I'm tougher than that!" I said, and rolled onto my side to face him as he lay, satisfied, on his back. "Besides, you lost that fight."

I pressed myself against the outstretched boy as he chuckled. I enjoyed the smell of his body—the scent of exertion, apples, and mint.

"Are you smelling my armpit?" he snorted. "You really are a savage, you know!"

He drew an arm around me and pulled me in closer, so that my head lay upon his chest.

And I fell asleep to the steady pulsing of his heartbeat.

No tears did I shed as I stood there, beneath that familiar crimson sky, and watched it all burn.

And as they reached into the darkening void above, the pillars of inky smoke carried with them the remnants of all I'd known, all I'd come to cherish—and all I'd come to resent.

I whispered no prayers as it all became nothing, for it seemed that the Spirits too had been burned away.

After a silent moment, I turned away from it, and looked down at the face of the child whose hand clutched my own.

The raging fire flickered in his wide green eyes and on his Hobgoblin features. He looked back up at me.

This was to be his legacy, but now he was spared the suffering.

"Slaves are we all," I told him. "But for now, we shall leave those shackles. We shall leave this place."

And we would. But before then, hand in hand, we would watch the last of the Sacharri presence in our lands burn—just for a while longer.

iii.

Anra was gone when I woke up.

In his place, there was a hound whom someone had let inside the chamber, and who caused me the briefest moment of confusion and fright, when I rolled over and came face to ugly face with it.

I assumed that duty had called, and so Anra had been required elsewhere in the fortress, but a part of me thought it was instead just sobriety. Perhaps the morning light had cleared his mind and vision, and so alerted him to his folly, and inspired a daring escape.

Whatever the reason, he was gone all the same.

My mind swam with glimpses of the previous night, and a blush began to overtake my cheeks. Once fully awake though, my skull felt as if it was going to explode, and my stomach churned and threatened to do much the same.

If I didn't know any better, I would think I had been thoroughly beaten by a horde of Kobaloi. It was like Azure all over again. Thankfully without as much mess, but unfortunately without a beautiful ocean to wash it away in too.

Why did I have to think about water?

I was unbearably thirsty, and when I breathed into my cupped hand, a foul stench made me think that one of those Kobaloi had perhaps shit in my mouth. Maybe that was why Anra had escaped.

"Miko. Fetch water..." I commanded the plains-hound, but he just looked at me blankly then resumed his sleep.

"Bastard."

I'd had a strange dream again. It briefly flickered back to me as I pulled on my overshirt.

I really needed to talk to Narod about some herbs or something—anything that would help my mind to remain quiet throughout the night.

Then I remembered where I'd last seen him.

I wouldn't be the only victim of mockery for last night's antics, after all.

With as much effort as I could muster, I dragged myself from the bed, relocated my discarded breeches, and pulled them on. Then I valiantly, though reluctantly, trudged off to face the cruel morning. I had only made it halfway down the hall, when none other than Manox Threydon himself strode up and blocked my path.

"I would have words with you, girl," he stated.

I squinted up at him through bleary eyes as he loomed overhead, but in my present state I was far too unwell to be as intimidated as I should have been—in fact, I welcomed death.

"I hope they're brief," I replied.

"First though, with whom did you spend the night?" he demanded.

Strange that I'd considered all of the mockery I'd have to face from my fellow Vulkari—and even some of the Sacharri garrison—but I hadn't once considered how Anra's father might react, once word had inevitably spread of last night.

By Yanghar, what a bad start to the day.

"Forgive me Commander, I was very drunk last night..." I began.

"I understand well the passions of youth, for I was once like he—but do not think for a moment that your childish romantics have any future. I'd not have it that the pet Kimora of Karthak ensorcell my only son so."

He towered over me.

"I see the maneuverings of your raid leader. And I shall not allow such a breach of station, regardless of our law. Enjoy your tryst, but remember that should anything come of your union, my name shall be prize to neither you, nor your... progeny. No matter how much Karthak might wish it."

I didn't know what to say. The impetuous, defiant spirit within me wanted to protest, but then, I had nothing to really protest about.

I wouldn't have put it past Karthak to have some strange plans that involved his son. It was unusual for her *not* to have strange plans, involving anything, really. But I wasn't some pawn to be used in her schemes, and I'd thought she was well aware of that by now. As far as

I was concerned, there was no great plot to bewitch Anra, so last night was simply… What *was* last night?

Perhaps it had all just been the inevitable outcome of our similar ages and situations, provoked by boredom, and the constant goading from my sisters and his comrades—and the liquor. Perhaps it had actually been something more. I couldn't say, and Threydon wouldn't have heard it anyway.

"You overestimate our affection, Lord Threydon," I said simply, and mustered as innocent an expression as I could manage through my crapulence.

The Goblin commander narrowed his eyes at me and leaned a little closer—brave, given my breath.

"Be sure of that," he said, then his features softened, and it was as though a whole other Hobgoblin stood before me. He even placed a gentle hand upon my shoulder.

"Now, tell me all that you remember of whom you saw at the Merchant's excavation site."

Taken aback by his sudden change of attitude and his interest in something that had happened weeks prior, all the same, I did as he bid, and detailed what I'd seen—in particular, the Hobgoblin who might very well have been his brother.

Threydon listened until I was finished, somehow unmoved by my heinous breath.

"And you are certain beyond doubt that he was the same man that you saw within my throne room?" he asked.

"Yes Lord Threydon, he looked like you, though not quite as handsome."

He didn't seem to care much for my flattery, and merely nodded sternly.

"Thank you, Vulk-child," he said, then raised a finger in front of my face. "Though remember what I have said of my son. I would rather that I did not have to forbid your company, but I shall, should last night be repeated."

Then the Hobgoblin lord stood and marched away, whilst I remained there stunned.

※　※　※

I waited until we were a day's travel from the Blackfort before I told Mazgar and Sarga about that night, and it looked surprisingly like they weren't going to make fun of me at all.

"I suppose that would explain why he was avoiding you," Mazgar suggested, hacking at the undergrowth we trudged through.

"Do you think Lord Threydon shall kill you?" Sarga asked. "You know, once he realises that his heir and only son is in love with you?"

I shrugged. Probably.

Mazgar looked confused. "Can Kikimora and Goblins make young together?"

Sarga looked at her like she was an idiot.

"They are the same thing. All Bare-Skins are the same, but with little differences; short, tall, dark skin, light skin, round ears, ears like spear-heads. They are still just Bare-Skins. Their weird babies shall just be a mixture of all the worst features of their kind."

Mazgar listened to Sarga's explanation then asked another question of me.

"So shall you be a queen or something?"

"She shall be a princess I think. Is Manox Threydon not still the king?" Sarga said.

"No," Mazgar began to giggle. "I mean once he dies of shame."

Maybe I was too hasty. I wasn't going to get away with no mockery after all.

"You are both horse-sons and shits! You're the ones who were goading him on," I reminded them. "I just said that—"

"That you thought he was beautiful, and would be a good lover?" Sarga was laughing now too. "Well, was he?"

"By the Mother, I wish I were bigger than you both. Then I'd thrash you soundly, and get some peace and quiet while we journey."

"Perhaps your child shall be bigger. Being half-Goblin and all." Sarga flicked my belly, and with that, my companions' relentless mockery began in earnest. For days it continued sporadically, and ceased only when we finally crested the last few hillocks that bordered the valley of the Mother.

Below us, almost exactly as I remembered it, lay the temple of Yanghar.

The compound consisted of an ancient stone ziggurat, encircled by mighty walls. It was all built from enormous blocks of carved stone, which looked to have been brought to the verdant hills from some far-off quarry. In fact, the entire temple looked out of place in that valley—as though picked up from elsewhere and placed in its spot by some colossal Vulkar hand that reached down from the heavens.

If Karthak were here, she would assuredly confirm as much.

She had sent a message to the Mothers within, to alert them to our coming presence. I wasn't entirely sure how though, since I'd not heard of any scouts or messengers departing for the temple recently. Nonetheless, as we approached the mighty walls of the temple complex, two Vulkari came out from beyond the burnished bronze gates to greet us.

They were clearly mighty raiders in a past life; both covered in the many scars of the raid, and one missing an arm from the elbow down.

"Little Sisters," the first spoke. Her voice was accented and soft. Almost soothing. "Praise Yanghar, that she delivered you safely to our door this day."

Both Vulkari bowed to us, and we three bowed to them in return.

The other, one-armed, guard looked us up and down—apparently unconcerned by the fact that I was a Kimora.

"You look to be exhausted. Come, we shall see to it that you are bathed and fed, then we shall present this season's claim," she said with an earthen rumble.

It was a strange way to speak of the new recruits.

We followed the two Vulkari through the same halls as our war-band had, seemingly an age ago. This time however, the carved stories on the walls made sense to me:

First, there was Yanghar. Hunting, sleeping, fighting other beasts—even mating—beneath the wide, starry skies of the plains.

Then, she sat atop a mound, and the stars above her this time took the shape of a figure. From it, wavy lines of Magick beamed down upon the lonesome plains-hound.

After this, the story went much the way Karthak had said; she birthed a pup, and herself became a constellation. The pup was raised by smaller hounds, who over the course of several walls, became as she—bipedal and Vulkar.

Then they took up spear and blade, and drove a score of smaller two-legged figures from the plains.

Eventually Vulkar too became a constellation, and her progeny roamed free beneath her.

Finally though, there was another carved panel—one which I had not noticed last I was here, or perhaps hadn't paid attention to.

There was a small figure, standing atop some sort of dias or altar. Below them were massed countless Vulkari, and beyond them burned some sort of castle, or city. Curiously, snakes rose from the conflagration.

More curiously, that figure was not Vulkar themselves, though the familiar patterns of the Vyshivka surrounded them.

And even more curiously still, was that in the centre of the small carved person, over their belly, was a spiral. It radiated those same wavy lines as had been bestowed upon Yanghar herself.

A strange warmth filled my lower abdomen as I gazed upon the carving—lit by the flickering glow of our escorts' torches. The warmth seemed to grow and spread within me, building to a near-painful heat.

Just as my insides burned, the wavy lines that emanated from the figure began to move. They danced around before my eyes.

"Zyntael..." came a distant voice. It was not enough to pull me from my trance.

My head swam. I almost smelt the burning town, heard the cacophony of Vulkar chants. I almost felt the elation of victory over some oppressive master, whose claim now smouldered around me. The voice came again, a little louder. Still I ignored it.

> *The skies burned crimson above me. A weight tugged at my core.*
> *There was blood on my brow, though it was not mine.*
> *Sarga was there beside me. As was Mazgar.*
> *I was excited. I was alive. I was strong. But I was also a little sad.*
> *Something terrible had needed to be done, for all our sakes, and I*
> *had done it.*
> *With this act of carnage and defiance, a crusade had begun. More*
> *violence would follow, but eventually so would true freedom.*
> *A hand reached down from the skies—dark, furred, and bejeweled.*
> *It grasped my shoulder.*

The escort held me firmly with her decorated hand, until I was fully present once more, before grasping my other shoulder and turning me away from the carving.

"And thus you understand, chosen pup of Karthak of the Crimson Star. Chosen pup of Yanghar," she whispered in that soothing voice of hers.

But I didn't understand. I knew, but couldn't possibly understand.

iv.

W e were indeed bathed and fed, then made to rest before we were permitted to visit the Mothers, and the pups.

Whilst we lounged around in a warm chamber, scented with a rich and soothing incense, I tried to explain what had happened to me in the hallway.

"So you have been having these... dreams... for a while now?" Mazgar asked, an intense look of concern on her face.

"Yes," I admitted.

"And you did not tell either of us?" She cocked her head, visibly confused. "I can understand not talking to the others, they are morons. But we are your best friends and closest sisters. We would not think you stranger than we already do!"

"I know," I began. "But for some reason these dreams always leave me feeling a sort of... I don't know. Maybe shame?

There's nothing in them that we haven't already been through. But there are these little details that set them apart from fantasies of raiding. Like, for instance, I dreamed of Karthak—slain by my hand. I wouldn't want to admit that."

At their insistence, I recounted as many of my dreams as I could recall. Sarga was nodding as I spoke about the dream in which I held Karthak's head, then quietly added her own opinion on it.

"You called her 'the betrayer' so I would assume, if these are not just fantasies, that she shall deserve it. You and me? We are both faced with the same prospect—slaying our birth mother." She caught herself. "Well, not *birth* in your case, but still, you know what I mean."

I did. But it still felt wrong. Still felt shameful.

"What of the Sacharri? Why are we fighting them?" Mazgar suddenly asked.

"Well, I don't really know. But I get the feeling that it's to free our-selves from them, somehow," I told her. "I get the feeling that I have started some great betrayal myself. Unlike Karthak, though, I am cel-ebrated—and not loathed."

"And you are with pup? In each of these dreams?"

"I am." I confirmed Mazgar's query, and she looked somehow proud. "In fact, in a dream I had, shortly before leaving the Blackfort, after uhh…" I trailed off.

"After Anra planted his seed in your belly." Sarga finished my sen-tence with words that I probably wouldn't have chosen myself.

"Okay, after that. Well, I was with a boy. He was older—no pup at all. We were watching the Solent fortress of Threydon burn. It wasn't some small village, but the entire city."

"So you slew Threydon?" Sarga asked, wide eyed and impressed.

"No. Or not then, at least. I got the feeling that I had slain some-one else, but it wasn't him. I got the feeling that whoever it was I'd killed, whatever it was I'd done, it had meant the last of the Sacharri presence in these lands," I explained.

We pondered the bizarre vision I'd had for some time, before sleep claimed us one by one.

In a stroke of luck perhaps, and in spite of the evening's discus-sion, I had only mundane dreams. There was no burning sky—no desolation of Sacharri territory. Instead I dreamt that I was chasing a painted hare. Only, once I caught it, I realised that it was not painted. Rather, it was simply outlandishly colourful.

Sarga and Mazgar were there too—tiny, and being chased by gi-gantic colourful hares. I chased them around for a bit too, before the dream morphed into another, and another after that. So it went—un-til I was woken by the sound of something metal, falling on a stone floor.

I sat upright, in time to see a very small Vulkar—smaller even than my friends had been when we'd claimed them—scurry from our room. It had made its way into our den, and had clearly made an at-tempt to retrieve my Sacharri blade.

Whether it simply wanted to examine the weapon or was attempt-ing a theft didn't matter. Whatever its motivation, the pup had fum-bled the dagger, and dropped it to the floor before beating a hasty retreat.

After much yawning, and stretching away the aches of our journey, I dressed myself and left the room to seek out the curiously diminu-tive pup.

I found a whole host of them.

I began to wonder where they might have come from, given that I'd never seen any pregnant Vulkari in the warband. Perhaps though, they carried their young in such a way that it was impossible to tell they were even with pup. Or maybe some of the many sisters who had come and gone over the seasons, had left us before the visible signs of young within her belly.

The little pups darted here and there—chasing one another, playing games with all manner of childish toys, and of course, fighting. They were minded by a very old Vulkar. She had milky eyes, patchy fur, and used a simple wooden cane to help her to stay upright. She sniffed the air when I entered the hall, and after squinting in my direction for a bit, she beckoned me over to her.

"You have the scent of something else, young Raid-Sister," she told me, with a voice that sounded as old and worn as she looked. Then, once I was close enough, she realised why that was. "Ahh. The Bare-Skinned Vulkar. I am honoured to meet Karthak's progeny."

I bowed to her, even if she probably couldn't see it.

"I am honoured to meet you also, Mother," I replied, and at this, the ancient Vulkar cackled.

"Child, I am no mother. I never could be, thanks to a raiding wound. There is no real shame in that though. I do my part in the way that I can."

She pointed out an old scar, which ran from hip to hip across her belly. I knew that there was shame in being barren, but wondered if that applied where the cause was injury.

"So you watch over the young?" I asked.

Again, she cackled.

"Perhaps 'watch' is not the term, but I can still track each pup with my nose and ears."

To demonstrate, the old Vulkar singled out a pair of fighting pups and corrected their technique—encouraging the losing pup to fight harder, and the other to finish her off before she had a chance to.

I laughed at how typical it was.

"So these pups, where did they come from?" I asked her.

"From other tribes…" she said. "These are all who remain of the Vulkari in the lands to the east. We have been all but eradicated. Driven once more, from our homes in the Wilds—just as was the case in Yanghar's day."

"By the Merchant Combine?"

"They and others." The Vulkar nodded. "Wherever we dwell, other creatures shall make their attempts to unpick our stitch from the Vyshivka of the world. They cannot abide our existence—whether threatened by our raiding, or simply loathing our freedoms.

Not all Vulkari do raid the other peoples, you must understand. Though it is the most common lifestyle for our people, there are—rather, there *were*—Vulkari who farmed, Vulkari who traded, even Vulkari who sought to integrate into the empires and kingdoms of the Bare-Skins."

I wondered why Karthak had never made mention of these ways of living. After all, it would certainly draw less ire from both Sacharr and the Combine—and whoever else dwelt where Vulkari did.

"To the south there are Vulkar pirates and merchants. Their integration, more successful than others have been," the matriarch continued. "But even they risk destruction, once civility and peace becomes the more profitable option to the empires. Some may survive in body, but the spirit of our people, the spirit of Vulkar, dies a little more with every treaty and deal signed onto parchment."

I was starting to understand Karthak's distaste toward Gill's opulent lifestyle, and why she remained so distrustful of the Legion.

"What's the plan then?" I asked. "If there even is one."

She cocked her head and shrugged.

"We must adapt, though remain ourselves. We must find the balance between our freedom and our survival." She was nodding to herself as she spoke, as though the words comforted her somehow. "All shall come in time, but you bear a burden that shall secure both."

I didn't like the sound of it, but it wasn't the first time I'd been told such, and I would have loved to stay there, listening to the wizened matriarch tell me of the world and the future—with her chalky voice and infinite wisdom. Soon, however, the time came to greet the Mothers and to meet the new recruits.

Once my friends and one of the escorts from yesterday had fetched me from the hall, we made our way into the antechamber that connected to the nursing room.

There we waited to be allowed into that great carved hall, where the Mothers sat upon their gilded thrones. Just as before, we were beckoned in after a prayer, and led before the hulking nurses by warriors who wore exquisitely ornate armour.

We each bowed before the Mothers—who all but ignored us as they suckled their pups. Far fewer pups than had been present the last time around.

Following the lead of the other Vulkari, I stepped forward to touch bulging bellies, and kiss bejeweled hands. It was a struggle to reach the mountainous Vulkari, but I made every effort to do it with as much grace and deference as I could display.

Beyond the hall where the Mothers sat, a smaller room held our awaiting pups.

There were eight of them.

⚜ ⚜ ⚜

"Runts. They are all runts. And we are expected to train these… runts!?" Sarga was fuming.

She'd used the word 'runt' at least fifteen times now. Pretty soon it would make up the entirety of her vocabulary.

I thought back to something Karthak had once told me, about how the more words one knew, the more power they could wield. I began to worry that my friend would become all but useless.

"Runts can grow to become fearsome, you know," I informed Sarga, and nodded toward Mazgar.

The sandy little Vulkar shrugged, and shook her head with a grin.

"I do not know about that, Sister," Mazgar began unhelpfully. "I am not exactly the strongest in our band."

I sighed.

"Well, you're still stronger than I am, and any Hobgoblin, for that matter," I said. "Besides, these pups will grow, and they will also be formidable—by Bare-Skin standards, at least."

The pups looked dismayed. It wasn't their fault, and from what the old matriarch had said, they were the last we'd ever get from their tribes anyway.

"Let us just be gone from here. We shame Yanghar by even considering such a claim." Sarga spat.

"No! We are taking these pups. We shame Yanghar by even considering the idea of abandoning our own kind," I stated, finally.

She grumbled, but she relented. There was no other choice, and Sarga knew it. I was sure she would understand once I told her of the dire state of our people elsewhere, but my friend was the product of a different, more violent Vulkar. It was hard for her to see strength in more than a physical sense—except, of course, in the case of my own.

Mazgar on the other hand, was overjoyed at the prospect of no longer being the weakest Vulkar in our entourage, and also our entire

288

warband—males notwithstanding. She took it upon herself to corral the pups, and where she went, they would go too.

After only one more day spent in the temple, we set off for the journey back to the Blackfort. The new pups were used as porters, and made to carry both our spare equipment, and our supplies.

Initially, I thought it a little cruel, but upon overhearing them chatter excitedly about how this was all part of a test—something that would see them become cruel and fearsome raiders like us—I figured I should act the part.

V.

Ragged, bleary-eyed, battle-scarred and starving. It wasn't just the pups, but me too—perhaps more so. Where they could at least consume the cooked meat from fallen Combine soldiers or peasants, I would have to go hungry.

It was almost funny to me that every one of our raiding party thought of me as Vulkar in all instances but this. I was glad for it though, and wouldn't have eaten the flesh of a Bare-Skin in any case—irrespective of my constant hunger.

When we trekked through wooded areas or near streams, I was sure to hunt or fish, but each settlement that we came upon was either outright deserted, or very close to. And so presently, we travelled over abandoned pastures and meadows—with not even rabbits and hares to be found.

The Combine had been careful to deny any logistical advantage to the Sacharri, being sure to drive away livestock and empty or burn food stores. And so I starved.

I was certain that my two closest friends were regretting their decision to venture out with me. Sure, getting to the Temple had been quick, clean and easy, but with eight pups in tow, we had turned southward once more and not a day into our journey, we'd been set upon by a detachment of the purple-clad scum.

Taken by surprise, and knowing full well that the eleven of us were no match for properly equipped soldiers, we dumped what we carried, split up, and dispersed into the cover of the frosty hills—each taking a few of the hopeless youngsters with us.

I lost two of my three. One was killed by an archer as we scattered, the other simply wandered off into the woods.

After half a day of searching for her, I'd found her mangled corpse. She had been half eaten by Spirits only knew what.

A stag bear perhaps?

Maybe they didn't only eat honey.

In short time, we regrouped in the mountains southeast of the temple—where I discovered that I had fared the worst in keeping my wards alive.

Sarga was trailed by three beaten-up, but still-living pups, and Mazgar had only lost one of her two charges.

Apparently the pup had fallen into a ravine and broken apart on the jagged rocks below, mere moments prior to them finding us.

Still, and despite their trial by fire, the five surviving pups were chatty and excited.

At least to begin with.

"That was a great idea. Meeting at this tall rock, no matter what happened," one said.

"The older sisters are so wise, and Raider Sarga killed one of the Bare-Skins that followed us," another added.

"May-gu did not make it out of the ambush. She walks with Vulkar and our Mother now."

"As do Ugtaya and Tannok. But we are favoured. We shall be raiders yet!"

We let them chatter amongst themselves and convened to plan our path south.

"What do you reckon? Make our way down from the highlands and traverse open terrain?" Mazgar asked. "I wager there are enemy soldiers crawling all over these parts."

"I don't know. That ambush may have been specific. Urga could have given the Combine the location of the temple," I suggested, then noticed Sarga's black expression. "We might be better served by sticking to the mountains. There are probably at least a handful of trails that we could follow."

Sarga kicked a rock.

"Filthy turncoat. I am ashamed to have sprung from her loins," she muttered.

"Your suggestion?" I asked her, once she had finished grumbling.

"Stick to the mountain. At least we shall have cover," she said.

"Then it is settled. I shall round up the pups. Do you think they shall all make it? I cannot recall being so hopeless," Mazgar said.

Neither could I, though I supposed I was probably just as inept—if not more so—when I first began training.

We spent the following days scurrying along treacherous paths and leaping across narrow chasms. We slowly travelled ever further south until, almost one week since we had left the temple, we were forced to halt.

A rockslide had blocked what had become the only easy way onward, and so after some deliberation, we elected to detour westward, down the mountainside, and into Combine territory.

Their lands really weren't any different than the Sacharri land, or at least, the frontiers that had only recently been claimed by the Legion. Further east, the plains were dryer, and the earth a coppery reddish hue of course, but the farmland and open fields, the forests, fens, rivers, and mounds on either side of the Stormhills were practically identical.

I didn't really know what I had been expecting in all honesty, but for whatever reason, I had held some small belief that there would be, at the very least, some difference.

Instead, we marched along past much the same scenery as we were used to, until we reached lands that we had been beaten to by the touch of war.

The first few hamlets looked to have been abandoned. There was no evidence of conflict, yet almost everything of worth was gone. Buildings were mostly burnt, and wells were either filled in, or spoiled with rotting carcasses.

We'd been travelling for quite some time now, and I wondered how the others were getting on with their raids. I regretted taking on the task of collecting the youngsters.

One of them—I didn't know her name yet—was wearing my spare bone breastplate, and it amused me that it actually fit her. I really was quite pathetic compared to Mazgar—and especially Sarga.

"Kikimor-Sister, do you need something?" the whelp asked, noticing my gaze.

"No, nothing. Though it occurs to me; I don't know your name."

"It is Feygar-Shar," she told me. And for some reason, she looked very embarrassed.

"Kimor-Killer?" I asked, and laughed. "Don't be ashamed of that—I have killed many Kimori, I'm sure. In fact, when I think about it, it seems to be pretty normal for people to kill their own kind. I've seen it done as punishment, in battle, and even just for the sake of it."

The small Vulkar looked a little relieved, then said "I have not killed anyone yet. Pretty pointless name."

"You will get your chance, I guarantee it. And if it makes you feel any better, my family name is Fairwinter. It seems to be a contradiction." I shrugged, and held a hand up to catch the early winter drizzle, which fell from the patchy clouds above. "Anyway, we will stop for a bit shortly. See that smoke? That's likely a village. Since you are already dressed for a raid, you can accompany me when we scout the settlement."

It felt good to boss the young Vulkari around. They looked up to me, even though I was barely stronger than they were.

We had assaulted a few smaller hamlets as we travelled, but between the last and now, had crossed nothing but desolate fields. I hoped that the smoke indeed signalled the possibility of a raid. Of food to be taken.

Sure enough, the smoke was from a village that bordered what looked to be a great forest. The buildings hadn't been razed, and the woods were neither cut down, nor burned. We halted, prepared ourselves, then crept onward—to scout the place out before the weak sun dipped too low in the grey evening sky.

❊　❊　❊

We approached from the north, and moved westward to skirt the edge of the forest and use the undergrowth as cover.

The village was larger than I had first thought, and the few buildings that we had seen from afar were only the edge of the settlement—the rest of the small wooden houses were almost entirely surrounded by the woods.

I wondered how good a defense the trees would make, and imagined that they'd offer a good vantage from which to spot approaching marauders, but hoped that the opposite was true and that we could use them as a shield for our raid.

Something bugged me, but I couldn't quite place what that was.

"Zyntael, circle further west. Take your shadow and this one with you. You are smaller and might be less likely to be spotted. I think it might be a Combine village. Garrisoned perhaps," Sarga whispered. "We should scout first, then meet up again to plan our assault—if it is possible."

I agreed and then motioned for Feygar-Shar and Okra—the other pup whom she had pointed out—to follow me.

Crouching low, I made my way across a short stretch of open ground, then pressed myself against a tree trunk and waited for the pups to follow suit.

"You two wait here. Watch all directions, and howl if you spot any soldiers. We don't want to fight a small army. If there are only villagers, then we will be fine. But soldiers will kill us, understand?" The two Vulkari nodded, their eyes wide and their spears gripped tightly.

I peered around the tree, and could see that a small rocky path ran nearby. It looked as though it meandered deeper into the woods in one direction, and back to the village—across a shallow stream—in the other.

I was scanning the edge of the treeline, looking for signs of life in the village, when I heard the unmistakable sound of pebbles crunching underfoot—someone was walking along the path.

I crouched low, and watched as two figures strolled along the path from the village towards the woods. The taller one was wearing a simple linen tunic and a work knife on his belt, the other was clad in a purple and grey hooded jerkin and carried a mace or club of some sort at their hip.

Both of them were Kimori.

"The Black Legion has broken through the defensive line in the east. They took the Vulkar fort," the Combine Kimora told the other. "You must abandon the village—there will be no stopping them, should they spread into our lands."

"Son. You know we won't leave. You may have joined the Merchants, but we will not. We will always belong here, and be free of outside influence. Already the Wardens are constructing defences and gathering supplies," the other replied. "I urge you to abandon your new fellows. I understand the appeal, but their ideas are folly."

The shorter figure let out a short, sharp sigh.

"You don't understand, Father. You have not seen the world as the Enlightened do. I have glimpsed it, but am only just Awakened."

"And here is that rubbish again. It is of the dark-arts. It is not natural. Our people don't need awakening. We have guarded the forests and the valleys for longer than the Goblins have had their cities."

The taller figure rested a hand on the short man's shoulder, and they both stopped only a handful of yards away from where I hid.

I glanced back at the two pups, who were peering into the undergrowth at me. I held a finger to my lips and hoped that they'd remain in place—and remain quiet.

"The Combine is the only chance we have. I have seen the raids. The carnage that the savage beast-men leave in their wake. I have seen them, Father. I was there when they took the Blackfort, and only just escaped with my life," the short one said. "It was far worse than the raid on us. Far worse."

"I understand it, Son, truly I do. I know why you went there. I would likely have done the same, were it your mother who was taken. But the girl is gone and probably dead—a victim of the carnage that the beasts so enjoy."

"But you heard what the Pixie told her father—She still lived," the younger man protested, but his father shook his head.

"Yes, she may have been alive then, but that was how many summers ago? She is gone. You must accept that, and understand that your people need you."

Just at that moment, a stick snapped behind me. I thought it was one of the idiot pups, and instantly regretted relying on them. When I turned to check though, I saw them both pointing and gesturing furiously at something off to my right.

It was a bear, and a rather large one at that.

I ducked low and heard the two men whisper to each other, then one threw a rock at the animal and shouted to drive it away.

I'd never known brown bears to be particularly aggressive, and thankfully this one didn't seem to be an exception. Instead of attacking, it simply loped away into the woods.

Unfortunately, the bear wasn't the only thing the men had spotted.

"Show yourself!" the father shouted out. I wasn't sure if he was speaking to me, or to the pups though. He whispered to his son "Fetch the Wardens—there is someone lurking in the bushes."

I couldn't risk an alarm being raised, so decided to act. As quickly as I could, I stood and hurled my spear. Then I scrambled after it, towards the men. The pups obviously understood my intent, and I heard them crashing through the bracken behind me.

My throw wasn't very good. The projectile merely grazed the larger of the two men. Luckily, it was enough to knock him off balance, and so I charged headlong into him to finish the job.

He was easily a foot taller than me, and nowhere near as starved, so only stumbled back a little. I twisted away from the man and slashed out at the other figure with my dagger as he struggled to wrench the mace from his belt. I caught him across the chest, but the blade didn't cut through the layers of padding—despite how well crafted my weapon was. Instead, it glanced off, and luckily clipped his unprotected knuckles.

He cursed and dropped his weapon.

The two pups reached us, and both attacked the shorter Kimora. They lashed out with their spears, but he managed to fend them off somehow.

The older man stood, holding his own short blade in his hand, pointing it at me. He seemed more confused than eager to fight.

Then, just as I readied myself to strike, and my two rookie fighters overcame his son, he shouted:

"Stop!"

And for some reason, we actually did.

In the short and confused reprieve, the son took the opportunity to run. The two pups were looking at me, so didn't immediately notice. I pushed past them and gave chase.

"Keep him there!" I called out to the pups. "Don't let him raise the alarm—but try not to kill him!"

I sprinted after the fleeing Kimora, feet slipping on the loose pebbles of the path as I went. He was quick—but I was gaining on him.

The path eventually opened up to a small clearing, with a pair of large boulders in its centre. The Combine soldier stopped to face me, and I crashed into him at full speed. This time, the momentum carried us both over and into the hard, mossy surface of the rock.

I pressed the advantage once again and began pummeling the Kimora, whilst he struggled to fend off my blows. I wasn't really sure what I was trying to achieve, short of maybe subduing my opponent—but at least in that regard, it seemed like I was succeeding.

Unfortunately it didn't last long, and somehow, he managed to wriggle free from beneath me. He retreated cautiously until his back touched one of the mossy rocks. Then he twisted around and hauled himself atop it.

He pulled a dagger from somewhere within the folds of his clothing, and I drew my own.

I lashed out at his feet, and he leapt backward across the gap between the boulders—over a stream which gurgled between the rocks.

I took the opportunity to leap upon the rock as well, and held my blade steady. He seemed more scared than anything, and his stance was clumsy and untrained. I thrust at him, gauging his skill. It was lacking.

He thrust back with three lunges in rapid succession: the first simply struck the air between us; the second was easily parried, briefly lighting the glade with a flash of sparks; and the final thrust actually managed to hit me. I twisted so that it bounced harmlessly from the bone armour I wore upon my chest.

He was panicking now. I could see it in his eyes—the only part of his face that I could clearly make out. He had blue eyes, and maybe a scar that was barely visible beneath his cowl. Maybe he had seen combat and prevailed, or perhaps it was a wound given to him during another defeat.

Those ponderings were fleeting. I resumed my assault.

I baited out another of his weak jabs, then ducked under his outstretched arm. Mindful of Karthak's desire to capture one of the Combine alive, I made sure that my blade cut only muscle as I slashed his bicep.

He howled in pain, and relinquished his grip on his knife. Without pause, I shoved him.

He pitched backward through the air, and landed hard on the ground below.

I lept off after him and held my dagger to his throat, but not before kicking him five or six times in the face.

"I yield, savage! Your Legion does not permit the slaughter of captive officers," he cried out.

"My Legion?" I asked. "I am no Sacharri!' I pushed myself to my feet, and kicked him again. Hard.

"You are a coward and a horse-son! Like all of your kind—easily bested, and weak!" I shouted at him.

The Kimora, his mouth bloody, looked up at me and then spat, so I kicked him one more time—for good measure, and for forcing me to chase him.

"Ah screw this. I should just kill you. My sisters could use the meat, and we could always capture another one of you." I pressed the tip of my blade against his neck again, then paused.

I hadn't actually had a good look at the Kimora until now, so consumed had I been with the task of beating him senseless. I figured he was the one who had been present when my companions were captured back at the Combine dig-site—but even back then, he had worn a cowl.

Now though, with his head uncovered by my merciless beating, and even despite the blood and swelling, I understood why he had been asking after who I'd presumed to be me.

Despite my promise to Feygar-Shar. it would be one of the only times that I did not want any of my companions to kill any Kimori.

And it would be the first time, in as long as I could recall, that I realised just how little I now resembled one.

I didn't need him to confirm—his unique birthmark, mess of golden hair, familiar blue eyes, and look of surprised realisation, were answer enough. But ask I did.

"Lleyden?"

vi.

There were scarcely words for what I felt. I was home.

Though that was the problem; I was also so far from it.

I could not stay there, despite a long-dormant aching that tugged at the very core of my being. I followed Lleyden back along the path to where I had left my pups and his father. I really hoped they hadn't slaughtered the man.

Luckily Feygar-Shar and Okra had been merciful, and instead stood over his prone and bound form. I was proud.

The two Vulkari turned to face me, surprised that Lleyden walked freely. I commanded them to circle the forest, and find the others, to tell them we would withdraw and discuss what to do next. I couldn't be responsible for a slaughter there. Unquestioningly, the pups bounded off into the evening.

"Father!" Lleyden rushed to his father's side and tried to untie his bonds. He struggled, due to the wounded arm that hung uselessly by his side, so I pushed him out of my way, and freed the man myself.

He rolled over and stared at me, before getting to his feet.

"Zyntael," he whispered, softly.

He made to embrace me, but I held my blade before him. It was strange; I could not remember his name.

"My family," I began, eyes locked on his "Do they live?"

"Your father and sister, yes. But your mother..." he began.

"I know. Fever," I told him. "Are they here? In this village?"

"*Your* village, Zyntael. This is your home! You have returned to us!" The man was almost pleading with me.

I shook my head.

"This is not my home. It should not even be yours—if you want to survive this war." I glanced at Lleyden. "The Combine has doomed you. The Legion is all-powerful, and will march on these lands in earnest soon. We Vulkari may raid, but the Hobgoblins raze—or occupy and enslave."

"You speak as though you are one of those... beasts... Those monsters!" the man said, then gasped as I thrust my dagger forward—mere inches from his throat. Lleyden started, but he was powerless to stop my wrath, should I have wished to draw blood.

"I am Vulkar," I told him, through gritted teeth. "You had best watch your words and your tone."

He was shocked. But then, so was I. These were my genuine feelings. It felt empowering simply to say them aloud.

※   ※   ※

If at some point I had hoped for a beautiful reunion with my family, those hopes were wasted.

After escorting Lleyden and his father to where my companions waited nearby, I resolved to head back to the village. If anything, I wished to barter food for a warning of the danger they were in. I understood that the Wardens of the forest may have attacked us, had I ventured in with the other Vulkari. Conversely, electing to go alone, I ran the risk of capture and imprisonment.

Whichever way I looked at it, the latter seemed the less risky of our options, and I was confident that I could escape if need be. Though of course, I prayed that it wouldn't come to that.

Thankfully, it didn't.

Instead, I slipped into the village unnoticed, and as though guided by Yanghar herself, found myself before a humble cottage. I hadn't lived there as a child, I was sure of it. I vaguely recalled that my birth-parents were wealthy. But this was the place.

When I peered within the crack between two wooden window shutters, I spied a beleaguered and frail man, and his young daughter—of perhaps six summers at most.

They sat next to a fireplace, and he looked to be reading a story to her. Or perhaps she, to him.

Without thinking, I simply opened the door and stepped inside the house.

The little girl, her hair a pale reddish blonde and her skin the same earthen brown as my own, leapt from her father's lap with a shrill cry.

He stood and positioned himself between she and I, and with empty hands held up before him, spoke:

"Please, we have no wealth worth taking," he pleaded. "We want no part in your war. If it is food and drink, then take what you will, and leave us be."

I would almost have called it pathetic were it not for his clear desire to protect his child. He was no fighting man. I knew that much. Strangely, I couldn't recall what it was my father actually had done for his wealth.

"I shall take your food, and will need more still. But I am not here to harm you. I am here to talk," I told him. My voice sounded almost alien to me—the command that it carried was uncharacteristic. I liked the feeling.

"Talk about what? Who are you?" he asked.

I looked at the little girl who hid behind his leg, her wide blue eyes almost overflowing with terror. She was pretty. And beside her skin, looked nothing like me.

"Are you not Zachya Fairwinter?" I asked her, trying to maintain a soft and non-threatening tone.

She peered up at her father with uncertainty, before nodding.

Strange that we bore no resemblance, but there she was, my infant sister, now a little girl.

I looked back up to meet my father's fearful gaze.

"Father," I said. "It is I, Zyntael."

Still he stood there, incredulity upon his face.

"Zyntael is dead," he said. In a whispered tone, he repeated it several times—as if trying to will it to be so.

I stepped forward into the clear light of their fire, and both he and my sister stepped back.

"I survived the raid, I survived Threydon's fortress, I survived all this time. Now I have returned," I reassured him. "Phobos Lend told you it was so, and he did not lie. I am very much alive."

Gradually, he lowered his hands and blinked away his fear.

"Oh the things I have seen, the things I have done!" I began, but he was clearly in no mood for tales of adventure and raiding.

Instead of fear, he now wore an expression of anger.

"All this time, all these summers, and now you return? Like this?" he stepped toward me. "Your mother lies, embraced by the forest roots, your betrothed has joined the cursed Merchant Combine to seek you out, our village is threatened by war, and you show up *now?*"

I didn't know what to say. It was either now or never, since only chance bore us to this village in the first place.

"Look at you! You wear the adornment of those beasts. Dressed as though a Wolf-man raider. How? Why?" He stepped a little closer with each angry question.

I winced at the words he'd used to describe my sisters, but I allowed him his slurs. He could not possibly know, nor could he understand.

"I am one of their number now. I came with them to seek food for—" He cut me off.

"You brought them here? Was one slaughter at their hands not enough?"

I had to calm the situation.

"Listen you fool. We did not come here to slaughter you. We need food for our journey back to Sacharri lands. But we also need you to leave this place. Come with us if you will, but no matter what—you cannot stay here."

I explained to him the things I knew of the Sacharri plan for securing the territory west of the Stormhills. They did not seek to simply subjugate the populace, but would garrison troops and take slaves too. Better my father and sister come willingly and be welcomed as family of an ally, than be captured in my absence.

He listened on as I spoke, then replied with a question.

"And you fight for these Eastern invaders?" he asked.

"No, I fight *with* them. I fight for our freedom. My sisters have our own goals, but for now they align with Sacharr—to oppose the Merchant Combine," I explained.

"Your sisters? Your *sisters!?* Zyntael, *this* is your sister!" He pulled a stunned Zachya from behind him.

"Oh Father, you cannot possibly know. There is more to the Vulkar than the flesh." I said.

I tried to at least help him see that Vulkari were not some great evil. Not beasts, but rather, people—myself one of them.

Eventually, reluctantly, the man accepted my explanation, but still I knew that yet again, he really couldn't possibly understand.

"I'm sorry Zyntael, we cannot leave our home," he told me finally. "You may take food, and I shall retrieve as much as you need from the stores, for your journey to come. But we will not accompany you into the arms of Sacharr. The Wardens have protected the forest and our lands since time immemorial, and they shall continue to do so."

I had hoped he would relent, but deep down, I knew that would be his choice.

After trying my luck a few more times, I gave up. I sighed, and sat upon a wooden stool at his dinner table. He fetched some bread, cheese, and a mug of rich forest wine, then came and sat beside me in silence as I ate.

For some time we talked, once I had satiated my gnawing hunger.

He spoke of my mother, and how she had passed from fever, several summers prior. He spoke of Zachya and how clever she had grown to become. She could even read—something which I one day hoped to do also.

We even spoke of Lleyden, and his fixation on my rescue. The boy had never let go of the hope that I still lived, and had joined some sort of priestly order within the Combine, once of age. It had been in some hope that they could teach him to divine my location.

I didn't know such a group existed—thinking Magick to be the domain only of the Spirits and those with whom they communed.

Of all the things that my father told me, I was most curious about this. It was a little odd that I was more interested in information that might shed light on my current enemy, than hearing of people who had become mere shadows in my past.

The gulf between who I had been—perhaps might still have been in his eyes—and who I really was now, was vast and complex.

I tried to force myself to question him of his and Zachya's lives, but as long as they were both alive and well, I almost didn't care.

"Were you not a merchant, or a…" I asked, struggling against the swirling fog of suppressed memory.

"Yes, and no," he told me. "We had wealth from lives prior. Here, we simply arranged and supported the trade between our village and others. Our time spent travelling was over long before your birth."

"Then you must have also seen fabulous sights." I said.

"Of course. But there was always a draw to the simplicity and comfort of our ways here. To the north, our people have their own lands. Remnants of a mighty empire—this village would once have been amongst its most southern points," he said. "Like Lleyden's parents, I was born there—in the old heart of the Faer-Reach—but when in the cities, when within the walls, all I could do was long for the forest."

"For some sort of freedom?" I asked. Perhaps, there was some small similarity between us, after all.

"Yes. I don't believe that the course of our lives can be determined by those who live lives so differently. How could I, as a wealthy man housed in brick, and surrounded only by structure, possibly truly un-

DAUGHTER OF THE BEAST

derstand the wild? The twisting, chaotic beauty of the forest?" He was almost sounding a little like a Vulkar. "I had to leave, to set roots into soft earth, not cobbled streets."

"I understand," I told him honestly. "That is the view of the Vulkari too. Perhaps not all of them, and not so much to set roots... But most simply want the freedom to choose their own path. As do I."

He nodded, and there was the smallest hint of pride about his features.

"I am truly sorry, Father. For all that has happened, and for all the pain you must have felt—in my absence, and after mother..." How did he put it? "After she became one with the forest."

I meant it too. I didn't want the poor man to suffer, and even though he might lament my current situation, I hoped he would take solace in the fact that I lived. That I was strong. That I was free.

We conversed for a little longer, and he slowly seemed to warm to me a bit—even reaching out as if to touch me a few times as we spoke. Though he never went so far as to actually make contact with my skin. It was as if he didn't want to confirm that I was no mere phantom—something he had conjured up in his mind.

After a time, Zachya even joined us, and showed me both her storybook, and her ability to actually make sense of its words. In an amusing twist, the book told the tale of a little girl whose mother had been eaten by some beast. The beast then took on the mother's role, in a strange attempt to eat the girl too.

Zachya carried with her a little doll, made from stitched cloth and stuffed straw. It had vibrant crimson hair, and green buttons for eyes. She showed it to me, and it reminded me of the strange little effigy that the Vulkari had made, presumably of Karthak's chosen pup, back during one of our many ritual nights. The doll's name was 'Zynnie'.

I showed her my Vyshivka, and the patterns that spoke of her and my family. I began to tell her of the raid, but my father's look of concern silenced me on the topic. Instead, I spoke of the Kobaloi—monsters that would be at home in one of her storybooks.

Before I left, I promised that I would plead with Threydon to spare their village the horrors of enslavement, but knew that my voice would likely go unheard. Perhaps Anra would be better suited to reach his father's sense of mercy.

Even as I crossed the threshold of their cottage, my father refused to touch me, so I left him no choice. I gripped his sagging shoulders, and then drew him into an embrace. Though taller than I was, he seemed so small and weak.

In turn, I crouched and embraced Zachya. She seemed far more accepting—her youthfulness lending her a flexibility to her emotions, and a curiosity that reminded me of a pup.

"Fear not the beasts in your stories," I told her. "For anything can be slain with a stout blade... and stouter heart."

And finally, laden with sacks of supplies, and filled with a strange mixture of both comfort and worry, I departed my old home—that humble little forest village—for the last time.

vii.

I had broken my promise to Feygar-Shar, but none of the Vulkari were disappointed when I returned. They may have thirsted for bloodshed, but even Sarga was probably too exhausted to fight.

They hungrily devoured some of the meat I carried with me, but we rationed the rest for the journey southeast. We even shared the load—allowing the pups a reprieve from their constant duty as pack-mules.

It was an awkward and unpleasant situation as far as dealing with Lleyden and his father went. First his father refused to let us take Lleyden back for interrogation, then he demanded to come with us. It was only after Mazgar suggested that we simply slaughter them both to save us the hassle, that he allowed us to depart with his son.

Lleyden assured his father that he would return, and as I had with my own father, tried in vain to convince him to leave the village. Whereas I had suggested they flee to the Sacharri lands, he of course spoke of safety amongst the Merchant Combine.

Sarga and Mazgar, both, hadn't helped his cause—mocking the Combine for their weakness in battle, and describing (in violent detail) every brutal death they'd inflicted on the Merchants' foot soldiers.

The poor man finally left us, heart likely filled with naught but fear for his son and his people.

After ensuring Lleyden wouldn't bleed to death from his wounds, we too made our way from that place, turning south and a little east, to follow the Stormhills back to the Blackfort.

The journey back was easier than it had been up until this point, even weighted down as we were with supplies. The Vulkari had already begun interrogating Lleyden, and before long, their attitude toward him had morphed from outright hostility, to a curiosity and perhaps pity.

"So why do you have the—what was it called, Sister?"

"An octopus."

"Right. An octopus. Why is that your sigil? It is weak and strange—not like the fist of the Legion, or the comet of Karthak," Sarga asked of him.

"I don't know," he said simply. The frustration in his voice, palpable.

"Alright. So what about that stuff you said of awakening? What does that mean?" She continued to press him.

"It is power. Some force of energy. You open your eyes and see clearly. Well, not your actual eyes, but sort of…" Lleyden was struggling to explain it, just as we were struggling to understand.

"Is it the Magick of the Spirits? Or the Vaela?" I asked.

He had no idea what the Spirit-talker was, by any name.

"Look, it is something that comes to you as you learn. All of the Enlightened in the brotherhood have the gift of sight. I don't think it is natural. At least, not entirely. But they can communicate over great distance, and they can see things beyond the waking world—through dreams had even when the dreamer is awake."

"Sounds fishy," Yezga, the largest of the pups said. The others agreed.

"If it isn't natural," I asked. "How do they do it?"

Lleyden produced a talisman from beneath his tunic. It was the same curved sigil as all his kind wore, carved into a disc of black crystal and bound to a cord of leather. Like the one Sarga had once claimed as a trophy, and which I'd convinced her to hurl into the Storm river.

It bugged me. Not simply because of the shape, but because of what it was made from. That strange mineral gave me a terrible feeling—one of dread and foreboding, that crept deep into my being. I remembered how angry the voices of the Spirits were, last I held some of that cold obsidian, and it began to make sense; nothing good could come of using their beaconstone as a conduit for conquest.

Were the Combine forcing the Spirits of the dead, and of the lands, into service as messengers? Were they using the rock to force their perverted form of order upon the wild worlds beyond this one too?

It was unnatural. Of course it would anger the Spirits, and it began to anger me as well.

"When you touch that stone, what is it that you feel?" I asked.

He held it up, and rubbed the talisman with his thumb.

"Well, nothing I suppose. I mean, I am merely Awakened, not Enlightened yet. I don't know exactly what it entails, but I had aimed to become so. In order to find you, if I'm honest."

He shrugged nonchalantly, to try to hide his clear embarrassment at his admission, but the blush that spread across his cheeks let slip his true feelings.

"Fiiiiiishy..." Yezga sang.

I agreed. It really didn't sit well with me.

Strange too, that he felt nothing at the stone's touch. It must have been the same rock, given the Combine's mining of it.

I reached out and touched it.

Sure enough, almost immediately, a seething, icy rage touched me back. It shocked me, and I recoiled. Lleyden looked at me, wide-eyed, with eyebrows raised quizzically.

"What was that?" he asked. Almost demanded.

"That was the Spirits. I feel them through your stone. They are beyond angry at this point." I sighed. "Whatever your fool ilk are doing with the beaconstone, it must be stopped. They can't possibly understand how wrong it is."

He was still caught on my reaction to his talisman, and there began to grow a look of envy upon his face.

"So you, who have had no training, who isn't even Awakened, presume to know more than the Enlightened? Than the Merchant Lords themselves?" He shook his head and looked up at the grim greyness of the clouds above. "I don't believe it."

"Well none of us care what you believe," Mazgar retorted on my behalf, and I shot her a smirk.

"I have a question," Ar-Goruk, another of the pups, informed us, then turned to Lleyden. "Why must you come into these lands? The Combine, I mean. You are from here obviously."

Lleyden explained what he knew of their plans. It seemed that there was something special about the Stormhills and the Ancient Wilds that the Merchant Lords wanted to exploit. I assumed it was the black rock of the Spirits, but perhaps the lands themselves held a power of their own.

We carried on travelling, and whether walking or camped, Lleyden carried on explaining things to our group. He was limited in what he knew, but was surprisingly forthright with his information. It occurred to me that he may have simply been seeking answers through the Combine, and was not entirely convinced of their ways. I might have shared a similar feeling when it came to the Sacharri, but I was Vulkar, through and through.

Finally, after what seemed like a lifetime of travel, we approached the foothills of the Blackfort. This time, from the northwest.

We were careful to scout ahead for enemy patrols or Sacharri presence, but we saw neither. Instead, whilst climbing the grassy hills on our approach to the fort, scrubby bush and long grass concealing our approach, there came a sudden howling. Crying out from above us, probably only thirty or so yards away, the sound echoed in the damp air.

We ducked low, and looked at each other. Lleyden was terrified but, we were confused—maybe a little embarrassed that we had forgotten our training on scouting protocol. I couldn't remember any of the calls that our scouts used, and I certainly couldn't mimic them, so I looked at Sarga and Mazgar expectantly.

Sarga pondered for a bit, eyes squinting, and a finger to her mouth. Then, after another cry echoed from above, she threw her head back, and howled a response.

It sounded a little like the tune that Karthak often sang to herself, and unfortunately, to me at times. Knowing her and her well-camouflaged sentimentality, it probably was.

The two lovers called out to one another in the night—separated by a vast and impossible distance, searching, regretting that they heeded not the Spirits and their hearts.

Sarga howled one more time in response to the next part of the melody, and I found myself singing along—with the words of the song:

"With the moon as silent witness, I speak words whilst worlds apart—but that moon she shall take them, and speak my words to absent heart."

Lleyden looked at me in confusion, the pups looked at me in adoration, and Mazgar and Sarga looked at me in amusement.

Then, as we made our way up to our scout sisters, our hearts filled with relief, we three began to sing the rest of the song.

viii.

"You must promise that he faces no torture. I beg of you." But Karthak seemed deaf to my pleas. She barely glanced at me as I spoke, perhaps disgusted by my display of pity. Star-Star, however, did not avert her gaze. She looked at me with a strange warmth, a sort of understanding—and a little reassurance. I hoped that she would sway Karthak. Just as I hoped that Anra would sway his father. Both to mercy, though she for Lleyden, and he for my family and former home.

Strangely, Karthak expressed little desire to harm the Kimori of the forest. She saw them better used as a source of peaceful tribute. Slaves were usually only needed for bartering, and the current alliance with Sacharr meant that there wasn't much bartering required.

Threydon, on the other hand, was resolute in his view that any village within Combine lands was his to do with as he pleased. I began to like him less and less.

On the evening of my return, I spoke with Anra. He seemed apologetic to my plight, but was far more concerned with Lleyden—with my childhood friendship with the Kimora, and with the idea that we had been betrothed. He seemed to think that Lleyden had always been one of the Combine's strange acolytes, and not merely a little boy with a perpetual desire to either be with me or be like me. Was it envy that spurred Anra on, as we sat together in his room and discussed our feelings?

He wouldn't admit it, of course, but it must have been so, for he almost hissed Lleyden's name when he spoke it, and seemed to wince whenever I did.

"Oh come on! We were pups!" I reassured him. But he was as stubborn as his stupid father.

I didn't want to like Anra less though, so I persisted.

"I bullied him. He was a brat and a coward." That much, I could clearly recall. "Besides, I have not lain with the boy," I said.

He shrugged and looked away from me.

"I don't care if you have. He's of your kind, and isn't unattractive," he muttered.

The latter was no lie, but the former most obviously was.

"You do care. And I think I know why." I grinned. "It is as my sisters say; you have fallen in love with me, and wish to claim me as your wife. A shameful romance between Kimora and Goblin! Should we elope? Lest your father take our heads for this betrayal of your station, Under-officer Manox Anra?"

He slowly began to grin as well.

"That isn't true. I couldn't take you as my Kimor-wife. Remember, you are never to marry! And though slaves are we all, in some way, you said it yourself; you will be slave to no man!" he said, and turned to share his grin with me.

"Aha! You didn't deny the romance!" I nudged him.

"Nor the love, it seems…" he said with a puzzled frown, then nudged me back.

That familiar warmth was growing in me again. My ears began to burn.

"Well then, it's only the slavery of marriage that is missing. I suppose it would be possible, but whoever it was with, he would have to be a really strong man to keep me. He would need shackles wrought tougher than even Urd, Feldspar, and Zentar together could forge," I told him, and shuffled a little closer to him.

"Would he not also need to be a little hard of sight?" Anra's smirk grew wider.

I stopped, confused.

"Wait, what? Why? Are you saying that you think me ugly, after all?"

He laughed.

"If the man could see clearly, he'd get naught done all day, but for staring at you. How could he labour in his duties under the Emperor if he were gazing upon the stars that speckle your summer skin?" Anra traced constellation lines between first the freckles upon my shoulders, then those which dotted my cheeks. It was such a stupid compliment, but my blushing beneath his tender touch threatened to consume me in flame.

I looked up at his eyes—a deep purplish colour, almost black. If I could see through them, I would have liked to. If only to understand how he saw me. I was a savage, or so he said, but those eyes saw me as so much more.

But any nagging doubts I had about my nature, and Anra's view of it, vanished like thin wisps of fog in the sunlight, when the Hobgoblin leaned down to gently kiss my forehead.

I could have sworn that little tears were beginning to well in my eyes. I had no clue why, but I let them, as he traced a line of kisses downward, along the bridge of my nose, and finally to my lips.

I kissed him back.

Then, in a moment of pause, he smiled at me, and spoke:

"Your sisters are right: I do love you."

How could that be? We barely knew one another. But I knew it was true, and let his words fill me with a gentle bliss.

Gradually though, something else began to well up within me—growing from low in my core, as we kissed. It built up—before long burning like a raging inferno. It was no longer peaceful, comforting warmth that I felt, but now intense consuming heat.

My body ached. Not with bliss, but with desire. And to Anra's and my own surprise, both, I let it take over.

Again we frantically stripped one another of our clothing, and once more fell into a passionate embrace. This time it was neither awkward, nor short lived—and I began to wonder if the electric pulsing that rendered my body almost paralysed by the end, would ever go away.

Not that I would ever want it to.

✖ ✖ ✖

The following morning, I awoke to find that Anra was still present, lying upon his back beside me. No hasty retreat had he beaten, nor had he been warded off by my foul breath—thankfully nothing near as horrific as it had been last time. Even so, I sipped water from a wooden cup on his bedside table, then worked my way closer to his warm body.

Manox Anra stirred, then rolled over to pull me into his arms—strong, but gentle and comforting. Again, he smelt nice. The faint hint of soap and oils, the perspiration of last night's deed, and an underlying scent—something natural, and masculine, and wholly his own.

I felt at peace, there in his company. Snuggled into his naked body and his blankets, I smiled to myself. I didn't care what his father thought. If this was to be my chosen fate, then let it be.

His heartbeat pulsed—firm, unending, and like the distant rhythm of Sacharri war drums. In the boy's chest, Sacharr would always live on.

Was it the case with my own heart? Was that what Karthak, the Shaman, that old matriarch in the temple had all meant? Did we really carry the spirit of our peoples within us?

A strange thought occurred. It was something I had joked about with my sisters, spoken of with the Warlord, and even dreamt of. But it was something I had never seriously considered the reality of:

Did I now also carry Anra's child? Did I bear the pup who would be heir to both the Sacharri frontiers, and the Vulkar home plains?

Somehow, I already knew the answer. Somehow I already knew of all the trouble it would cause. But even so, as Anra opened his eyes and beamed at me in the morning light, as he began to gently kiss my face, and as we once more began to work ourselves back up to that desperate, stirring passion—the weight of that future reality began to melt away.

THE SIXTH STITCH

DESTRUCTION

i.

"And do they also drink ale?" Oya asked me.

I shook my head and looked at her like the buffoon she was.

"They are children," I reminded her.

She was really struggling with the concept of a birthday celebration. She understood that it was a novel excuse for feasting, but was totally lost beyond that. It really didn't help that Uya had fully understood, and now confused her twin further by attempting some sort of explanation of her own.

"Tell me again Sister; why do they give a gift to the Kimor-pup? What did it do to deserve it? Does it barter one of its own things in return?" Oya pressed me.

I regretted making mention of the topic. It would be best to forget that within the next few weeks, I would count the sixteenth anniversary of my birth—though technically, I would remain sixteen summers of age for only a few more months.

Each winter I had thought about that fact—perhaps one of the small slivers of Kimoriness that remained in my core. Though I had only made mention of it because Lleyden had.

He dwelt mostly in a locked room, near Karthak's solar—though there had originally been the intent to shackle him within the dungeons beneath the fort. I had pleaded with Karthak to no avail, but as was her way, Star-Star had said or done something to soften the Warlord's heart.

Of course, Karthak had made out that her act of mercy was actually one of pragmatism—explaining to me one drunken evening that it was only because we may need allies in various regions, or a spy within the Combine itself, that she would spare the young Kimora. I went along with her charade, glad that for whatever reason, my old friend would not suffer as I had so long ago. Then again, since Urga had been ousted, even the dungeons of the Blackfort were more hospitable.

I had spent a fair bit of time speaking with Lleyden, much to Anra's silent disapproval, but I was curious as to so much.

One such time, he confessed to me that every new winter, on the anniversary of my birth, he had put aside some small gift for me. The thought filled me with both joy and sadness. It was cruel that he so clung to such longing for me. I could scarcely understand why either. I had been unkind to him as a child, though perhaps those were the only memories I still held of that time—few as even they were. Perhaps his memories were happier ones.

I fetched him food and drink, and sat with him for hours at a time, listening to him talk. His life seemed so easy compared to mine, but still he treated it as such an arduous journey. Each trivial obstacle was, to him, a great burden or some deathly challenge. Yet he had no tales of combat other than the taking of the Blackfort by my sisters, and our own duel.

I regaled him with stories of my own—of the violence and excitement of the raid. Three or so summers of it. I even tried to speak of Azure.

Sadly, he wasn't much impressed, and would almost always change the subject.

He was curious instead, about things that I considered mundane—from the Vulkari disdain toward most malefolk, to their aversion toward bows, and a host of other things that didn't even concern Vulkari at all. Mostly though, he wanted to talk about me.

In time, I felt a desire to help him from his plight somehow. As far as I could see, he was where he was through simple boyish infatuation—it was hardly his fault, and something of a compliment to me. So for all the trouble I'd caused him, perhaps I owed him that much.

The trouble I had caused Anra, on the other hand, had not been so drawn out.

Perhaps knowing that he held no real sway over me thanks to the presence of Karthak, Manox Threydon had turned his ire on his own son.

He indeed forbade the boy from keeping my company, and saw to it that Anra's duties kept us apart as much as possible. This was, of course, after a most heated row between the two Hobgoblins—an exchange heard almost throughout the entire fortress.

As stubborn as his father, Anra had shrugged it off, and still we slipped off in the dead of night to meet in the shadows and secret places of the Blackfort, where we shared our love for one another excitedly.

As the weather grew colder, the rains began to subside. There was a dry and icy sharpness to the air tonight, and so we had made plans to lay furs and blankets on the rock overlooking the bastion, then to keep each other warm beneath the cold glitter of the stars.

I was excited, and a little nervous even, but all I could do was wait.

Presently, I was occupied with teaching the new pups how to stitch their tales of our journey south into their Vyshivka. Between their ineptitude regarding stitching, inability to express themselves with anything more than simple lines, and the twins' constant interruptions, it was tough work.

Was this the life of Star-Star and Kovvik-Shar when we had been mere pups?

I could forgive the older sisters their occasional brutality.

"Okay, okay, I think I have got it!" Uya exclaimed.

"You already had it. Oya didn't," I reminded her, and she and her counterpart began going over their understanding of birthdays once more.

Whilst I listened to them completely confuse each other, and watched a pup, Yarog, prick herself repeatedly with her needle—neither distraction keeping me from my daydream of the coming night—the door to the chamber opened.

Sarga strode into the room, dried blood upon her chest and around her maw. She smelt awful.

"Sisters!" she bellowed. "Another raid, another success!"

I envied her. Due to her size and strength, she was more and more often sent out for days at a time with the older raiders. They would attack the Combine scouting parties who frequented the hills, and return with stories of fearsome slaughter and glorious victory.

Mazgar sulked during these times. Even as the runt of our claim, she still towered over the Goblins and I, but she resented not being chosen for much more than training the pups. Even patrolling would have been more fun, as far as she was concerned, but the Hobgoblins seemed to do the bulk of it.

"How many did you slay this time, Sarga?" I asked my friend, a little excitement building in me by proxy.

She sat on the floor, and the pups gathered around her in a small circle to listen to her tale.

"We stalked westward until we found their camps. There are hundreds of hundreds of them—and maybe a hundred more. Ar-Tarak and the older sisters are telling Karthak and the Legion now. I do not think I have ever seen so many banners, nor so many tents. I have certainly never seen so many... brelts, were they?"

Uya and Oya looked genuinely excited. As did the young pups, though their excitement was tinged with a little fear. They had seen only the slightest combat; during the Combine ambush on our party, and once or twice when we stumbled upon a village that hadn't been completely abandoned. It was no preparation for real fighting.

I was also a little worried, in truth. The Legion invasion force yet marched from the east. They had already sailed along the redirected Solent river to Threydon's fortress city, and sent word that they were en route, but it would still be some days before their arrival.

"How many day's travel did you say it was?" I asked my friend.

"Oh... It was only three or four at most. You know how it is—the anticipation of the raid makes the journey there go quicker, and the anticipation of the tale makes the journey back quicker still!" Sarga shrugged. She continued her story—likely embellishing it for the sake of the young Vulkari, who listened with wide grins and wider eyes.

I listened too, as she described their daring raid on a group of men who wore robes not unlike Lleyden had. Sarga and her companions had easily slain the group, as well as their handful of guards, then claimed a prize of their charts and parchments to return to our leaders.

I found it worrying that these so-called 'Enlightened' would be present in such numbers—especially after Lleyden's explanation of their abilities. Did they need no physical spies, if indeed they bent the Spirits' sight to their will?

More worrying still, was that their army amassed so near by. If our reinforcements didn't arrive soon, we might face overwhelming numbers—I didn't like the idea of a siege.

That evening, whilst we ate in the hall, an older Hobgoblin made me like it less.

"Glorious?" the Legion veteran laughed a bitter, wheezing laugh. "Did songs and poets give you that idea? What would those cowards know?

"Glorious... No, simply singing of the spectacle isn't enough. Bearing witness isn't enough.

"Oh you need to breathe the acid smoke of flesh rendered from bone beneath a torrent of burning pitch. You need to hear the screaming. The begging and wailing.

"You need to cower behind the crenellations—slick with blood, and puke and shit. You need to cower as a hail of arrows break themselves around you, or find homes in the bodies of your comrades.

"You don't fight in a siege, you don't win one. You simply survive it. Oh a siege. A proper siege, in all its majesty and horror, would certainly never make the centrepiece in any mummer's spin, had they actually lived through one!

"Those gilded minstrels who pay mere lip service to the chaos and carnage, would keep quiet, had they too starved for so long behind their walls that their own children and wives—or the recently dead of their friends—began to make their mouths water.

"How many dead friends they would have seen too, if they were actually there!

"To see a tower trundle ever onward, wreathed in flickering fire; to be shaken from your feet by the pounding of the ram at the gates; to hew ladder and grapnel from the walls and cast the climbers back into a moat of pikes—that is to survive a siege, and you wouldn't be excited if you'd done it. Glorious. Ha!"

The old warrior looked at his mug, before finishing the ale and sighing. "But that does sound glorious to you, doesn't it? It always does to the young. And to the Vulkar."

Mazgar's amber eyes sparkled with excitement at the old Hobgoblin's tale. Of course it sounded glorious to her. Nothing was more so than violence and terror and the testing of one's mettle.

"Well, I have more stories you might like. About the Northeastern campaign—against the Kimori and their 'Faer-Reach.' But first—" The veteran pushed himself away from the low wooden bench, and staggered to his feet "I've got to take a piss."

It was the second, or maybe third time I'd heard of some kind of Kimorin empire. It was always spoken of as though a thing from times past, however. Maybe they had been defeated and absorbed by the Hobgoblins, just as Feldspar had said.

I recalled that he told me of the Merchant Combine—that they dwelt back east also, and wondered how it was that they now came from the west. Did their empire stretch across the land to the north or south, or did it loop all the way around the world?

Karthak once told me that it was only the Vodyanoi who believed the world to be a flat plane—even Vulkari knew that with enough time, one could journey eastward and arrive back where they started from the west. Apparently, one uncharacteristically brave male had even done it.

What I wouldn't give to take with me my sisters, Anra—even Lleyden—and do the same. What I wouldn't give to escape the cloying threat of some other's war, to see far-off places with all their wonder and novelty.

But deep down I knew the truth: the only way out, was through.

I sighed and pushed my still half-full plate across the table to Mazgar. She was eating far more than normal, which for her, meant a considerable amount. It was some forlorn effort to grow as large as Sarga, but instead I feared she would end up like the Mothers in their temple.

She took the plate, glanced across the hall to where Anra was eating, then raised her brow at me.

"Later," I told her, with a blush and a smirk. In the meantime I meant to converse some more with Lleyden, then perhaps make another plea to Karthak for his release.

"I shall expect to hear the details tomorrow morning then," Mazgar said, as I pushed myself from the table. She made a rude gesture with her fingers to simulate the act. It made me smirk more, but didn't make me blush any less.

⌘　⌘　⌘

As always, Lleyden sulked in his chamber. At times he paced around, muttering curses and thumbing his creepy medallion.

"You know, Zynnie, I do wonder if it would have been better if you had slain me," he said, and if he kept calling me that, I just might. "I fear for my family—for yours too. I have not forgotten Kyrill, even if you did so easily."

The boy dwelt almost entirely in the past, and in worry. It was exhausting.

"Lleyden, you need to let those fears go. You cannot forge a path for yourself if you are constantly looking backward. A friend of mine once told me that if you wait in the forest—caught in uncertainty—you will be claimed by the things that lurk in the dark," I told him sternly.

He looked confused.

322

"It's a proverb, stupid. A Pixie one. It means that you should always move forward. Sure, you can reminisce—I certainly do—but it isn't going to help you, unless it is to teach a lesson."

"What lesson is to be learnt from this? That the Vulkar and the Legion are as I thought? Villainous?"

"Oh come on! If we were all so cruel, you would be tortured for your information, not simply subjected to conversation with Karthak." I paused and grinned. "Though that is a torture of its own kind, is it not? Has she sung songs for you yet?"

He began to grin too, and nodded.

"Is that what you call them?"

"Did I tell you that she used to make me groom her? It's not as though she was ever lacking in slaves or malefolk to do the duty, but still. I would trim her claws, and I would scent her fur with oils. Though, it was never quite enough to diminish her menacing presence of course. Eventually I was freed from that service, though every once in a while, if Star-Star isn't with her, I will steal into her chamber at night, and douse her with perfume."

He laughed, then stopped and looked confused.

"Is 'Star-Star' Garok? Why the different name? And is she not female also?" he asked.

I explained that Star-Star was simply the common Solent translation of Garok—which literally meant 'Two Stars.' I didn't actually know why she preferred her name spoken in another's tongue, and why Karthak almost refused to do it entirely. Nor why she spoke of herself as if another.

"Yes, she is female. And before you ask, something of an intimate companion to Karthak instead of some whelp. I believe it is more than that though. Obviously I have never really asked why they don't take males as their mates. They could have any they wanted, should they wish it, but perhaps it's that there are none worthy. Perhaps it is more than simply physical."

I shrugged. I supposed that they must've still felt those physical urges, but would not wish an inferior pup to take root within them, should they be relieved by the use of a male.

I realised that I was tenderly stroking the painted skin of my stomach.

Mazgar had insisted we scrawl a spiraling pattern around my belly button—with the pigment of Yinnik and Otrek. It had been a strange, but somehow heartfelt little ritual one evening, and I knew my sisters' strength now flowed within me.

The older Vulkari noticed the colourful patterns, and would occasionally stoop to trace them with a clawed finger. More often than not, whispering prayers of strength too.

Karthak beamed with pride and knowing at the sight of it.

Lleyden was oblivious to all of that, and merely continued his queries.

"So there is nothing strange to you, about a female lying with one of her own kind?"

"No, why would there be? It seems almost logical to me—given the worry that a weak pup may result from real mating. Though, I'll admit that we could use all the pups we can get."

A sudden worry that Urga had betrayed our temple to the Combine struck me. As much as she resented the 'old ways' surely even she would not be so vile as to wish them annihilated.

I thought of the old Vulkar, the happy little pups, and the giant Mothers with concern. Then I remembered how fearsome those well-armoured warriors had been, and how impenetrable and sturdy the stone walls were. They would surely be safe from assault, at least whilst the bulk of the Combine force was focused on us.

"What of you?" Lleyden asked.

"Sorry?"

"What of you?" he repeated "Have you taken a mate? You are of the age to bear a child."

I had wondered whether he would ask, and had even wondered whether I should tell him of Anra and I—if anything, to quell the childish feelings he still held for me. They felt a little like ownership to me. A little too much like shackles.

I didn't answer for a while, though I got the sense that my silence was tacit admission in his eyes.

"I suppose I have," I finally confirmed.

"Who? The Goblin boy?"

His pretty face was cold, lips a tight vertical line as he looked at me. It wasn't his business, but perhaps it was for the best, so I told him anyway.

"Manox Anra. He is Threydon's heir. I don't know what that would make me..." I began.

"A whore," he said.

I was taken aback. What a cruel, spiteful, childish, and petty thing to say.

An anger began to rise within me. A cold anger.

"How *dare* you," I hissed.

And just as we had when we were children, we argued. This time though, the words and insults were nothing a child might have said.

He took it to be some great betrayal, of him and our families, and of Kimori in general. He seemed to be labouring under the delusion that, since we had been, we still were to be betrothed.

I called him a coward. I called him weak and pathetic—and stupid too. I informed him that Anra and I were both Bare-Skins, so the same, and I informed him that no man would make me a slave. Only, where Anra had turned it into an avenue for compliments and kindness, Lleyden spoke with disdain.

He declared that I would make no suitable wife anyway. That I was somehow spoiled, and that I was—he put it bluntly—'a waste of good seed.'

I didn't know why I remained—arguing for as long as I did with the foolish, selfish, jealous boy. Any one of his vile insults could have spurred me to leave—slamming the door behind me, and never looking back—but, for whatever reason, there I stayed.

Back and forth our words cut—a far more balanced duel than the one we had danced over the stream between the split rock near our old home.

"Still you think of me as some wealthy brat?" I questioned him. "I met my father. He was no rich man. And he was as weak as all of your kind."

"Your kind too. You may dress like a beast, paint your filthy skin, stitch your stupid Vishy-whatever, and play at being a warrior, but you are still a Kimora!" he raged "They will never accept you!"

"They already do! Do any of them—malefolk included—seethe so, over Anra and I? Do they claim to somehow own me? Call me ruined and worthless now, as though I were some mere prize to be had?"

"They are beasts, Zynnie. They don't do anything but lie, steal, and deceive!"

I strode forward and pointed a finger at his face.

"Don't call me 'Zynnie!'" it was a stupid childhood name, and I was no child. I hadn't minded Zachya's doll bearing the name, but I refused to.

"Or what, *Zynnie?*" He stressed each syllable in the most annoying, juvenile way.

I punched him in the face.

I wasn't entirely sure what would happen, and hadn't even really meant to, but instinct took over, and so my fist connected with his jaw. To his credit, he actually fought back.

Where my wrestling with the Vulkari was always in good fun, and the mock-fights between Anra and I were of a different sort entirely, this was a real brawl.

He attempted to throttle me, whilst I beat him about the head and chest. He was larger than I, though lacked the spirit of the Vulkar— so without the advantage that weapons would give me, we were somewhat evenly matched.

I bit his knuckle where he gripped my shirt, then head butted him when he let me go.

Lleyden shoved me away, then punched me square in the mouth when I charged forward again. I reeled from the blow, tasting blood on my tongue. Then I spat it in his face, and whilst he blinked in surprise, I tackled him into the shelf against his wall.

Wood splintered beneath our weight and the force of the impact. Bottles and trinkets soared across the room.

I pushed myself off him and began to stomp on his chest. It wasn't as if I hadn't slaughtered his kind before—boys, Kimori, Combine—whichever way I looked at it.

I was winning, and in no state to stop myself, but as usual, that was to be my downfall.

He rolled to the side, extracting himself from the broken furniture as I brought my foot down, then whilst I was off-balance from the missed attack, he swept my other leg from under me.

This time, he straddled my chest. It was all I could do to protect my face as he battered me. His punches weren't particularly hard, but they still hurt.

I finally managed to throw him off, and staggered to my feet, then he ended the fight. A single blow to my stomach dropped me to my knees. Panic spread through my body.

It hadn't been a very impactful strike—it barely hurt at all, such was my enraged state. But it wasn't the pain that I cared about anyway.

I held up my hands in surrender, as the boy stood over me.

Then, seeing me clutch my patterned belly, seeing the panic that was probably very clear on my face, Lleyden softened.

"By all the Fae, Zyntael," he said, voice a hoarse whisper. "You carry his child."

※　※　※

Something changed in Lleyden from that moment. At first, he sat quietly—dejected and lost in thought. But then he began to blink away the bitterness. It was as though he realised that he had just lost some imagined battle between Anra and he, between Hobgoblin and Kimora, even. And he resolved to accept his defeat graciously, and with dignity.

He helped me to my feet, and placed a trembling hand upon my own, over my belly.

"I'm sorry Zyntael," he said. Tears threatened his cheeks. "If I had known."

I accepted his help, and though terrified at the prospect that he had somehow harmed the life within me, opted instead to make light of the situation.

"Whilst I am glad that your blows are so weak, Lleyden, I think the pup is hardier than that." I silently prayed that it was.

He smiled reassuringly and nodded.

"Even diluted with Goblin, the blood that flows within you will surely make it so."

"Now aren't you glad I didn't say it was a Vulkar?"

He laughed heartily, and again, I felt that kindness from the boy. It still carried with it a certain sadness, but no longer felt like the product of longing—instead of genuine concern.

We sat in silence for a while, then once more began to speak—this time about the future, and what the war might mean for the two of us.

He held no illusions about his unlikely survival, but I begged to differ. I told him that Karthak would relent. I felt confident that she would be more agreeable to my desires in general now. The issue remained that the Merchant Combine would attack at some point, and he would be seen by the Legion, as a liability at best, and an enemy at worst. I didn't suspect there was much even Karthak could do to convince Threydon otherwise.

I promised my friend that I would simply help him to escape, if it came to that. But I hoped that it wouldn't.

After some time spent in conversation, I made to depart. Lleyden stopped me with a hand upon my shoulder, then drew me into a lingering embrace.

"I'm sorry Zyntael," he said, softly.

"Me too."

✠ ✠ ✠

As promised, I sought out Karthak. According to Ar-Tarak and Narod, she was in a chamber off one side of the throne room—with Star-Star, Kovvik-Shar, Tan-Shar, and some of the other veteran sisters. Sarga was there too.

They were gathered around a large round table, wrought of hearty wood and covered with the maps and charts that the recent raid had acquired for us. They were attempting to decipher the Combine plans, and I wondered if the Legion commander and his advisors and officers had been made aware of the spoils yet.

I cleared my throat to announce my presence when I pushed open the door—so wrapped up in their discussion they were. Star-Star beckoned me over to sit between Sarga and she.

I looked over the largest of the parchments—a beautifully drawn map of the lands laid across almost the full table. The chart differed from the many I had seen Karthak pore over in the past. It seemed to show those lands that she had planned our travel and our raids in, but it also showed others—to the east and west, but also to the north and south. There was more to the world than I'd actually realised—even in spite of my many fantasies of travelling to far-off locales, or of sailing from Azure on some Vulkar pirate vessel.

Each land had been dyed in thin shades of colour, with the ones I recognised mostly uncoloured. On the right hand side of the map, lay what I assumed to be Sacharr; a massive crimson continent, stretching far and wide, and dotted with many cities, towns, castles, and forts. Bordering it to its north, and cutting a swathe through a green area, a purple section began. It was as I had pondered; the Merchant Combine almost circled the world.

There was also a land to the south, almost entirely a yellow-gold colour, and separated from the rest by a wide ocean—serpents, octopuses, and worse lurked in the waters between, grasping ships and dragging the sailors to their doom.

In the lands I recognised, where no colour touched, there were lines drawn—not of the same ink that painted the original map, but added later with charcoal. Perhaps the intended movements of the Merchant's invaders.

Karthak frequently traced her own lines upon the map with a claw, most often around or from a small drawing of a castle. There were words written above it in curling script. I guessed they spelled out the name of the place, but they could have been anything for all I knew. Despite not knowing how to read, it wasn't hard to understand that the image must have represented the Blackfort. It was surrounded on both sides by the small curved lines that marked low hills, and above it, more lines grew ever taller as they spread northward—eventually becoming mighty snow-capped mountains. The Stormhills.

I traced the range upward then looked to the right of them, and with a sense of relief, noticed that there was no secret valley present—no temple. Our Mothers and our pups would surely be safe.

I was impressed and a little worried by just how large the two warring factions' territories were. No wonder Karthak feared being caught in their war—no wonder Phobos Lend had warned me not to be crushed between them when they collided. But here, on this magnificent map, it remained clear as day—that was exactly where we were.

A curious bit of land suddenly caught my attention, and as I stared at it, it seemed to stare back. To the northwest of the central landmass, beyond the coast, there sat a strange island, once painted green, but now tainted with purple, so that it was a dull, dirty brown. It almost looked as if it was an eye—complete with spits of land that represented eyelashes. How curious it was to me that such a place could exist naturally, and I wondered what strange sights one might behold there.

Star-Star interrupted my musing with a hand on the top of my head—just an idle gesture of affection, but it broke the spell that my imagination had cast upon me.

I looked up at her and she squeezed her eyes closed in a sort of smile, then grinned proper.

"Do you not wish you could read?" she asked.

I nodded and laughed.

"A man back east, Grunwald, told me he would teach me. He actually tried once or twice, but I think I might be too thick between my ears," I told her. "In fact, that was almost exactly what he said."

"Star-Star knows Janos Grunwald. She parlayed with the rascal when he held the Solent. She much enjoys his stories and tales, though she suspects that they may be myth."

I agreed.

"Star-Star has much fondness toward the man. Even if he were more of a scoundrel than he is, she still would," she told me. "He makes the best stew in all of the world. It is fit to feed Yanghar herself!"

"Apparently Threydon's grandmother makes better, so I can only begin to imagine how that must taste," I told her. I began to wonder how the old man was. Did he oversee things in Threydon's absence?

Surely there would be a Legion officer in command, but it was always as though Grunwald still ran the fortress anyway—even under Threydon's occupation.

I hoped that I could return to my friends there. I would so love to show the trio of smiths my dagger. They would be proud of how well I kept it, and how sharp the blade was, and they would be curious to see how I had adorned it with the pigments of my fallen sisters—even Feldspar would surely approve.

Then a sudden memory sprang to mind. I recalled the adventure that Sarga, Mazgar, and I had taken to the Shaman of the Whispering Cavern—to the Vaela. She had spoken of a flight to the east. She had not been wrong about my pup, even if the version of myself whom she had portrayed was far stronger and better equipped than I was.

I wondered if she was right about the rest of her prophecy.

ii.

Planning. Preparation. Drills. Routine.

With the recent arrival of a full host of reinforcements, it was as though the spirit of Sacharr was infecting the Vulkari with some sort of ailment. Only instead of making them sick, it was making them disciplined.

Mazgar thought that was worse.

I was, of course, swept up in the new regime, and could barely find time to sneak away from it all, to spend a moment with Anra. He usually wished to tell me some news, or talk in hushed whispers, about feelings and plans and love; I didn't want to waste time that could be better spent with physical affection. For my impatience, he called me a savage. But I knew it was a compliment, for not once did he protest.

There was an edge of uncertainty to it all. A slowly creeping fear and dread that made everything we did—every moment we shared—feel as though it could be our last together.

Alongside that horrible urgency came a worsening of the winter chill. The hearths and braziers of the Blackfort burned night and day, and I was thankful to the Legionnaires who had spent the first months of occupation harvesting massive stockpiles of wood from the nearby forests.

I wondered if the Vaela had been mistaken in her prophecy as the anniversary of my birth rapidly approached. The first full frost had come days prior, and each morning since, the earth was painted with a crisp white—a pure, unstitched Vyshivka, which awaited the threaded lines of orderly footprints. Instead, it was quickly trampled into a slushy brown muck.

I'd never seen so many soldiers before, and neither had most of the Vulkari. Small groups of us would frequently gather at that same rocky overlook, to gaze upon the ocean of tents, banners, fire pits, equipment, and beasts, which made up the Sacharri camp.

Some of the higher ranking officers dwelt within the fortress, but most of the army would have to make do with their thick-walled tents and carefully managed fires to protect them from the worsening chill.

As cold as it was outside, Karthak seemed to grow warmer with each passing day. Unfortunately this meant that I was subjected to more of her atrocious singing as she fussed over me occasionally. But, if that was the price I was to pay for securing Lleyden's freedom, then I paid it gladly.

She released my friend from his detention, though ensured that he remained under guard by a few of the new pups. Even as small as they were by Vulkar standards, they would probably have no trouble killing him if he made any attempt at sabotage or escape. I hoped that Fey-gar-Shar would be able to overcome the temptation to live up to her name.

Luckily, Lleyden remained un-slain, and was permitted to eat with my friends and I—his escort enjoying the fact that it meant they too could spend their evenings with the proper raiders.

During the day, when the Legionnaires trained and prepared to march west, and the Vulkari battled to overcome their new-found sense of duty, he was relegated to helping Narod in the kitchens. With the addition of the ever-present pups, it made it somewhat cramped apparently, and Lleyden reported that were it not for Ar-Tarak's frequent absconding with the male provisioner, there would be no room to actually work.

The boy seemed to appreciate the freedoms he had been given, and even made an effort to befriend Anra. In an attempt to fit in, he had taken to wearing a crimson gambeson that he had somehow acquired. He still wore the horrible disc of black rock though, and would occasionally rub it idly between finger and thumb when he was distracted.

I hated the necklace, and much preferred the one that Anra wore. Though it too was made from a black stone, it didn't feel cold nor filled with malice, but rather seemed to store some of Anra's body heat, or perhaps the warmth I felt for him.

I wondered if it was the same mineral, and whether maybe the Spirits within could somehow sense the purpose of the pendant. I liked to think that they could tell the difference between a gift from an esteemed daughter of Yanghar to the future lover of her pup, and some vulgar effigy—wrought of pillaged crystal for the purpose of subjugation.

Somehow, I knew I was right, but fate—and I supposed the Spirits themselves—would offer me solid proof.

⚐ ⚐ ⚐

The Legion army departed on the morning of my birthday, and despite an unexpected gift of some of Narod's wine from Lleyden, there was nothing particularly unusual about the new day.

As the sun rose, weak and watery in the crystalline sky, Manox Threydon led his force westward. He was mounted upon a fearsome black horse, and wore a sparkling suit of jet scales. He would almost have looked like a carving made from onyx—or even the beacon-stone—were it not for the impatience of his steed.

Before he left, he addressed his son in his typical stern manner—though in an uncharacteristic twist, actually leant down and patted the boy on the shoulder. Then to further confuse me, he even rustled Anra's hair—just like the Vulkari did.

Finally, after much pomp and ceremony, the Legion soldiers, and a retinue of Vulkar 'shock-troopers' and their plains-hounds marched out, followed by a cavalcade of supply wagons. Anra returned to where I stood with Mazgar, Sarga, Lleyden, and his pups to sip my birthday wine, and watch them go.

"What was that?" I asked him.

Anra was blushing. My friends began to mock him by mimicking Threydon's affectionate gesture upon one another's heads.

Anra blushed more, and stumbled over his words.

"My father told me that he rides for our honour… Mine and his, I mean. And, well… uhh, whatever happens. He told me that the frontiers were in good hands—my hands—should the worst come to be." he shrugged his usual nonchalant shrug.

"Well let us hope it does not!" Mazgar said, and rustled Anra's hair.

"Stop that, you foul beast!" Anra was grinning as he slapped her hand away and then kicked her for good measure.

"That's actually pretty nice of him," I offered. "Though I do also hope the worst doesn't come to be—I'd never get to spend time with you if you had to take up his boring duties!"

The Vulkari cooed and jeered, as was to be expected, but before I could threaten them with violence, Lleyden quieted them, then turned to the Hobgoblin.

"Anra, what exactly is his duty?" he asked. "Surely there is a ruler in the east, in Sacharr. But is your father beholden to them when he is here?"

"Of course! All in Sacharr are beholden to the God-Emperor. But each Nomos—that's like a region—is a sort of sovereign entity. We pay taxes to the Empire, and they provide men and equipment and the like," Anra told him.

The Vulkari lost interest and began to speak of raiding.

"So if you were to inherit the... throne?" Lleyden began.

"So to speak."

"Would you be free to rule the region—the Nomos—as you wished?" Lleyden finished.

Anra shrugged again.

"I suppose I would, within limits of course," he said. Then frowned and shot Lleyden a skeptical look.

"Why do you ask?"

"My village," Lleyden admitted, and glanced at me. "Our village."

Anra laughed.

"Of course your village would be spared. It already will be! Do you truly think my father so cruel as to slaughter or enslave the family of his own son's friends? He thought to use it as leverage over me, but he relented."

A wave of relief flooded over me. Why had Anra not told me before though?

I asked him as much.

"I never got the chance. You don't want to talk whenever we get to spend time together," he said, and I couldn't be angry, such was my relief—nor could Lleyden be jealous, such was his.

Before I could move to show Anra my gratitude though, Lleyden had already swept him up in a spirited embrace. Anra was stunned, and only blushed when I joined them. He begged for mercy when the Vulkari did too.

Once we released the poor Hobgoblin, we found a spot to sit and enjoy the morning sun as it found its strength and began to warm. We laughed and joked and chatted about all manner of trivialities as the previous night's frost began to melt into a lingering mist around us.

There was still a small garrison of Legion soldiers stationed within the Blackfort, and most manned the walls with their ebony bows. With the majority of the Easterners gone though—and with them their infectious sense of order—the Vulkari would soon begin to lounge around and grow bored, and a fresh desire to roam and raid would grow within them.

Karthak would have a lot of convincing to do, to keep us there, and presently sat on the steps of the keep with Star-Star and Kovvik-Shar. They were chatting and adding delicate stitching to their already-full Vyshivka.

I decided to talk to our leader, to ask her what she made of the Vaela's words—that strange premonition that bugged me more with each passing hour.

Even as I made my way toward her, thunder rumbled in the west, and drew the attention of all present. The sky above the hills was dark with clouds and it looked as though rain or hail streamed down from them. I dreaded what Manox Threydon's army were set to face.

More worrying than the weather, were the eddies of shadow that seethed and writhed in the ominous storm. The occasional flash of a strange light—too blue a shade to be lightning—contrasted the bizarre groping darkness against the fog around it. The more I tried to focus on the shape within, the more my head began to hurt, and the less I could see it clearly.

There was a sudden cry from one of the pups behind me, and I tore my eyes from the alien sight. As I turned toward the source of the noise, Karthak leapt to her feet.

Holding her spear before her, Feygar-Shar was backing slowly away from Lleyden, who was standing on the very tips of his sheep-skin boots, contorted in a horrifyingly unnatural way. It was as though he was being held up by cords of invisible rope—barely able to touch the ground. His eyes were wide with terror and panic, and his mouth opened and closed as though he were a suffocating fish.

He shuddered and twitched and slowly turned his face toward the Warlord, as she strode forward—her cleaver in hand.

Tears of black welled up within Lleyden's blue eyes, until they were polished orbs of beaconstone within his skull. Froth spewed from between his lips, and through it he spoke:

"Behold, beasts of the raid, men of the Legion! Behold the Frost-blade! Behold your doom!"

The voice was not his, but rather, many others—booming from within him, as if one, repeating the words as a mantra.

He convulsed and gagged, clawing at his neck.

Sarga and Mazgar stood frozen, abject terror in their grimaces. Anra turned to me, his hand gripping his blade.

I strode forward. I had to help Lleyden.

Still he shook, and still his nails scratched at his throat—desperately trying to dig out the voice. No, that wasn't it. It wasn't the voice itself he was groping at, it was how it was speaking through him—how all of their 'Enlightened' spoke.

My stride became a dash, and before any Legionnaire or raider could simply drop him with arrow or spear, I reached Lleyden.

Frantically, I tugged at the collar of his shirt, and with my dagger, I sawed away at the leather cord that held his tunic. Then finally, I grasped the foul talisman of the Merchant Combine, and tore it free of Lleyden's neck.

The voice stopped immediately, and the boy dropped to his knees. Anra unexpectedly rushed to his side and raised a palm to the gathered soldiers to stay their arrows.

Mazgar and Sarga had moved past us and were trying to hold Karthak at bay.

I barely saw it though.

It was as if I was looking through a blanket of mist. Or perhaps more like a swirling drop of black ink, suspended within a bottle of murky water.

I could hear those voices, and could almost make out the speaker.

I looked up toward the sun, hoping to let enough light into my eyes that I might burn away the vortex of shadow within them. And then I could see it—it was no creature of the Fae—no Goblin, Kimora, Vodnik, or Pixie. Nor was it something like the Vulkar.

It was a mass of seething fog, distorting and writhing—groping the pathetic morning sun with tentacles of smoke. It was an octopus made of pure, eldritch evil. It was wholly alien. And now it spoke to me:

"As you see us, from the unblinking eye, we see you also. You are marked. Your Warlord shall not save you. Your Legion shall be destroyed."

The voices were like many individual shards of fire and ice both—deathly cold, yet each searing into a different part of my mind, like red-hot needles.

"We shall take your lands. We shall take your freedom. We shall take your living. And we shall take your dead. Your Spirits shall be ours, one and all. The Throne shall crack, the Spire burn, and the Forest shall grow only death. The Well of Souls has been opened once more. Your time has come."

It took every last shred of my will, every fibre of my being, and all of the rage that ever burned within me, to resist the spell and to cast that accursed disc of rock to the ground.

It shattered into a hundred pieces, and I stomped it into a thousand more.

iii.

"Know that when the frost grips your sixteenth eastern sun; beware the violet scourge."

That thing in the talisman had called itself the 'Frostblade' and most certainly had gripped the sun; but as far as that damnable prophecy went, there was more to it—something about fleeing to the Solent fortress. I couldn't remember why though.

How the Combine could possibly threaten the Blackfort when Threydon stood between it and them, was a mystery to me. But I reminded myself that stranger things had happened. After all, I had somehow breached the Combine lines myself—shrouded by an inexplicable fog.

That had felt different though. Still alien, and not of the waking world, but natural all the same. There was something strange about these lands, something ancient and far beyond my understanding, and it made sense why the Combine wanted them so. I had the dread feeling that they might have somehow found a way to claim its powers already. I couldn't spend more time pondering though; Karthak opened her chamber door and beckoned me in.

"Your friend was their spy all along!" she hissed. "Were it not for your sake, I would have had him killed sooner. Who knows what the Merchant forces now know, thanks to him. Thanks to you."

"Karthak, you are wrong about him," I protested. "That wasn't Lleyden, that was that amulet. Made of the stone that the Spirits whisper through. I was so relieved to be back that I forgot to mention it, and I'm sorry for that. But it's destroyed now—you saw me do it."

She paced back and forth as I continued.

"I saw something when I tore it from him, though. It was—" She stopped suddenly.

"Saw something?" Her white eyes were wide with surprise. "Pup, the beaconstone does not convey sight. Only the voices—the intentions—of the Spirits. You cannot have seen something."

She could tell me that all day, but it wouldn't change the fact that I had.

"It was as their banner. Some octopus thing, with tentacles like smoke. It was reaching out to me, and speaking directly into my head."

"And? What did it say?"

"It said a throne would break, a spire would melt, and a forest would die. And it said that a well had been opened and that it was watching me with unblinking eyes or something. It told me that I was marked. That it was going to kill us all—or strip our freedoms away. That it was going to claim the lands, and the Spirits too!"

It could have been some idle threat, but I very much doubted that.

Karthak had stopped pacing now. She stood next to the mighty blade of black meteor iron. She traced its sigils with a talon, then slowly turned to face me.

"You saw it. And it was not of the Bare-skin?"

I had just told her. I got the feeling there was something putting itself together inside her head. Some typically devious, and ultimately secret plan was being formulated as we stood there.

"Yes, Karthak. I saw it. It was exactly as the Shaman said; 'when the frost grips your sixteenth eastern sun.' I looked at the rising sun, to try to clear the fog it put in my eyes, and it wrapped its form around it. Like an eclipse in reverse," I informed her. Still she remained silent, tracing those lines, those prayers, that blessed her cleaver.

"I need to know, Karthak. By Yanghar herself, I need to know; what is the Shaman, and does it speak the truth?"

Karthak turned suddenly away again.

"It is not of this world, that much should be clear to you already. It is one of the Vaela; more than a mere Spirit," she spoke in a hushed tone, almost reverent. "Mavka, the spirit of nature itself, it has come to me as… though that is but one aspect."

I wasn't quite satisfied and the frustration on my face must have been visible without even looking. Karthak continued.

"Before the lands were lived in—even before Yanghar's kind—there was a power. It held within it, all of the potential, all of the Magick of life and the living. It contained the Spirits before they were ever born into bodies. All within one… entity. The Vaela is that. That primordial force that gives life, and claims the Spirit back into itself once the life is spent. It is not a being, so much as it is also a place for beings to be. It is, in a sense, the Spirit world itself—with a will of its own."

She took up a bottle, half-full with brown liquor.

"This is the Vaela." She waved her hand around the bottle. "Not just this, or this, or this, or even this." In turn she tapped the glass, the cork, the peeling label, and the liquid within. Then she opened the bottle and drained its contents.

"I think I understand. It is like how the Sacharri believe Sacharr is each person and also the whole thing—each nail in the ram, or link in the chain," I said, and Karthak looked at me like I was stupid, shaking her head then rolling her eyes.

"It is a poor comparison, but if it helps you understand," she sighed. "If what you say is true, and what that thing said is also true, then there is far greater cause for concern. The Spirits have been angry. We know that, and have done for some time. But precisely why was a mystery.

"It is a shame that you destroyed the Kimora whelp's talisman. I would have liked to observe this so-called 'Frostblade' for myself. Tell me again, what it looked like, what it sounded like, and *exactly* what it said."

Again I relayed what I had experienced. This time, Karthak seemed more receptive to the possibility that I wasn't mistaken.

She began pacing again, though this time in thought rather than rage. Until, finally, she stopped next to me and placed her massive hands upon my shoulders.

"It may well be that you saw the thing because it has a physical form. Perhaps if it occupies both the Spirit world and our own, it brings some of that form with it. Or perhaps it is not a single being itself, but rather the intention of many made as one. And perhaps their intent was for you to see them. 'Behold!' the whelp said. It, or maybe they, might indeed have wished for you to behold them. Why, though? That is the question indeed..."

I stood quietly whilst Karthak babbled. Better that she was telling me her thoughts, incoherent as they were, than simply hiding them behind riddles.

"What of Lleyden then?" I asked, seizing my moment.

"Bah! It matters not, does it? He has served their purpose. And unless he carries a spare trinket, or some more of the beaconstone, may as well be useless to them and to me."

I took that as permission to have him set free. Though for now he rested next door, under guard by Feygar-Shar and Okra.

"What about the rock I took from their mine?" I asked Karthak.

She looked momentarily surprised, or maybe amused, before nodding.

"We could try to use it, yes. Attempt to scry that mystery foe through its power. Good thinking pup, you shall make a fine Warlord yet," Karthak exclaimed, then like Threydon had with Anra, she ruffled my hair. Though, she frequently did these days.

※ ※ ※

It had been at least half an hour, having sat there holding the black stone, but still nothing was happening. I opened my eyes and looked up at Karthak's expectant face. I also opened my mouth to tell her this idea was a waste of time, but she silenced me before I began.

"Shhh shhh. Close your eyes! Focus!" she demanded.

So for another quarter of an hour or so, I sat there. Like an idiot. Until I'd finally had enough.

I opened my eyes and shook my head, then tossed the rock to Karthak.

"Nothing," I told her. "Not even the cold."

She looked somewhat dismayed but nodded in understanding.

"So it is for you also. I hoped that it might have been different," she admitted.

So she had clearly already tried this herself—yet the crafty old wretch acted as though it was my idea, was she leading me to it earlier?

"What does that mean then? Is the stone ever silent?" I asked.

"To some, it is always silent. But to those who share a connection with the world beyond, or the Spirits therein—the Vaela—to them, it is almost never so," she told me. "Perhaps it is truly as you say; perhaps the Merchant Combine has claimed our Spirits."

For a short while longer we spoke of the Spirits. I told Karthak once more of the Vaela and how it had shown itself to me. What it had said—or at least as much as I could remember of it. As with each time I did, she barely tried to explain it—only going as far as to tell me that it was for me alone to interpret.

She was concerned with the warning it had given me though, specifically the part about escaping to the east. She insisted that I ready myself to depart, claiming that if the Spirits deemed it important enough to instruct me, I would be a fool to disregard it.

I protested, and demanded to remain. There was no risk of attack any time soon, and for all we knew, Threydon would drive the Merchant Combine all the way back to the coloured bit of the map.

If not, and if Anra's mentioned worst should happen, then it made my choice even easier:

I could not abandon my sisters and friends, to flee like some craven whelp. Vaela be damned, I would stitch my own Vyshivka. I would choose my own path.

iv.

The earth trembled underfoot, throwing soldiers from the walls and scattering them across the slurry of the courtyard. With the deafening cry of metal bent beyond its limit, and the thunderous roar of obliterated wood, the southern gates were breached.

The armoured brelts punched through the first line of defenders, both Vulkar and Legionnaire alike—splintering pikes, and trampling warriors underfoot. The Legion soldiers who were still standing, locked their shields together, lowered their spears, and braced for impact. Those behind them, nocked arrow to bowstring.

Karthak bellowed commands to the raiders around her and they surged forward, hurling countless javelins as they went, and releasing their plains-hounds from their shackles.

The mighty brelts were eventually brought to the ground under a hail of projectiles, but even as they fell, the next pair crashed through the reformed line. They were followed by a horde of purple-clad warriors.

Vulkar, Hobgoblin, and Kimora fought beside and against one another. A desperate and brutal melee raged on in the mud-slick courtyard of the Blackfort—the sides apparent only by the colour they wore.

From the western wall, three of the pups and I took up javelins and threw them into the fray. From the east, Anra and his retinue of Legion archers did the same with their bows. One after the other we picked off targets where we could, but it proved almost impossible after only a short while. The fear of felling one of our own slowed our aim, and for each Combine fighter we struck, more spewed forth from the rubble of the obliterated gates.

We could do little to help those who fought within the walls, and were forced to turn our attention back to the soldiers outside. We cowered behind the black stone of the crenellations as the Combine arrows rained down, then we responded with thrown spears. Anra's well-disciplined Legion archers loosed arrows as well—staggering their shots so that there was no pause that might allow a return volley. The effect was deadly.

With the advantage of height, and the protection of the walls, we were inflicting far more losses than we were taking. I prayed to Yanghar that the same was true for those who fought below.

"Zyntael! Sister! I have almost run out of javelins!" Yezga cried out. I only had three left. Yarog and Ar-Goruk only had a few as well. I took up my remaining spears and passed them to the pup, then, praying that the Mother would understand, scooped up a Legion bow, and nocked an arrow.

I was no archer, having only used a bow for hunting—and even then, fairly infrequently—but loosing arrows into a crowd of enemies negated the need for much accuracy or skill.

I let arrow after arrow fly, pausing only to collect more, to hack away grapnel ropes, kick down ladders, or to press myself to the Blackfort's wall when the Combine arrows came our way. They were coming more sporadically now, though whether because we were thinning their numbers sufficiently, or they were reluctant to hit their own vanguard, I couldn't tell.

It felt like hours had passed up on that wall, the fighting below gradually turning the way of the defenders. My heart swelled to know that despite the discipline and bravery of the Legionnaires, it was through the sheer power of my sisters that we were winning. Urga's Vulkari were few in number, and even supported by Vulkari I didn't recognise, the Combine were outmatched by the might of our warband.

In the chaos below, Kovvik-Shar, Star-Star, and Sarga tore the enemy limb from limb—isolated islands in a sea of carnage—the latter, slaughtering her way toward where Urga fought alongside her vanguard. Mazgar, Ar-Tarak, Uya, and Oya fought as a group, pushing the Combine flank back along the wall below us. To where the pups and I dropped heavy stones down upon the poor bastards—crushing metal and bone both.

In the thick of the fray, carving wide arcs through the enemy ranks, towered Karthak herself. She was drenched in violence—her eyes wild, and a frothing spittle dripping from her gaping maw. The meteorite cleaver sang out as she swung it, and where the mighty slab of Magickal black iron met flesh, gouts of steaming crimson erupted into the frigid air.

She was cackling with a terrifying glee that filled me with a burning excitement, and spurred me on. I wasn't dropping rocks now, I was hurling them. Snarling and roaring and cursing the scum that they struck.

When an enemy managed to somehow climb a Combine ladder and made to haul himself over the edge of the wall, I drew my dagger and thrust it through his throat or hacked his hands away from the blood-slick rock—now cackling with manic fury too.

The enemy were still making attempts to mount the wall, even as below, they were pushed back through the gates they had breached. Armed with the blades and axes of fallen soldiers, my pups and I defended our position with violent fervour. Nobody would take the wall from us.

And nobody did.

※　※　※

That old Hobgoblin veteran was a liar; the siege had indeed been glorious. Terrifying, that much was true, but there was no real time to dwell in that fear. Perhaps his tale only applied to some long, drawn out affair—not a blistering assault on the walls by a horde of enemies led by living siege engines, which rendered wood to splinters with the great axe-heads upon their brows.

We had lost a fair few of our number, though only several Vulkari had fallen, and despite still standing, almost everyone else sported some injury or other.

Amongst the dead was Tan-Shar, but nobody else with whom I was close. She had been kind, and had taught my friends and I how to cheat at card games. I hoped her pigment would be like the green of her mischievous eyes.

The siege began only two days after the fell warning we had received through Lleyden. First, a billowing fog rolled in, alongside a terrible chill. Then forward scouts had hurriedly retreated into the fortress, and told Karthak and the acting Legion Commander, Valishar Sakorm, that a massive host approached from the south. They had either defeated or bypassed Threydon's force somehow, and would arrive within the day.

Bells rang out, and soldiers scurried about—ensuring that barrels on the ramparts were adequately stocked with ammunition, fires were lit beneath great cauldrons of pitch and sand, and every Legionnaire was at his post.

Karthak spoke with the gathered warband in the throne room. She told us that this would be no ordinary fight. We would not have the luxury of open space, nor the possibility of discretion. If we did not repel the horde, and if we allowed ourselves to become trapped in the Blackfort keep, we would likely perish.

Should it come to it, if the worst came to pass, she told us that she would lead a charge, out of the gates and deep into the enemy ranks—cutting a path for as many of us to escape as possible. Sarga was among those bravest and fiercest of raiders who volunteered for the tip of the spear, and I hoped against the stitch of fate that such a sacrifice would not be needed.

So far, it hadn't been.

The dead had been gathered, and the wounded moved into the fort—where Narod and the other males laboured to stitch and bind wounds, or ease the passing of those who were too far gone. The corpses of the massive Combine siege beasts had been pushed against a makeshift gate, along with countless beams and rocks—it wouldn't hold up to much abuse, but it would slow a renewed assault.

I was glad that Uya and Oya had finally seen their brelts up close after all. The latter having been thrown some twenty feet across the muck by one. I chuckled at the thought—thankful she was unharmed, but amused nonetheless.

The twins now sat atop one of the fallen animals, wrenching arrows and spears from its grey hide. We would need all of the ammunition we could collect; the scattered horde beyond the walls was reforming into organised formations once more.

I climbed down from my station to fetch water for the exhausted trio of pups. They had fought bravely, and whilst their training had been truncated, were as valiant as any raider in the warband. I told them as much as they drank, then circled the battered defences to find Anra.

Even covered in blood and sweat, he was still a sight that warmed me inside. I pressed myself against his filthy body, and he gently wiped blood or spittle or something else from my lips, then kissed me.

"Are you hurt?" he asked, though he was looking at the sheet of bone and wood that hung over my torso, scuffed and battered, but intact.

"We will be fine. And what of you?" I reached up to touch his arm, near where an arrow or blade had cut through his sleeve.

"I barely feel it. Whoever forms the rings of our maille is a true master!"

I'd remember to thank Feldspar, next I saw him. It couldn't have been one of my terrible attempts, else the boy's arm would be gone.

We couldn't spend any more time together, as much as I wished it though, and instead busied ourselves with our duties. There would be another assault—they had simply been testing our defence, and our resolve.

As we worked to clear the courtyard and resupply our positions, the tendrils of fog once more stretched overhead—grasping from west to east, and smothering the noonday sun, then creeping ever earthward.

Again, the air grew almost painfully cold, and took on an unnatural thickness, which hummed and crackled with an unpleasant power.

Another attack would follow.

But before it did, a shrill horn sounded from beyond the broken southern gate.

There, in the midst of a circle of heavily armoured Combine soldiers—more dangerous looking than any who had tried to break our defence thus far, and much closer than the other soldiers dared wait—there stood a horse.

It was a pale colour, painted with swirling sigils of rich purple. Atop the steed sat a mighty Hobgoblin. I recognised him from so many years ago, and from the Combine dig site. He wore a suit of shining metal, layered with a violet cloth, and carried upon his back, a mighty, ornate blade. In his hand, he clutched something far more terrifying. Plain for all to see from where we stood, the Hobgoblin held aloft his trophy, and cried out for our surrender.

The Combine general held aloft the severed head of his brother— the head of Manox Threydon; Legion Commander of the Eastern Frontiers, right fist of the Domovoi war machine, and Anra's father.

Anra let out a roar of rage and hate and despair. Several of the Legionnaires scrambled to where he stood and dragged him away from the sight. Several others loosed arrows at Manox Thrinax, but his bodyguard raised their triangular shields to protect him.

⚹   ⚹   ⚹

Within minutes, the second assault had begun. This time, the Combine warriors pushed contraptions of wood and metal into place. Then as one, they launched gigantic, metal-capped arrows into the walls. I would have expected some sort of traditional catapults, something to knock the walls down with, but these were different.

Each of the bolts, which now protruded from the black rock, had a rope attached to it, and the enemy engineers somehow used them to winch wooden planks through the air. They formed ramps from which their soldiers could pour over our walls.

Panic set in, and we desperately tried to cut the massive stakes apart. It was made difficult by the steady rain of arrows that clattered around us and embedded into the shields we held overhead.

Ar-Goruk squealed in pain, then pitched off the wall and into the courtyard below—struck between her ribs by a Combine arrow. An older Vulkar scooped her up and carried her back to the keep, and I silently hoped she would survive.

We couldn't dislodge or destroy all of the anchors, and soon the enemy ramps were in place. With shields held up in front of them, and bristling with spears, scores of the purple-clad attackers advanced.

"To the walls!" Karthak cried out, gesturing to several of the largest radiers. And with the mighty Warlord, they came to our aid.

They pushed us back and away from the approaching onslaught, and they took up defensive positions in our stead.

All along the wall of the Blackfort, Vulkari and Sacharri warriors together repelled the Merchants' storm, but our enemy's numbers were seemingly infinite. Below, the gates were straining against yet more brelts.

Their massive bony protrusions capped with iron, and making wicked axes of their skulls, the gigantic beasts were demolishing what little remained of our makeshift doors.

They were protected from above by immense plates of metal, and were it not for our desperate need to see them slain, I would have pitied the creatures for their discomfort.

Slain they were though. Through the gaps that the brelts had carved in the wood, and during a lull in their crushing blows, Sarga, Star-Star, and Kovvik-Shar slipped out and beneath the two beasts. The mighty one-eyed veteran threw herself upon the exposed throats of the brelts. One after the other, hacking and hewing with weapon and fang, whilst the other Vulkari slaughtered the gathered Combine beast-herders, and any who moved to defend their brelts. The gates would hold this time, but Kovvik-Shar paid the price with her life—bringing the final behemoth down upon herself and a score of Combine warriors.

Her name meant 'Slayer of Great Beasts' and Yanghar saw it to be true.

※　※　※

Victory was not to be so easy this time, and whilst the gates remained sealed, too many enemies mounted the walls. More and more of their devious gang-planks went up, and more and more of their troops came over.

There was little to be done but hack and stab with any weapon available—several times resorting to rocks or even fists, as weapons became lodged in flesh and torn from my grip to fall into the moat of spikes below the wall.

There was a sudden lull in the fighting, and Karthak looked out over the wall, ears pricked. I followed her gaze to see a group of robed figures, standing in a ring and surrounded by a wall of shields.

Their heads were thrown back to the sky, and their arms were held aloft—one straight above them, the other angled to the side slightly. Although I couldn't see it from where I was, and for the blood that blurred my vision, I knew the men were chanting.

I could hear it. We all could.

"Behold!" the voice boomed from the heavens. "Behold, beasts of the raid, men of the Legion! Behold the Frostblade! Behold your doom!"

And as the oily tentacles reached from the tempest, trailing their foul smoke behind them, ice-blue fire began to rain down upon the Blackfort.

V.

The Blackfort was burning. Not just the wooden beams and woven carpets, but the rock itself. It ran in rivulets of searing liquid that engulfed anything nearby in bluish flames—whether object or flesh.

I paced along the corridors, up to the northeastern wing—inky smoke burning my eyes and lungs, and leaving a swirling trail behind me.

I had to rescue Lleyden and his guards. They would not die here.

The walls rumbled from the sound of another of the bolts hitting the building. Dust dropped through the seething smoke and burned up in sparkling, hissing fire.

I rounded the final turn, and darted up the stairs. A burning beam fell near me, and clattered down the steps, then another, and another—and just as I emerged on Karthak's floor, the rest of the staircase ceiling collapsed. The way back was blocked.

Lleyden's door was open and within his room, there was only carnage. Falling timber and rock had crushed poor Okra, and Feygar-Shar was desperately clawing at the rubble. She turned to me as I sprinted into the chamber.

"Sister, Okra is dead, and our Kimora whelp is buried! Please help me rescue him!" she cried.

I joined her in unearthing my friend.

Through some miracle, Lleyden had survived, although half the room lay atop him. The posts of his regal bed had taken the initial weight of the falling rock, and somehow dispersed it in such a way that there remained a cavity, large enough for him to fit.

It looked as though he had a dislocated arm, and even in his dazed and semi-conscious state, the boy cried out in pain when we hauled him free.

"Quick, grab a sheet or a hide blanket. We must carry him between us!" I commanded Lleyden's bodyguard and saviour.

The pup did as I bid, and together we managed to haul him out of the room before it fell in on itself entirely.

We were trapped though, and I could barely see for all the smoke that filled the hallway. There had to be some other way—we couldn't die here like this. I couldn't leave my friends and sisters, Mazgar, Sarga, and Anra.

A brief memory of the Goblin boy sprang to mind. A touching and wistful one, but exactly the one I needed. We were arguing about women and their place—on Karthak's balcony.

It overlooked part of the wall, so with luck and skill, we might be able to climb down the side of the keep to safety.

We burst into Karthak's kingly solar, and made for the balcony. But just as we reached it, I halted. There was something else I needed.

As quickly as I could, so as not to cause panic in the pup, I tore open Karthak's chest. Casting aside the scented oils that would be sorely missed, I recovered my prize—still wrapped in its crinkled brown cover: the Kimor-pup.

Our escape from the keep was not an easy one, and had it not been for Karthak herself, it may not have been a successful one.

She spotted us somehow, as her warriors battled the Combine and the fire. Below us, she began to make her way back toward where Feygar-Shar and I struggled to haul Lleyden over the stone railing. I clambered over first, and gripping the rough wall with burning fingers and sheer desperation, I was reaching up to hold my friend. But I had no idea how to proceed.

We couldn't carry him, since we would need to hold onto the wall. It wasn't working, so I hauled myself back up.

"Tie him to yourself, Sister. As you would a stag," Feygar-Shar suddenly suggested. She was a genius.

I stripped off my armour, and withdrew one of the belts, then linked it to the one I held my dagger with, and wrapped it around Lleyden. I pushed my back against him, and had begun to fasten the belt around us, when I was suddenly thrown off balance. Lleyden levitated away from me, and I sprawled to the balcony floor.

I turned to see Karthak, holding herself upon the edge of the balcony with one hand, and carrying the boy like he was a child's doll with the other. Then, without a word, she gripped his crimson gambeson in her teeth, and began to clamber down the wall.

I was halfway down, drenched in sweat, and trembling when she returned for me. I could hold on a little longer so begged Karthak to carry the exhausted pup down first.

Once she had, I finally let her take me.

⌘　⌘　⌘

The battle for the Blackfort still raged on, but it was clear that we had lost. Karthak's Vulkari withdrew from the walls to regroup behind a wide wall of Legionnaire shields and spears, in the courtyard before the keep. The worst had come to be.

Under-Commander Valishar Sakorm stood with an arm around Anra's shoulder. He was clearly not long for this world.

"Take Threydon's heir," he implored Karthak, his proud face pale, and stained with blood and soot. "You must see him delivered to the Solent."

In a strangely caring gesture, Karthak touched the man's cheek.

"I shall do so, brave Hobgoblin, Sakorm. And know before you fall, that had your skin borne fur, I would have had you as a mate. You have been a good friend, and I shall remember you fondly." I was confused, but assumed that the pair must have shared some typically complex and unexplained history.

The Legion warrior smiled gratefully, and a little wistfully, then allowed Anra to lower him onto the steps of the battered fortress. He caught me watching him and smiled.

"You smell like a warrior," he told me, then turned and began to address Anra and his remaining officers.

It seemed that the Sacharri Legion had been made aware of Karthak's plan—though to begin with, I'd assumed it a gambit meant to save only our people and had worried that Anra would be left to die amongst his fellows.

As honourable and fearless as ever though, the stoic men of Sacharr agreed to act as a diversion, and launch a suicidal assault of their own—meant to concentrate the ranks of the Combine where they would strike. That way, the resistance to Karthak's spearhead would be slightly thinner, and we might just have a chance to reach the rapids nearby.

From within the burning building, Narod and a few of the other males and injured raiders had escaped. Alongside Sacharri servants, they took up weapons and readied themselves for the final assault. Narod carried with him a sack filled with the memorial pigments, as well as a finger from each of our fallen sisters, from which their pigments could be made.

Before the attackers overran us completely, the malefolk and the Hobgoblins who were too wounded to form the shield wall, cleared the rubble that blocked the southern gate.

█ █ █

"For the God-Emperor! For the Obsidian Throne! For Sacharr!" They cried out in unison.

And the Sacharri Legionnaires, led by a mortally wounded Valishar Sakorm, cast their spears and shields away, drew their blades, and charged out to throw themselves upon the surprised enemy, in a desperate, suicidal frenzy.

Then, as those heroic men became engulfed, and the enemy occupied, we poured out and veered off toward the Storm river. A bloody path was carved by my sisters, and I ran for my life.

For the second time, I found myself scrambling down that hill—bracken and bramble clawing at my legs. For the second time, I prepared myself for the icy plunge into the surging waters below. This time though, the waters would be that much colder. And this time, I would actually reach them.

As I leapt from the bank, I turned to see my companions leaping too—Mazgar, Sarga, Ar-Tarak. They had all somehow made it, though Sarga was haggard and bloodied. Star-Star and the three surviving pups came next, and Anra followed.

I was already in the frigid water, struggling to stay afloat against the clawing current, when—cradling Lleyden in her arms—Karthak leapt. She was followed by Uya and Oya—though the first was half-dragging the second with her.

With relief, I heard more Vulkari break the water's surface behind me, as I was swept downstream, toward the ancient forest.

vi.

O nce Oya departed to walk with Yanghar, she was laid to rest beneath a tree. Out in the open, so that the forest scavengers could make a feast of her strength.

It was unusual not to burn her to ash, and mix her with colour, but Uya told me that she needed no pigment to commemorate her twin. She assured me that she was always with her anyway—since the same blood, and the same Spirit dwelt within them both. And with a sad little grin, informed me that she had forgotten which one of them she actually was.

"Treya," I told her, and pointed out the three dots on her head; one of darker fur, and the others, marks of her sister's blood—where Oya had gently stroked her face and bid her goodbye.

In the early morning of the following day, the warband lingered in an ancient copse of knotted trees. Shrouded in fog, the Vulkari rested amongst the onyx stones that sprouted hither and yon. Whilst the raiders bound wounds and fastened equipment, Karthak gave my sisters and I time to say our goodbyes—despite the unease that potential pursuit carried with it.

Before she did though, she took me aside and informed me that I was to wait in the Solent fortress for her arrival some months later. They would do all the warband could do to harass the pursuing Combine force, whilst she investigated the mysterious appearance of the black rock, and the disappearance of the voices within. She would seek out the Vaela, and all the Spirits of the wild, and would have answers and—as to be expected—a plan.

She warned me of the Legion, and that there would be those who would contest Anra's claim—particularly in lieu of his relationship with me. With a wry grin, she told me to always have a slave test my food and drink, before I took it.

I tried to give her golden statuette back to her, but she bid me keep it—a reminder of what it meant to be a mother. She had a feeling I'd need it.

"Carry well the chosen pup of Yanghar, Zyntael," she commanded, her voice stern and her white gaze unwavering.

"I shall."

"She carries within her, the future of us all." Karthak held a great and powerful hand over my entire belly whilst speaking those same words someone had once spoken of me. "It is through these trials, through your own, that your pup shall gain her strength."

I didn't have the heart to tell her that, for whatever reason, I already thought the pup a boy.

"Remember that Yanghar walks beside you, defiant in the face of the Combine's grip on her world. She shall bear you safely east—and guard you until I return."

I thanked the mighty Warlord for her kindness, for saving Lleyden, and for saving me. I thanked her for all that she had taught me—good and bad alike. Then I thanked her for letting me go, to face my chosen path.

She rustled my hair for perhaps the last time, and chuckled.

"If that is what you call the stitch of your Vyshivka, I shall not begrudge your blatant Bare-Skinned ignorance," she said, then she retreated into the gloom to address her raiders.

Star-Star also spoke with me. She told me that she was proud of me, and of Mazgar, and that she had bet upon the best of our claim. She told me that should she not survive the coming seasons, I would find her with Yanghar—roaming the coasts of the ocean.

She told me to seek her where the sand and the sea was most golden—indistinguishable from the glow of the horizon—and that we would meet as equals beneath an eternal sunrise.

She told me that we would eat and drink and roam wild, and maybe even do a bit of gambling. And she told me to bring my friends.

I embraced the sandy Vulkar and thought it just a little touch of Magick that no matter how far from the water, she still carried with her that salty scent of freedom.

Ar-Tarak didn't say much to me. Instead she merely held me by the shoulders, and looked into my eyes. She nodded whilst she stared.

Then finally, she cocked her head to the side and simply said: "You are my Raid-Sister, and always shall be."

It was possibly the nicest thing she could have said. I tried to return the compliment, but she brushed it off, and shooed me away so that she could speak with Narod.

"Look after yourself," he said to me before I left them.

"You too…" I replied.

"Horse-son," we both said together.

Finally, it came time to speak with Sarga. She was to stay, as Karthak required all of the strongest of the raiders for the brutal times to come.

Beneath a gnarled and twisting tree that blossomed with delicate flowers of the onyx crystal, I held Sarga's hand and peered into her sparkling black eyes. Mazgar joined us, and together we three stood.

"I will find you," I told my friend, my sister.

"I shall find you first, because your backwards legs carry you too slowly to track me," Sarga replied with a smirk. "Besides, we have unfinished business we must see through."

"Adventure business," Mazgar added.

Through my tears, I laughed.

"Indeed. And there is still the matter of revenge to be had upon Urga. I would not wish to take all of it for myself!" Sarga told me, then held me close against her strong, russet chest. I did not want to let go.

Once I finally and reluctantly did, Mazgar and she pressed their foreheads together and gripped each other by the hands. They held their thumbs upright and unmoving. They remained like this for some time, not a single word spoken between them, until finally, with a grin, Sarga tucked her thumbs down, and let Mazgar pin them.

"Take care of her, Smallest," Sarga whispered to her best friend and closest sister.

"I shall. Take care of Karthak, and of Garok," Mazgar asked in return, and for the first time since I had known her, it finally occurred to me who her birth mother was.

❈ ❈ ❈

Before the warband departed, Karthak addressed us all, her voice thick with emotion.

"Sisters! Brave and mighty raiders of the Crimson Star! We have triumphed and we have lost. But never forget, either way, we have fought! The glory of our people is eternal, and our sun of true freedom shall rise soon. But for now, we must stalk the lands once more in shadow. Once more as beasts of the wild. We must strike at the invaders, and drive them from the hills and valleys. We must slaughter them in the forests and glades. And we must consume them where they fall. We shall tear their strength from them, and we shall show no mercy!"

The uneasy feeling of earlier was quickly forgotten as the mightiest Vulkar ever to walk the land spoke. Her voice echoed through the forest, causing even the oldest of trees to tremble with fear.

"My glorious Sisters! We shall restore the natural order. We shall wrest the taint from the world of our Spirits, and we shall liberate the Vaela!" A sudden breeze could be heard all around, though no wind was felt.

"Here I pledge to you all; that none shall pass on to walk with Yanghar, without her price being paid in the blood of those who defile us—those who seek to defile our Mother.

I pledge now, to honour those brave men of the Legion, who sacrificed themselves so we may yet claim their price too. They are heroes, all and each of them, and shall be reborn as wild and free as shall we all!"

The warband cheered—a wild cacophony of whooping and cackling that seemed to hold time in place. Anra cheered too.

Then, without another word spoken, the Vulkari warband of Karthak—my sisters and my friends, and my home for so many of my summers—dispersed into the misty woods.

Where they went, wild and ethereal howls rang out. They were as fell Spirits—they would strike terror into the hearts of all they found, and all they slew. But that sound did not fill me with terror. It was only love that I felt.

The tears did not cease their flow until well after the last of the warband was out of sight in the gloom of the forest. They did not cease until well after Mazgar, Anra, Lleyden, and I stalked further into the woods ourselves—and like Spirits too, disappeared into the east.

vii.

Old. Knotted. Forgotten by the world.
I dreamt of a tree with roots that burrowed deeper than living
memory could manage.
Down into the cold depths of the earth, it clawed at places that were
perhaps passed from history for a reason.
The tree fed on those impossible secrets, its sap carried upward, the
darkness from within the dead soil.
Cold, resolute, unnatural—crystalline flowers began to bloom on the
old tree.
Although it had sought life in the deep, now only death blossomed in
its creaking, whispering boughs.
Death that would soon ripen and fall, to sprout anew.
Death that would spread as icy pollen on the winds, and soon cover
all the lands in its onyx embrace.
But I wasn't afraid. I was sad.
And I was lost.

"Shh! Fool, you will wake her. And by all the Fae, you kept her awake long enough last night!" Lleyden was chastising Anra, still the subtlest hint of covetousness in his whispered voice.

I didn't even need to open my eyes to know that Mazgar was doing that lewd gesture with her fingers. The resulting laughter from Anra and she was enough to confirm it.

"I'm awake," I told them, though still I refused to open my eyes. I was glad that the dreams I'd had of late had not taken place beneath a burning crimson sky, but by now I was positively sick of that stupid tree. It wasn't a premonition if I'd already seen the accursed thing.

I'd stood under it. We all had. And it wasn't the only tree that sprouted the strange mineral. The whole forest had been filled with them. Other plants too—flowering in winter, with petals of black glass. Where there were no plants, the bizarre crystals had simply sprouted from the earth.

Luckily, it had been some days since we had escaped the grasp of that ancient forest, and I was glad to walk under the pale, clear sky instead of the swaying boughs of sickly wood.

Still, the damned thing followed me in my sleep. Appearing each night, as I battled with the mists of my memory—trying to clutch the moment where the Vaela had given me her warning.

"Know that when the frost grips your sixteenth eastern sun; beware the violet scourge. Make haste on that morn, with the three parts of who you are, to the Fortress of the Fist."

I said it out loud, and my companions groaned in unison.

It helped if I sang it like a song. Mazgar said I was becoming Karthak. And Lleyden agreed. Anra pretended to like it, but I knew he thought it was terrible.

He was so sweet. Initially, I worried that he and Lleyden wouldn't get along. But, perhaps due to some secret bond that existed only between men, they were becoming fast friends.

They would banter and mock one another, of course, but they seemed to share a love for historical trivia—Mazgar and I simply nodded and smiled politely when they spoke of it all. Then again, it was mostly me who was subjected to their waffle. Mazgar was happy to tell them to shut up, or would change the subject to things more her taste: violence, vulgarity—the usual things she and Sarga spent the last however many summers chatting about.

I wondered how Sarga was, as the morning meal was cooked. It made sense that she would need to stay with the warband, but something struck me as a little odd. Karthak had never felt it necessary to split up our trio before, even when the warband was faced with danger.

A small part of me (and probably a very accurate part of me, knowing Karthak as I did) suspected that it was some type of leverage. The prospect of being reunited with the missing member of our little group, would drive me to grow bored of the Solent fortress—or at the very least, ensure that I was not likely to remain comfortable there. Especially if the warband was delayed—as frequently they were.

I gave up on my slumber and forced myself to rise. The weather was milder today—the worst of the winter chill now fading as though the season did, as we ventured further into the east.

We still had a fair way to go, based on my memory of travelling to and from the fortress. But I was glad to see that the trails that the warband had cut, and the bridges they had repaired still remained to make our passage easier. Better still, but a sad reminder, were the new tracks made by the Legion as they had marched westward to our aid. And to their doom.

We also passed by some settlements, Mazgar and I had looked at one another with fire in our eyes—each daring the other to suggest a raid. How that would have been received within the Sacharri territory though, was not hard to guess. Not that Anra or Lleyden would have let us terrorise some farming folk for fun and food anyway.

Instead of stolen livestock, we ate a breakfast of stolen eggs. Claimed, I assumed, from some incredibly large lizard or snake, since they were tough and bitter. Lleyden suggested dragons. Anra mocked him relentlessly.

Once fully fed and refreshed, we gathered our belongings and trekked on. There wasn't a lot to see as we made our way into the vast plains of grass that bordered the arid lands of the Solent fortress. I wondered whether they would remain arid—now that the river flowed freely through them. The dusty summers in that city were only slightly more bearable than the rains and the sludge that came with the spring melt in the west.

As we journeyed ever closer to that place, my thoughts lingered more upon its occupants. Would they be glad to see me? Would they even be able to recognise me? Anra had been—in both cases. I wondered why, and resolved to ask him when out of earshot of the others.

It was strange that he found me attractive, even as Goblin-like as I looked, and especially since, as he'd grown, he looked more and more like his father.

His father. I hadn't even spoken to Anra of Manox Threydon. He was hiding it well, but it couldn't be easy for him. Especially since with his father's death came a whole new set of responsibilities for the boy.

As far as I knew, the sons inherited the father's station in Sacharr, though there was some requirement that they be no lout. As long as he was some sort of officer, or decent man, a boy of the Legion would assume his father's role when the elder perished.

I wouldn't want that. Karthak, and even the Vaela had suggested a life as the leader of a warband. But in all honesty, I was tired.

I also felt a little sick. No, I felt *very* sick.

"Is it fever?" Mazgar enquired as I vomited for the third time.

"No you flea-ridden simpleton!" Lleyden sighed. "It is probably the child. It's normal, and will come and go over the seasons. Mostly in celebration of the sunrise. I'm surprised it didn't start sooner."

How he knew any of this was a mystery to me, but then, Narod was also well-versed in this kind of thing, and he was male. Actually, he had clearly been making some things up. I hoped Lleyden wasn't.

"Will she be alright today?" Anra asked.

"If not, I could carry her. Like a little nursing pup. Ohh… So adorable and small. So sweet and tiny." Mazgar mimicked a nursing mother, first coddling her imaginary child, cooing and speaking in a weird, cutesy tone. Before pausing and looking, horrified, at her hands.

"So… pathetic and weak! Ugh! On second thoughts…"

She drop-kicked her imaginary baby into the undergrowth.

I laughed. More breakfast came up.

It was the last of it, so I drank from a nearby stream to wash away the foul taste and probably fouler smell.

"Alright. I think I'll be fine. We must hurry onward, lest I slow our journey to a crawl."

I apologised to my friends, but they were all patient and concerned.

"You must be sure to eat at least *something*. No matter how hard it is to keep in your belly," Lleyden informed me, but I tried to refuse.

"Do Bare-Skin pups not want to be large?" Mazgar asked with a dismissive shrug. It was a rhetorical question.

We carried on, and as the day stretched out behind us, I relented. I made sure that I ate what I could, and kept up a steady intake of water. All the time, dreading what fresh new horror my body would bring.

❈   ❈   ❈

Whether because of the better trails, the lack of raiding and interruptions, or the relentless Sacharri pace that Anra kept us to, our journey was so much shorter than it had ever been with the entire warband—and before the first sunset of a fourth week, the city came into view.

With its high earthen walls and dusty streets, it seemed to shimmer a little with the beginnings of springtime—even though the weather still didn't seem hot enough, and there was almost a whole moon left in the season. It felt surreal to gaze upon the place again. Were it not for the weight in my body, and the strange pull I felt from the rolling plains and wild hills at my back, I would run the rest of the way.

But we needed to stop. I needed to rest.

I did not dream of the tree that night. Instead I merely fell into a quiet, comforting blackness. Within the void, I reflected on my life— or what I could remember:

I thought about the raiding, the adventures and the chaos of the Vulkar. I thought of all they believed and all they were—the spirit of the Wild, made flesh. All of the beauty that entailed, and all of the horror too. I thought of how they struggled to be, in a world that would sooner fall into ordered division. And I thought of Mazgar.

Next I thought of the Sacharri, of how structured and disciplined, cold and sharp, and yet fiercely brave they were. I thought of all they would do to pacify the lands. I thought of the honour they carried within them. Their strength and their hope for a world that reflected their ideals. They could be so villainous, but they were also heroes. Anra swam into view, and my heart warmed.

Finally, my strange dream-like state carried me back. Back to the furthest reaches that my blurred memory would allow. I saw a simplicity. A sense of ambivalence. Perhaps ignorance. But a little of long-ing—of nostalgia for some long-lost greatness. I felt the desire to hide away from the world. Neither to follow destiny, nor to pacify it. I saw my father, not as frail as he was now—but a fuller man.

And I almost saw my mother. Just as I tried to focus on her image, it was gone—leaving Lleyden in her place. He was undeniably hand-some, but when I looked upon his features, I felt only a wistful sad-ness. A touch of regret. A swell of fear—felt on his behalf, for all around him.

Then it all melted away to leave only darkness, and a curious reali-sation:

Here I was, travelling my chosen path. But it ran almost exactly in line with the Vyshivka stitched so deftly for me by the Vaela. Was I really in control of my future? I would like to think so. But then, again here I was, travelling with the three aspects of myself and my life made flesh—each an avatar of the essence of their people.

There was something else still bugging me, something I had not yet done. I was supposed to be somewhere, to meet someone. Why was I going back to the fortress again?

It came back to me. Spoken by the mouth of a colossal plains-hound who towered over the land, and seemed to struggle just to be—to struggle against a great and dark cloud that yawned behind her:

"Know that when the frost grips your sixteenth eastern sun; beware the violet scourge. Make haste on that morn, with the three parts of who you are, to the Fortress of the Fist. There you shall find your deliverance—and find your true path to greatness."

I whispered my thanks to Yanghar as she was consumed by the mist, and I awoke. I was ready to reach the Fortress of the Fist, with all three parts of who I was. I was ready to find that deliverance, and the greatness too, but I'd take no path but my own—even if I was a little late.

❈ ❈ ❈

No nausea struck me that morning—so excited was I, to reach the familiar brown fortress.

After a rushed breakfast and lively chatter, we got ready and started the final day's trek.

The road was well maintained, since it serviced the surrounding farmland. Even though the soil was dusty and light, workers still toiled in the fields—embroiled in their small, unknowing lives. They reminded me of bees that danced from flower to flower in endless labour. I did not envy them, but I could respect them for their simplicity, and for their perseverance. I would never know such a life, of that I was certain.

As we approached the city, and spied the river boats bobbing in the waters of the Solent—a novel sight for all four of us—the words of my dream came tumbling back into my mind. Perhaps prompted by some long held desire to escape the weave of the Vyshivka by boat. I tried to decipher those words, to defeat them somehow.

'Deliverance.' That's what the Vaela had called it, and I was to find it in the Fortress of the Fist, alongside my true path to greatness. I wondered if that actually was to be my chosen path or yet another wrought for me by someone else.

Even as we strode closer, and the mighty walls of the fortress loomed overhead, I was lost in thought. But I was still aware. Past familiar sights and new, we marched. Mazgar, Lleyden, Anra, and I; a mismatched party of friends—heading right where we needed to be.

As the Legion soldiers of the expected escort approached us, I smiled at my friends in turn. This was it. This was where it would all change for us: Anra would be swept up in his duty and all of the things his station would entail; Mazgar would face boredom, once the sights and sounds and smells grew dull; Lleyden would likely feel lost—as I once had. Taken from his home by a Vulkar warband, to become a captive. And then something else entirely.

Of my own fate, I couldn't say. I would know it when I saw it, and glanced around expectantly whilst we were escorted up that familiar road, and toward the fort itself. The sun was in my eyes as I squinted up at the gatehouse that marked the entrance to the place I had once called home. I expected to see the silhouette of Grunwald, and whoever happened to be on guard duty that day. The former talking both ears off the latter in turn, then talking some more.

I couldn't stop thinking about my supposed 'deliverance'—what did that even mean? What was I supposed to be looking for?

Was it the Sacharri Legion? Some specific Hobgoblin? Or perhaps even the fortress itself?

No. It was none of those.

But then, as the sun was blocked by the boughs of a tree, and I could see the gatehouse clearly, there I saw those figures.

My heart leapt in my chest and a surge of emotion threatened to wash away my ability to behold the sight. I knew what I had been looking for. I finally understood the words of the Vaela.

There, up on the wall beside the figures of my dear friend Janos Grunwald and his poor Legionnaire victim, above the fluttering black banners and the mighty gate, sat another figure whom I had not expected to see.

There sat the bastard who was to blame for all of this. The reason I walked my chosen path in the first place.

His tiny form perched atop a crenellation; one leg swinging idly below him, a lazy coil of smoke issuing from his long, curved pipe, and his kindly emerald eyes sparkling in the light—there sat the Murdering Sausage-path Horse's son himself.

There sat my deliverance:

Phobos Lend. The Darkrunner.

NEXT IN THE VYSHIVKA TRILOGY:

SISTER
OF THE
DEAD

The Vulkari do not belong within the walls of a city, and Zyntael Fairwinter is no different.

So when a perilous quest into the heart of the Old-Reach is planned, Zyntael jumps at the chance to join it. Together with her closest allies, she embarks on a journey to travel beyond the mysterious "Mortuary-City" of Quaresh—to cut off the source of the Merchant Combine's Necromancy.

But there is a reason they call it the Mortuary-City.

Between dangerous arcane rituals, pirate attacks, bar fights, and battles—death lurks at every turn.

And, to make matters worse, only a few short moons remain before Zyntael's pup is due.

Sister of the Dead is available in Paperback, Hardback, and E-book formats.

(Visit ECGreaves.com for more!)

ABOUT THE AUTHOR

The weave of Ed Greaves' Vyshivka began in Solihull, UK, though he now resides in Christchurch, New Zealand.

Besides pouring his imagination out into the pages of this book and others, he also spends his time developing indie horror games, composing music, building and modifying old vehicles, and drawing.

That is, when he isn't trying to figure out a way to smuggle raccoons into the country, of course!

AND A FINAL WORD FROM ME

First, and most importantly:

My warmest thanks to you for reading my book!

I truly hope that you enjoyed it, and if you did, please consider leaving a review on the Amazon store, Goodreads, and wherever else you can think of.

Obviously I don't have the giant marketing budget of a traditional publisher behind me, so positive word of mouth (as well as some cheeky algorithm manipulation) is a HUGE help!

If you'd like to stay abreast of anything related to my writing, feel free to give me a follow on social media, or visit my website.

Twitter: @GreavesEC,

Website: www.ECGreaves.com

Once again, thank you from the bottom of my heart.

And finally:

May your path be free of brambles, and may moss ever cushion your footfalls!

~ Ed